The Last Entry

A NOVEL

The Last Entry
A NOVEL

Jim Hamilton

Working Title Farm

an imprint of River's Edge Media

This is a work of fiction. Names, characters, places, and incidents are a product of the author's imagination. Locales and public names are sometimes used for atmospheric purposes. Any resemblance to actual people, living or dead, or to businesses, companies, events, institutions, or locales is completely coincidental.

The Last Entry
Based on the screenplay 'Sang by Glenn A. Bruce, Story by Jim Hamilton & Glenn A. Bruce
Copyright © 2019 by Jim Hamilton & Glenn A. Bruce

All rights reserved. No part of this publication may be reproduced, distributed, or transmitted in any form or by any means, including photocopying, recording, or other electronic or mechanical methods, without the prior written permission of the publisher, except in the case of brief quotations embodied in critical reviews and certain other noncommercial uses permitted by copyright law. For permission requests, write to the publisher, addressed "Attention: Permissions Coordinator," at the address below.

Working Title Farm
6834 Cantrell Road, Suite 172
Little Rock, AR 72207

Edited by Shari Smith

Cover design: Silvinia Hamilton
Cover photography: Jim Hamilton

The Last Entry/Jim Hamilton — 1st ed.
ISBN 978-1-940595-71-9 (Hardback)

For Silvi, Cristian, and Lucas

Foreword

Every school kid here in the mountains learns about Daniel Boone—the woodsman, the trapper, the frontier hero. Where I'm from, old-timers still tell lots of stories about him, different stories than the ones in the history books. Daniel Boone didn't just trade in furs. He was a forager, too; knew every plant and herb in the forest. What can heal you, what can kill you ... and what can earn you a dollar.

Ginseng, or 'seng as they call it here, is a special plant. Only grows in certain places ... old, deep hollers where it can hide from man. Some years it's there, some years it's not. The Cherokee say you won't see it if it doesn't want you to—if you don't respect its hills and trees. The most valuable roots are just like the old-timers who still hunt them. Wise and wrinkled ... with their own stories. This one's mine.

~ Jim Hamilton

Every time I think I have a grasp on understanding ginseng as a plant, I realize there is so much more to learn about it. Ginseng can and will constantly surprise you, no matter how much you think you know about it. Western North Carolina is one of the most biologically diverse places on the planet, and of all of the important botanicals that grow here, Wild American Ginseng in particular, is truly at the crux of history and culture, market and demand, and the future of an entire species.

Sara J.
Bat Cave, NC

Part I

One

Tucker and Danny hopped into the truck at the end of the gravel lot of Mount Zion Lutheran Church. Paw Paw had taken them to the late-morning service each Sunday since the boys and their parents moved in. Tucker was a few months from turning thirteen and old enough to keep still during the sermon, but his younger brother could never stop squirming, even through the chorales. The red-faced preacher dabbed his forehead throughout the hour-long homily, his flock fanning their faces, warding off the heat as much as unconfessed sin. Danny bolted out of the pew, escaping the cramped nave as soon as the last hymn ended.

The engine in the D-100 growled to life as Paw Paw unbuttoned his dress shirt while shucking his loafers and slipping on boots. He was as ready to go as the boys, and grinned as he put the truck into drive. They made their way along miles of winding dirt roads, weaving between potholes and braking for the chipmunks before finally coming to a stop. The rusty frame of a long-abandoned Forest Service dozer marked their parking spot at the end of one of the overgrown byways that Paw Paw had memorized over the years.

The boys jumped from the truck, changed out of their church clothes, grabbed their water bottles, and fumbled through the half-full box of Swiss rolls on the dashboard. Paw Paw folded his shirt and set it in the floorboard. Before Tucker shut the door, his grandfather reached behind the bench seat and pulled out the old service sidearm that he always wore in the woods. Tucker had practiced with the dulled-chrome .45 in the woods behind their house under Paw Paw's watchful eye. The sharp report had made him jump the first time. Even though Tucker's hands barely wrapped around the grip, the pie pans he hit from twenty feet away didn't stand a chance after he got used to the kick.

"Just in case," Paw Paw said as he shoved it into his belt. "Never know if Mr. No-Shoulders might be out and about."

Tucker shuddered. Snakes. Only the rattlers made him nervous, though. Sometimes it was hard to see the ground through the thick brush, so Tucker kept keen eyes on each step. He hadn't seen a snake all summer—just the skin of a black snake under the porch. But black snakes were harmless. Miss Tincher, his sixth-grade teacher, kept one in a glass cage behind her desk. Tucker volunteered to hold it first, just to seem tougher than his classmates. It felt both slick and rough at the same time, and calmed in the warmth of Tucker's hands, but he shivered every time it flicked its tongue. "Y'all be careful, now, or it'll barf up the mouse it just ate," Miss Tincher had warned. Her kin were local, but she had been raised in Georgia with her mother, and the boys giggled every time she said "y'all" instead of "you'uns."

After hiking for over an hour, following fresh deer trails and the landmarks known only to his grandfather, Tucker grew more excited. He stopped and stared at the lush mat of green in the holler just below him. His Paw Paw sat down next to him at the base of the enormous oak at the top of the ridge. The massive tree, misshapen from a large heart-shaped burl, bulged at its center, thick enough to throw shade over them.

Paw Paw pulled a worn journal out of his knapsack. After a couple of glances at the yellowed pages, he looked up at the tree's contorted knot and then at Tucker.

"Been awhile," he mumbled as he put the book away, satisfied he had found the same place he had made notes about when he last visited over twenty years ago.

Fall was arriving quickly there in the southern Appalachians. The leaves on the maples and birches were transitioning into the warming shades of autumn color, even as the afternoons and evenings became chilly and mostly-black woolly worms inched across the blacktop. These signs told Paw Paw that it was time for them to hunt 'seng.

"Berries are good 'n red by now," he said.

Ginseng, or *'seng* as everybody called it, was the low-growing plant they were after. This time of year, it gave away its hidden locations in the understory as its leaves turned a conspicuous golden yellow between the streaks of green in its fading veins. Its top cluster of once-green berries turned a lucent, blood red before falling to the ground to begin a decades-long cycle to reproduce mature plants with big roots. Money roots.

Many Appalachian natives relied on foraging 'seng and other *goods from the woods*—as Paw Paw called them—this time of year. Ginseng was a poor man's bank account, withdrawn from when times were tight. And times had been tight for the Trivette family. The 'seng that Paw Paw and the boys found paid for the new school shoes for growing feet and kerosene for the heater, which would be burning through fuel soon enough.

The full moon competed with the sun, slipping behind the tallest spires of the tree tops on the most distant mountain. Although he broke a sweat during the long hike, Tucker didn't regret bringing the sweatshirt tied around his waist. It felt like the temperature dropped fifteen degrees as he sat in the cool shadows for a few moments to sip water and catch his breath.

Tucker looked back for his younger brother, wandering away from him and Paw Paw as always. Danny stooped over at the edge of a rocky outcrop inspecting the greenery. Tucker saw him reach down quickly and then slide a fistful of something into his pocket with his one good hand. Berries.

"There'll be more than a bunch down this way, son," Paw Paw said. "Best you keep up with your brother and me." But his youngest grandson did as he pleased. Danny, young as he was, had a quiet fierceness to him and seemed most at home in the forest. He moved deliberately and quick like a feral child born to the wilderness, through even the thickest of brush, despite lacking an arm since birth. Tucker, the more cautious and obedient older sibling, kept a responsible pace with his grandfather, asking questions and hanging on every word that his elder uttered, eager to please.

"You remember what it looks like?" Paw Paw asked him.

"Yessir," Tucker said. "I'm lookin' for them prongs." He had only hunted ginseng this far away from the home place a time or two before, but he felt confident in his ability to pick it out from the other herbs of the forest.

"Make sure you look for them other plants, too." Paw Paw said. "The 'seng will be nearby."

Tucker immediately complied, bending over to scan the ground—training his eye for the plant that "paid the bills" as Paw Paw said.

Tucker spotted bloodroot first—the easiest. Its single, rounded and deeply lobed leaf stood out against the backdrop of the forest floor like an emerald orb. By early fall, its green faded to yellow, but during the spring, Tucker picked it out on the road banks from the passenger window of Paw Paw's truck. Its white, star-like flower perched on a spike about six inches off the ground. Locals still made tinctures from its nodules for mouthwash and salves to heal nicks from barbed wire. Danny, however, streaked its crimson dye on his cheeks as his war paint while foraging. "I'm a Cherokee!" he hooted as he stalked through the brush.

Paw Paw had showed the boys how to find bloodroot and ginseng's other companion herbs. "Bloodroot and 'seng are like peas in a pod," he'd said. So was poison-ivy, it seemed. Everywhere he dug 'seng, Tucker awoke the next morning with itchy fingers and forearms—the sap from unseen tendrils of the toxic vine blistering his skin. A little jewelweed rubbed between the joints could take the itch away and numbed the welts from stinging nettle, too. The woods were an endless apothecary, and Paw Paw knew all of its healing secrets.

As Tucker made his way down the slope just ahead of his grandfather, he noticed other telltale plants of ginseng's cohort that Paw Paw had taught him. Jack-in-the-Pulpit's larger cluster of red berries sat atop its short stalk and jumped out at him like ginseng at first glance. Tucker also noticed blue cohosh with its dull indigo fruits, the wispy fronds of maiden-hair fern, and still more and more fading bloodroot. They were in a prime spot.

"Look here," Paw Paw said just above him—pointing at the forest floor. "You stepped right over this bunch."

Tucker stared at Paw Paw's feet and shook his head. "That's a nice one," Tucker said as he walked upslope and carefully removed the small ball of red berries from the stalk at the center of the plant.

"Can't believe I missed it. And look! There's three more bigguns around it." Tucker knelt down, excitedly scraping away soil from one.

Paw Paw shook his head. "One at a time, now," he said. "Need to give each plant its proper respect. They've been growin' here long before you were born. God's gift." He grabbed his hand-tool and grubbed away the weeds from the green and purplish-stained stalk. It stood upright and knee-high, the largest of the plants there. "Be sure to plant them seeds back," he said as he swung the worn hoe into the ground a foot away from the base of the stem, patiently loosening the soil as he encircled it.

As Paw Paw worked, Tucker walked a few steps away and made a depression in the soil with his index finger. He mashed a berry and dropped its two seeds into the shallow hole, covering it back up with dirt and leaves, as Paw Paw had showed him how to do it, then walked a few zig-zag steps repeating the process until all were safely planted just under the soil.

"That way, we'll have 'em to come back to someday," Tucker said, repeating his grandfather's lesson.

When Tucker turned back around, Paw Paw shook the loose soil from the fresh root. Two large earthworms, often present around big ginseng, wriggled in the small crater at his feet.

Paw Paw cut the stalk off at the neck with his pocketknife and handed the root to Tucker, then he jammed the stem in his teeth. His facial expression changed as the bitter flavor hit him. "Hmm. Strong. They say the Indians 'round here used to chew on these before battle. I can see why," he said then turned to Tucker. "How old you reckon that one is?"

Tucker held the root at the base of its neck close to his face. He paused and admired the tightly compressed rings that encircled the top of the root and felt the indentation where it had wound against an underground rock.

"One, two, three …," he mumbled, examining each turn and crook of the root's three-inch-long neck, counting the dimpled scars left over from each year's previous stem. Then he guessed: "Twenty-five?"

Paw Paw chuckled. "At least twice as old as you. Might be older. Big 'seng like that don't come up every year. Only when the woods are right."

Tucker grinned and gave the root back to his grandfather who dropped it into a dirty zip-lock bag that he shook from his knapsack. "First one of the day," Paw Paw said contently.

Tucker nodded to Paw Paw's tattoo peeking from his shirt sleeve. "Bigger than that one, too," he said, referring to the ginseng root sketched into his grandfather's arm.

Paw Paw rolled the sleeve farther up and flexed. While the ink under the skin had faded over the years, an unmistakable three-prong ginseng plant snaked down his arm. Its miniature leaves and berry pod began just below Paw

Paw's shoulder, and its stalk traveled a couple of inches before ending with a small, tentacle-like root above his elbow.

Paw Paw stared at the body art. "Yep. Lucky for me, this was the only bleedin' I took in the war."

"Did it hurt?" Tucker said as he ran his finger along its outline.

"Naw. Just stung a little."

Tucker smiled then turned away to search for more, farther down the hillside. He caught a flash of Danny's shirt behind a maple tree a good way down the holler, stooped over again. "Dang it, Danny," Tucker shouted. "Stay close."

Danny glanced up at his older brother and held up a handful of berries. Tucker looked away, though, and Danny shoved them in his pocket, already damp from the other handfuls he picked.

"Slow pokes," Danny said out loud as he sauntered back towards his brother and grandfather, gliding over downed logs and hopping over bushy ferns like a deer. Looking up at the early fall canopy of the trees above him and following its shadows back down to the forest floor, Danny didn't notice the cub until it stood up directly in front of him.

Paw Paw and Tucker heard the squeals first, but they weren't coming from Danny. The terrified young bear gave a succession of yelps as it ran to a nearby locust and scampered into its branches.

"You stay put," Paw Paw yelled to Danny. "Mama's around here somewhere, and she ain't gonna be happy."

Danny froze.

As soon as the words left his lips, huffing and clacking grabbed their attention from the other side of the holler. Tucker and Paw Paw turned to see a large sow standing on her haunches. She popped her jaws again, gnashing her teeth, and stared directly at them.

Tucker moved closer to his grandfather and noticed the pistol on the ground next to his pack. Paw Paw had removed it from his belt to dig. The mama black bear grunted twice at them, before lowering herself to all fours and cautiously moved towards her distressed cub. Tucker looked around to find Danny, but Danny had disappeared.

While Paw Paw began walking down the hill with his eyes on the sow, Tucker quickly picked up the gun and followed right behind him, frantically scanning the woods for his brother. As the large, jet black female moved closer, now between the two of them and the young bear, Tucker noticed Danny's small figure in the fork of a maple—fifteen feet off the ground, next to the treed cub.

"What is he doing!" Tucker whispered loudly.

Paw Paw glanced up to see what Tucker was talking about.

"Git out that tree, little *bar*!" Danny said, shaking a limb at the cub. "Go on. Git!"

Danny bounced the limber stems of the maple as Tucker and Paw Paw both stared with gaping mouths.

The sow bear regarded all of them with additional grunts and pawed at the ground—still chomping her jaws while quickening her pace. Black bears notoriously postured and bluff-charged when nervous, but this was different. Her cub was treed by some other critter—a small human one.

Tucker felt goose bumps on his arms and made up his mind. He raised the pistol with both hands, pulled back its hammer with his thumb, and put the sights in the center of the sow's head, which was bigger than a pie plate. His hands began trembling. This was different than target practice. The sudden thought of orphaning the cub added ten pounds of weight to the barrel.

Paw Paw heard the clicks of the pistol cocking and spun around, then slowly put his hand on Tucker's arms and pushed them down.

"No need for that, yet. Give it a minute," Paw Paw said without any tension in his voice as he stared at Tucker, whose eyes remained glued to the approaching mama bear.

Without any other prompt, the cub suddenly shimmied down the trunk of the tree and bounded towards its mama. As it rejoined her, Paw Paw picked up where Danny had left off—waving his hands and kicking at the ground.

"Soo-wee!" Paw Paw shouted. "Go on, now. Soo-wee!"

Reunited, and free of any additional threat, the two bears galloped off into the deeper brush.

"Well now. That'll get your heart pumpin'," Paw Paw said, wiping his brow. He watched the bears retreat to the other side of the holler and over the next ridge. "You done good, son. Protecting your brother," he said to Tucker.

A wave of pride and relief washed over Tucker as he slowly passed the pistol to his grandfather. "I thought I was gonna have to shoot her."

"I know. But you did the right thing. She just wanted her little one back."

Tucker nodded then asked, "Is that what you say to scare off a bear?"

"Well, it works for shooing off pigs … or calling them up. Can't remember," Paw Paw joked. Tucker laughed along and then turned to see Danny climbing down from his perch, jumping the final six feet to the ground.

"That mama bear can climb trees, too, you know," Tucker said.

"Not as good as me," Danny said as he trotted back up the hill to join them, unfazed by the whole affair. Tucker shook his head as Paw Paw lowered the hammer on the pistol and tucked it back into his belt.

"Why don't you'uns stay a little closer to me from now on," Paw Paw said.

Danny shrugged.

They spent the rest of the afternoon walking the holler a few steps at a time, finding the perfect ginseng plants as they went, carefully removing the roots from the loam to keep them intact, and planting back the seeds from the wads of ripe berries. Danny wandered off again but stayed within sight this time.

Other than the close encounter, it had been a good day. Between them, Tucker and Paw Paw had filled three bags full of large roots. Judging by the bulges in Danny's pockets, he had discovered his fair share of plants, too, even though he hadn't dug a thing.

As dusk smothered the holler and the crickets cranked up their chirping, Paw Paw decided to call it a day. He pointed up at the stars, visible even with the strong light of the moon. "So, that one is Orion. See those three stars in his belt?" he said. "He rises in the east, sets in the west. So, which way's home?"

Tucker pondered the night sky for a moment longer, then guessed, "That way?" He pointed to his left and looked to his grandfather for a reaction.

Paw Paw ruffled his grandson's hair. "Taught ya good, didn't I?"

Feeling the weight of decision-making lifted, Tucker smiled and put his arm around his little brother's shoulder, resting his hand on Danny's stump under the shirtsleeve. Danny quickly pulled away, shrugging off the affection, and the three of them headed west through the dark woods back to the old truck.

Two

By the time Paw Paw reached the silhouette of the small log house, both boys were sound asleep in the cab. In the dark of night, with a soft yellow glow from the single-pane glass windows, the old cabin didn't look too awful bad. The dew-laden night air softened the edges of his vision and memories, but the Trivette homeplace had known better days.

It had once been a tidy and respected landmark—a symbol of the grizzled determination for which these hills were known. His grandfather, Tucker Paul Trivette, had hewn the logs for the structure himself using trees timbered off the side of Salter Mountain back before the turn of the century. Everyone around still called it Paul's Peak, after the hundred plus acres of Trivette land that stretched from the house to the rocky bluffs surrounding its summit. Tucker Paul had manned a skip hammer and single buck saw on every logging crew that worked the county, methodically harvesting the mammoth old-growth woods for four mountaintops in any direction—until one of those trees got the better of him. Buck Trivette shook his head at the memory. Now a grandfather himself, he hadn't felled a tree in over thirty years.

The boys slowly awoke upon hearing the lowered idle, a sign they were home. As Paw Paw parked the rust-stained Dodge pickup, he let go a deep sigh that was a mix of fatigue and pride ... and loss. Madigail, or "Maddie" as he called her—his wife of 52 years—died a few years back. With her went his will to maintain much of anything, including the house. His do-nothing only son, Ewing, and crippled daughter-in-law, Ruth, had moved in with the two boys in tow after the furniture mill downsized and eventually shut down. Ewing fell victim to the first round of lay-offs, while a slip on the factory floor tweaked Ruth's hip into disability.

Tucker was six at the time and healthy as a horse. Poor little Danny had just been born with only one good arm; his other shriveled to a nub where he should have had an elbow. Ewing didn't even have the decency to name him, referring to the newborn instead as the "one-armed bandit"—until Paw Paw gave his youngest grandson a stronger namesake: Daniel Boone Trivette. Ewing blamed his wife's drinking for the birth defect, but she'd been dry at the time. So maybe it was his fault. Whoever was responsible —God, maybe —the house was everyone's responsibility, but only Paw Paw owned up to it.

Then he gave up.

Where had it all gone? Paw Paw shook his head. While long walks in the woods energized him as much as anything could, the miles traveled in his accumulated years had taken their toll. Overlapping cushions of moss growing on the wooden shingles and a patchwork of clapboard hid what needed to be fixed. The porch sagged more each year, along with Paw Paw's spirit every time he looked at what had become of the once-proud Trivette homestead under Paul's Peak. A generation lost, his only two grandsons all too likely to await their turn in the welfare line.

When Paw Paw cut off the engine, the boys stirred at the silence. "We're home," he told Tucker. "Grab your brother up." He paused to look at the slow, blurry images inside. "See what's goin' on in there tonight," he said, preparing for the nightly set-to.

"Yessir," Tucker said and reached for Danny. But Danny jerked away, using his good hand to open the creaky truck door while nearly falling out onto the ground.

Paw Paw chuckled, "You okay there, little one?" Danny said nothing. He just waved the two of them off and headed for the light of the house.

The tranquility of the sojourn and quiet hike back through evening woods and the sleepy, silent drive home ended as soon as Danny opened the door and barged in with Tucker and Paw Paw close behind. The boys' mother, in her disheveled flannel robe, hobbled toward them with one hand on her hip. The untreated hitch in her giddy-up gave her an almost comical gait.

Her voice pierced the night, carrying into the next valley. "Well it's a-*bout* time!" she screeched through the cigarette glued to the corner of her lips as she glared at their dirt-stained clothes. "You boys are *filthy*."

Danny cut a bee line for the kitchen. She snatched for a sleeve, but he yanked free and darted past, stomping clay from three hollers on the floor as he went.

"I swear. You get back in here!" Ruth yelled then turned to Paw Paw. "Where in creation you been?"

Paw Paw was silent.

"Well, you can clean 'em up, then. It's *late*."

Then she looked at Tucker: "And sweep up this floor. It's a mess."

Paw Paw looked around at the mess—the same mess as when they left in the morning. "They can wash themselves. I'll tend to the broom," he said.

While Ruth continued her rant, lighting up another smoke from the butt of the last one, the boys' father remained seated on the drab, velour couch in the corner of the living room. He stared with bleary eyes at Tucker who shed his worn pair of boots and hopped toward the kitchen. Ewing Trivette took a draw from the glass on the rickety table next to him and set it down with a loud *clunk*. It had been filled and drained multiple times throughout the evening from the near-empty Mason jar on the floor beside him. Reaching for it and finding it empty, Ewing chose to stand, if unevenly.

Tucker gritted his teeth and cringed, expecting a lick to follow soon.

Paw Paw stared at Ewing. "Don't start," he said as he held the front door half open and swept away the clods from Danny's shoes.

Ewing sat back down abruptly and waved at the moth that snuck in the open door towards the only light. "Quit takin' them boys off," he muttered in Paw Paw's general direction. "They ain't got nothin' left in 'em to do no chores."

Paw Paw mumbled under his breath as he took off his boots. They had both given up in their own ways. "No harm done. Had a good day of it but my back hurts. Can't get in and out of the woods as quick as I used to. Dug a pile of 'seng, though. Boys were a big help."

His son mumbled back, "Well, not around here. Chickens ain't fed."

"And the clothes been on the line all day," Ruth added. "Gonna come a shower in the morning."

"Well heaven forbid you get wet." Paw Paw glowered. "What you think pays for them clothes?"

As the back and forth between the elders continued in the living room, Danny snuck outside through the back door. He emptied his pink, wet pocketsful of ginseng berries, stashing them in a metal pail half-full of moist sand hidden behind a back-corner post.

While Danny was outside, Tucker rinsed his hands under the kitchen faucet and wrapped a towel over a cold plate of leftovers that had been sitting on the edge of the sink for the better part of a day. A click and three beeps from the dirty microwave signaled that their dinner was ready. Tucker still marveled at the machine that they now used for most of their meals since Paw Paw brought it home last Christmas, taking the place of the ancient wood stove where the unwashed pots collected.

Paw Paw finally shrugged and turned away from the bickering in the living room as he walked into the kitchen and calmly took a seat at the table. While nibbling on a stale biscuit, he pulled out his journal and jotted down notes and sketches from the day in the forest. Ruth, having said all she had to say, scoffed and limped into the bedroom, sucking on her ever-present cigarette.

After scarfing down their shared meal, the boys took turns washing up outside from the dry-rotting hose behind the house. Shivering in their damp towels from the clothesline, they tip-toed to their room, changed into their pajamas, and hopped into bed without drawing any more attention—a well-rehearsed routine in the Trivette household.

Ewing, drifting into his nightly stupor, stared blankly at the wall on the other side of the living room. His gaze passed over the black and white photo of Paw Paw, then a young man in uniform on the deck of a ship. Beside it hung the family portrait of him, Paw Paw, Ruth and baby Tucker that Maddie had taken not long after Ewing and Ruth signed their courthouse papers. Ewing grunted, closed his eyes, and within a minute slumped over, snoring. He'd come to sometime in the middle of the night and amble into bed. Or not.

Paw Paw finished with his note-making, stood up and stretched stiffly. He walked into the room he shared with his grandsons, turned down the other bed and closed the door.

Three

Paw Paw roused the boys early the next morning. The couch was empty and the other bedroom door shut. Ewing and Ruth wouldn't stir before noon. Paw Paw removed the sack of ginseng from the refrigerator and pulled the boys' breakfast from the oven. Tucker and Danny unwrapped the aluminum foil from the salty ham biscuits as they left the house and loaded into the truck.

Danny took his customary place in the middle hump of the bench in the '68 stake bed. He almost immediately fell back asleep as Paw Paw tuned the radio to the morning news and pulled onto the main road for the half hour trip into town. Tucker's attention piqued at the broadcaster's mention of the President. Miss Tincher had made the whole class write get-well cards after he got shot. He was better now, though. While the commentator droned on about matters that didn't concern him, Tucker began sorting through the cool bag in his lap. Mr. Gragg would like these.

Gragg's Pelt and Herb Mercantile didn't stand out much, architecturally. A simple, square two-story building on the edge of town, its sturdy locust columns supported a small eave and a creaky wooden porch. Tiers of adobe dirt dauber nests clung to the century-old, wormy chestnut boards, encasing one corner of the rusty Dr. Pepper sign whose colors blended into its timbered exterior. The screen door groaned when it opened and slapped a warning against its warped trim every time it shut.

Jim Gragg ran the Pelt and Herb just as the earliest of five generations of Graggs had before him, back when the area was just a trader's outpost, carved out of the woods, connecting the settlements to the expanding veins of logging roads. Gragg's kin had brokered skins, furs, and forest herbs since before timber crews clear-cut the mountains. Pioneers on this end of the southern Appalachians stopped in to swap their hard-won bounties from the wild rivers and frontier borders trading for homesteading supplies like gunpowder, tools, and nails. Small bands of Cherokee even passed through to barter hand-crafted beadwork and baskets for store bought trinkets before retreating to the darker reaches of the country.

The fur and herb trade all but dried up after the train quit running, soon after the furniture mill shut its doors. These days, only a handful of old timers and cash-strapped locals familiar with the land still worked the woods to eke out a few extra dollars trapping an occasional beaver or hauling in leaves, bark, or the roots of plants that held long-standing folk medicine value.

American ginseng still fetched the best price. It weathered the ups and downs of the forest herb market due to high demand from Asia. The medicinal root had been shipped from Appalachia north and south for over three hundred years and was among the goods sent to the Far East on the *Empress of China*— the first American flagship to sail to the southern Chinese port city of Canton in 1784.

Roots from thirty- to fifty-year-old wild plants fetched a premium. A pound of old ginseng could sell for thousands of dollars in the Hong Kong markets. However, trophy roots like that were harder to come by. Each year there were fewer, but they endured, due to the stewardship of the plant that traditional harvesters followed—those from whom dealers like Jim Gragg bought and then sold up the chain.

Paw Paw parked in front of the Pelt and Herb and pulled out his journal. Tucker watched him slowly turn each page, pausing briefly at a drawing of a big tree on the side of a mountain. Tucker recognized the sketch of the burl in the middle of its trunk.

"That's the tree with the heart on it. We were just there," Tucker whispered as Danny nuzzled his head against Tucker's lap, still dozing.

Paw Paw nodded as he thumbed through other pages, stopping to touch-up the penciled images grown fainter through time. He and Tucker both looked up as Zebulon Greene approached the shop, carrying a bag similar to the one Tucker held in his lap.

Zebulon, or Z, as most called him, leased a small cinder block building on the other side of town. The sign on the outside of his shop said "Pawn and Gun." But it was rarely open. Most of his business conducted by appointment only. A special type of mountain entrepreneur, he traded guns, knives, gold jewelry and any other under-the-counter item that one had a hankering to unload for quick cash. This time of year he frequented the Pelt and Herb, usually by himself, but always with a bag or two of root, acquired under questionable harvest.

Most locals maintained a patch of ginseng transplanted into their own woods, some sown from seed taken from wild stashes. Z spent enough time in the shade of the forest to know where to find these "hidden" patches. Most folks had a set church-going routine which took them from home long enough for him to sneak onto their land and dig. It was rumored that Z even conscripted a small band of younger boys to work the woods for him, for a percentage of the haul. They could clean out a patch quickly, moving on to the next, unseen—cashing in on years of work and patience of their neighbors, even family.

Z glanced at Paw Paw, giving a quick nod as he held the door for two others with him: a man in his early-twenties and a boy close to Tucker's age, with dirty pants and a rat-tail hanging out of the back of his ball cap. He followed behind the men. Tucker knew the boy from school—a reliable troublemaker—and he knew what they were bringing in, too. It was digging season.

"We goin' in yet?" Tucker said, impatiently.

"Hold your water," Paw Paw said, as he continued studying and sketching, not even looking up. But after another minute, he finished his notations and closed the little book. He leaned over Danny, still asleep, and placed the journal in the glove compartment. He then opened the truck door quietly, as did Tucker, and they got out and headed toward the store's screen door.

The moment they stepped inside, Danny's eyes popped open. He hadn't been asleep at all—just pretending. He opened the glove compartment, took his grandfather's journal, and began poring over it with intense fascination. Page after page of words and numbers, many of which meant nothing to the boy. But Danny didn't care about those. His eyes lit up at the sketches of plants and places that he *did* recognize, trees, rock fences, the occasional waterfall. The pictures were the best part. To him, they were better than any of the picture books in the school library.

Inside the Pelt and Herb, a smell of the woods hit Tucker, as it always did, as soon as door rattled shut. While there were dried goods and other country store essentials, the animals mounted on the wall caught Tucker's attention first. No less than a dozen deer heads and shiny trout adorned the entryway. A couple of recently tanned deer hides hung against the interior walls. Flies buzzed around bits of yet-cured strands of pink flesh clinging to the skins. A stuffed bear stood in one corner with an open maw, its claws resting on a five-foot tall stump. He shuddered at the recent memory.

In the middle of the store sat a cast iron, potbellied stove which kept the Pelt and Herb toasty during the frigid winters. Most any Saturday night, the local bluegrass pickers gathered around it in rocking chairs with their banjos, fiddles, and mandolins.

Beyond the stove and past the aisles where the general groceries ended, other containers filled the store with earthy pungency. Tucker followed his grandfather past the barrels, burlap sacks, and wooden racks filled with all manner of dried bark, root, and herb. The aroma of the black cherry fruit itched his nose as he scrunched away a sneeze. He thought about the days, the *weeks*, it must have taken to find, collect, peel, dig, cut, haul, and dry it all.

Mr. Gragg leaned behind the counter peering at the needle on a balance scale upon which a pile of ginseng roots lay heaped to one side. Jim's only daughter, Allie, stood on a wooden crate beside him. She swayed back and forth, wagging her pigtails, and studied the men in front of her. Their hands and fingernails were caked with dirt, and the tips of crusty screwdrivers stuck out of their back pockets.

The boy with the rat-tail shuffled around the store as the older men conducted business. Allie kept her eye on him, waiting for him to stash something in his pockets, but he made his way back to the counter, peered at her from behind the other two men, and made a smug face. She knew the kid from school, too, and returned his look with a quick poke of her tongue. Then she fixed her eyes on Zeb Greene again. He maintained a calm gaze that betrayed his sharp jawline and thin brows—made him look sneaky.

Jim finished weighing out the roots, punched some numbers into the calculator on the glass counter, then paid in cash, as he always did, after exchanging few pleasantries. Z lingered a moment while he counted the ten-dollar bills, never purchasing anything with the proceeds except for an occasional box of ammunition that he marked up for resale at his own shop. Satisfied, Z grunted, passed some cash to his cohorts, and the three of them strolled toward the door without a word between them. The kid with the rattail shot Tucker a sneer as he slinked off. Tucker smirked back.

Tucker and Paw Paw waited a moment behind them. As he casually looked around the shop, attempting to play it cool, Tucker tried not to make eye contact with Allie. They were in the same class at school and, *Dang!* He'd caught her glance a moment too long. She rolled her eyes, then giggled as she jumped off the crate and skipped to the other end of the store.

"Wonder whose patch they was into this time," Jim said to Paw Paw after the trio left the shop.

"Guess some poor soul's gonna find out soon enough," Paw Paw said. While many referred to Z and his like as poachers, Paw Paw called them what they were: *thieves*. "Sorry rascals. You stay away from that bunch," Paw Paw said to Tucker. "They's trouble." Tucker nodded, looking back at the door before hefting the bag up to the counter.

"Not waitin' around to sell it dry this year?" Jim asked Paw Paw.

"Boys are growin' outta their clothes. Needin' more school supplies, too," Paw Paw said.

Jim understood. He knew enough about Buck Trivette and his family to know that the old man couldn't sit on his harvest. Sellers this early in the season needed the cash—others, though, brought in just enough to chase their next high.

"So ... whatcha got today, son?" Jim asked Tucker, politely.

Tucker dumped the roots out from his bag onto the scale and watched the needle settle while Mr. Gragg looked over their condition. "Looks like just over forty ounces. These are real nice. Look at the neck on this one." Gragg held up a monster. "Must be over thirty years old," he said to Tucker, then to Paw Paw: "These all look nice. You know I pay more for good 'seng like this. How does one-eighty suit you, Buck?"

"Sounds about right," Paw Paw said.

"Reckon you might wanna share directions?"

"Reckon not," Paw Paw said, but he knew Jim was just pulling his leg.

Mr. Gragg smiled and hit a button on the cash register, which dinged loudly, and proceeded to count out a stack of bills as Tucker watched on intently.

Paw Paw thanked Mr. Gragg and folded the wad into his wallet after peeling off a dollar bill. He handed it to Tucker, who wasted no time heading to the front of the store to pick out a treat.

As Tucker browsed the candy aisle, the front screen door opened again. Sheriff Hicks waltzed in, a toothpick flicking between his lips. He nodded towards Paw Paw and Jim Gragg.

"Mornin' fellas," he said.

"Sheriff," Jim nodded.

"Just got a call from the Cornetts," Hicks said as he casually glanced around the shop. "Len said he ran off some boys back behind the house yesterday. Says they got in his 'seng."

Tucker saw Jim and Paw Paw look at each other and shake their heads.

"It's a comin' in as it always is this time a year, Marty," Jim said. "No way I can tell if it's stole or not."

"I understand," Hicks said, waving off any innuendo. "Just doin' my due diligence."

Marty Hicks had grown up in the county, no stranger to the intricacies of 'seng huntin', moonshining, and other pastimes that he could do little about, or even wanted to fool with. Poverty and desperation brought more nefarious things into the county. It was hard for him to get worked up over a few missing plants in someone's backyard, unless someone got shot over them. And that hadn't happened in a while—not as long as he had been Sheriff.

"You'uns have a good day. Stay outta trouble," He tipped his hat and mussed Tucker's hair as he left the shop.

After paying Jim for candy and a can of soda, Tucker handed his grandfather the change as they left the Pelt and Herb. Tucker crawled into the truck and handed his brother, now wide awake, a handful of wrapped caramels, Danny's favorite. Tucker popped the top of his RC and slurped up the soda before it fizzed into his lap.

Paw Paw slid into the driver's seat and pulled out his journal again, noting the quantity and price of what they had just sold, and put the truck into gear.

"You think Z and them boys stole that 'seng?" Tucker asked.

"Who knows," Paw Paw replied. "But that ain't our business, is it."

"Hmm," Tucker said, thinking about it for a moment. "Guess not. Where're we goin' now?"

"We gotta go see Mr. Clint about gettin' you boys started on that shearing work," Paw Paw said as they pulled away.

Tucker nodded and sipped on his drink while Danny smacked a mouthful of sweets.

Four

Tucker stood at the bottom of the second row and squinted up the hill trying to guess how many were left in just this one. Beads of sweat gathered on his forehead. Though the humidity was low this time of year, the late September sun bore down like the heat lamp on the incubated eggs in Miss Tincher's class. *They'd hatch quicker out here*, he thought.

Tucker counted seventy-five trees, more or less, before he could take a break. At the rate he was swinging the knife, he *might* finish before sundown.

Christmas trees had become a more common sight on the hillsides in the higher altitude reaches of the western part of the state. Fraser firs had replaced the vacant slopes of farmland that used to yield cabbage and taters by the ton, before blights and falling prices emptied wallets and the slopes.

The early 1950s ushered in a new Appalachian industry as frustrated farmers pulled wild seedlings from neighboring mountaintops on the Tennessee border for transplant into their fallow fields. Before long, beds of Fraser starts appeared in river bottoms alongside tobacco, and the practice spread like kudzu. Within a couple of decades, a few hundred tree growers were planting and harvesting Fraser firs in seven to ten-year cycles to supply a new market of fresh-cut Christmas trees. Since then, each November saw tractor-trailers rolling down the winding roads, piled high with stacked bundles of Christmas greenery headed off the mountain to shopping centers and tree lots up and down the East Coast.

Paw Paw sent Tucker and Danny down the road a piece to help Clint Winebarger finish shearing the thousand or more Fraser firs that dotted his hillsides. For a century, the Winebargers and Trivettes shared the narrow, gravel route. Clint remained as the last of his hardened forbears who settled in the high hills at the beginning of the Civil War to escape the fray—a practice common at the time.

Clint and Paw Paw had enlisted together, serving on the same destroyer in the Navy during the Korean War. The boys and Paw Paw spent many an afternoon on Clint's front porch enjoying his swashbuckling tales with a glass of sweet tea. A self-taught historian of the Revolutionary War and a voracious reader of Naval classics, Clint read to the boys on more than one occasion.

"Ah, there is nothing more enslaving than life at sea," he would say, and Tucker would daydream about life on the ocean. Clint was the cool and calm sort with a dry sense of humor, but according to Paw Paw, he'd gnaw the barrel off a pistol if anyone had the notion to put one in his face.

His quick wit and chipper demeanor masked the melancholy of family tragedy. Clint lost his only child over a decade ago, the boy's dirt bike meeting a wayward tractor trailer in the middle of a blind curve. Clint's wife never got over it. Deep depression led to the note left under the empty bottle of pills. Clint channeled the grief of his lost family into the land, becoming a full-time farmer. Along with Christmas trees, he grew a half acre of burley through a family allotment, kept an immaculate garden, and sold produce at a roadside tailgate market. He apparently "dripped corn," too, which never made any sense to the boys when Clint and Paw Paw whispered about it.

The trees required an annual trimming to maintain their desired pyramidal form and sturdy branches on which to hang ornaments. Clint desperately needed help and offered to pay the boys well for their labor. It was not easy work, but it built character, according to Paw Paw. Jim Gragg sent along Allie to help with the shearing, too—even though Tucker didn't think a girl could handle that kind of work. She could. And she didn't let Tucker forget it every time she got close enough to comment on his work. After a short while, young Tucker hung back at the end of his row, letting her get ahead to avoid the biting criticism:

"You're doin' it wrong, Tucker." "Trees don't have shoulders, Tucker." "You're cuttin' 'em too tight, Tucker."

"She's right," Clint added with a wink as he passed from the other row. He continued, raising his eyes to the sky: "*I don't like work ... but I like what is in work—the chance to find yourself.*"

Tucker rolled his eyes and half-heartedly resumed the monotonous swing of the shearing blade—a slender, light-weight machete shaped like a butter knife, but with an edge fierce enough to shave knotwood and kneecaps. The dull ache in each step a reminder of his first careless swing.

"Yep," Clint had said, unspooling the duct tape. "This'll stop the bleeding. But that'll leave a nice scar for you. A man's scars define him. Betchya won't do it again, though."

While unhappy about the eventuality of ripping away the homemade dressing—and working under the brutal gaze of the sun—Tucker learned his lesson, never again swinging the knife anywhere near his body. Still, even he had to admit, he was not a natural for this kind of work. Danny, however, had picked up the skill quickly and wasted no time in his rows, easily keeping up with Clint. Tucker pouted at his younger brother's deftness in the tree field. The boy cruised up and down the fir-speckled hills as effortlessly as he sprinted through the forest—never seeming to tire and sculpting the trees perfectly, his one arm working like a mincer as he danced around each one.

Danny and Clint finished their rows and had even sheared the last dozen in Tucker's.

As Danny met his older brother with a jug of water, Tucker approached the last tree. "You missed one," he said, raising his blade to swing at the first branch, but Danny blocked the tip of Tucker's knife with his own, the tinny ping echoing.

"Wouldn't do that if I was you," he said, nodding to the other side of the tree. "Look in here," he added.

Tucker took a couple of steps to his left and glimpsed at the football-sized, gray orb suspended in the branches. He backed away slowly, watching black worker hornets zip into their dime-sized doorway. The nest's guards turned robotically, tracking Tucker's movement.

"They'd a gotcha good," Danny said, handing him the water jug as they headed to the shade next to the fencerow. Tucker continued to step backwards, staring at the winged demons and contemplating the close call.

Danny leaned his head toward the adjacent cove of hardwoods on the other side of the fence. "Mr. Clint's got him a big patch of 'seng back there," he said out of earshot of anyone else.

"How do you know that?" Tucker said, looking over his shoulder.

"I know a lot more than you'uns think," Danny said as he took a last swig of water and set off to trim his next row. Tucker stared into the woods and the dense greenery below the trees, but couldn't see a thing.

Allie caught up to him a minute later. "You're 'bout as slow as Christmas, Tucker," she said, as she started down her next row singing *"Get out the way, old Dan Tucker, you're too late to come for supper. Supper's over and dinner's cookin', old Dan Tucker just stand there lookin' ..."*

Tucker couldn't help but grin at his and Danny's favorite tune. The old men played it around the stove of the Pelt and Herb on weekends when he and Danny visited with Paw Paw.

Tucker hummed along while he swung his blade, as Allie continued lilting: *"Now old Dan Tucker come to town, swinging them ladies all around. First to the right and then to the left, then to the gal that he loved best."*

Allie peeked around a tree and winked. Tucker blushed and shook his head. Maybe she wasn't so bad after all.

For a girl.

Five

 The boys huddled together with gloveless hands shifting from one pocket to another as they blew vapor-smoke from imaginary cigarettes until the bus arrived. Paw Paw made sure they were waiting at the rusty mailbox at daybreak. As the farthest house on the route, the Trivette brothers were first to be picked up when the weather cooperated and the buses ran. With Spring appearing in earnest, school had returned to a normal schedule.

 The last pile of gray, melting slush made sucking noises under their boots as Tucker and Danny stomped off the bus and up the front walkway that split the school buildings. Built by hand from smooth river stones in the twenties, Chestnut Cove Elementary had once been the only school in the county. A few years back, the county scraped together enough funds to construct an unsightly brick and vinyl addition that looked like a Quonset longhouse to carry the eighth through twelfth grades.

 Tucker would begin junior high after the summer, so his teachers stacked on more homework, getting his class ready for high school, and for some, a shot at moving on. Most of the teachers were local-born and knew every cove from which their students hailed. While they did their best to keep matriculation at state benchmarks, college was a long shot at best for most. And even then, despite the lack of jobs, the mountains pulled most folks back anyway—their identity tied to the peak or holler of their kin, for better or for worse. A lopsided frame outside of the principal's office acknowledged the only three full-scholarship athletes that the school had produced. One of them had even pitched in a few minor league games.

Tucker wondered what that must have been like. He had thrown a mean curveball back when he played with the Baptist boy's league. Even though the town kids made fun of his cleats from Roses and the Catfish Hunter glove that Paw Paw found at a yard sale, he played tough and pitched hard. Tucker cried to himself the night Paw Paw told him he couldn't take him to practice anymore.

"Too expensive. And we don't go to the right church."

Tucker didn't understand what religion had to do with it. But in most small towns, it did.

While he hated leaving the sport, he found new purpose working on his neighbor's farm. Clint kept him busy. Allie too, often to Tucker's chagrin. When she wasn't stocking shelves at the Pelt and Herb, her father sent her to Clint's to gain an appreciation of *real* work, farm work. It was true that Clint needed all the help he could get, but Allie also had a better eye for the detailed top-pruning. Clint referred to the two as Archie and Edith; she and Tucker squabbled as much as his favorite TV couple.

Allie and Tucker suckered, stripped, staked and hung his tobacco crop in the summer and early Fall, and teamed up during tree harvest season come November. They sawed and dragged fresh-cut Frasers from the field to bale and tie onto cars for frostbitten tourists who made the drive from Charlotte to get a taste of snow and pick out a tree. That work kept Tucker and Allie so busy they didn't have the energy to bicker like they normally did.

Allie's competitiveness carried into the classroom even more than on Clint's farm. She kept at least a letter grade ahead of him in every class and had no problem giving him a hard time about it.

"Don't worry, Tucker," she taunted. "I'll hire you to clean up the shop when I get back from college."

At least she left him alone at recess. While Tucker and other boys from his class threw the football or traded baseball cards, the girls thumbed through magazines that Allie snuck from her father's store.

The other kids—the rough ones—kept their distance from everyone, except to torment any loner they could gang up on. Harlan Ward was the worst—just plain country mean. Known as "Rat" for the stringy, braided appendage that began in the back of his head, cascading to just below his left shoulder, Harlan threw a punch at anyone calling him by his given name. Rat received his first suspension in the third grade for charring the substitutes dress with a cigarette lighter as she wrote her name on the chalkboard. After that stunt, Rat attracted a following of other derelicts and soon-to-be dropouts for any sort of mischief he could think up.

Rat's family tree sprouted from a holler of bad soil. His father was serving time for grand theft, and rumors abounded that his mother had run off with the parole officer after her own stint in the county lock-up. So Rat's only family consisted of a delinquent older brother. They shared a run-down, twice-repossessed trailer near the auto body shop where his brother and friends worked part time—liberating parts from vehicles they were supposed to be fixing.

Rat and the other troublemakers hung out in the far corner of the recess field closest to the woods, where the principal couldn't see them sneaking drags off the stubby butts scrounged from the teacher's parking lot.

As Tucker stuffed a banana peel into his book bag, a racket erupted on that end of the empty lot grabbing his attention.

A mob gathered around two boys on the ground. Tucker jogged over with a couple of classmates, shoving his way into the circle to see who Rat and his minions were wailing on this time. Turned out it was Danny. Rat pounded on him in the grassless arena formed by the ring of bodies. "Take it back ya' damn retard," he yelled.

Tucker stepped in and shoved him off. "He ain't a retard!" Tucker said. "He's missin' an arm, not a brain."

"He called my mama a whore," Rat said, pushing himself away from Tucker and moving back toward Danny.

"Well ... she *is*," Danny said, spitting pink from his lower lip.

"Shut up," Tucker said to Danny. "You don't even know what a whore is."

"I do, too," Danny shot back. "His MAMA!"

Rat turned red and reared back for another swing. Tucker caught Rat's arm at the elbow and slung him around into the growing crowd that now included Allie and her friends who pushed their way in to watch.

"You want some of this?" Rat shook his fist at Tucker, then looked back at Danny.

"I don't need your help, Tucker!" Danny bristled.

"Two fists are better'n one," Tucker said. He wanted a piece of Rat himself.

"One's enough for me," Danny said. He looked back at Rat and said: "WHORE." Rat charged.

Danny stepped forward quicker than Rat expected. As Danny reared back, feigning a swing with his good arm, he stabbed Rat in the eye with the nub of his other. Rat collapsed grabbing his face, yowling. "OWWW. Nasty stump! He stumped me!"

Allie and the other kids laughed but scattered as the principal threw open the cafeteria door and jogged toward the melee.

Rat stumbled away with one of his mini-gang, hurling obscenities at Tucker, Danny, and anyone else he saw. "Sons of bitches! You just wait," he yelled as he limped off. "I'll git you all! Every one of ya!"

"You're twice his size, pecker-head. Got what you deserved!" Tucker yelled back.

Tucker grabbed Danny, slinking away in the opposite direction. "You don't need to start crap like that with those boys. Gonna get your ass whipped one of these days and it ain't gonna be pretty. Rat and them'll come after you."

"I ain't scared of 'em," Danny said as he tore free. "And I don't need your help, neither."

Tucker let him go, shaking his head, then turned around to see if any teachers were heading his way, almost colliding into Allie.

"You shoulda kicked his dumb butt all the way to Clemson," she said.

"Huh?" Tucker said. "Why Clemson?"

"Because I'm going there someday, and you're not."

He stared at her, confused.

"That's right, just stand there looking stupid, Tucker Trivette. And shut up," Allie said as she pushed him then ran back to her giggling friends.

Tucker stood bewildered, fired up, and speechless all at the same time. "Why don't *you* shut up, Allie," he said out of earshot, then trod back to class.

Tucker spent the long ride home sprawled across the entire back seat of the bus scribbling out the answers to math problems while Danny leaned against the window gazing through the hole he repeatedly rubbed and fogged over again with his breath.

The bus kicked up a fine sheen of dust from the shoulder of the road where it U-turned after dropping off the boys. Tucker and Danny raced each other from the mailbox, slapping the branches of the sagging willow that all but hid the house from the road. Danny outpaced his brother handily, even faster on gravel as he was in the woods.

As they reached the house, Ruth stood up from her crate seat next to the steps. The cherry on her cigarette glowed hell-orange as she took a long drag, still in her nightgown. Smoke dribbled down her chin as she spoke. "What happened to your face?" she said, noticing Danny's puffy lip as he blew past her.

Danny tossed his book bag on the porch without stopping and ran inside through the open front door. Ten seconds later, he jumped back through the doorway as fast as he ran in, ignoring her again as he vaulted the railing and skipped up the hill towards the forest.

"He's alright," Tucker said.

The front door swung open and Ewing shouted at Danny, already halfway to the fence line. "Where you goin', boy? Get back here. You got chores."

"I'll do 'em," Tucker said, choosing to keep quiet about the fight, even though any other father would be proud of his boys whooping the school bully.

"Take a strap to him, he don't come back before dark, again. Sneakin' off all the time. Lazy, worthless ..." Ewing mumbled as he turned back for the open door.

"Where's Paw Paw?" Tucker said.

His father waved towards the coop. "Tend the chickens, now. Ain't gonna tell you twice."

"There's dishes in the sink too," Ruth said as smoke rolled out of her nostrils.

Tucker glanced up the hill as he picked up the rusty pail of feed and ambled towards the hen house. He saw Danny duck under the fence and disappear into the forest at the top. No one would bother him up there.

He headed for his favorite spot, far beyond the cabin. Paw Paw had taken the boy there—only him—the year before. Danny learned the complicated way in one trip, never to forget. Just before reaching the last crest of his destination, he paused at the stacked stones just off the whisper of the trail. The marker. A shiver began at the base of his neck and rose to the peaks of his ears as he remembered what he and Paw Paw had buried beneath it:

The creature had appeared suddenly, just ahead, in the middle of the path, materializing out of the opaque blankets of clouds drifting across the escarpment. Danny, while fearless of anything else with four legs of the woods, instinctively stepped behind his grandfather as a low growl gurgled in the beast's throat, an effervescent sputum dribbling from fangs showing within a quivering maw— its ears gnawed ragged and asymmetrical by things from the forest even more sinister, its otherworldly eyes, red orbs, with black centers. Danny shuddered, seeing into its soullessness.

Paw Paw stiffened and pushed Danny even farther behind him without saying a word. Shouts of warning or displays of aggression would do no good, Paw Paw knew.

This creature was different than its origin. Transformed from some deliberate cross of curs, the patches of mange that dripped from its haunches created a wraith of leathery rind and fur from what had once been a formidable bear dog, a Plott hound perhaps bred with something more menacing, abandoned or lost, but beset by viral demons.

Though it happened quicker than a primer igniting gunpowder, Danny remembered every detail: the mongrel lunged and Paw Paw stepped forward to meet it. In what seemed like one fluid motion, he unsheathed the buck knife at his side with his right hand, grabbed the dog by the scruff at the thick collar buckle welded into its neck, and plunged the blade deep into its sternum, slicing upward. He released his hold and backed away, feeling behind for Danny, who had not flinched, as the gurgling death-bays of the writhing animal subsided, its warm viscera emptying into the duff.

Confident that the creature would move no more, Paw Paw turned to Danny. "Always keep your senses sharp and your knife sharper," he had said, wiping the stained blade on his pants leg. "Nothing else you can do for that kind of evil. We need to bury it, though. Less it spread."

Danny gazed at the stones a moment longer, remembering Paw Paw's words, but putting the memory behind him as he went on his way.

Using his one arm to balance, Danny scuttled over large rocks and continued up the side of the mountain. The grey, granite stones had been made smooth by time, enveloped with a patchwork of pale lichen after tumbling from ragged peaks, eons ago—victims of countless winter freezes, thaws and flowing rivers. Only trickling waters remained in the crotches of the long-settled mountains. And Danny knew every spring, creek, and crossing with firm footing to avoid soaking his only pair of hand-me-down boots.

After a while, he came to the familiar outcropping of immense boulders, set back into the hillside. To the untrained eye, they appeared to be freestanding and unfettered by the earth's clutches, but to Danny, they spelled deep comfort. This place, his secret.

He entered through a cleft in the rocks, stepping across the fine silt of its opening, like a welcome mat, worn thin from time and the footsteps of ghosts. This place had only known his feet, and Paw Paw's for a hundred years or more—and maybe those of the occasional bear.

When Paw Paw first showed the cave to little Danny, he did so with quiet reverence; he had discovered this place fifty years earlier as a child himself. Inside lay shards of tempered pottery and flakes from the working of arrowheads. That and black smudges from bygone hearths provided evidence of those who once called it home—a deep crevice in the old rocks leading into the earth, kept dry by its primeval walls.

After touching each side with the same respect his grandfather had shown, Danny stepped out again, returning through the front slit, and climbing atop the roof of the stone fortress. Thick forest prevented distant views, but to Danny, it was perfect. If he held his head just right, and focused his eyes on the farthest horizon through the widest crack between the towering chestnut oaks, he could see the peak of the next mountain.

He thought: *I can see Injuns comin' a mile off.* The isolation and protection of this sanctuary gave the boy great comfort, the troubles of home far away. He lay back with a broad grin on his small face, to take in the high canopy, and the blue sky beyond. After a suitable amount of gazing time, he sat up and opened the poke by his side—a cloth sack he made himself, just like the one Paw Paw carried to gather herbs—or as close as Danny could get to it, using his one good hand, his teeth, and one of his mother's few sewing needles.

Opening the sack, he pulled out the dull, maroon book. Paw Paw's journal. He had snuck it from the nightstand, as he did when he wandered the backwoods alone—just like his grandfather would. With the same care given to the walls of the cave, Danny caressed the cover of the ledger, then opened its stiff binding.

One by one, he examined each entry front to back. His eyes passed quickly over tracings of landmarks near the homeplace, the creek dividing the holler behind Paul's Peak, and the precipice of stone he sat upon. Every place Paw Paw had taken him, and many he hadn't, traced in graphite—rough-sketched images of peaks and forest rarely seen by man or his saws. Paw Paw's clues to the wilderness. They all meant something. Danny had sought out many of the hidden hollers on his own.

He flipped to the end of the journal, and stared at the one sketch he couldn't place, a big one. The details of the illustration stretched across the last two sheets. Danny's eyes crinkled. The image portrayed a cluster of trees drawn from a distant perspective, encircled entirely by a ring of what Danny thought to be shrubs, laurels maybe. However, the meaning of the faintly penciled numbers in the margin alluded him. He turned the journal sideways and upside down trying to figure Paw Paw's code, glancing up occasionally to get his bearings. In the middle of the drawing, in the crotch of the spine, the outline of a long, gnarled ginseng root stretched from the top of the book to the bottom. His grandfather's secrets whispered to him within its pages.

Danny ran his finger across the image and grinned. Then he stood up, put the book back in his poke, jumped off his perch and began walking.

It wouldn't be dark for hours.

Six

Paw Paw handed over the keys to the old Dodge truck just after Tucker's seventeenth birthday. "Early graduation present," he said. "A man your age needs his own wheels."

Tucker grinned widely at his *new* ride. Paw Paw had made him work on the truck for a whole year before letting him in the driver's seat. On the weekends, with Paw Paw's guidance, Tucker learned how to change the oil, work on the brakes, tweak the transmission, and make the other adjustments that the well-worn pickup demanded.

After months of running the mechanic's gauntlet, Paw Paw put him behind the wheel—first, on flat farm roads to learn the finesse of the clutch and gears, then on the steep, winding routes in the back country. Having his own truck meant no more hours on the bus, but now Tucker was responsible for getting himself and Danny to and from school.

Danny lounged on the long cobblestone wall outside the annex, enjoying the sunshine and waiting on his ride. He snuck out of P.E. early, cutting through the hedgerow at the edge of the playing field. For Danny, his long afternoons in the woods gave him more physical education than he could ever get at school. Even as a seventh grader, he outran most of the seniors without breaking a sweat.

The brakes squawked as Tucker pulled up beside him. "Hop in. We gotta git," Tucker said.

"Where we goin'?"

"Gragg's. I need new spark plugs."

Danny stretched, taking his time sliding off the rock perch. He knew why his brother was in a hurry.

"Come on, I ain't got all day."

"Afraid she'll be there?" Danny said. He laughed at how jumpy Allie made his brother. She still put Tucker on the spot any time they saw each other.

"I wanna get there before she does," Tucker said, looking through the rearview. "Don't feel like hearing her lip."

"I think she likes you," Danny said, smiling.

Tucker huffed. "Has a funny way of showing it."

Danny slid onto the bench seat and Tucker peeled off.

Ten minutes later, Danny lurched forward as Tucker came to an abrupt stop in front of the Pelt and Herb and sprinted inside. Danny followed quickly behind, grabbing a Cheerwine and a pack of Nabs.

"What's the hurry, boys?" Jim Gragg said as Tucker rushed straight to the auto parts rack and returned to the register where Danny waited with his snacks.

"Tucker's gonna teach me how to drive," Danny said. Tucker shot his brother a surprised grin. Well-played. Danny winked at him.

"Never too early to learn," Jim said as he handed Tucker the change.

The boys jogged back outside, hopped in the pickup, and backed away from the store just as Allie pulled behind them, blocking Tucker's exit with her much-newer truck.

"What are you doing, Allie?" Tucker said through the window.

"Oh, sorry. Thought you might need a tow or something," she said. "You sure that antique can make it back to your place?"

"Very funny," Tucker said. "It runs just fine."

Allie persisted, grinning. "For now. Be happy to give you a ride, you know, when it breaks down."

Danny giggled and Tucker stared straight ahead with his tongue gouging a hole in his cheek, gripping the steering wheel.

"Bye, Allie," Danny said.

Tucker waved without looking as she drove around to the back of the store.

"Yeah, she likes you," Danny repeated as Tucker reversed away from the Pelt and Herb.

Near where the pavement ended, Danny pleaded to finish the trip at the wheel. Tucker finally gave in, patiently showing him how to change gears, use the brake, and keep a steady speed. While his feet barely reached the gas pedal, Danny steered the country roads one-handed with enthusiasm as he peered over the dashboard. As they passed Clint's place, something inside the engine rattled.

"I didn't do nothin'," Danny said.

"I know. I'll check it out at home," Tucker sighed. "Dang sure ain't the spark plugs this time."

As soon as they pulled into the driveway, Danny jumped out of the truck racing upslope, headed for the woods to find his grandfather. While the arthritis had caught up with him, his stoop even lower to the ground, Paw Paw still piddled with ramps growing in the forest close to the house, moving clusters of the rhizomes from good soil to better soil, ensuring the patch of wild leeks would spread. Mr. Gragg sold them to a real sit-down restaurant at the resort the next town over whose chef paid top dollar for the garlicky-flavored sprout to garnish fancy dishes. Danny liked them just fine fried up with eggs.

Tucker lifted the hood on the Dodge in the front yard and fished around inside the engine, checking loose cables and any one of the hundred parts of the ornery engine that could rattle for no apparent reason. Fan belt, he guessed. As he looked up to grab the spanner lying on the battery, he noticed Danny at the top of the hill, in a slow and deliberate descent.

Tucker paused, craning his neck. Something was wrong. Danny and Paw Paw rarely came in until well after dusk.

Danny limped down the mountain, his head lowered, swinging his arm like dead weight.

"What's goin' on?" Tucker said as Danny reached the truck.

"He's up there," Danny whispered, nodding towards Paul's Peak. "Barely made it past the fence line."

"Huh?" It took Tucker a second to catch on, but when he saw the tears welling up in his brother's eyes, his chest tightened and ears tingled as the blood left his face. "What do you mean, Danny?"

"I don't know." Danny's shoulder's lurched forward as he sank to the ground, wrapping his arm loosely around the back of Tucker's knees, before letting go. He rocked back and forth on his ankles, curled in a ball as if gut-punched. "I don't know," he repeated between sobs. "He ain't moving. I didn't know what to do."

"No, no, no," Tucker said as the wrench slipped through his fingers and rattled off the engine block as he dashed up the hill into the forest. Panting as he dove under the fence, he darted from one side of the trail to the other, more frantic at second that passed.

"Paw Paw!" His voice cracked into a moan as he yelled, fearing each round of silence as his echoes passed. "Where are you?"

Dread of the inevitable churned his stomach as he stepped over the low-growing border of vegetation just below the main trail and saw the gray and white checkerboards of his grandfather's flannel shirt flecking through the forest's green. Paw Paw sat slumped over at the base of a blackgum, a handful of ramps spilling from his grasp. For a moment, it looked as if he was napping. The same comfortable repose of a sofa slumber after a big Sunday lunch. Tucker approached slowly, from behind, and reached out to touch him, but stopped—as if scared to wake him.

The wind of a coming front took the burn from the heat on his cheeks and Tucker looked away purposefully, wiping the mist from his eyes and staring through the canopy to the now-gray sky. As the gust subsided, he stooped to shake his grandfather's stiff shoulders, before erupting into sobs as he dropped to the ground and hugged his Paw Paw as hard as he could, one last time.

The editor of the six-page weekly paper, who attended every viewing in the county, gazed at the ceiling from the back row of mostly-empty chairs seeking inspiration for the obituary.

Paw Paw's body lay in state in the open casket at the front of the chapel, a tradition that still gave Tucker the willies. At least they didn't have him packed in ice like they used to during warm-weather wakes. He and Danny waited in the receiving line while Ewing fussed with Daryl Hollars over the cost of the service in the nave, even though Paw Paw had paid for most of his own arrangements years ago.

From where he stood, Tucker could see the white bridge of Paw Paw's brow just above the lip of the shallow coffin. The overhead light touched one bead of glue at the base of an eyelid just right, resembling the tiniest of tears. He thought his grandfather looked uncomfortable in a tie, but the undertaker had insisted.

The bile rose in Tucker's throat from the dank smell of the chamber, causing sweat to dampen his forehead. He wiped it away with the sleeve of one of Paw Paw's old wool suits—the only article of clothing from the attic not riddled with holes from moths or mice. Tucker squirmed in the tight, itchy jacket, as his high school growth spurt had transformed him from boy to young man almost overnight.

Years had passed since anyone in the Trivette family had occasion for formalwear. Ruth wore a brightly colored sun dress and a scarf that didn't fit her nor the occasion. Danny's borrowed outfit once belonged to Clint's son, who had been a bit older than Danny at the time of the accident. While it made Danny uncomfortable, Clint had been emphatic that he wear it. The quick hems that Ruth tried to stitch had failed, and the pants legs swallowed his shoes as he shifted in place while the few attendees patted shoulders and offered polite condolences to the Trivettes.

After the viewing, Sheriff Hicks led the hearse and a small entourage of pickups to the cemetery near the stone church where a long line of kin had been baptized, married, and buried. Paw Paw would lay next to Mamaw Maddie in the Trivette plot—a family reunion of modest granite and marble markers dating back to the 1800s. Danny and Tucker lifted one end of the wooden box alongside their father. Jim Gragg, Clint, and a Marine Sergeant from the VFW hefted the other side of the casket, and together, they set it on the bier. Ewing did his best to keep his hands from shaking. He hadn't had a drink all morning.

The preacher concluded his brief eulogy, extolling Buck Trivette's virtuous relationship with wife and family, his love of the woods and hills, and the earth to which he was being returned. Clint removed a medal from his neatly pressed uniform and carefully laid it next to the small wreath of plastic flowers. "Goodbye, old friend," he said without a tear, tapping the casket. He gripped Tucker's shoulder as he walked past, looking hard through hazy eyes. "Your grandfather was a fine man. Always proud of you boys. Make sure it stays that way."

As Ewing and Ruth passed, they both tossed a handful of soil scraped from the burial mound into the grave. Danny followed, reaching into his pocket and quickly throwing in a handful of seed, his own tribute to his grandfather—making sure some of the woods went with him. A stoic Tucker stared at the simple pine box, still stunned that his grandfather was gone.

Allie, standing next to her father, tenderly touched Tucker on the arm as finally turned away from the grave and walked past. Tucker stopped for a moment to shake Mr. Gragg's hand, and Allie reached up, giving him a tight hug. "I'm so sorry," she said.

"Thanks, Allie," he said. Their childhood angst and rivalry peeled away for a moment, and it surprised him at how mature and pretty she looked, even in black.

"Will you be okay?" she said.

"I'll make it," he said. "Danny's taking it pretty hard, though." They both turned to see him making a beeline, head down, towards the truck.

"How about your dad," Allie said.

Tucker cringed. "What about him? And Mama's only talked about his stuff. What she's gonna do with it. Ain't even in the ground yet." He shook his head and nodded to the parking lot. "Look at 'em."

Allie turned to see Ewing and Ruth strolling to the waiting Lincoln the funeral home provided. Ruth opened up a new box of Pall Malls as she limped to the car, while Ewing promptly opened the pint bottle smuggled to the service in his jacket pocket. Tucker remarked at the unseemliness of the two as the driver held the door. Ruth bumped her head as she ducked in.

Mr. Gragg intervened. "Listen. You let me know if you and your brother need anything, okay?" he said. "Anything, now. Buck was one of a kind."

"Appreciate it," Tucker said. "You still buying ramps?"

"I'll take all you got." Mr. Gragg said with a smile, winked and patted him on the shoulder. Allie squeezed Tucker's hand with a sorrowful look before walking away. Then Tucker entered the small fellowship hall next to the cemetery. After shaking the preacher's hand, Mrs. Gragg handed him a foil-covered pan— casseroles being the side-dish of death.

He left the church carrying the dish and opened the door to the truck. Danny's suit lay neatly folded in the passenger seat. Tucker looked up and noticed his brother already in a pair of jeans and boots on the dirt road from the cemetery heading in the direction of Paul's Peak.

Tucker pulled the truck alongside his brother. "You need a ride somewhere?"

Danny remained mute, eyes fixed on the gravel, and kept walking. Tucker followed him for a moment in silence, then drove past, to let his brother grieve in his own way.

On returning home, Tucker shoved the casserole into the refrigerator and walked into the bedroom to change clothes. He stared at Paw Paw's bed. Still made. His pillow centered and squared perfectly with the headboard and the clean but worn bedspread tightly tucked between mattress and box spring, rubbed smooth of any crease. Neat but empty, as it would be forever. Tucker opened the closet to rehang the suit and thumbed through the other garments, sliding each threadbare pair of pants towards the other side—remembering Paw Paw's deliberate gait in every outfit. Mismatched patches were rough-sewn onto the elbow of each shirt, like bandages, covering the casualties from the blackberry thickets and hours spent on bended knee prying root from soil.

At the end of the rack, tucked into the far corner, hung the uniform. Tucker hid behind it as a kid, playing hide-and-seek with Danny or evading his father's belt. The stiff bag draped to the floor offered perfect refuge. He had only seen Paw Paw wearing it in the living room photo that no one seemed to notice anymore. Tucker pulled the twill jacket and trousers from the hardened plastic and held them up facing the mirror on the armoire. The stark, formal whiteness of the garments contrasted everything else inside and outside the house. Other than a light sheen of bronzed green tarnish on the buttons, it looked like it had been starched and pressed yesterday.

Tucker's wheels began to turn. His glory days of high school, if he could even call them that, were quickly coming to an end. What would he become if he stayed here, in town, in this house? A farmhand at Clint's or a janitor at the Gragg's shop like Allie had always said? Or his dad? *No way in hell.* But there weren't any good jobs to speak of. He made a little money working for Clint, and his grades were okay, but not nearly good enough for a scholarship. He hadn't even bothered applying to the community college the next county over.

But the military loved small towns. Recruiters from each branch were setting up interview booths in the counselor's office next week. Tucker and his fellow seniors had just taken the ASVAB test. He had even finished first, completing the three-hour exam in just under two, but hadn't given the slightest thought to enlisting—until now, with the dress whites in hand.

He held up the uniform again and thought, *I'd look pretty good in one of these.*

Seven

Tucker returned home from Clint's late in the afternoon with a sack of potatoes that thudded on the loose boards in front of the door. Clint had been providing glass jars of canned vegetables and stewed venison from his ample root cellar since Paw Paw died. The boys had fended for themselves, which they were used to, but Tucker appreciated the groceries. Clint had plenty.

Nobody stirred inside the house. Danny, brooding and distant since the funeral, rarely came home before midnight. While usually in bed when Tucker woke him up for school, he spent most of his time in the woods doing who knows what.

While the butts inside Ruth's overflowing coffee-can ashtray still smoldered, she was gone, too, off to see Gloria. Ruth's only first cousin had just moved back to town. Her most recent ex-husband left her to find Jesus—with a younger member of his Bible study. So she returned to the holler where she and Ruth were raised, not far from the Trivettes. She called the day she moved back needing help to re-situate the empty house.

Their mothers, twin sisters, had borne Ruth and Gloria out of wedlock within a year of each other, raising the girls together like siblings. Gloria's extroverted, busy-body personality contrasted Ruth's quiet stiffness. While Gloria thrived on being the center of attention, Ruth's introversion had kept her in the shadow of her cousin, her only "sister" and best friend through school. Gloria set up Ewing and Ruth on their first date her junior year, and the two married soon after Ewing dropped out of high school. There had been love there, once, or the closest thing they knew to call it at the time. Ruth broke the news that she was pregnant after the first month of "courting;" Ewing resigned himself to signing the papers at the courthouse when Ruth was almost to term with Tucker.

Upon hearing of Gloria's return, Ruth jumped at the chance to spend time with her again—a reprieve from the dulling routine at the Trivettes. She left each day around noon to the dilapidated cabin where they had both grown up, left vacant since the aunts passed within a week of each other over a decade ago. There, Ruth dusted away cold cobwebs and helped unpack Gloria's things while her cousin began her new teller job at the small branch of High Mountain Bank.

After the funeral, the cousins swooped in like vultures over fresh road kill to pick through Paw Paw's meager belongings. They took two trips to the weekend flea market across the state line, hocking antique furniture and a Victrola discovered in the upstairs alcove, returning with mismatched décor and boxes of sundries for Gloria's 'new' house.

Ewing's bender since the funeral left him passed out on the porch or in the yard, when he came home at all. He sobered up just long enough to see about the flats on the Plymouth that Ruth and Gloria had driven nearly to the rims returning from Tennessee.

"Bring that lug wrench from the truck," Ewing barked at Tucker as he dragged tread-bare replacements from under the porch.

Tucker tightened the nuts on the rear wheel of the moss-colored coupe backed against the strands of chickenwire. The beat-up Valiant matched the sorry state of the patch of vegetables Paw Paw had transplanted in just before the last frost. After changing the tires, Ewing and Tucker both stared into the fenced plot. No one had paid it any attention. Tucker felt a pang of guilt. He had always helped his grandfather mound the soil around the starts, plucking the ever-present weeds that plagued them. Even Ewing shook his head at its state of disrepair. The Trivettes had always had a garden, even a meager one, and it just seemed wrong somehow to let it go.

A few sprouts of corn, bean vines, and greens peeked through the poke and burdock choking most of the edibles. Chickens fluttered to the crooked posts as Ewing made weak passes to shoo them off. Tucker took the hoe hanging by its broken handle from the rusted fence strands and made a few stabs around the small hummocks where the potatoes seemed to be struggling the most.

"We don't get some rain soon, ain't even gonna be worth weeding," Tucker said.

Ewing glowered in a semi-sober state as he stooped to pull up thistles smothering one corner of the plot. Watching his father mope around the garden, flailing weakly at the chickens, the last of the Leghorns that Danny had hatched in 4-H, Tucker saw only bitterness. He wanted to tell him the big secret, but knew Ewing's reaction wouldn't be pride. It never was.

Tucker had passed his physical readiness exam and spent the last two weeks meeting with the Navy recruiter. Since he hadn't yet turned eighteen, he nervously forged Ewing's signature on the consent form in the school bathroom. After taking the oath of enlistment, the recruiter told him he'd be off to basic after graduation and on a ship before he knew it. He was in.

"See if that hose will reach out here," Ewing said.

"I'll check." Tucker rehung the hoe and walked towards the house, wiping sweat off his cheeks and surveying the disrepair of the grounds of the old home place, the low afternoon sun drawing attention to every pathetic detail.

"Just a few more weeks," Tucker mumbled to himself as he approached the corner of the cabin and uncoiled the kinks near the spigot. As he pulled the rest of the hose from under the crawl space, the nozzle hung.

"What now?" Tucker said as he peered below the house. Sand poured from a large, metal pail that the hose had knocked over, and there were two more full ones beside it. He pulled the half-rusted tin containers from under the porch, spilling more.

Feeling a different texture between the grains that ran through his fingers, he separated a few of the small, bead-like objects and rolled them into his palm. It took him a second to realize it was seed—ginseng seed—and a lot of it. Tucker scratched his head. He had squeezed them from ripe berries each fall, but always replanted them next to the mother plant. *Dang! Where'd he get all these?* he thought. Then he remembered. Paw Paw always said it took two winters for the seed to sprout after falling to the ground. If he had picked these last fall, they were ready to plant.

Damn shame, Tucker thought as he grabbed the buckets and drug them up to the stoop. As he ambled back to the garden with the leaky hose, he looked up at the forested hillside above the house, then back at the full buckets. *Why not?*

he thought. *No need for them to go to waste.* The garden might not make it, but Tucker would make sure that Paw Paw's last seed did.

The conversation about the Navy with Ewing could wait.

Tucker sifted the sand from the last pail and stared at the mound of seed. *Gotta be over ten pounds, here.* Staring at the huge pile of potential, Tucker contemplated what it would take to get it all in the ground. At least a couple acres. He gazed at the dense undergrowth of the forest for long, agonized minutes—then dove in.

Laurel thickets crowded much of the understory in the lower section of Paul's Peak. He hiked just past a barrier of brambles, then began hacking at trunks and dragging limbs downslope into discreet piles—attempting to make his efforts less obvious to anyone like Zebulon Greene and his conscripts who might roam the woods in search of what he was planting. But these woods were far enough off the main road, he thought. Nobody would bother it out here.

Each day after school, Tucker worked hard and steady. On the morning of the second day, his arms felt like jelly. By Day Three, he hurt to his core. The underbrush came by its nickname honestly— "green hell." Clint's recounted stories came to mind of rebel guerrillas retreating into the thick stands to avoid detection from the Red Coats, while sniping at them from within. Tucker now fully understood why. On certain sections of the mountain, he could barely see beyond the next shrub.

Early on the fourth day, Tucker found the first yellow jacket nest in a bare spot, warmed by afternoon sun. The ten-foot long limb he drug across its hidden entrance in the hard-pack roused a few hundred of the meat-bees. He kept his distance from their underground nest, knowing that as long as one didn't find him, the rest wouldn't pursue. "Don't even know I'm here," he marveled as they rose into a buzzing dust-devil, searching for the interloper.

Yellow jackets are just plain dumb that way. Not like hornets, thankfully. *Those things'll chase you for miles.* Since they hadn't pegged him, Tucker took a live-and-let-live approach and moved on, careful not to brush the hole again.

On the fifth day, he wasn't so fortunate. Tired from the work and the heat,

Tucker stooped to wipe his dripping temples, and only then realized that he was standing squarely on a new hole, a different hive, in a similar hot spot, but on the far side of the widening clearing. Before he appreciated what was happening, yellow waspers mobbed him in their vortex like a mini, inverted tornado—angry and bent on revenge.

When the first one popped him, Tucker swatted—and smashed it. The others gave chase. Before he could get ten feet away, they peppered him even through the denim. As he jigged away, swinging fists like a schoolyard brawler, one popped him just under his left eye, bringing tears. "That does it!" Tucker cried, headed for the shed.

He returned with a can of white gas and a book of matches. "We'll see who wins this one," he told his still-swarming enemies, and ran past, splashing as much gas into the hole as he could hit on the run—a sizable amount, as it turned out. Carefully lighting a crisp laurel twig until its popping leaves ignited the branch high in flames, Tucker stepped as close as he dared and tossed it at the busy hive.

FLOOF. He felt the heat of the vapor ignite as he ran.

"Fire in the hole," he laughed, as flames tore into the ground and up into the air, cooking everything in front of the hole, and melting the bees in the ground. There wasn't enough left to feed a small skunk.

"Take that," he said, victorious and swollen.

After cleaning the hillside, barely able to bend over after dragging out the remaining brush, Tucker raked rows out of the leaf litter from the top of the now park-like clearing and worked his way down. He sprinkled the seed sporadically through each row, tilling the seed into the soil a bit with the broken garden hoe, then blanketing the beds with the leaves from the row above—the only method that made sense given the amount of seed.

Rake, sprinkle, hoe, cover—repeat, again, and again, row after row. Late afternoon shade from the canopy above provided some relief from the sun, but after sowing the last handful, Tucker Trivette was drenched and exhausted—if satisfied. He walked over each bed once last time, tamping down loose leaves and soil before finally collapsing against a maple tree at the bottom of the hill, surveying the tribute to his grandfather.

"This would have taken Paw Paw all year," he said to himself, drinking the last of his sweet tea, and canteen-water from the spring, and the small bottle of store water he'd found in the shed next to the gas. While still thirsty, he beamed at his efforts. Now he could rest. Aching from scalp to toenail, Tucker stood to gather his tools and headed down the hill, confident this secret 'seng spot would someday become a cache of giant roots.

Not too far away, Danny slipped back into the woods from behind an outcrop of rocks, having watched his brother toil the whole week. He crept away silently and unnoticed—grinning.

Eight

Ewing's open palm landed hard across Tucker's face from the other side of the kitchen table. It stunned more than hurt. His father hadn't swung at him like that since Tucker had grown big enough to be reckoned with. Clint's farm had worked the childhood softness out of him. But Tucker's announcement didn't go over well.

Ruth lit up a cigarette and retreated to the bedroom, knowing what was coming. Danny watched in silence from the tattered sofa. Tucker had told him on their way back from school that he was going to share the news, and Danny came in early for dinner just to see the reaction, but had second thoughts now as the first fist had flown.

"The *hell* you say, boy?" Ewing shouted.

"It was good enough for Paw Paw, it's good enough for me, too," Tucker said, rubbing his cheek with one hand and pointing at the Navy photo on the wall.

"I don't need his help. He's gone now. I need you here at the house, dammit," he said, as he swigged from the nearby bottle, then pointed at Danny. "That worthless freak of nature don't do nothin' around here except run off to play in the woods."

"Don't put that on Danny. It's because of you he ain't got—" Tucker began, but Ewing interrupted.

"Why you little sonofabitch. Ain't nothin' wrong with me. It was *her!*" he yelled in the direction of the bedroom.

"Shouldn't talk about Mama like that," Danny chimed in, glaring at his father.

Ewing quickly turned and hurled the bottle at Danny, who ducked in time as glass and liquor spattered the room. Danny leapt out of the chair and through the front door as his father lunged to take a swing at him, too.

"You'll get worse, I swear!" Ewing said as the bedroom door latched shut. Ruth wasn't about to intervene.

Now it was just him and Tucker.

"This is what you're gonna get, boy," he said, with a finger in Tucker's face, saliva dribbling from one side of his mouth. "You'll show me some respect and take your whoopin' like a man." His dad glowered with red eyes.

Tucker stood resolute, his own eyes widening seeing his father making good on his threat. As Ewing charged, Tucker dodged to the side and shoved his father to the floor with all his weight, stabbing one knee squarely in the middle of his spine and pressing Ewing's jaw into the hardwood slats.

Tucker hissed between clenched teeth: "You ain't never hittin' me again, old man. And you ain't never touchin' Danny or Mama no more, neither. I'll have you hauled away. Or worse. You hear me?"

"Get off me!" his father howled.

Tucker leaned in close, with steel resolve. "Soon as I graduate, I'm gone. The *hell* outta here. I ain't gonna be like you. I'm gonna *be* something, you damn drunk."

"I'll kill you where you stand," his father whimpered—still angry, but weeping in his foggy, beaten state.

"You ain't doin' *nothing*. No more. *Never!*" Tucker rattled his father's head into the floor one good last time, and stood. "Mama, you hear me?" Tucker shouted towards the bedroom. "He as much as touches you or Danny again, it's over."

Tucker, through his focused rage, heard some vague muttering from the bedroom, as Ewing Trivette picked himself up, woozy and disoriented. He paused as he dabbed at the blood dripping from the side of his face, staring at his fingers with defeat and disbelief—and maybe regret—which had extinguished the fire.

"You shouldn't have done that," he mumbled, as much to himself, as he staggered to the bedroom.

Tucker let him pass, still tense and half expecting another round to follow. His mother, though, opened the door and shot a pitiful and weary look as she turned away to help Ewing to bed.

As the door closed, Tucker sank into the old sofa, shaking, and looked up at the old photo of his grandfather. *Thanks for your strength. I'm gonna do you proud.*

"We're gonna be late. Clint's waiting," Danny said as he leaned out the passenger window and opened the mailbox. "Nope. Nothing."

Tucker's shoulders sank. "Recruiter said it would be here by now."

"Just kidding," Danny said as he passed Tucker a pale yellow envelope.

Tucker snatched it out of his hands, ripping the seal like a kid at Christmas. "Great Lakes Naval Training Center," he read aloud. "Never been to Illinois."

"You've barely been out of state," Danny muttered to himself.

Tucker glanced at his wristwatch. "Damn, that's in three days," he said as he slapped the ticket against his thigh. As they pulled out of the drive, they saw Clint ahead, walking to them with a book in hand.

As Danny slid to the middle, Clint climbed in.

"He got it," Danny said as Tucker held up the bus ticket.

"I thought something was up. I could see his teeth grinning from the road. Congratulations are in order, then," Clint said as he turned to look out the back window. "Not coming, are they?" He frowned, but tried to sound cheery.

"Nope," Tucker said as he adjusted the mortarboard on his head. "Don't matter."

Clint grunted, then turned to a folded page in the book and began reading: *"The sea has never been friendly to man. At most it has been the accomplice of human restlessness."*

"Sounds about right for the mountains, too," Tucker said.

In the weeks since the fight, not a word had been uttered at home. Tucker had made his peace with himself. There was nothing left to say. He felt ready for anything the Navy could throw at him.

But he had to graduate first.

Illuminated by stadium bulbs, caps flew into the evening sky like the murmuration of so many starlings rising and diving. Tucker had squirmed in his chair as the valedictorian's hope-for-the-future musings for the class of '92 droned through the staticky speakers on either side of the dais. His future was set, and he was chomping at the bit to get started.

After shoving the rolled diploma into his back pocket, Tucker saw Allie in one of the family clusters gathered around their new graduates. She saw him coming and raised her eyebrows while crossing her arms.

"Heard anything from Clemson yet?" Tucker said.

"Clemson?" she sniggered. "Where have *you* been?"

"I thought that's where you wanted to go."

"Once upon a time," Allie said. "Didn't even apply there. State has a real good program. At least that's what the counselor and Mrs. Tincher said. Sent my application off months ago."

"And?" Tucker said.

"Wait-listed," she huffed. "Got into ECU and Western, but there's no way I'm gonna be a pirate or a 'catamount'—what the heck's a catamount anyway?"

"Yeah, the 'wolf pack' makes more sense for you. Need to practice your howl, though." He lifted his head and yowled as he mock-pawed at her gown.

"Stop it," she said, punching him on the shoulder. "And what? You just weren't going to tell me you joined the Navy?"

"Well ... " Tucker kicked the ground in front of him, searching for the right thing to say.

"You didn't think I'd find out?" Allie said. "Dad hears everything at the store."

"Sort of just decided it was the best option," he said. "Ticket just came. I leave in a couple days. Probably be away six or seven *years*."

"Couple days?" Allie said. "Six or seven years?"

"It's not just a job, it's an adventure, right?" Tucker thought he saw disappointment in her eyes. "I was meaning to tell you," he said. "But with everything going on, and this happened so fast ..."

"I'm just glad you finally realized you're not cut out for farming," Allie joked. "Clint's trees can rest safe knowing that the 'Fir Butcher of Paul's Peak' is leaving town."

"Good one," Tucker replied.

"I don't blame you for getting out of here, though. Nothing much for anyone to stick around for."

"You have the store, at least," Tucker said.

Allie huffed. "Yeah. My life's goal is to sit behind a counter hawking beef jerky and buying leaves and twigs off folks like you and yours."

"Ooh," Tucker said. "That one hurt."

"Sorry." Allie bit her lip, softening some. "You know what I mean."

"I guess I do." Tucker shifted nervously, changing the subject. "Well, I thought we can write, at least—let each other know what's going on?"

"That would be nice. You'll have to send me your address when you get to where you're going. What is it, like an APO?"

"I think so. And I will. Once I find out where they send me. Never know where we'll end up."

"The 'world is our oyster' now, right?" Allie said, winking.

"More like a *mountain* oyster." Tucker laughed, happy to have a civil conversation with her for a change, but then he blurted out: "And since you didn't get in to State, you can keep up with Danny for me."

Allie's lips pursed. "What?"

"Well, you just said you didn't get in. Wait-listed means waiting, right? I'm gonna be long gone and while you're *waiting*, you can keep an eye on Danny for me," Tucker said.

Allie's lip curled even more.

"What?" Tucker shrugged.

"Yeah, I'll do that," she said with the nasty tone that he was more accustomed to. "I'll just sit here and pine away, waiting with bated breath on your correspondence from *all over the world*."

"That's not what I meant," Tucker said.

"Sure sounded like it to me. You think this tiny-town, hick girl from the mountains *ain't goin' nowheres*," Allie mocked.

Tucker scoffed. "I didn't say that. All I was saying is what if you don't get in at all?"

That did it.

Allie shook her head. "Enjoy your row boat, Tucker. Do you even know how to swim?"

"Better than you, I bet," Tucker said—even though he still held his nose underwater.

"Congratulations. Save your postcards for someone who cares," Allie said and stormed away.

"Well, that could have come out better," Tucker told himself.

"Boy, you sure have a way with words," Clint said as he walked up with Danny. "Congratulations are due, nonetheless," he said, "On your graduation." He shook Tucker's hand firmly.

"What did I say?" Tucker said as they headed to the truck.

Clint replied: *"Well you know, being a woman is a terribly difficult business since it consists principally of dealings with men."*

"Conrad?" Tucker said.

"You betcha."

Time passed through the night like honey through cheesecloth, as Tucker stared at the ceiling, his laced boots draped off the edge of his already-made bed. He glanced occasionally at his brother, hoping he was awake, but Danny snored away.

An hour before the sun even rose, Tucker looked over the packing list from the Navy for the fourteenth time, of everything *not* to bring along, which didn't leave much. After quietly throwing some last-minute garments into an old duffel from under the bed, Tucker shoved his brother, who joined him on the porch step a few minutes later. They sat together in the darkness without words.

As the first distilled glow began to backlight the hills, the brothers heard an engine crank in the quiet dawn. Clint pulled in a few minutes later. Danny hopped into the truck first, rubbing his eyes, and scooted to the middle as Tucker pitched the bag into the bed of the truck and shut the door.

As they left the driveway, Tucker caught a glance of his mother—still in her robe under the single bulb of the porch—watching, with a ring of smoke over her head. Just before they were out of sight, he saw his father join her.

Tucker turned to the windshield and didn't look back, putting home and his past in the rearview.

They arrived at the bus station in Johnson City an hour and a half later. Several other new recruits milled about—hugging girlfriends and teary-eyed mamas. Clint gave Tucker a firm handshake as he got out of the truck and handed him a wrapped package.

"What's this?" Tucker said.

"Ah, just a couple of sea tales to help you bide the time. You can guess."

"Appreciate it, Clint. And everything."

"Chin up, sailor. Anchors aweigh. Make the best of it." He added, "Time gives us time to reminisce, but not to live again."

"That Conrad?"

"Nope. That's Clint," he said with a wink as he left Danny and Tucker to their goodbyes.

As Tucker stood there with Danny on the bare polished concrete of the depot, Tucker noticed that his little brother stood a little taller, and it seemed like peach fuzz had appeared on his upper lip overnight. Tucker had been so focused on his own future, he hadn't really stopped to think much about Danny. What it would mean with his leaving. But Danny emitted his own strange confidence and Tucker hoped his independence and quiet determination would be enough without big brother around.

Danny seemed to read his mind. "I'll be okay, you know," he said.

Tucker agreed, but still: "Anything happens at home, go to Clint's—or call Sheriff Hicks."

"I ain't worried," Danny chuckled. "I'm quicker than Dad, anyhow."

Tucker laughed, "I know you are."

"Dang straight," Danny said.

"Take care of the old truck for me," Tucker said, mussing Danny's hair and pitching him the keys. "You remember how to drive it, right?"

Danny creased his lips and nodded as Tucker skipped up the stairs of the coach, duffel in hand, giving his brother and Clint a final salute from the back window as the bus pulled away, headed for his new beginning.

Grandpa always said "search for ginseng looking downhill. It's easier to spot those big berry pods." As growers, we do so because we love the plant, the heritage and the memories in the woods. It takes some pressure off wild ginseng as well. My bliss is found in the hills of southeast Kentucky, scouring for that forest gold.

Marcus S.
Hazard, KY

Part II

Nine

Petty Officer Tucker Trivette stood on the forward observation deck of the USS *Independence* as the ship came into view of the Hong Kong skyline—a dense urban forest of steel and glass erupting from the small patch of land seemingly incapable of supporting the weight of such a city. The carrier dwarfed the assembly of multi-colored sails of the sampans circling in the harbor. Waves and yellow grins from barefooted fisherman greeted its wake as the navigation team began the docking maneuvers to bring the 1,100-foot behemoth into port. Tucker, off duty for a change, and ready for a much-needed shore leave, gawked at the scale of the skyscrapers on the shoreline superimposed onto the verdant backdrop of the island hillsides behind them.

During the course of his seven-year hitch, he had become a man, packing on twenty pounds of muscle and growing three inches taller. Standing over six feet now, he took in the vista thinking about how far he had come and the things he'd seen. Somehow the city in front of him seemed like the capstone of his adventure, and he itched to take advantage of this last port-of-call. The years had flown by.

As a recruit, Tucker's intuitive sense of direction and basic understanding of things celestial—gleaned from the countless excursions into the wooded hills of home with his Paw Paw—earned him an additional nine weeks of A-school for training as a quartermaster. The history and tradition made him proud of the ship's wheel emblazoned on his shoulder patch, the sextant now a part of his identity.

The ocean's limitlessness was a far cry from the mountains of home where he knew the name of every peak that broke up the horizon, but Tucker had transitioned easily from dry land, to simulators, to reliance on the stars as his escorts on the open ocean. He would leave in a few weeks with confidence and determination, his Navy brothers now family.

Tucker and three other men worked five and dime shifts, mainly on the bridge—five hours on watch and ten hours off. Johnny Kelly was the rowdy one. A Yankees-fan hard-ass from Navy Hill, Johnny was destined for the service. Growing up, all he heard were the stories from uncles and grandparents who built ships there before McNamara closed the Yard in '66. Tim Brown came from Amish stock farmers just outside Sugarcreek, Ohio. The first day of basic, the drill sergeant named him "Tiny," which stuck. Standing six foot six and weighing in well north of two-fifty, Tiny, like Tucker, had never seen the ocean until arriving at San Diego to board the *Independence* for his first commission. While more straight-laced than most of the crew, Tiny quickly learned how to party hearty like the rest of them.

"Blind Sam" Hutchinson, Tucker's best friend, came from a family of Bessemer, Alabama textile workers. While a student athlete and all-state swimmer, the economics of college proved too high a hurdle. A hitch in the armed forces was a more direct opportunity for a job and maybe a degree later. So, Sam signed up, and despite the thick glasses that kept him out of a pilot's seat, he saw the world from the ship's navigation deck.

Assigned as bunk-mates, he and Tucker hit it off almost immediately. Their mutual agreement on livermush and molasses being the sole toppings worthy of gracing a scratch biscuit sealed the deal. Although, Sam argued, anything sweet or grease-fried on a biscuit worked for him. Tucker made it through swimmer qualification only with Sam's help. Before boot camp, Tucker had only ever dipped in waist-deep creeks. Within an hour in the pool, Sam had him cruising down the lanes in a confident crawl and treading water without pinching his nose. Sam always joked that the Navy had a sense of humor pairing up a "hillbilly farmer" with a "city boy from the hood" like himself, but with all prejudice left at the boot camp door, the two became fast, inseparable friends.

Sam's large frame and solid build seemed at odds with his passive demeanor, and his horned-rim glasses, which didn't seem to fit his head right, betrayed his athleticism, grit, and wit. During their third week of training,

Tucker made a bet with some *real* rednecks that Sam could out-swim every one of them—past the buoys at Nunn Beach. Since those boys had all grown up believing the stereotypes, they threw in their full weekend allotments into the wager. Sam won handily, finishing the last twenty yards pulling two of the half-drowned cowboys through the breakers back to the Lake Michigan shore. So much for the clichés. Tucker bought the first round then and after the pair finished A-school near the top of their class.

As quartermasters, their hours on the bridge afforded them the impressive view of the expansive Forrestal-class flight deck—the best seats in the house to observe the take-offs and landings of the fighter jets. While Tucker appreciated the talent of the pilots from a distance, Sam lamented his poor vision keeping him from the cockpit.

The pair's talents with navigational gear and willingness to learn made them popular with senior officers. Their proficiency with the technology, new and old, and their prowess reading oceanic charts and the complex calculations involved in maneuvering an 80,000 metric-ton ship, the last of its kind, made them a team to be reckoned with. Just a year ago, they had guided the ship back to Japan with the Carrier Air Wing after its third deployment to the Arabian Gulf, earning accolades and extra shore leave. Now they had returned. The final deployment of their commission had taken them to Guam and Malaysia for a battery of exercises with the ship docking in Hong Kong to refuel, and the crew released for some well-deserved R & R.

"You ready to see King Kong take on Hong Kong," growled a voice behind him.

Tucker dodged the jab to his ribs he knew was coming, feinted to the right, then grabbed his shipmate in a headlock before Johnny could land a sucker punch. "You know I'm quicker than *that*," Tucker said.

Johnny scrambled out of Tucker's grip, readjusted the Dixie cup on his head, and smoothed out his dress whites. "Come on, now, Tuck. Don't mess up my get-up," Johnny said. "Ain't nothing finer than *this* in a uniform. Those Chinese ladies ain't never seen nothing like it before."

"I'm sure they have," Tucker said. "And this is Hong Kong. It's British. Not Chinese."

"Same difference," Johnny said, then grabbed his crotch. "I'm ready to release the Kraken."

Sam and Tiny shook their heads. "Check your side-arm, sailor," Tucker said. "Don't want that thing going off and scaring the locals."

"Personally, I can't wait to eat me some authentic cuisine," Sam said. "You think I can find General Tso's Chicken?"

"Why? He lose it or something?" Johnny said.

Sam rolled his eyes and Tucker said: "They'll have anything you want here. Chicken and pigs in the windows, noodle shops on every corner—more than even *you* can eat. And the ladies—Johnny, you'll be in 'horndog heaven' is my guess."

"That's what I'm talkin' about," Johnny said, making quotation marks in the air: "Get me some Chinese 'take-out' ... I'm starving. Been too long on this boat with you boys."

"I'm sure you'll find something you'll need a shot for later," Tiny said.

"Bring it," Johnny said, grabbing his package again.

They all stopped to stare for a moment at the bustle of humanity surging around the dock as the gargantuan warship came to a rest. Tucker, having been on bridge duty during the last two ports of call, was excited to step onto dry land for a change. The well-worn copy of the travel guide from the ship's library bulged in his back pocket, although he'd already memorized a navigable route through the city.

Tucker and Sam high-fived their crew as more sailors gathered and the all-quarters horn sounded as they fell in line with an ever-growing mob heading below deck to debark. They flashed their IDs to the watch officer, saluted, and left the ship in a cascade of white uniforms.

"Where we going first?" Sam said.

"I heard the Peak Tram is pretty cool. They say you can see the whole city from up top," Tucker said.

"There's also the famous 'Fu-King' Deli," Johnny said, winking at Tucker. "I know you'll like that."

"That sounds more like it. I'm ready to eat, man," Sam said, rubbing his belly and ignoring the joke. "I wonder how they do barbecue here."

"Ah ... patience, *Sam-san*," Johnny said in a horrible accent while bowing. "Confucius say, '*You are what you eat, which is why your head look like big peck-ah*'."

"Shee-yit," Sam said in his deepest 'Bama drawl.

"Need to hit the ink-shop before the line gets too long," Johnny said. "We can get our drank on afterwards."

"Aren't you supposed to get lit *before* they put the needle to you?" Tiny said.

"What's the matter? Afraid it'll hurt?" Johnny said, mock-wiping tears from his eyes. "Guy from the mess said there's a place close to the dock."

"Let's get this over with, then," Tiny said.

The four friends left the pier and meandered through the narrow roads closest to the port, their nostrils clogged with the stench of diesel and stagnant sea. Sailors in various states of sobriety stumbled through the streets. Buses overflowing with passengers honked in unison at streams of mopeds and bicycles, passing rows of street vendors hawking everything from music CDs to counterfeit designer clothing and watches, VCR tapes and American movie posters—in Cantonese symbols—and live animals in cages, right next to the grills.

"Bam! There it is," Johnny said, pointing to a storefront with flashing neon symbols.

"What does that even say?" Tim said.

"That's the Chinese word for 'hepatitis'," Sam said, eliciting a frown from Tim.

"You're not gonna do it?" Tucker said.

"Negative, ghostrider," Sam said. "I'm rather fond of my liver function. I'll hold Tiny's hand. You know, emotional support."

Tim rolled his eyes as the four of them hustled into the dimly lit shop, the buzzing of tattoo guns drowning out the punk-rock music coming from a boombox dangling from a wire coat hanger rigged to the ceiling. Other clients sat stone-faced and sweating in their chairs as their artists worked. While Johnny and Tim looked over the massive collection of artwork in plastic sleeves tacked to the walls, Tucker sat down as one of the men vacated a chair. The sailor winced a smile as he slapped cash into his artist's hand.

"Place looks safe enough," Tucker said, nodding to the blue-colored jars of chemical-soaked needles on the tray next to him.

Sam grunted. "You say so."

Tucker fished the folded drawing he had sketched on a napkin out of his pocket and placed it on the armrest. He took off his shirt as the artist took the chair next to him. "So, this is what you want, eh?" the man said with an Australian accent, which surprised Tucker. He looked stereotypically Asian, with a dull-green mask of tribal ink coating his entire face.

"Can you do it?" Tucker said.

The small-framed man removed a delicate set of round spectacles from his shirt pocket, placed them low on his nose, and draped the thin wires around his ears while he inspected Tucker's handiwork. "Ooh, I don't know, mate. All I do is anchors, hearts, and 'mums'," he said as he grinned. "Just joshing. This'll make a nice one. Unique."

The man swapped out cartridges in the machine, wiped Tucker's canvas with an alcohol swab, and flipped the switch to his gun. Tucker gritted his teeth as the needle sang into his upper arm. Sam shook his head, then went over to harass Tiny and Johnny who were settling in for their session.

After an hour, Johnny wandered to Tucker's chair, flexing to show off the still-bloody calligraphy stretching across his shoulder blades. "Whadya think?"

"Semper *Fart*-is. Hmm. Nice touch. You do that on purpose?" Tucker said.

"You better be joking," Johnny said as he craned his neck to make sure. "*Fortis*, bitch," he mumbled as he leaned in to examine Tucker's arm, scrunching his face. "What in the *hell* is that?"

"My grandpa had the same one. Family tradition," Tucker said as he strained to see the finishing touches.

"Looks like a bush tied to a turd. Good looking bush, though."

"Thanks, man."

"Anytime. You done with Betty Boop, over there?" Johnny yelled to Sam. "His damn face is gonna be stuck like that for a week, you know."

"Y'all thought I was joking. I can't feel my hand," Sam joked as Tim's tight fist shook around Sam's while he stared straight ahead in a Zen-like trance of agony as the needle continued to hum along.

Tucker turned as the constant sting in his arm suddenly ceased. "There you go. Quite enjoyed that, actually. Something different for a change," the artist said as he held a mirror for Tucker's approval.

"Looks perfect. I think you nailed, it," Tucker said.

"I know I did, mate. That'll be fifty quid," he said as he rubbed a coat of

Vaseline over the tender skin, then taped over it with a large square of gauze. "Keep it oiled and covered for a couple of days. Enjoy."

Tucker paid the man as he, Johnny, and Sam cheered on Tim's final touches. "Well, if that isn't the fanciest anchor I've ever seen," Johnny jeered with a lisp as Tim finally stood up, his knees slightly wobbling.

"I need a drink. Several, actually," Tim said, wiping a stream of perspiration from his forehead.

"Now we're talking," Johnny said. "You and Tucker coming?"

"Time to eat," Sam said. "You and Tim enjoy your date."

"Oh, we will," Johnny said, batting his eyes. "Come on, Wonder Bread. Time to be wasted seamen." Tim dipped his head with a subtle shake, following close behind Johnny as escort and designated accomplice.

As Tucker and Sam left the parlor, they wound their way deeper into the city, shoved forward by the pulsing crowd, and with Sam's nose and appetite guiding them. After a couple of blocks, they turned onto another busy thoroughfare cramped with outdoor seating. The tang of exotic odors blended with cigarette smoke, stinging the nose from the fog of steam and spices wafting in the air.

"Found you some appetizers," Tucker said, nodding to a rack of scorpions on skewers. "Heard they taste like chicken."

"Nope. No bugs. That's a rule," Sam said as his radar locked onto a platter of noodles and street meat. "Now, that's what I'm talking about."

As Tucker turned to flag someone down for a seat, he noticed a young woman on the opposite corner of this plaza, standing totally alone for a frozen moment. Her sleek black hair matched her dress, which made her stand out from the generic droves who now approached from either side as the buses crossing in each direction had temporarily paused the pedestrian mob. Before she became lost again in the obscurity of the street-crossers, she locked eyes with him and smiled—or at least he thought she did—but then she turned away, crossing the avenue down another feeder road and blending into the swell of the crowd.

"You see that?" Tucker said. "Gorgeous."

"Yessir. Looks delicious," Sam said, still drooling over the passing plates.

"No, man. That girl," Tucker said.

"What girl?" Sam said staring into the distance.

"She smiled at me."

"Damn, Tuck, you *have* been on the boat too long. There's like a million people here. I'm sure a couple of them did look in the general direction of your pasty white ass."

"Go on and get us a table," Tucker said. "I'll be right back."

"Okay, but I ain't waiting," Sam said.

Tucker slapped Sam on the back, scanned the crowd again, and darted across the street, hoping to intercept the girl in the black dress as quickly as he could, fighting his way through servers and packed bodies, even thicker here than near the docks.

"Where'd you go, Beautiful?" he mumbled as he straddled curbs and hopped over sewer grates. " ... There!"

As he looked to his right he saw the same black dress and long black hair. He pushed his way just behind her and tapped the ivory skin of her shoulder.

"Hi, I couldn't help but notice ... you ..." Tucker paused as an older woman, probably in her sixties, still very elegant but not the same girl, smiled pleasantly as she turned. "I'm sorry," Tucker said. "I thought you were someone else."

"I know. We all look the same, don't we ... So do you," she said with an accent and a wink. "The massage parlors are that way, sailor."

Tucker blushed and apologized again as the old woman went on her way. Looking over the heads of the crowd, he saw the young woman again—he hoped—and went in pursuit, trying to keep track of her in the masses as she adeptly maneuvered her home turf.

Tucker lost her again as she cut in front of a minibus and turned onto the next block. Tucker glanced at the sign above as he followed. *Wing Lok Street* it said in English with unreadable characters below it. Tucker remembered the locale from the guidebook—the seafood and herb district. An intense odor of earth and ocean confirmed it, as did the shop windows full of fish, bird's nests, and wreaths of dried plants.

He rounded the corner almost at a full sprint, hurdling to avoid a panhandler squatting in the middle of the sidewalk. As he recovered from the near collision, the girl in the dress appeared just a few steps in front of him. He took two more quick strides, and as he reached out to touch her shoulder, she spun around and lashed out with a solid punch to his arm—squarely in the middle of the bandage.

A jolt of electricity exploded up Tucker's shoulder into his temples. Through the wall of pain and stars in his vision he heard her shout: "Why are you following me?!"

Tucker staggered backwards, instinctively gripping his upper arm. Then he peeled the collar of his shirt over his shoulders, expecting to see a river of blood running down his arm. "Sorry!" he grunted as he knelt to the sidewalk, half-topless. "Godalmighty, that hurt!"

Within a few seconds, as the sting began its slow fade into a numb ache, he gathered his bearings enough to stand and face the girl, whose expression changed from anger to cautious sympathy. He was taken aback as his eyes cleared from the tears—she was much prettier than he had noticed from afar. The contrast of her jet-black hair mingling with her milky-white skin just seemed too perfect.

"Are you okay?" she said.

"Tattoo." It was the only word that came into his head to say.

"Excuse me?" she said. But Tucker was too focused on her green eyes. Then she nodded up the street. "If you want one, you need to go that way."

Tucker shook his head. "Uh, no," he stammered as he slowly peeled away the bandage to check the damage.

"Oh. You *have* one?" she said, finally understanding.

"Yep. Or did," he said dabbing at the angry wound.

The girl squinted for a closer look, and Tucker saw her eyes widen with curiosity. Or fear. He couldn't really tell.

"Sorry for scaring you." Tucker's manners took over, converting the pain in his arm to as much charm as he could muster. "I just saw you from across the way and wanted to meet you. You know, being on a ship with a bunch of guys …" He extended his hand. "Tucker Trivette. I'm from North Carolina … in the United States. Of America."

"I see that," she said, nodding at his uniform.

Tucker babbled on as he continued to stare, "I'm getting out soon. Going back to North Carolina. That's where I'm from."

"Yes. You mentioned that," she said.

"Uh, yeah, I did say that already didn't I?" Tucker took a breath and regrouped. "Let me start over."

"Please do," she said, noncommittally. But at least she was smiling.

He dabbed at his arm one last time before covering it again with the bandage. "My Paw Paw—my grandfather—had one just like this. On his shoulder. Of a 'seng plant. Gin'seng … Ginseng."

"Ah, *ren shen*," she said with the correct pronunciation in Chinese. "Really? Was he in the Navy, too? Did he get his tattoo here in China?"

"Yes. In the Navy," Tucker said. "But he got his in Korea, I think. Or somewhere else. On a boat, maybe? Not sure where he got it. Why?"

"Yes. *Why?*"

"Oh, well, we dig it. Back home," Tucker said. "It grows in the mountains, natural. I planted bunch before I left, too, a long time ago. Almost forgot about it. Should be big by now."

"In North Carolina," she said, amused.

"Yes," Tucker said. "It's in the South. Below Virginia and above South—"

"I know where it is," she interrupted. "And you *grow* ginseng there?"

"Yes. Well, we hunted it mainly. In the wild. Lots of folks back home dig and sell 'seng—or, how did you say it?"

"*Ren shen*," she repeated and looked around the street. "We have a lot of it, here, as you can see." While there were glass jars full of impressive ginseng roots in the shop windows surrounding him, Tucker hadn't noticed.

"You're right. That sure is a whole lot of *rin shin*," Tucker drawled.

"You can say ginseng," she said. "I know what you're talking about."

"Whew, good. I don't speak Chinese."

She raised her eyebrows into a smile and said: "Come. Walk with me. And I'm sorry for hitting you, but, you never know. Some of your *associates* can be quite *forward*."

"Sure. I understand. And yeah, we can be. Most of us are decent guys, but I probably would've slapped me down, too, the way I was coming at you," Tucker laughed nervously.

The girl nodded slightly in agreement and said, "Tell me more about your ginseng story. It's interesting."

"Well, one of my favorite stories is about when Daniel Boone ... You ever heard of him?

"Daniel Boone," she said. "Vaguely. From American history?"

"Yes!" Tucker said. "That's him. Anyway he used to—Daniel Boone, my brother's actually named after him— back around 1800, he dug a bunch. No time at all, he had him a barge lined up, just full of ginseng—barrels of it—to send to China. And it sank in the river. But there was so much in the woods back then he just went back and dug some more."

The young woman stopped walking. "I think I may have heard part of that story. There was really that much?"

"Oh, yeah," Tucker said. "It grows everywhere. Well, it did back then. Now you gotta know where to look for it, or grow it in the woods. I planted a patch of it, too. Need to check it when I get back home. I'm out of the Navy soon. Did I say all of this already?"

"Yes," she said. Then: "Are you hungry?"

"Starving."

"My name is Wei," she said and put her arm through his. "It means *rose* in Chinese."

"That's ... cool," Tucker said. "I like it."

"And 'Tucker'," she said. "I like that."

"Cool," he said again. "It's my grandmother's last name, but hell, I don't even know what it means."

"So, Tucker," Wei said, snugging her elbow into his. "How would you like me to show you the real Hong Kong."

"You mean, like a tour guide?" he said.

"Exactly like a tour guide," the beautiful woman said to him.

Feeling euphoric, Tucker grinned so hard his face hurt. "Cool," he said for a final time, because no other words came to his addled brain.

As she escorted him past the row of restaurants where they first saw each other, Tucker saw Sam seated at a table, by himself, plowing through at least three plates of unrecognizable chow.

He seemed happy enough.

Ten

After two blocks of attempting a conversation over the din of the street noise, Wei led Tucker around a corner to where a car and driver waited for her. The small man wearing a black suit and tie stepped around the slick, gray Rolls before Tucker even realized he was there, with the door open and a polite bow.

He straightened up for Tucker, who smiled and hesitated before getting into the fanciest car he had ever seen. The driver closed the door behind them, scurried around to the driver's door, got in, put on his blinker, and blasted into traffic.

"Jesus," Tucker said. "Does he ever look before he goes?"

"People make room when they see the car," Wei said. "It's our way."

"You mean, 'get outta my way'?"

"Something like that, yes," she said, rocking naturally with the speed-lane driving of the silent, small man in front who never smiled.

Tucker reached for his seatbelt.

Wei said, "You needn't worry. He hasn't hit anything in years. Or is it months? I can't recall. My mind is a little slow from the last crash."

Tucker had to look to make sure she was kidding.

Wei laughed and shoved him playfully. "Have you never driven through a city, before?"

"Not one like this," Tucker said, looking out his window at the colossal buildings packed against each other tighter than the oldest poplars on Paul's Peak—and ten times as tall.

"They are all the same," Wei said. "New York, Beijing, Tokyo."

"I wouldn't know," Tucker mumbled, watching the city zoom by.

After less than ten minutes of what to Tucker felt like a stock car ride at Bristol, the sedan came to a quick stop and, before Tucker could get his seatbelt unhooked, the little driver opened Wei's door open and bowed for her to exit.

"Follow me. I want you to meet someone," Wei said.

Tucker reached for his door handle and Wei advised, "Get out my side. If you want to live."

Tucker glanced at the dense traffic whizzing past, inches from his door, and followed through her door. He smiled again at the driver, who turned away.

"I don't think he likes me."

"He loves everyone. He just prefers not to express it."

Tucker looked back to see the man glaring at him. "Oh, yeah, I can see that."

The ride up the elevator—56 floors—took less than a minute. Tucker said, "That elevator is faster than your car."

"You should ride in my brother's Porsche. He's a maniac."

"I can't wait," Tucker said as they exited the elevator into a plush lobby.

While Wei and the receptionist exchanged niceties in their native tongue, Tucker found himself standing in front of a large painting. "Is that an original?" he said. It looked like one he had seen in a book.

"Of course. My father loves Picasso," Wei said. "This way. I know he'll be interested to meet you."

Tucker shrugged as she led him down a hallway festooned with artwork including more paintings, glistening ceramics, and antique hand-weapons, and directly into a lavish office at the end with a view so incredible it appeared false, as if from a photographic mural.

Tucker followed along, patiently, as Wei called out the same words in Chinese several times, while checking around the office, in the boardroom off to one side, and what appeared to be a black marble executive bathroom. Then she said, incredulous: "He's not here."

With that, she spun on her heel and exited.

Tucker trotted to keep up, asking as he nearly ran, "Your father? Where is he?"

Wei did not answer him, but instead read the riot act to the receptionist—without slowing her pace. The demure woman bowed her head and mumbled, but otherwise seemed unbothered. Wei walked in to the private elevator with Tucker on her heels and pushed the button for down—never letting up on her excoriations for the secretary.

Wei groaned as the marble and gold box went into freefall.

"Was he expecting us?" Tucker asked.

"He's always there," Wei said.

"But ... " Tucker wasn't sure what to say.

Wei said, "He will be there next time."

The elevator stopped and Wei marched toward the outside door. Again, the little driver saw her coming, got out, ran around, opened the door, bowed, and let them in. Moments later, they entered traffic again and sped back through town—the little man in the suit never looking as he switched from lane to lane.

Tucker marveled: "He just hits his blinker and goes."

"What else should he do?" Wei said, then gave sharp, concise directions to the driver who crossed three lanes of blowing horns, and turned onto a side street.

A few minutes later, the car came to a quick stop again and Wei said: "Wan Chei. My favorite part of Hong Kong. Lots of shopping."

Her door opened and she stepped out, followed by Tucker. This time he spoke to the driver. "Thank you for the ride."

The man said, in perfect English, "The pleasure was mine, sir," and slammed the door.

"Come on," Tucker heard Wei call. When he looked, she was already almost a block ahead.

After running past high-end shops speckled with brash colors and designer logos, he finally caught up. "Where are we going now?"

"My place," she said with a devious smile.

After a similar ride in a similar elevator—though slightly smaller and slower—the bell dinged and Wei turned right through the dim lobby corridor to the only door on that end of the floor. After digging in her handbag for a frustrated moment, she found her key and opened the lock, striding in ahead of Tucker.

"Make yourself at home," she said, stopping at a phone answering machine to hit the play button. Rolling her eyes with each message, Wei fast-forwarded through the foreign gabble—which sounded even more comical to Tucker when sped up—then said, "I'll be right back. Drinks are over there."

Tucker wandered over to the refrigerator and plucked out a bottle of beer—at least it looked like one—from between the wine crammed into the door shelves, found an opener on the counter, then strolled to the floor-to-ceiling windows that offered an even more spectacular view than the one in her father's office: the entire harbor, all the way to Macau.

"Wow," he said, turning back, but she was still gone.

Then he heard, "Very nice, yes? My father found it for me. He'd like me here more often."

"He, uh ... He pays your rent?" Tucker didn't want to offend.

"I work for it," Wei said, kicking off her shoes. "This one and the other."

"Other?"

"I'm not here as often, anymore. I live in San Francisco, now. I went to college at Berkeley. Have you heard of it?"

"Good school, right?"

"Great place," Wei said. "I love it there." She opened the refrigerator. "Wine?"

"I found a beer, I think." Tucker squinted, trying to interpret the label.

"Beer," she said. "Ah, yes. So *gweilo*."

"What?"

"It means 'westerner' ... *foreign devil*." She made a scary face.

Tucker chuckled. "You don't really sound very ... Chinese."

"I worked hard on my accent. Most Chinese study *Ingrish*," she joked. "Same can't be said for Americans, eh?"

Tucker laughed. "I took Spanish in high school one year. Not a lot of Chinese teachers where I come from."

"I've yet to meet *gweilo* who speaks it well," Wei said while deftly uncorking a bottle of chilled white. She took a sip and said, "Ah. I needed that."

She flopped on the couch. "Are you any good at rubbing feet?"

Tucker looked to see her rubbing the toes of her left foot along the inside of her right calf.

"No," he said, moving closer. "But I'm a fast learner."

"I'll bet you are," she said, offering her foot as he sat on the red leather beside her. As he took her foot in his hands, she closed her eyes and moaned softly.

Tucker was enjoying her foot—too much he thought—so he asked, "So, what exactly do you *do?*"

"I buy ginseng," she said matter-of-factly.

"Really?" Tucker sat up. "No way."

"Yes, way," she said as she pulled back her foot and jumped up. "Are you hungry? I'm famished."

"Works for me," Tucker said. "As long as it isn't monkey brains or something."

Wei smirked and opened the refrigerator again, taking out a white ceramic container, pouring half of the contents into one bowl, half in another, and throwing both in the microwave.

Tucker watched her graceful movements as she removed thick noodles, and meat of some sort, and passed him chopsticks. As Tucker fumbled with the bamboo utensils, she said, "Let me get you a fork."

"No, this works fine," Tucker said, as ramen slid through the sticks.

Wei returned with the fork and handed it to him. "We are not uncivilized in Hong Kong. It's okay."

"Thanks," he said after taking a large mouthful. "This is good. What is it?"

"Cobra testicles," she said.

Tucker choked.

"Just kidding, silly," she said. "Chicken."

"I thought it was chicken," he said, turning red.

"No, you thought it was snake balls."

"I did. You got me," he giggled.

Wei took a bite, using her chopsticks better than Tucker could use his fork. "Should I get you a spoon?" she asked after he dropped a piece of chicken into his lap.

"No, I got this," he said, spearing it. "So, how much ginseng do you buy?"

"Tons."

"Tons?" Tucker said, astonished.

"Of course," she said. "That's why I go to California. We export from there to here."

"I see," he said. "Well, if you're looking for more, I know where a bunch is. Could probably put you in high cotton."

Wei cocked her head. "Ginseng *and* cotton?"

Tucker chuckled. "No, sorry. It's a saying from the South. Like, 'It'll make you rich'."

"Ah, rich," she said in a sultry lilt. "Rich is good."

Wei quickly put her food aside and straddled his lap before he could put down his dish. He didn't complain. If Tucker knew anything at his ripe old age of twenty-four, he knew not to turn down an advance. "I think I like Hong Kong," he murmured.

Doing better with her dress zipper than the chopsticks, he reached up and around—pulling her against him. As she kissed his neck, Tucker slipped the silky strap of one side of her dress down to her forearm, while his other hand made its way along the small of her back, and lower.

"Much better than a foot rub," she said, pulling the other shoulder of her dress down to her stomach, freeing her arms.

Keys suddenly rattled in the doorway and two men stepped inside. Wei snapped a look around—and began screaming. Not in terror, but anger.

As Tucker stood, turning away to tuck himself back in, Wei pulled her dress back to her shoulders in one swift move as she crossed the room reading the men the riot act in full-blown Canton fury.

One of them, the younger one, turned his head away quickly and stepped just outside the apartment, but the older man took another step inside, balled his fists at the hem of his jacket and stared. Tucker saw the man's face turn crimson from across the room as Wei stepped between them. The man hurled a stream of syllables at her and then turned his attention back to Tucker—who moved to the other side of the glass living-room table to keep his distance. The older man followed Tucker once around the table while continuing the tirade until Wei brought his attention back to her. The only words Tucker understood were *Carolina* followed by *ren-shen*.

As both of them paused to take a breath, Tucker extended his hand across the furniture.

"You must be Wei's father," Tucker said, nervously. "I'm Tucker, sir. Tuh-ker. Pleased to meet you," he continued, loud and slow, still holding out his hand. The man's eyes widened again as he fired off another explosive volley in the native tongue.

The man stopped momentarily as he looked back and forth between Wei and Tucker. She said: "*Bába*, this is Tucker. Tucker, my father, Andy ... Ling."

Tucker nodded and dropped his hand when it became apparent it would not be taken. *That's fair*, he thought, since he hadn't yet zipped his pants.

"Why don't we have a seat," Wei said. "And you can speak English now, Pa," she said, then turned to Tucker. "Don't let him fool you. He's fluent. And can be pleasant … if he chooses."

As her father took a seat at the head of the table, Wei poured shots of whiskey and set the heavy crystal glasses in front of the two men. Tucker waited for Wei's father to sip his and mimicked the motion. After a few moments to allow for the desired effect, Wei's *Pa* said: "So, you have seen these fields."

"The ginseng fields? Yes. Yessir, I mean. Well, they're not fields, actually. It's in the woods. The forest. That's where the ginseng grows. I planted a lot. Of ginseng. Seed. So they're my *fields*." Tucker couldn't tell if Andy squinted to understand his drawl or was still thinking about how to kill him.

Wei smiled at him and her father grimaced as Tucker looked back at Wei. "Is that what he wants to know?"

"Hong Kong is the largest market for ginseng in the world," she replied, and then looked at her father. "Father lives here in Hong Kong."

Her father snapped back with something quick in Chinese and Wei responded likewise. Then she looked at Tucker: "A few families manage the trade of ginseng into China. My father now leads one of them."

"Sorta like Michael Corleone?" Tucker said jokingly as he tried to piece everything together. Neither got the reference, but Andy added, "North Carolina ginseng is very valuable here. Brings good price. Hard to find reliable sources."

Tucker furrowed his brow and Andy continued: "We are interested in purchasing. I will buy all that you can produce, all that you can find, all that you can acquire for me."

"Won't be a problem, sir. My grandfather knew a bunch of places. Kept a journal before he died. Places in the mountains where it grows." Tucker spoke more confidently as he rambled, seeing the potential. "I'm sure I could get you however much you want. It'll all be in full glory by now."

Both Andy and Tucker paused for a moment before Andy stood up. Tucker followed suit.

"Then we have an arrangement," Andy said. "I will be in touch," as he offered his hand to Tucker—finally.

Wei corrected him: "*I* will be in touch."

Andy shot her another harsh look, then sighed heavily and moved away from the table.

"I will let myself out."

"It was nice to meet you, sir," Tucker grimaced.

Wei's father nodded without emotion then said to Wei: "Don't forget. Your brother. You're already late." Wei looked at her watch and winced as her father closed the door behind him.

Tucker stared at Wei, confused. "Late for what?"

"I have to meet my brother now," she huffed. "Lost track of the time. Will you come? I'd like to show you something."

"Sure," he said. "I'm game."

"Perfect," Wei said and grinned. I think you will be interested."

Tucker was more interested in picking up where they had left off, but instead said, "I don't have to be back to the ship until dark."

Wei's driver let them out in a wide alleyway not far from where they first met. Wei pushed open double doors from the front side of a modest brick façade which betrayed the size of the interior, then said something to the effect of *"He's with me"* to the two guards strapped with compact submachine guns. They replied with curt nods.

After Tucker adjusted his eyes to the dim light, he saw that the cavernous warehouse stretched for half a block. He followed Wei down a central aisle of racks of open containers—full of dried ginseng.

"Whoa. There must be a thousand barrels in here," Tucker said.

"Almost," Wei said. She nodded to their right at wooden tables stacked with roots being picked through by a small army of women in blue uniforms, each wearing rubber gloves and manipulating scissors and tweezers, speedily and focused. Not a single one looked up from their task. "This is where we sort the roots by shape, size, age, and unique qualities."

"Where do you get it all?" Tucker wondered.

"All over," Wei said. "But most comes from Korea, Canada, the United States."

Tucker had never given any thought to what happened to the roots he dug after Jim Gragg scooped them off the scale at the Pelt and Herb.

"After that, much of it goes to auction, then it's shipped all over China," Wei said as she continued the tour. "We supply around ten percent of the market of *wild* ginseng. My brother wants to push that number to twenty-five, but it's getting harder to find. My father is skeptical, but perhaps it's possible—with your help."

"I'd be more than happy to oblige," Tucker said with pride.

They reached the end of the warehouse and Wei opened a glass door to an interior office. A young man barked into a phone, ignoring them. He wore acid-washed skinny jeans and a bright orange, button-up shirt with a popped collar. Carat-sized diamond studs in each earlobe reflected the open bulbs on the ceiling like Christmas ornaments.

What a douchewhistle, Tucker thought.

Wei crossed her arms and stared at her hipster brother, tapping her foot impatiently. "He loves making me wait," she said to Tucker, in a raised voice, causing the man to look up. "This is my brother, Chin."

Chin shot her a look, unleashed a final torrent into the phone and hung up, turning his attention to his sister, followed by a thickly accented: "What you want?"

"Oh look! He's trying to impress you with his English," Wei said to Tucker. Then to her brother, mockingly: "Not bad for Rosetta Stone."

She extracted a small ream of papers from her handbag and slapped them onto his desk before flicking her fingers at him. "Here. Run along and tell Father you have them, now."

Tucker suppressed a giggle and attempted to make his own introduction, but Chin turned away, spewing a litany of Chinese at Wei, which she returned. Finally, she turned to Tucker and said, "Okay. Let's go."

"Nice to meet you," Tucker said as genuinely as he could muster, and followed Wei out of the office. Chin glared back, picking up the phone again and immediately shouting into the receiver.

"You two seem close," Tucker joked to Wei.

"He's a bully. I can't wait to get back to San Francisco," Wei said with a sigh. "Where to next?"

"Let's ride the Peak Tram," Tucker said. "I've been wanting to do that since Manila."

Wei's eyes rolled into the back of her head at the thought of being stuffed in a cable trolley with overweight *gweilo* tourists, but gave in. "Okay."

After the tram-ride, Wei gave Tucker a windshield tour of the historic district as they headed back to the ship. They stopped at one of several of her family's retail herbal shops where she showed Tucker the many forms that ginseng took after it left her warehouse. Packages of diced, sliced, and powdered ginseng lined the shelves along with whole roots preserved in rice whiskey in large, glass apothecary jars. While she spoke, customers drifted in and out sampling skin creams and ointments with pieces of the root suspended in them. It seemed like everything from candy to tea contained some form of ginseng.

"Americans consume coffee everyday—or chocolate. Chinese prefer ginseng," Wei explained. "As you can see, it's very popular here. Good medicine, too."

"There's so much of it, though," Tucker said with astonishment. "Why is your dad so interested in mine?"

"Think of it like wine," she said. "What you see here on the street is like cheap chardonnay that comes in a box."

"All I've ever had," Tucker mumbled as Wei's driver opened the car doors for them.

"Most of this ginseng is grown on farms. Very fast. Cheap. The wild ginseng that you are growing is like a fine vintage wine from France. Only the wealthy can afford that ginseng. Wild grown ginseng. *Your* ginseng."

"Cool," Tucker said, pondering the economics of it all as Wei's driver came to a stop at the docks. If the rich could afford the ginseng that waited on his return home, he'd be in good shape.

Wei said, "Here is my card," and handed it to Tucker. "That is my U.S. number. I will be there in a month or so, and that is my email address."

"Don't have one of those yet," Tucker said. "Don't even have a computer. Guess I'm behind the times."

Wei gave Tucker a sad, patronizing smile and a quick kiss on the cheek. "Call me when you get home. Then perhaps we can ... catch up. After your harvest. And sorry, again, about hitting you, earlier."

"If you hadn't, we wouldn't have become friends."

"Business partners," Wei winked. Then she pecked him on the cheek again before Tucker climbed out of the limo. Her driver quickly closed the door and scuttled for his seat. "Thanks," Tucker said; but the little man said nothing, hopping in and squealing into traffic before the words had fully left Tucker's lips.

With Wei's card in hand and swooning about the potential, Tucker trotted back to the wide gang plank of the ship with a wide grin, passing a disheveled Johnny and Tiny at the top of the stairs, the duty officer giving the two a tongue-lashing. Tucker could smell a vapor trail of liquor emanating up the stairwell.

That'll be a good story, he thought.

Eleven

After a quick stop in Okinawa to top off fuel and supplies, the *Independence* headed east, back to American soil. Between duty shifts on their way to Navy Base San Diego, the crew told and retold the stories of their final shore-leave exploits. Johnny and Tiny began their odyssey at a karaoke bar, winning a tequila-shooting competition; Johnny ate every worm. Neither of them remembered how they wound up at the Hong Kong Zoo, but Johnny convinced everyone it was Tiny's affinity for farm animals. Sam spent most of the next three days in the head, suffering ills from the culinary tour of the city he took after Tucker disappeared. Tucker kept quiet about his outing, swearing to everyone that nothing happened.

Now they were headed home. To what, neither Tucker nor Sam was sure. They had grown enough to know that in their years away, a lot could have changed. Though the short-timers acted thrilled about ending their hitches and returning to the States, they were all nervous, if they were ever honest about it.

Sam was returning to Alabama to help out his mama and daddy and working his way into a position at the new Mercedes plant just outside of Birmingham. Two of his cousins worked there, so he had an in, or hoped he did. And while he loved the Navy, duty to family was stronger. His time at sea was done.

Tucker remained skeptical about what he'd be coming home to. He didn't really know. During recruit training, which seemed like a lifetime ago, he phoned home twice to check in—mainly with Danny. The first time, his father hung up. The second time, Ewing passed the phone to Ruth for a brief and awkward conversation—too much distance already between them. When he asked about Danny, "Who knows" and long pauses were Ruth's only responses. So Tucker quit calling.

It was easier to write. He mailed a few postcards, mainly to Danny, but never got anything in return—which didn't surprise him; he rarely had seen his brother pick up a pencil. Tucker wrote more detailed letters to Allie, addressing them to the Pelt and Herb in the hopes that Mr. Jim would pass them along. However, when Allie didn't respond, Tucker gave up. But Allie finally wrote back—once—to let him know that she was indeed at State, enjoying college life and her studies.

A few years later, Tucker won a satellite call off his XO by slow-playing a full house in the monthly officer-versus-enlisted poker game. He used the precious minutes to call the Pelt and Herb, hoping Allie might be there. Mr. Gragg answered. According to him, she was doing well. She had decided to go on to graduate school, hopefully to land a job with the USDA—and had a boyfriend, even talking marriage. Tucker felt a rock land in the pit of his stomach; unsure as to why, he lied and told Mr. Jim that he was happy for her. Gragg went on to say that Danny dropped by occasionally. All seemed to be as normal as it could be with the Trivette family as far as he knew. But that left a lot of room for speculation, which Tucker chose to avoid. But he didn't bother calling again. That was over two years ago.

His world had expanded, and trying to keep up with the folks back home seemed like throwing bottled messages into the sea. Instead, he concentrated on his tasks on the ship, doing them the best he could, and tried not to think about home and family. And Danny. Deep down, he almost hoped that his brother moved away and started fresh, like he had. But he doubted that likelihood.

As the California coastline came into view, Tucker thought, *maybe things have changed*. He frowned at the memory of the fight with his father an eternity ago, hoping time had healed that wound by now. Maybe the years had softened him—maybe even sobered him up. Tucker knew that he himself was a different person and expected a cordial reception, at least, after all this time. The look on his parents' faces as he strolled home in dress whites might make it all worthwhile, allowing them to move on to a better future. Maybe even a happy one.

Meeting Wei gave him hope that he had made the right decision. Perhaps a chance to continue in his granddaddy's footsteps and make a life from what the land could provide.

After pulling into the San Diego port, Tucker returned his personal gear—minus the compass and sextant he had used since A-school. Uncle Sam wouldn't miss them. The soon-to-be veterans cleared medical after Johnny received an extra round of penicillin from the "pecker checker," and the Career Transition Officer signed off on the final pages of their discharge paperwork.

They were free.

Tucker picked up the phone in the CTO's lobby to call home, hoping to let his parents know that he was coming, but only heard a bleeping tone repeating in his ear. With others waiting to contact their families, Tucker hung up. He'd see his soon enough, anyway.

Tucker and Sam booked flights home with similar departures, and shared a last beer at the airport before boarding.

Sam downed two drafts before Tucker sucked the head off his first. "Easy, there, partner," Tucker said.

"Don't like planes," Sam said as he waved to the bartender for another.

"Thought you said you always wanted to be a pilot?"

"Pilot's different. Not a fan of *riding* in a damn aluminum tube."

"Stewardess won't be a fan of you, either, if you hurl in the aisle."

"Won't bother me a bit if I'm passed out," Sam said.

Tucker laughed. "What's the first thing on your agenda?"

"After kissing the ground? Well, Ole Bob Sykes better have the hickory smoking," Sam said. "Best ribs in 'Bama. This west-coast shit just don't cut it. Travesty they even call it barbecue. Might as well be damned sushi. What's next for you, hillbilly?"

"I got something in the works." Tucker winked. "If you end up needing a loan or anything, give me a call."

"Yeah, right. You win the lottery or something?" Sam said.

Tucker shook his head and leaned closer. "Remember that girl I chased after in Hong Kong—"

"I *knew* it!" Sam said. "Was wondering when you were gonna cough up the juicy details. You didn't ditch your wingman just to ride some damn trolley. I knew that for damn sure!"

Grinning wide, Tucker said, "You remember those stories I told you about that plant I used to dig in the woods back home and sell for cash?"

Sam said, "Vaguely. You talked a lot of hillbilly nonsense over the years."

Tucker chuckled. "Turns out that girl was more than just a hot date. Her family buys it—a lot of it. And it's gonna make me rich. Soon as I get home, I'll be in the woods, digging out, and cashing in."

"I like the man's confidence," Sam said, patting him on the shoulder. "Good luck with that. I'll be installing fine leather in Benzes. In air-conditioning."

Tucker laughed again. "I'll give you a call when I figure it all out—just in case that doesn't work like you planned. Might need your help, like I said," Tucker winked again. "You know: spending all that money."

"We'll see about that," Sam said and laughed in return. "You got my folks' phone number?"

"Right here." Tucker tapped his shirt pocket as they heard Sam's boarding call over the speakers.

"Stay in touch. I mean it." Sam lifted Tucker off his feet in a bear hug before heading across the terminal for his flight home.

Tucker looked down and called out. "Hey, Sam. You dropped your glasses!"

"Those are Navy glasses. I'm getting real ones, soon as I land." Then he ran into the side of the jetway.

Tucker laughed a final time, looked up at the menu, and ordered a second beer. "Can't be too careful," he said to himself, and set to planning his future.

Twelve

After seven years of monotone vistas of gray bulkheads and the blue sea beyond, Tucker saw the mountains of home finally come into view as the bus meandered through familiar countryside. From the new lane on the main highway, steel skeletons of nascent apartment buildings and strip malls emerged from scraped, red clay at every exit. A steady column of dump trucks all but grazed the bus as it headed northwest from the Charlotte terminal.

Progress.

After the bus all but emptied at its first stop, Tucker scooted to the front, peppering the driver with questions. A burly native of the foothills, the man popped a wad of sunflower seeds into the jaws hidden within his shaggy beard and nodded at changes without lifting his grip from the steering wheel. "Lot of new construction. Up in the mountains, too. Rental cabins are popping up quicker than horseweed," he said as he spat husks into the Solo cup in his lap. "Snow birds been buying up everything this end of the state. Woods I used to coon hunt turned into neighborhoods. Driveways steeper than a cow's face."

A Lexus blasted around them without a turn signal. He pointed to its Florida license plate. "You'll see them and the Coupe De Villes start showin' up in June. They leave the North, retire in Sarasota or some damn place, then move up here for the summer. Guess it gets too hot down there. Half-backers. One of them runs you off the road, you'll wish 'em *all* the way back."

Tucker snickered, but deep down wondered how things had changed farther up the escarpment. As the bus's engine strained, beginning its final climb to the High Country, gates on stone posts appeared at each turn with quaint names in calligraphed iron that sounded like truly wonderful places to live: "*Laurelwood Meadows,*" "*The Vista at Gray Oaks,*" "*Ridgemont at Poplar Cove.*" Tucker gawked at the "For Sale" signs and rows of shiny new mailboxes decorating the turn-offs that had once only led to four-wheeler trails and drinking spots. He passed the time thinking up monikers more reflective of the area: "Bear Scat Holler," "The Peak at Old Fridge Dump," and "Broken Bottle Ridge."

After another hour of winding switchbacks, the silver and blue Greyhound finally reached the outskirts of town. Air brakes hissed as it stopped right in front of the Pelt and Herb. Tucker smiled.

"Wish I could get you all the way home, but I'm due in Johnson City," the driver said as he opened the door.

"Appreciate the ride, sir," Tucker said as he handed over a tip and stepped off the bus. He waved as it pulled away, checking his wallet before tucking it back into his pocket. While down to his last few bills, he wasn't worried. The desk officer in San Diego had assured that his final check was on its way. Tucker had survived just fine on the allotment he set up after basic, never touching the rest of his pay while at sea—most of his last years of service. He'd saved a nice nest egg for this next chapter of his life, enough to get started, anyway. Maybe Danny could help.

Tucker stood for a moment and took in the scenery. Very little had changed. Other than the hum of the bus leaving town and the sound of his own breath, the streets were quiet. The screen door on the Pelt and Herb still hung slightly crooked—exactly the same as he remembered. He would've hurried over to say hello, but it was Sunday, and the store, along with the bank and everything else in town, was shuttered.

Invigorated by the cool, mid-afternoon breeze, Tucker hefted the duffel onto his shoulder and began walking. In less than a minute, a longbed pickup pulled up beside him. "You're lookin' like you need a lift, soldier." The man, dressed in overalls, spat on the pavement through his open window and grinned.

Tucker nodded at the Plott hound he could see stretched across the passenger bench. "Yessir. That'd be awful nice. If your pup don't care, that is." The gray-whiskered dog looked up with a low growl.

"Betty ain't too much for company," the man said. "But if you don't mind the back?"

Tucker didn't mind. He'd have wheels of his own soon, maybe the Dodge in the meantime. *It's gotta be Danny's by now.* He smiled at the thought. Eager to get to the home place, he hopped into the truck's dusty bed, stepped over loose coils of barbed wire and sat on a half-licked salt block next to the cab.

After a half hour, the truck turned slowly off the pavement onto the dusty gravel that led to the base of Paul's Peak. Tucker leaned in to the back window. "Just up ahead."

As they passed Clint Winebarger's property, Tucker remarked at his neighbor's Christmas tree farm, now expanding across the entire hillside. "Dang. Ole Clint's been busy. Must be forty acres up there, now," he said.

"More in the ground every year," the driver said.

Tucker smiled and tapped the roof of the truck. "This here'll be just fine, thank you."

The truck stopped and Tucker hopped out, stepping across the overgrown fescue draped over the shoulder and down the center of the byroad. As his shiny dress shoes met the familiar path leading to the home place, he turned down the driveway with a snap in his step and noticed the rusted mailbox overflowing with rain-stained envelopes. *Good lord. When was the last time they ... checked ... the ...*

A quick wave of nausea grabbed Tucker's gut. The house was gone.

In its place, charred ruins lay piled in the yard. Tucker's eyes narrowed and cheeks flushed as he processed the image. Only blackened timbers and crumbled stone remained—scattered across a low mound of coals and gray, bare earth.

Off to one side, Paw Paw's truck leaned crookedly on cinderblocks. Its dull-to-begin-with paint job peeled away to bare metal on the side nearest the rubble, leaving side panels of muddy-orange rust. Another car, or its frame, rather, sat in front of where the porch had jutted from the main structure. It looked like the body of a convertible. With the tires melted off, its steel skeleton appeared to sink into the gravel. "Whose is that?" he said aloud to the car, which was too wide to be his dad's old beat-up coupe.

Tucker's mind churned. *"What the hell happened?"* He saw that fresh, green stalks of orchard grass had crept into the fringes of the cold mound of debris. *This happened a while ago.* But when? Where were his parents and Danny, now? Surely they were okay. Someone would have let him know, *right?*

Needing answers, Tucker dropped his bag and cut through the woods for Clint's house. After trotting up the porch steps, he banged on the front door and peered through its small diamond-shaped window. Nobody appeared to be home. As he turned around, he noticed a small stack of mail under a stone on the rocking chair next to the door and a handwritten note that said, *"Fishing. Back in a week or so."* Tucker sighed and decided to head back to town. He simply had too many questions to wait around.

After jogging over a mile down the main state road, he knelt down at the top of one of the few straightaways to adjust his socks and rub his heels, his scuffed Oxfords already rubbing blisters. As he stood back up, Tucker noticed a bubble atop a car in the distance. As it approached, Tucker waved with both hands and the cruiser replied with a single spin of its light. As it came to a stop, Tucker trotted over and smiled when he saw who it was. "Howdy, Sheriff," he said as Marty Hicks stopped in the middle of the empty two-lane road, turned the engine off, and stepped out.

"Tucker Trivette. Well, I'll be. Long time, no see," Hicks said as they shook hands. "Barely recognized you."

"Yeah, it's been awhile."

"Was wondering when you might show up. If you'd be coming back at all."

Tucker gave him a curious look. "Yessir. Just rolled into town," he said, and motioned towards Paul's Peak. "I suppose you can tell me what happened?"

Hicks exhaled strongly, turning solemn as he placed his hat on the hood of the car. "It was a bad fire. I was at Myrtle Beach with the wife when it happened. Been around ten months or so. Call came in around midnight. Structure was totally involved by the time the volunteer squad showed up. Old houses like that are like a tinderbox." He took a deep breath and continued: "They pulled your father out. Severely burned. They took him to Winston, but he's back at Memorial, now, last I heard."

Tucker stood in shock for a moment, then quickly said, "What about Mama and Danny?"

Hick's paused. "Your mother didn't make it out, son. Coroner had to match her hip and dental records," he said somberly in his official capacity.

Tucker's shoulders sank. Hicks waited another moment, then continued: "Your brother's remains weren't recovered."

Tucker looked up, hopeful.

"But witnesses say he was in there. Fire was so hot, he could have immolated completely. That's the thinking. I'm real sorry, son."

The color left Tucker's face as he stared blankly at the Sheriff trying to fully fathom what he was hearing: his brother was gone.

"And there's something else." Sheriff Hicks took another deep breath and spoke carefully. "There was talk around town, Tucker—not sure from who, maybe EMS—that Danny ... may have started that fire."

"What?" Tucker said, shaking his head. "There's no way he would—"

"I know, I know," Hicks interrupted. "Fire Marshal ruled it accidental, and he's good at what he does. I agreed with the assessment. It was a bad, tragic event. But I wanted you to know first in case you heard it from someone else."

Tucker turned away and walked to the other side of the road. "I just can't believe it," he said running his hand through his hair, staring at the ground.

"Nothing you could have done, son," Hicks offered. "Bad things happen. No rhyme or reason sometimes."

"Didn't even get to ..." Tucker paused, lost in hazy images of his mother on the porch through the rearview mirror and Danny waving goodbye from the bus station. "Damn ..."

Tucker stood in silence on the deserted road staring at the outlines of the most distant peaks while the Sheriff leaned against the cruiser. After a minute, Tucker slowly turned around. "How come nobody told me?"

Hicks raised his eyebrows. "We tried to get your contact information from your daddy. But he didn't cooperate. Well, he couldn't at first. Had him drugged up from his injuries for a month. Bad burns. When they transferred him back up here, I went to see him. Tried to get something out of him. He just kept saying you were long gone. Wouldn't say another word." Hicks shook his head. "Stubborn old cuss."

"That figures," Tucker said. "I quit calling. Every time I did, he'd hang up ... if he picked up at all. I thought things might've gotten better. Guess I was wrong."

Tucker pondered at the road's edge for a moment longer, then asked, "Can you take me to see him?"

Thirteen

Sheriff Hicks pulled under the front portico of the medical center and let Tucker out as the police radio chirped and the county dispatcher said: *"Marty, deputy needs your assistance at the Millers. Dogs again. Neighbors called."*

"Call A.C. I'll be right over," Hicks said into the mic. Then he turned to Tucker: "Might be a bit, but I'll give you a ride to wherever you need to go." Tucker thanked the Sheriff and shut the door, then stared anxiously at the hospital doors as the cruiser turned the corner out of sight. Other than disaster drills and first aid training, he hadn't dealt with injury and misery up close and personal.

"Suck it up," Tucker said to himself as he walked through the automatic doors to the admissions desk. A candy-striper signed him in, pointing the way to the ICU wing. "Past the pharmacy counter and to your right."

At the nurse's station around the corner, a stocky, pleasant middle-aged nurse greeted him, apparently having been alerted to his arrival. "Hello, Mr. Trivette. I'm Debra," she said. "This way."

As she escorted Tucker down the long hall, he glanced into the few open doors they passed. The patients, all elderly, either asleep or unconscious, lay in beds framed by stainless steel bars and flanked by blinking monitor carts. The muted televisions in the rooms cast eerie, flickering shadows down the dim corridor.

He wondered in what state he would find his father. The nurse seemed to read his mind. "Your father received grafts and wound care for his burns at

Baptist before they brought him back here. Then he had a stroke. He's mainly under palliative care, now. Just trying to keep him comfortable." She stopped before opening the door to the ICU. "My brother's with EMS," she said. "He was on-shift that night. Said the only thing they found was your mother's hip replacement. Titanium." Thinking better of her blunt clinical observation, she added, "Sorry."

Tucker said, "She had her hip replaced?"

The nurse smiled wanly and pushed open the door.

As they reached the bed, she touched Tucker's arm. "Don't expect too much. He's been fairly unresponsive lately," she said and left. Tucker took a deep breath and pushed the curtain away.

Wires and IV tubes connected to the monitors snaked around the blankets supporting his arms and head. Atop the pillow, ripples of marbled tissue blended features and strips of hair together in what was remained of a barely-human face. Tucker heard himself gasp at the broken and withered body in front of him, dying. Nothing menacing remained of the bitter man Tucker remembered. His father's scarred eyelids were closed, a crust of spittle in the corners of the taut pink outline of his lips.

"It's me, Dad. I'm home." Tucker sighed, not knowing what else to say.

Ewing's short lashes fluttered for a second, then closed again.

"I was just out to the house," Tucker said. "Sheriff Hicks told me about Mama. And Danny. I didn't know. Nobody told me. I feel terrible. You ... " Tucker stopped and stared out the window for a moment, then cautiously patted his father's arm. It hardly seemed worth it. He doubted Ewing could hear him anyway. Realizing he had nothing more to say, Tucker took a last, uncomfortable glance, then closed the curtain and started for the door, suddenly needing some air.

As Tucker hurried out through the sliding doors with his head down, he brushed against someone walking in. "Sorry," he said without looking up.

"Tucker?" a familiar voice said, as a hand grabbed his forearm, stopping him in his tracks.

Tucker glanced up and stared at the young woman for frozen moments. It took him that long to recognize her. She was skinnier than he remembered and with short hair—no more pigtails.

"Allie?" It was all he could muster.

"You're back!" she said with surprise.

"Uh, yeah," Tucker blinked away the fog. "Pulled in earlier today. I just ... found out what happened. Sheriff brought me over. Filled me in."

Allie's brow furrowed. "Oh, God. I can't imagine what you must be going through," she said and touched his hand. "I'm so sorry about your mom and Danny." After a quick second, she added "And your dad. How's he doing?"

"He's in bad shape. I don't know how much longer he'll make it like that."

"I'm so sorry," Allie said again, retrieving her hand.

"It's okay," Tucker said. "I'm still sorta in shock, I guess. What a homecoming, huh? Definitely wasn't what I expected. It's nice to see you, though. You look ... good. Different."

"Thanks," she said with an awkward smile. "I guess."

"What are you doing here?"

"Picking up some medicine for dad." She pointed to the pharmacy window.

"It didn't even cross my mind that you'd be here. In town."

"Yeah, well, Dad's having a few health issues of his own."

Not knowing what to say or ask, Tucker nodded, trying to look sympathetic. He was saved by the sound of Sheriff Hicks' cruiser pulling up next to them.

"Guess that's my ride," Tucker said.

"Well, let me know if there's anything I can do," she said. "Come by the shop sometime. I know Dad would love to see you. We can ... catch up."

"That'd be nice. I will," Tucker said as he opened the passenger door and slid in. Hicks nodded a polite hello to Allie, then put it in gear and drove away as she offered a last wave.

"You looked surprised to see her," Hicks said.

"First good surprise all day," Tucker said flatly, staring out the window.

"You alright?"

"I'm okay," Tucker said. "It's just—never expected to see Dad like that."

"How's he doing?"

"Not good," Tucker said. "But he never was."

"Hmm," Hicks said. He understood. While he didn't know Ewing Trivette very well, he knew the type.

"You hungry? Sadie's might still be open. It's just as bad as before you left," Hicks said to lighten the mood.

"Thanks, Sheriff," Tucker said. "Can't say I have any appetite."

"I guess not. You got a place to go in the meantime?"

"I think I just need to sort everything out," Tucker said staring out the window. "I'll be fine. Can you take me ... home?"

Fourteen

Hicks drove to the edge of the Trivette lot and put the cruiser into park. Then he reached between his legs pulling out a small but heavy wooden box and handed it to Tucker. Tucker shot him an inquisitive look and flicked the small latch to open it.

"Your grandfather gave it to me not too long before he passed," Hicks said, as Tucker lifted the Colt pistol out of the box. "Kept it at the station for him. He was worried about your dad doing something stupid. I thought he'd have wanted you to have it."

Tucker inspected the pistol for a moment and grinned. "I figured they'd probably sold it."

"I kept it oiled. I assume you know how to use it," Hicks said as he fished a box of rounds from the glove compartment. "Not that you'll need to, but around here, you never know. A little rough on this side of the county these days." No sooner had he spoken, the radio chirped. Hicks muted the receiver and sighed. "See what I mean."

Tucker gave a weak grin, opened the door, and stepped out of the car.

"If you need anything, just let me know, okay?" Hicks said.

"Appreciate it," Tucker said and closed the door. Hicks waved and picked up the receiver again as he put his car back into gear.

Tucker watched the dust waft across the drive as the patrol car pulled away, then wandered to the end of the driveway where he had dropped his duffel in front of the mailbox. He pulled what felt like five pounds of bills, flyers, and catalogues, some moldy and stuck together, and stuffed them into his bag. At least he'd have some kindling if it got chilly. Then he walked to his grandfather's truck, opened the creaking door, and tossed the duffel onto the driver's seat. Tucker coughed out the moldy humidity that wafted into his throat. Finding a cinderblock nearby, he flipped it upright and sat down, exhaling a heavy sigh.

Jesus. What a mess, he thought as he stared at the rubble. After years of order, routine, and constant drills with a like-minded crew, all working toward a common mission, being alone with nothing to hold on to was a foreign notion—the confusion he felt upon first seeing the destruction now replaced with resignation.

After a few minutes of introspection, the discipline and pragmatism of his training kicked in. Tucker stood up, determined to do ... something. *This ain't so bad*, he thought, reassuring himself. *I helped move a carrier from one side of the world to another. I can do this.* "Semper Fortis," right?

Tucker stepped over the ruins of the old home. The stacked-rock chimney had collapsed over broken chunks of black timbers that had once supported the roof. The stones that served as the footers of the house tumbled over into small piles—the remaining structural elements of the house scattered over themselves in ash and coals. He poked through the slag with a brittle stick of tarnished wire he pulled from the debris. Nothing of any value remained, not even a swatch of cloth.

He returned to the old Dodge and fished out the granola bar bought at the bus terminal earlier that morning. Tearing it open, he looked at the oats and raisins a short second, then tossed it back. Though he hadn't eaten all day, he still had no appetite.

Tucker walked to the front of the truck, reached under the grill, and popped the latch. As he lifted up the heavy metal hood, something flew at his face. Tucker ducked so quickly, he couldn't tell if it was a bird or a bat.

"Little bastard!" he yelped, then under his breath: "Scared shit outta me."

Holding up the hood, Tucker looked at the engine then tugged on the wires and belts. Everything seemed to be intact, though rusty and worn. Figuring the battery was long dead, he walked back around to the passenger side and tugged on the door. Its handle came off in his hand.

"Perfect," he said, then walked around to the driver's side and leaned into the truck, peeking under the driver's visor. Nothing. He checked the window crank, which rolled halfway down. At least that worked. Then he climbed in and reached across to the glove compartment. The knob was stuck. "Dammit, open up," he said and gave it a strong yank. The little door came free and Tucker face-planted into the seat cushion, which spewed a fresh puff of bluish-green spore into the cabin.

Hacking phlegm and muttering curses under his breath, he dug around the grungy contents of the compartment, locating the expired registration papers along with a wad of shredded stuffing pilfered from the seat cushions—a mouse nest. "Bingo," he said as he grabbed the spare key from under a pile of droppings and stuck it in the ignition, hopeful. He turned it. Not a sound. No surprise.

Tucker gave up on the truck and walked around the yard in a wide circle, gazing at the property beyond the remnants of the house—and his past. In the side yard, the overgrown orchard grass hid the disintegrating chicken coop. One section of the garden fence still stood, tall weeds the only crop remaining within its limited confines. The old, broken hoe clung tenaciously to the sole remaining strand of barbed wire, giving Tucker pause. Feeling warmth, he looked up. The edge of the setting sun peeked through passing clouds whipping above Paul's Peak, bringing his attention to the hillside above the house and ...

The woods.

Tucker snatched the hoe off the fence and ran toward the forest in long strides to see what seven years had produced from his ginseng planting. *At least I have that*, he thought as he used the rickety tool to hack through the layers of shrubbery, grown back thick while he was at sea.

He struggled through the dense understory as his deck shoes slipped on fallen limbs and moist ferns. *Should be plenty big to sell to Wei*, he thought.

As he tripped through low-lying mounds of decaying branches, he stopped to get his bearings, trying to remember exactly where he had sown those pounds of seed so many years prior. He crept forward slowly, complimenting himself on the careful planning that kept the site well-hidden. *Too well-hidden*, he thought. *Where is it?*

There. Tucker took two steps towards his first sighting of the "green gold" he was counting on. *Dang ... Sarsaparilla. Still fools me.*

Tucker pushed further into the holler. Limbs slapped him in the chest as he grew ever more impatient and stomped over rotten stumps. Each patch of promising green he saw turned out to be Virginia-creeper or some other worthless weed as if the woods were teasing him. Finally, after zig-zagging up and down the hillside for the better part of an hour, he broke through a thicket and stood for a few moments in the open forest. Still nothing.

As his eyes adjusted to the dimming light of dusk, he realized he was standing in the middle of a barely discernible row of sparse—too sparse—ginseng plants. Small ones. *This can't be it ... could it?* Only a couple of average-sized plants dotted the contour of the slope, interspersed with an occasional seedling or two. Hardly the mature plantation that should have blanketed the entire grove. Following the slope up the hill, he noticed another meager lot—then another. Just a few tiny clusters. From the tens of thousands of seeds he planted over seven years ago, barely anything remained.

Panicking, Tucker dropped to his knees by the largest of the stubby growths and stabbed into the ground with the broken hoe. The dense soil of the hillside jarred his arm with each swing. Finally, he extracted a small root—barely an inch long. Unsellable. *It can't be.* Tucker raced to the next cluster of plants—most having only two small prongs of leaflets—and swung his sad garden tool again. The head broke off. He stared blankly at the handful of puny tubers left scattered on the ground.

"*Shit!*" he howled, as he hurled the broken handle into the woods. Even that didn't work. He ducked as it hit a poplar trunk and bounced back at him faster than he had thrown it. Defeated, Tucker slumped onto the ground and grabbed the sides of his head, staring at the acres of nothing he had counted on to jumpstart his future. To be his future.

"What happened?" he said to himself. The answer came quickly: *Someone found it! Damn poachers. They got it all! How did they know? What did I do wrong?* Stunned, Tucker stood slowly and meandered hopelessly around the edge of his worthless plantation. All the same. Mere runts. His spirit fell quicker than the sun.

Tucker took a last look around and sighed. He ducked down the mountain as the wind began to pick up, sudden thunder signaling a quick-moving front that would be on top of him soon. Thick drops began to cascade from the leaves above as he solemnly trudged back, hoping to make it before the bottom fell out.

He didn't. The deluge caught him just as he emerged from the field behind the crumbled remains of the house. Running for the truck, he slipped less than five steps away, leaving a streak-track of mud on the ground and soaking his pants.

Groaning with frustration, Tucker threw open the driver's door and dove in, then turned to roll up the half-open window. The crank broke off in his hand with a foot to go.

"Give me a break!" he yelled at the storm—which answered back with a blast of thunder and a slapping sheet of rain.

Ripping open his duffel, Tucker snatched out his poncho, opened the door again and draped it over the window, then flopped over to the dryer passenger side. Anger and exasperation welled up over his predicament and lost lot. His broken dreams. His plans of greatness.

As the storm hovered over Paul's Peak, Tucker nibbled the soggy granola bar, contemplating the next move out of this hell. His prospects gone, his spirit sunk, he drifted into troubled sleep with dreams of disaster on land and at sea—sure that his future could be no darker.

Fifteen

Beams of sunlight hit Tucker's face through the half-fogged windshield, and the clucking of a chicken nearby signaled reveille. He wiped the sleep from his eyes and peered through the window at the bird pecking in the wet grass on the edge of the yard. *Where'd you come from?* With no shortage of hawks, snakes, and other varmints prowling the countryside, untended poultry never lived long outside the coop.

Tucker's stomach growled. The hen seemed the best chance at a meal. He'd worry about how to cook it later. Tucker quietly fought the passenger side door before remembering it was jammed. As he slid back to the driver's side and shoved the door open, his poncho fell to the ground—settling on the surface of a puddle. Tucker waited on the hen to move a little closer then steadied himself inside the cab. As he sprang forward, his left foot slid on the poncho, sending him into the mud. Tucker jumped up quickly, cursing, and scrambled toward the clucking bird, which artfully dodged his grasp each time he lunged. When he went left, it went right, the two of them dancing across the yard with Tucker howling expletives after each diving miss. Finally, his breakfast grew weary of the ground game and fluttered off, squawking into the woods.

"Great," Tucker said as he watched it go. He walked back to the truck, yanked off a moist sock hanging from the rearview mirror and smeared the grime off of his face. Then he pulled some clean clothes out of his bag and changed.

After tightening up the laces to his boots, Tucker stuffed everything into his duffel, threw its straps around his shoulders, and started walking. Within a half hour of hiking the blacktop towards town, a yellow and orange VW bus swerved around him, parking on the shoulder. An arm extended through the driver's window and motioned for Tucker to hop in. As he jogged to the passenger side, the door popped open.

"Sorry about the mess," the man inside said, leaning over and raking away a mountain of newspapers, sandwich wrappers, and foam cups from the seat. "Waiting to get the propane hooked up at the barn. Gives me an excuse to eat out."

The older gentleman's cheerful demeanor complemented the bright tint of his ride. Tucker heard a strong northeastern accent, which juxtaposed with the man's dirty overalls and short, gray beard and a thin ponytail that protruded from a straw farmer's hat.

"So which of the five last names in this county do you belong to," the man said, grinning at Tucker before grinding gears to pull back off the shoulder.

"I'm a Trivette."

"Interesting ... don't think I've met a Trivette, yet."

"There aren't many left," Tucker mumbled.

"Seems like there's no shortage of Wards, Greenes, and Graggs around here. And what the heck is a *Whine-burger?* One of those is my only neighbor," the man said. "Grows the Christmas trees. You know him?"

"Yes, I do. That's Clint ... *Wine-barger,* though," Tucker said.

"I see. Haven't had the pleasure of meeting him yet," the man said. "Or you. I take it you're not hiking the A.T.? You're a long way from the trail."

"Headed to the bank, sir."

"Don't 'sir' me, please. I'm not *that* old. It's the mileage," he said, lifting his eyebrows.

"I know what you mean," Tucker muttered.

The man chuckled, then said: "Bank, huh? Don't trust 'em. The only crooks I ever knew were bankers. And a few lawyers. Couple of doctors, too, now that I think of it. And accountants. Never mind. I guess I knew a lot of crooks. The schmucks." He laughed again. "No car, huh?"

"Needs some work," Tucker said. "That's my business with the bank."

"I see."

Tucker sighed then said, "Got discharged last week and came back to a burnt-down house and a broke-down truck."

Tucker lurched forward as the man hit the brakes and the van slowed to almost a crawl.

"That was *your* house?" he said. "Wow, I'm sorry. I could hear the sirens from my place that night. Heard it was a bad one. Anybody make it out?"

"My dad did—barely," Tucker said, then changed the subject. "So, you're not from around here sounds like."

"Saul Levitt at your service. Not many Levitts *here in these parts*," he attempted with a mountain accent and a snort. "Haven't met one yet. Staten Island via Port St. Lucie. Retired there a few years ago. Came here to escape the humidity and to get away from all the *other* Yankees. Wanted a hideaway in the mountains where nobody could find me."

"So, are you running from the law or like a prepper or something?" Tucker joked. "You don't look like one."

"None of us ever do," he winked. "Never know when the proverbial 'shit's' going to hit the fan, though. Saw the property advertised in one of my magazines. The ole bus here is home and office until I get the barn rebuilt and bury my freighter container. Those things make great bunkers. Hook up some solar panels and you're off the grid. I built houses before I retired. General contractor. You wouldn't happen to know anyone good at dozer work?"

Tucker shook his head: "I've been away too long."

"What branch?"

"How'd you know?"

"You said you were discharged. Plus, I could tell by the haircut," Saul said.

"Ah. Navy. You?"

"Semper fi," Saul replied, hitting his chest. "You boys gave us the good rides back in 'Nam."

"Yeah, yeah. Haven't heard that one before," Tucker replied. "How many tours?"

"Two," Saul said and cocked his head. "Forward observer. The views are definitely better in *these* mountains. And the weather. Locals can be just as friendly, though." He lifted his head and laughed loudly as they went down the road.

Saul pulled into the bank parking lot. "Enjoyed the company. Be happy to give you taxi service for the time being," he said. "At least until you get your own wheels. Come by the coffee shop when you get done."

Tucker looked around. "We have a coffee shop? I *have* been away too long."

"Opened a few months ago. A couple from Charlotte renovated the old jail, downtown. They even roast their own beans."

Tucker grunted. "Progress, I guess."

Saul frowned and said: "Yeah, but their bagels need some work. Southerners."

Tucker chuckled. "We do biscuits around here. With liver mush."

"*Yeesh.* Philistines," Saul said. But he was grinning.

Tucker smirked back, got out of the van, and waved thanks as Saul pulled away. Then he walked into the one-story, one-teller, brick bank. Glancing around, he saw no one manning the front desk. But he could hear a voice coming from the only open door inside the tiny building.

Tucker approached the office and nodded hello to a young man chatting on the phone who quickly removed his crossed feet from the top of the desk. Tucker glanced at the nameplate on the door: "Artie Helmsworth, Branch Manager." Tucker didn't recognize the name but guessed the guy to be straight out of college or wherever it was that bankers came from. The *kid* held up a finger letting Tucker know he wouldn't be long.

Tucker took a seat just outside the office door in one of the two bare, wooden chairs in the lobby. While waiting, he clicked through the mental checklist of essentials needed to tackle his new reality. First, the basics: food, shelter—a motel key away—and food. Some new pants and shirts would be nice, too. The clothes he wore already smelled like stale onions.

The young banker hung up the phone, straightened his tie, and motioned for Tucker to come in. "Sorry about that. Only call I've had all morning. Have a seat. How can I help you?" He shook Tucker's hand.

"I need to make a withdrawal."

"Easy enough. I can certainly help you with that."

"Don't remember my account number off hand. Set it up before I left for the military. Didn't need to get into it much. Just got back."

"I see. Well, welcome home and thanks for your service. Just need your license and a social."

Tucker pulled out his near-empty wallet and handed over his Navy ID card.

"Hmm. Let's see here ... Tucker Tri*vette*." He put the accent on the last syllable of Tucker's surname—like most out-of-towners—which made it sound like a French dinner roll. After clicking a few keys, he said: "Well. That's interesting. There doesn't seem to be anything here. The only account listed under that name shows a negative balance. Looks frozen, actually."

"What do you mean?" Tucker said.

The banker looked up at him: "There's nothing here."

Tucker chuckled—had to be a mistake. "You spelled my last name right?"

"Two T's. Yes. I see your account; there's just nothing in it. In fact, it's overdrawn." The banker shot him a wry look then looked back at the screen and tapped the keyboard again.

Tucker anxiously said: "My paychecks have been going in there since I enlisted. Direct deposit. Haven't taken much of anything out in a couple of years. Allotments. There should be like fifty grand in there."

"Hang on a minute," the banker said. "Let me check something."

He quickly tapped a couple of keys. "I'm sorry, no. There's nothing there."

"Check again." Tucker gave a stern look at the banker as his chest tightened.

"Let me pull up the transaction history," the banker said, his eyes darting nervously between Tucker's and the screen. "I can see where monthly deposits were made, but then withdrawn—regularly. There's checks made out to cash, which cleared until around a year ago, and the other withdrawals are automatic transfers to what looks like a loan company. Paid out until the balance hit zero. Triple R Auto Finance? Ring a bell?"

"*Jesus Christ.*" Tucker's vision began to blur. "Who signed them? The checks," he asked, even though he already knew the answer.

"There are two co-signers listed. Looks like you and a Ewing Trivette?" He spun the monitor around for Tucker to see.

Tucker stuck his tongue in his cheek and nodded slowly as his vision blurred. His brain couldn't fire fast enough to process what he was hearing. He had forged his father's name when he opened the account—just as he had on his first enlistment form. His mom's cousin, Gloria, had done all the paperwork for him ... "a family favor." Tucker didn't give it a second thought at the time. *Gloria* told them about it. *That. Bitch!* He almost screamed it out loud.

The front door to the bank opened and closed suddenly. Tucker and the manager looked around as the short, stocky woman scurried through the lobby carrying a small to-go bag and a drink holder with two cups. Her heels made skid marks on the tile floor as she stopped in front of the manager's office and met Tucker's glare. One of the cups slipped out and splashed open as it hit the floor. She didn't look.

"Tucker Trivette?" Gloria's eyes went wide. "My goodness. You're ... back!"

Tucker saw red as he struggled to keep his composure while his fingernails dug into the armrest under pale knuckles.

Gloria's expression morphed from surprise to fear. "I'm so sorry about—," she began.

"*What?*" Tucker seethed. "That you let mom and dad *steal* from me? You knew that was *my* money."

"Well ... Ruth's hip. She needed ... " The woman stuttered, then sobbed: "Your mama could *walk* again. And she loved that car! Excuse me, I just can't!"

"They took everything, just so you know!" Tucker shouted at Gloria's back as the stout traitor retreated into the office next to the teller counter and shut the door, latching it behind her.

Tucker threw up his hands and shook his head at the banker. The bank manager looked pale as he rubbed his temples and exhaled. "I'm very sorry," he said. "There's really nothing I can do."

"Me neither. They're dead." Tucker stood up and shoved his chair back into the office wall, leaving a dent in the sheetrock. Fuming, he left the lobby, kicked the front door open, and stormed out of the bank. Pacing back and forth in the empty parking lot, he cussed the bank, Gloria, the sky, and then his parents. "That explains a lot!" he shouted at the teller window. He saw the blinds lower quickly. "Yeah, that's right! Keep 'em shut!"

Never in a million years did he think that they, would stoop *this* low. His own *family*. Sure, it had been years and he hadn't left on the best of terms; but despite the mixed feelings about coming home, he had held on to a shred of hope, until now. Now, *everything* he had—gone. Tucker chuckled to himself as he tried to calm down. *How's that for a last laugh.* Homeless, broke, and utterly defeated, Tucker wiped angry tears from his eyes and began walking to the only other place in town he felt like he could go.

Sixteen

Tucker swung open the screen door of the Pelt and Herb and entered the building that had been central to so many of his good childhood memories. He took a deep breath and inhaled the lingering, earthy aroma that still filled the old store, distracting him from desperate thoughts of returning to the bank and murdering his aunt.

The inventory in the front had shifted around since the last time he'd been inside, but everything else felt the same. Deer antlers still adorned the walls, and the pot-bellied stove hadn't budged. For just a moment, he felt twelve-years old again.

Jim Gragg stooped over the counter in the back, turning pages of a newspaper. He looked up as Tucker's footsteps creaked on the wooden floor. "Well, look who it is!" Gragg said as he took off his reading glasses. "Now, there's a sight for sore eyes. My goodness, son. Looks like they fed you well."

"Yessir. Never missed a meal. Good to see you, too." Tucker smiled, then frowned as he saw Mr. Gragg lower himself into a wheelchair and roll his way towards the front of the store. "What happened?" Tucker said, pointing at the wheelchair.

"Ah. Pinched nerve in my back. Too much time leaning over that counter, I reckon. Getting old got the better of me," he said with a weak smile, the furrows on his forehead looking more like scars than wrinkles, and his hair having changed to a shock of white since the last time Tucker saw him. He beamed, though, as he gripped Tucker's arm, looking up at him.

"Allie was hoping you'd stop in sometime," Jim said with a wink. Then he turned somber. "Said she saw you at the hospital. How you been holding up? With everything."

"It was a shock, that's for sure," Tucker said. "On top of it all, turns out Mom and Dad cleaned out my bank account."

Jim grimaced. "Hmm. Was wondering how they got that new car."

"Left me in a tight spot."

Jim shook his head sympathetically, and Tucker went for his pitch: "So, Mr. Jim, I've got a check coming from the Navy. Not sure when it's getting here, though. Last pay and bonus."

Jim nodded, willing to listen.

"Do you think you might—," Tucker continued, but Jim interrupted, shaking his head.

"Sorry, son. Business has been real slow. I could give you a few bucks. Might get you through a day or two at best. You know, Sadie, at the barbecue joint, will do you a quick turnaround cash loan," he said. "She does that for folks in-between paychecks."

Tucker smiled. "I wasn't gonna say that. Appreciate it, though. I was going to ask if I brought in some 'seng if you'd give me a fair price. You always bought everything Paw Paw dug."

"Well, harvest season ain't come in yet," Jim said. "Won't be legal for another month."

Tucker's face crinkled. "What do you mean, legal? There's a season now?"

Jim chuckled as he tried to remember the last time Tucker had been in the shop with Buck Trivette. Had to have been just a boy. "There's been a legal season since before you were born, son—first of September. You never had to know, because your granddaddy always hunted in season when the berries were red. To replant 'em. Lately, price is up and folks are diggin' too early. Off Federal land, too. Can't be hunting it there no more. The law's cracking down. They're even puttin' dye on the plants that makes the root glow. They'll put you away." Jim reached under the counter and pulled out a flashlight with a green lens. "I'm supposed to use this to check. Can see the dye clear as day when you run the light over them."

"You gotta be kidding me." Tucker put his head down and sighed. "I can't catch a break."

"So, you think you know where there's a big patch?" Gragg said.

Tucker lifted his head up quickly and said with confidence: "I know I can find one."

Jim looked at him for a moment and laughed out loud. "Son, there ain't no more big hauls of 'seng left within a county's walk no more. Every no-good poacher's done gone and picked the hills clean. Got dug out hard last season. Price is supposed to be even higher this year. It's got to where I don't even wanna carry the cash to pay the diggers. I worry about gettin' robbed."

"Price is that good?" Tucker grunted.

"Highest it's ever been," Gragg said.

Tucker's eyes widened. A high price *could* work to his advantage, Tucker thought—if he could find a few of his granddaddy's old patches. The hidden ones. But that might take some time. "Well, I gotta make some money in the meantime," Tucker said.

"Well, you can always *grow* you some 'seng," Jim offered.

"I already tried that," Tucker said. "Didn't turn out so good."

"Oh yeah. I heard about that."

Tucker looked up at him, confused. "What do you mean?"

Jim rubbed his head and chuckled, "Ah, heck, son. All the diggers around here knew about that patch."

Tucker's mouth dropped open.

Jim saw the surprise and hurt in Tucker's ego, and tried to soften his tone: "Sorry. It's just, you know, local gossip. I wouldn't take it seriously. Maybe they weren't talking about yours after all."

But Tucker could tell Jim was lying. Homeless, broke, and now a laughing stock. Paw Paw would roll in his grave.

Jim tried to change the subject. "You know, you could go down to the Ag Office and see if they could give you some ideas. On the 'seng or something else. I hear the Ag Agent is an expert on that stuff," he said with a wink.

"Thanks, Mr. Jim. Sorry to bother. It was good to see you, though. If you see Allie, tell her I came by."

"I will," Jim said. But something else was on his mind. As Tucker turned to go, Mr. Jim gripped Tucker's arm again. "Son, I know you got dealt a tough hand. As tough as anyone could've been dealt. Knowing your granddaddy, though, and how he raised you, you'll be fine. I'm certain."

"Thanks, Mr. Gragg. Appreciate that."

Jim nodded. "You might try talking to Clint. He's done planted the hillsides full of firs. He's usually looking for help—unless the Mexicans all done got it." Jim grunted at the thought. "Can't hurt to ask."

"Might have to do that," Tucker said, trying to sound respectful—and serious. Shearing Christmas trees was the last thing he wanted to do.

"But if you *were* to happen on a good patch of 'seng between now and then ... talk to Z," Mr. Jim said cryptically as he turned to wheel himself back to the counter.

"Z's still around, huh?" Tucker said.

"They haven't caught him yet. And I hear he's always in the market. Sells starter roots these days, too. Just, uh, keep an eye out."

Before Tucker could say anything else, Jim rolled himself past the counter and into the back storeroom, leaving Tucker to his thoughts. He had always followed the law—Paw Paw had made sure of that. Dealing with Zebulon Greene could change all of that in a single transaction. But it might be his only option.

Tucker left the Pelt and Herb and strolled aimlessly down Main Street, his confidence withered and pride wounded. Despite everything he had worked for since leaving his small hometown, his future—his options—seemed now bleak at best.

He stopped in front of the county's Public Services Center, a split-level brick building that housed the two-ambulance EMS service on the lower level and the agriculture offices up top. He had never even been inside. With his grandfather's knowledge of the woods and Clint's wisdom of all things farming, he never had cause to. While he contemplated a visit, per Jim's suggestion, Tucker quickly changed his mind. The liquor store just down the street seemed a better option—its "Open" sign flashed below the large, red ABC letters. Easy enough.

"I told you!" Saul exclaimed, riding high on the extra-large cappuccino he sipped while he and Tucker rattled down the road in the Vanagon. "I bet that bank is in cahoots with the car company *and* the payday loan outfit. Just more than happy to help mom and pops screw you out of your life savings for a nice kickback. Granted, your parents were horrible human beings, God rest their souls, but you should sue."

Tucker laughed out loud. "Nobody around here does that. I don't even know if we have a lawyer in town. Serves me right for signing my father's name to begin with. Twice. Should've known Gloria would tell them about it." He shook his head and looked out the window at the passing farmhouses and the invasion of tall weeds overtaking the medians.

Saul waved his hand. "Ah, stop with the poor Appalachia self-loathing crap. You served your country and what do you get for it?" He waited for Tucker to look up and acknowledge him. "A foot in the kiester. That's what you got. It's a shame. You seem like a good kid. You wanna hear about mistakes? I'll tell you about mistakes."

As the curves rocked the top-heavy vehicle back and forth towards Paul's Peak, Saul expounded on his own life lessons—including the first ex-wife—and the two others. Then selling his 1970 Boss 302 Mustang for the raggedy Volkswagen bus. He ended each story with: "What was I thinking?"

Before the asphalt turned to gravel, Tucker noticed a tow-behind travel trailer parked by the road with its hitch resting on a single concrete block. The "For Sale" sign, taped to one of its windows, read "$2,500 OBO," hand scribbled in black marker. The camper sat in front of a small, neat brick house with an American flag waving in the breeze just off the porch. Tucker's neck craned back at it until the next curve.

"Not a bad deal," Saul said. "They've dropped the price on it, too. Looked at it myself when I first rolled into town. Had too many investments to make at the new place, though. Plus, the cot in this thing sleeps like a dream." He reached up and tapped the panel above, which hid the stowed sleeping quarters. "Gotta love German ingenuity—methodical sons of guns."

As they turned off from the main road and passed Clint's property, Tucker stared at a group of men spread across the farthest hillside above Clint's house, making their way down endless rows of Christmas trees. Glints of steel flashed as arms swung in the sunlight—shearing knives. Tucker dreaded the thought, but figured he'd give in and call on Clint.

"Thought about setting me out some of those, too," Saul pointed out the window and laughed. "Wouldn't that be a sight. Doubt there's many farmers around here who read the Torah."

"Are Christmas trees even Kosher?" Tucker joked.

"Good question," Saul said.

As they reached the Trivette mailbox, Tucker nodded. "This is me. Home sweet home."

Saul made a wide arc to turn around and stopped to let Tucker out. "Damn," he said, looking at the ruins. "You weren't kidding."

Tucker shrugged.

"Seriously. Let me know if you need anything," Saul said. "I'm just up the road a couple miles. I'd be happy to let you hang your hat there for the time being."

"I appreciate it," Tucker said. "But I gotta suck it the hell up, I reckon."

"True, but don't be ashamed to ask for help."

Tucker thought for a moment then said, "Where'd you say you lived?"

"Just up the road, around that mountain," Saul pointed. "Borders the National Forest."

"You got a map of the place?"

"I'm sure I do somewhere under the pile of closing papers. What for?"

"Get my bearings. Might be interested in takin' a peek in your woods. Better to stay on private land these days, apparently."

"No problem. Whatever you need. What are you looking for?"

"There's a plant that grows around here—"

"You don't say," Saul lifted his eyebrows.

"No, not *that*," Tucker chuckled.

"There's another one I'm looking for. You ever heard of ginseng?"

"Like in the tea?"

"Yeah, I suppose. I never drank it, but it grows around here. Or used to," Tucker said under his breath. "Might bag a squirrel or two while I'm at it."

"Yeesh. You mountain people. Have at it." Saul grinned. "I'll see if I can't find that map. In the meantime, if you need a loan ..." Saul tipped his hat as he began driving away.

"Thought you said not to trust bankers," Tucker replied, tapping the side of the van. As the dust from the VW settled, Tucker wasted no time removing the square bottle from his paper bag and cracked the seal as he walked to Paw Paw's truck and sat on the tailgate.

While he had learned to hold his own after many rowdy evenings with his fellow crewmen at the Navy bars, the fear of becoming like his father always loomed in the back of Tucker's mind. His regimented self-inhibitions weren't slowing him down tonight, though. *I've earned this drunk.* That's what he told himself, anyway.

Before long, he swirled a half-empty bottle.

Tucker whistled "Blow the Man Down"—realizing he never actually sung the tune while at sea—and hopped off the tailgate to relieve himself. The liquor hit him faster than he thought, and he immediately bent over to throw up. Straightening up while struggling to keep his balance, and wiping a trail of vomit-drool on his sleeve, Tucker fumbled for his zipper and got it halfway down. Good enough.

"Heave HO!" Tucker shouted as he urinated in the dirt, trying to spell his first name. Deciding it read more like TIOJI, he finished dribbling on his shoe, stumbled back to the truck and slumped into the cab, passing out before he got the door fully closed.

A vivid, troubling dream came upon him. Piloting a schooner heading straight into a storm, he sped along at ten knots. Menacing dark clouds and crackling lightning up ahead signaled rough seas. His crew had abandoned ship and Tucker found himself alone trying to keep a firm grip on the helm to maintain course—directly into the black, tossing waters. Frantic, he looked down for modern navigational controls. But his was an antique boat, something out of one of Clint's novels—creaky and wooden with three masts under full sail, the acre of canvas flapping loudly. On the deck, a Jolly Roger unfurled and snapped violently in the wind—the scarred face of his father, with bright bones crossed beneath, on the black flag. Lights flickered behind him followed by the reports of cannon, a bigger ship, a frigate, at his stern in stout pursuit. Something whistled overhead and an explosion took off the bow, leaving only a column of seawater to splash over—

Tucker jerked awake to realize that the water cascading over him was real—real rain, pouring in through the kicked-open door and his poncho flapping in the wind. With a loud grunt, he reached over to grab the handle and yank the door closed. Although soaked and with a chill in the air, he felt no pain. Tucker tried to keep his eyes open as the dome light above spun around and around before he finally blacked out to sail the pirate seas again.

Seventeen

The roar of the approaching vehicle awoke Tucker from his slumber with a start. Though more than a half mile away, the muffler-less engine rattled his dehydrated brain as it got closer, Garth Brooks' "Rodeo" blaring through open windows. He lurched up to the driver's side of his truck just long enough to see the rural route carrier stop at the mailbox. After a moment, the Subaru hatchback took off again in a cloud of gray exhaust that blended with the morning mist—the ground fog reminding him of Paw Paw's bean jar. Each foggy morning in August, his grandfather's dried pintos, dropped into an old pickle jar, predicted the number of snows for the coming winter.

Is it already August? Tucker thought as he rubbed his head—*liquor flu*, as his crewmate, Johnny, always called it. The pasty acridity in his mouth coupled with the throbbing in his skull made him queasy. He fumbled for the near-empty water bottle in the floorboard, swigged the dregs, then kicked open the driver's door, squishing across seat cushions turned sponges from the night's downpour—his clothes soaked through.

Rivulets of mud squished over his feet as Tucker tip-toed across the saturated yard, his back stiff and aching from sleeping in the cramped cab. Trying to stretch his calves, he made his way to the mailbox and pulled open its battered aluminum door, then fished out the sole parcel—a crimped mailer addressed to Petty Officer Tucker Trivette from the United States Navy.

Tucker ripped open the envelope. His final check.

"Thank God," he said aloud. It would be more than enough to pay for the parts needed to get the truck up and running—and a big plate of ribs from Sadie's, once his stomach quit turning.

Tucker hobbled back to the truck and changed into his other pair of mud-streaked pants stretched across the dashboard to dry. Then he slung the duffel onto his shoulder and began the trek to the main road. After a half hour of dry heaving every few steps, he heard the rickety mail wagon making its return trip. He could hear the chorus from "Just Call Me Lonesome" a mile away. At least they have good taste, he thought. Tucker stepped out with his thumb in the air. The beat-up Subaru came to a stop next to him.

"You know, we're not supposed to pick up vagrants," the driver said to Tucker through the passenger-side window of the retrofitted, right-hand drive. The woman's frizzy bangs engulfed most of her acne-pocked face. She slouched low in her seat, shoved so close to the steering wheel that its matted, dull-pink plush cover pressed into her crotch. She stared straight ahead, avoiding any eye contact.

"I understand, but I'd really appreciate a ride. Just going to the bank, ma'am," Tucker said.

"You ain't on no drugs are you?"

"No ma'am."

"Smells like you been in the sauce."

"Last night," Tucker admitted.

"You look like hell, too."

Tucker glanced down. He couldn't disagree. "It was kinda rough."

She grunted. "You that Trivette boy from back there next to Winebarger's?"

"Yes ma'am."

She grunted again. "I'm Grace. Marty Hicks' niece. He said you might be out and about this a'ways. Told me to check in. I don't know you from Adam, but he said you'uns was alright. I'm done with my run, so get on in."

Tucker walked around the car, opened the door and sank into its torn, vinyl seat. He set the mostly empty, plastic mail tub in his lap as Grace put the car into gear and sped down the road. It felt odd as a passenger in the driver's side, but the rushing air through the open window relieved the ache in his noggin. The noise from the wind and the mistimed engine made conversation nearly impossible, which was fine with him. Grace didn't say another word until she pulled into the parking lot of the bank, not in any hurry. Now.

"Payday, huh?" she said, still avoiding eye contact.

"Guess you could call it that," Tucker said. "Last one."

"Postmaster had to sign for it. All official. Ain't seen that before. Must be big."

Tucker chuckled. "Just big enough. Glad you brought it. And thanks for checking in on me."

Grace grunted a final time as she stopped in front of the main door of High Mountain Bank. Tucker slid out of the car, and she drove away without saying anything more. He took a deep breath to steady himself on still-wobbly legs, then opened the door.

As Tucker entered the lobby, he noticed the same, young bank manager chatting with a drive-up customer through the tinny speaker at the teller window. Luckily, there was no sign of Gloria. Good thing. Tucker had a few more *thoughts* to share with her, but it appeared the manager was the only person in the bank.

After the client at the window pulled away, the young man turned around with a start as he met Tucker's glare from the other side of the counter. "Um. Mr. Trivette," he said, nervously. "Listen, I'm really sorry about—"

Tucker slapped his hand onto the teller counter and slid the folded bank note across the faux-granite top.

"What's this?" He made quick eyes at Tucker's disheveled hair and the duffel hanging to the floor. "You're not gonna—" Eyes wide, breathing heavy, he opened the check.

Tucker cocked his head.

Seeing that it wasn't a ransom note, the kid said, "Ah, okay! Your final payout."

How the hell did everyone know about that check?

Wholly relieved, the banker smiled and said: "So, would you like to open a new account with this?"

"Really?" Tucker scoffed. The kid hung his head as Tucker told him to "Just cash it, *please*."

The young banker quietly complied, pulling out a small stack of bills from the cash drawer, riffling it through a counting machine, and slipping it into an envelope. "Appreciate your business," he said almost like a question. "Um, let us know if we can help you with anything else."

"You've done plenty, thanks," Tucker told him. "And please, tell Gloria I said hello." He gave a parting smirk, snatched the envelope off the counter, and began walking to the Pelt and Herb.

Jim Gragg nodded toward the counter as he looked through the items on Tucker's list. "Most of what you need is here near the register. Grab you a cold drink from the cooler, if you want. On the house."

Tucker rummaged through the ice and dropped a few half-melted cubes into his mouth before pulling out a Dr. Pepper.

"There's some denim in your size over there." Jim pointed to a small rack of clothes hidden in the corner of the store under the detergent shelf. "Clean t-shirts, too. Allie had me order them for the tourists."

Tucker glanced at his dirty clothes, then around the shop. "Allie not around today?"

"She should be coming by soon. Bringing her old man some lunch," Jim said as he worked the wheels of his chair to the back of the store. "I think I have some plugs and a battery that'll work back here. Don't sell a lot of car parts anymore these days since that Auto-World opened up off the mountain."

Tucker's stomach growled at the mention of food, but was glad that Allie wasn't there to see him, or smell him, like this. He scratched his nose with his shoulder, cringing at the sniff of his own armpit—a shower, or dip in the creek at least, long overdue. He found a bar of soap and dropped it into his basket along with boxes of ramen, some canned beans, and stew.

Tucker swigged down the rest of his soda, then pulled the last three quart cans of motor oil from the long-undusted shelf along with a few basic tools he guessed he'd need. When Mr. Jim returned with the spark plugs and battery, Tucker paid him quickly, and Jim pushed a box of Twinkies across the counter. "For the road," he said with a wink.

"Thanks, Mr. Gragg," Tucker said as he stuffed the goods into his duffel.

"Well, thank *you* for the business," Jim said with a grin. "Sure you don't want to stick around?"

"Appreciate it, but I gotta use the daylight while I can."

As Tucker walked out of the old store, adjusting the duffel's strap, an SUV pulled in. It was Allie. She parked and stepped out holding a bulging, grease-stained paper bag. She was neatly dressed in khaki jeans and a button-up shirt with a petite purse dangling from her shoulder. Her bobbed hair bounced as she walked to the steps. Seeing her in the full sunlight, Tucker remarked to himself how attractive she looked.

"Hey, stranger. It's about time you dropped in to say hello," she said. "Dad said you came by the other day. Sorry I missed you. How've you been getting along?"

"Okay, I reckon. I mean, well, I've been busy," he said, hoping the words didn't sound as pathetic outside his head as in.

"Doing what? Huffing glue and rolling in mud," Allie said, looking him up and down and chuckling. "You look awful. You sure everything's okay?"

"Thanks?" Tucker said with a weak smile. "Had a run-in with a chicken yesterday. Long story."

"If you say so," Allie said, shaking her head. "You need anything?"

"Just got it." He shook his full bag, which clunked on the wooden porch. "Good to go."

"Are you staying at home? I mean, back at your place?" Tucker saw Allie cringe at hearing her own words. At least he wasn't alone in that regard.

"It's all good," he said, kindly. "Baby steps. Getting things settled. Your dad set me up with car parts. And … groceries." Tucker showed her the Twinkies, then caught himself staring at her paper sack. He changed the subject to get his mind off cheeseburgers. He could smell them. "So, what about you? We didn't get a chance to talk much last time. Are you here for good? I figured you'd be married off by now, with little Allies running around, or … you know."

"Uh, no?" Allie laughed. "You sound like my parents."

"Sorry," Tucker said. "Didn't mean anything by it."

Allie hemmed a bit, then said: "Well, to be honest, there was a guy. A few years ago." She paused as if remembering some bad times. "Didn't work out."

"Sorry," Tucker said, earnestly. "Still, I thought you would've moved to the 'big city' by now, at least. I mean, you went to college and everything, right? Or could you not find a job?" He could tell by the look on her face that his jab didn't sit well.

Allie cocked her head and took a breath. "Actually, I made the *decision* to come back after school to help Dad. Worked out just fine. My office is down the street in the county building."

Tucker glanced down the road at the unadorned brick complex. "Cool. That's convenient. I'm glad things worked out for somebody."

Allie glared at him, then softened. "Well, you're one to talk. I thought you'd be on the seven seas for good."

"Nah. I finished my hitch. Thought coming back home was the right thing to do. Like you. Just didn't know what I was coming back to. Wish someone would've given me a heads up on that." He didn't say *Allie;* but his intent was clear. "Might have made different plans. You know."

Allie bristled. "I tried, Tucker. Called three bases to track you down after the fire. Even sent a letter, too. Post office returned it. 'Old address' it said. 'No longer at this location.'" She said it as if mocking the words on the envelope. "Besides, the last time we talked you didn't sound like you wanted to come back. Ever. So, you know, I gave up, okay?" She turned away, huffing as much as her pride would allow.

"Sorry, Allie, I was at sea, serving my country," Tucker said with sarcasm.

"And we're *so* proud," she bit back. "If you hadn't quit writing, I might have—"

"You never wrote back!"

Allie rolled her eyes then lit into him like they were kids again matching his sarcasm: "Oh, poor little Tucker Trivette. Heaven forbid the world stop revolving around you. Like I didn't have anything else to do? And I *did* write you when I could. I even read your letters to Danny. The ones you wrote to me too. He'd come into the shop every week just to see if you'd written. Bet you didn't know that. Or didn't care."

Tucker hung his head for a second, but clung to his point. "Well, you still could have written more. To let me know what was going on."

"Sure, yeah. Okay. I could have, if I'd known *where the hell* you were!" Allie paused and shook her head. "Anyway, that's not even the point."

"But I'm sure you have one, right?" Tucker said.

"You know what, Tucker? I'm not even gonna bother," Allie said bluntly. "I am truly sorry about your family. But that's all I have for you. You're not the only one who got a raw deal. Did you know *my* mama died while you were gone? From cancer."

Tucker sagged as Allie continued: "And Daddy's in a wheelchair. Did you even notice that? Huh? I don't know how long I'll ... " She choked up a little. "... how long I'll have him."

"Jesus, Allie, I'm sorry. I didn't know." Tucker reached for her arm.

Allie retreated a step and shook her head at him, dabbing at an eye with her greasy lunch sack. "No sir. Don't act like you care about what's going on with me after all these years. Life goes on. *Mine* went on. I'm sorry for what you came back to, but nobody here gets a parade! So, you can take your funky hair and your whiskey-stink dog breath, and just go."

Tucker stood silently, hanging his head.

"What's the matter?" she said, regaining her composure. "Still at a loss for words? Didn't learn any good comebacks in the Navy?"

Tucker threw up his arms. "What do you want me to say?"

"Same old Tucker," Allie huffed as she brushed passed him up the stairs. He had said enough, obviously.

Tucker heard the screen door slam before he turned back around. *What the hell was that all about?* He stood alone on the porch, rewinding. *I'm the one shit-out-of-luck. What was I supposed to say? Shit, I hadn't even asked about her mom.* Tucker kicked himself, regretting his selfishness. It didn't help that Allie looked really good. Better than he remembered. But her fuse seemed as short as it used to be.

He continued the inner conversation as he slogged his way down Main Street. After leaving the package store with two more fifths, he noticed Saul's van parked where he hoped it would be, his shoulder cramping from slogging the full bag across town. Now, he had to run with the dang thing.

Saul was leaving the coffee shop as Tucker reached the door out of breath.

"Ah, look who's here," Saul said.

"That offer for a ride still stand?" Tucker said.

"Of course. Let me buy you a latte for the road. They're decent enough here, even though they don't steam the milk quite right."

"No, thank you, I'm fine. Went to the bank. Again."

"You remember to ditch the dye-pack and homing beacon, there, Butch Cassidy?" Saul said, glancing at Tucker's stuffed satchel.

"Yep. Clean escape," Tucker said, playing along—even though the thought had crossed his mind, briefly, when the banker gave him the evil eye.

Maybe if Gloria had been there.

"Well, I'm too old to be the Sundance Kid," Saul laughed as he banged on the hood of the van. "The getaway car is gassed up, though."

Tucker grinned and tapped the envelope in his front pocket. "Last paycheck from Uncle Sam. This helps, but it's already spent."

Saul slugged down the last of his cappuccino, wiped the foam from his beard, and pitched the cup onto the mound of others behind Tucker's seat as he put the clunky Volkswagen into reverse and spun the bus around for the ride home.

While the charred remains of his childhood home marred the view of Paul's Peak, the serenity of the farmland and its reassuring familiarity afforded Tucker some solace. At least it was quiet, other than the distant clucking of the lone chicken as it foraged at a safe distance. He tossed the two bottles of green label into the cab and removed the spark plugs, wires, a new battery, a grease gun, and a set of wrenches from his duffel. Tucker set the tools on a makeshift bench he quickly assembled from chipped cinder blocks and opened the hood.

A refreshing breeze tempered his mood somewhat as he went to work on the rusty engine. As he got elbows deep into the repairs, Tucker felt back in charge of his own destiny. He *almost* forgot his set-to with Allie—but found himself arguing with her again inside his head more times than he would have liked. Each time, he said, out loud: "Stop it, man. She's not worth it."

Even if she was.

But she was back in town, busy taking care of her father and—*Jesus, how could I not have thought to ask about her mother?*—at her *new* job *"just down the street,"* and he was here, trying to get this damn rust-heap to run again.

At least she *had* a job. "All I got's this!"

He threw his new crescent wrench, angrily—and far. It took him thirty minutes to find the dang thing, which in turn gave him an extra half-hour of *debate* with Allie.

"Dammmiiittt!"

Shouting at Paul's Peak made him feel a tiny bit better and cleared his head. After sweating under the hood undeterred for an hour, he tried the ignition. The old motor turned over and over while the interior light flickered and all of the needles moved—except the one for the fuel gauge. Empty.

"Duh," he said. "It's only been sitting here for who knows how long." Tucker shook his head.

As he removed the blocks from under the axle and lowered the truck to the ground, each tire sank to the rims. Apart from the worn tread, three of the tires were dry-rotted beyond repair, and one had a gash that ran clear through to the other side.

Probably a bullet from some drunk—*maybe Dad*. Or kids, kids that needed something other than beer and a gun.

Tucker kicked the side panel of the truck in frustration and strolled to the edge of the woods to relieve himself. Where could he go from here? Being land rich wasn't any better than being cash poor without options. Selling the property crossed his mind, *but then what?* And who would buy it anyway? There were plenty other "For Sale" signs for much nicer digs. Nobody'd see the curb appeal of a pile of rubble, weeds, and a decrepit chicken house this far outside of town. He gazed up at the sky, into the forest, then around the entire perimeter of the ridges surrounding Paul's Peak.

"This is home," Tucker said to himself as he zipped up his pants. And it was the truth.

He walked slowly back to the truck, taking in the panorama. Being back at the home place, despite coming back to nothing, felt right in an odd way. The mountains defined his sense of being and bound him to the place, every lump of the hillside and curl of the vista past the tree line a benchmark in his past. His childhood, while harsh, had made him who he was, and the memories he chose to remember were the fond ones. While he wouldn't trade the open seas and his adventures over the past few years for anything, deep down he knew he belonged right here. Proving that to himself *here* was the priority now. And nobody was left to hold him back.

Cicadas interrupted his quiet introspection as they unleashed a late-afternoon cacophony in the nearby woods. Tucker smiled as his thoughts drifted to his brother. As kids, he and Danny used to catch the big-eyed bugs as they circled the naked light bulb on the porch at night. He tied lengths of old kite string or sewing thread—whatever they had on hand—to the creatures' bodies so Danny could fly them around like remote control airplanes. The ones that escaped lived a few more days above ground before their brief life expired. Tucker shook his head. Nothing here was easy or permanent—for insects or men.

Eighteen

"Body work" was hand-scribbled on a two by four below the sign that read "Tires & Repair," which hung crookedly on the front of the building where Grace let Tucker out. She had pulled in at the Trivette mailbox earlier in the morning for another check-in as Tucker gathered himself to come into town yet again.

"You're a life saver. Thanks again for the ride," Tucker said as he tried to hand her a ten-dollar bill.

"Keep your money. I ain't no taxi," she said, waving him off before nodding toward the garage door of the shop. "You watch out for them boys." Tucker gave her a curious look at the warning, but Grace just grunted before pulling away.

The cement on the shop's floor glistened slick and dark from years of accumulated oil drippings. Three stacks of tires in various sizes and states of wear leaned against the wall in one corner, while empty cardboard Valvoline boxes spilled over themselves in another. A Ford sedan with no wheels or back bumper rested head-high on the shop's only lift. From the layer of dust on its hood, the sad Fairmont had languished there for months. A NASCAR pin-up calendar on the back wall afforded the only color in the small, gray shop.

Tucker heard some voices out back as he tapped the greasy bell on the small counter with a muffled "ding." A lanky character in stained Dickies coveralls emerged from the rear door. Tucker dropped his head with a sardonic grin when he recognized who it was.

"Well, look here," Rat said with a sneer as he eyeballed Tucker up and down. "Mr. Army Boy, come back all humble and ... what's it called ... *world weary*."

"Navy," Tucker corrected. "Been a long time, Harlan."

Rat cocked his head slightly and sucked his teeth. "Navy," he said as his rat-pack of no-goods moseyed inside. "That's where all the pussies go, right?"

They all laughed and Rat soaked it in.

Tucker mock-chuckled at his old nemesis. The same braided rattail fell from the side of his head, but Rat looked even sketchier than the last time Tucker had seen him. He appeared to have put on twice the years but none of the weight since high school. Thin and drawn, he grinned with a yellow smile and skeletal cheeks. The straps of his coveralls clung to bony shoulders coated in grime and tiny scabs, like freckles. His "prison tats" homemade. Ink by *Bic*.

"I see not much has changed around here," Tucker said.

"Nothin' ever does." Rat and his crew of sycophants laughed some more.

Tucker recognized the same cronies Rat had dragged around since middle school—just lankier and skankier. Rat was right: nothing had changed.

Just gotten worse.

Opting against pleasantries—there were none to share—Tucker shot straight to the point: "I'm trying to get my old truck running back at the home place and—"

"Yeah, I heard about that shit out yonder," Rat interrupted. "Too bad about your family. That smokin's dangerous. Shit can kill a man." He pulled a pack of Winstons from his shirt pocket and began tapping its butt on his wrist. "Buddy a'mine was cooking in his trailer and blowed the whole damn thing up. Fumes got him. Had that raggedy plastic hangin' up all over inside. Melted all over him. Burnt the kids up pretty awful, too. Real tragedy."

"He burned his kids up?" Tucker frowned. "What was he cooking?"

Rat's boys looked at each other and laughed.

"Well, it weren't damn spaghettios," Rat said. "What do you think?"

"You need some?" said one of the sidekicks.

"Shut up!" Rat glared at the man. "Hell's wrong with you?"

"You know. Thought he came in for—"

"*Him?*" Rat shook his head and said, sarcastically, "Ole Tucker Trivette here's too goody-two-shoes to stoop as low as that."

While the rest of them laughed at Rat, Tucker turned to walk away. Surely there was another place in town to get tires, he thought.

Rat, seeing a client and cash leaving, caught up to Tucker before he left the garage. "Hold up, now. We ain't had no one show up all week. So, uh, what'cha need? I'm at your humble service."

Tucker hesitated but knowing there wasn't a set of new treads before the next county, he turned back. "Tires. For the truck. I need someone to come out and put 'em on, or I can bring the wheels in. Whatever."

"We can do it out yonder. You got the size?" Rat said.

"Ah, shoot," Tucker said. "Can't remember."

"You're a real mechanic, aint'cha? What'd they teach you in the Marines? Nothing?" Rat mocked.

"I steered a ship. The *Navy* taught me celestial navigation."

"Sexual nava-*what?*" said another one of Rat's bunch with a stupid look on his face.

Rat shook his head at Tucker and then rolled his eyes at his counterpart. "Damn, son," he said to Tucker, then turned to the closest dumbass. "*Stars,* dipshit," he said. "On the ocean."

Shaking his head some more, solely for the effect, he turned back to Tucker: "That'll do you a lotta good around here won't it."

Rat's gang laughed again.

"We got stars here, too. You want the work or not?" Tucker looked at the boneheads as if to say, *Keep it up and I'm outta here,* and they shut up.

"Bring the wrecker around," Rat motioned. "He'll need 235-15s." Then to Tucker: "You want new or used?"

"Used are fine."

"Out front," Rat said as he walked out with the others. "We'll go check her out. Be sure."

Tucker exited the garage and hopped into the back of Rat's tow truck with another one of the crew. Tucker avoided eye contact during the drive but could sense the dope-head sizing him up the entire ride. These boys were bad news, just as Grace alluded, and he was probably making a mistake. But they had what he needed to get rolling.

Tucker and Rat's gang stood around the old pickup with the flat tires mired in the spongy ground. Two of them leaned casually against the wrecker while

Rat circled the old Dodge and inspected the job site. The mud. "Guess we're gonna have to take 'em in after all. Can't hardly work in this mess." Tucker remained silent.

"Strip 'em off, boys. Get the jack and see if it'll even work in this pig waller," Rat ordered. "G.I. Joe here can't change a tire."

As the others kneeled, straining at the rusted lugs and slipping in the mire, Rat stood next to Tucker and pulled a joint out of his shirt pocket. He lit up and took a long, even drag before offering it to Tucker.

"No, thanks."

"Kill many towel-heads over there?" Rat said, trying to hold in the smoke.

"I was on a boat in the China sea, mostly."

"Hmm ... Kill many Chinese?"

"Ah, nope ... peacetime mission. Drills, mainly."

"Drills," Rat repeated slowly, as he exhaled a sour plume. "What's the fun in that?" Then he sauntered around the pickup again while the others stuffed the wheels between the winch arm and the tailgate of their truck. One of them took a used milk jug full of gasoline and splashed it into the Dodge's tank.

Rat evaluated: "Whatta piece 'a junk. Lucky if you ever get it running again. But I'll take your money, alright." He bounced over to the driver's side, looked through the window into the cab, then quickly opened the passenger door and drew the pistol from the map pocket in the door before Tucker even realized what he has doing.

"Well, holy hell. Look here, boys!" Rat said, brandishing Paw Paw's Colt semi-automatic. "He's packin'. Don't wanna come messin' around here of a night, now do we."

Rat quickly racked the slide. "Oooh. Careful now. She's hot!" He waved the gun around in an exaggerated motion with a twisted grin—then pulled the trigger, firing into the air.

The booming report made everyone duck.

"Jeezus!" one of the boys shouted. "What the hell you doin'?"

"Yeah!" another said. "Scared piss outta me!"

While Tucker ducked his head, too, he managed to keep his cool. He had seen plenty of bluster from fellas a lot scarier than Rat, especially during basic before the DI's beat it out of them with extra PT, latrine duty, and general humiliation.

Rat laughed. *"I didn't know it was loaded,"* he said in a mocking falsetto. "Be careful with this, son," he said as he dropped the magazine, unchambered the live round in the receiver, and slowly depressed the hammer with his thumb without breaking Tucker's gaze.

Rat snickered at his own bravado and tossed the Colt and its magazine back into the cab. Then he noticed the square shape in the paper bag on the dash. He slid the bottle out of the sack ceremoniously. "Store bought!" he whooped. "Well, dang, boys, let's get us a Beamer on."

Rat quickly tore the top off the bottle and took a swig. Tucker didn't intervene, allowing Rat to get all of his strutting in.

"This is real hospitable of you Tuck-Tuck. Boys?" he said while he waved a load-em-up sign to his gang. "I'll consider this your security deposit," he said after another chug.

"You have my *wheels*," Tucker said. "How long?"

"Yeah-boy. We'll get 'em back before you miss 'em," Rat yelled through the window as he left, spinning the tow truck in a wide arc in the driveway, slinging mud, grass, and gravel.

After the sound of the engine faded down the road well past Clint's house, Tucker turned to look at Paw Paw's old truck—back on blocks again, but this time without wheels. He grunted and ambled to the passenger door, digging out the other bottle he'd slid under the driver's seat. Just in case. That made him chuckle as he twisted off the cap and stared at the sky, hoping for a dry night.

As evening approached, peeper frogs began tweeting their mating calls, giving the cicadas stiff competition. Tucker swirled the bottle after taking another draw and checked his watch, resigning himself to the fact that he probably wouldn't be driving anywhere anytime soon. He sighed as he remembered something his granddad had once told him: "If you have low expectations of everyone, you'll never be disappointed."

Rat and his crew did not disappoint. It was midnight before Tucker decided to turn in. They still had not returned with his wheels. Tucker leaned into the cab again and gradually fell asleep watching gnats circle the dome light.

Nineteen

Moisture-laden clouds drifted across the mountain peaks as the sun rose, which kept the light at a pre-dawn hue. Sleeping weather. Tucker dozed through half the morning in the steamy truck cab, his face pressed against the fogged-over passenger window. He thought the idling engine noise he heard was part of a fading dream, but popped awake at the sharp rapping on the side panel.

"Rise and shine, Cinderella!" Rat said, thumping the windshield. "You ain't on China Beach no more. Don't get to sleep in all hours. Get up, now, and take a look at your new *rims*, man."

Tucker sat upright on the still-soggy seat-cushions and rubbed his eyes to focus on Rat gesturing at the two gangly knuckleheads by the tow truck.

"So, they did show," Tucker mumbled to himself as he watched them offloading his wheels.

Before reaching for the door handle, Tucker grabbed his grandfather's Colt from the open glovebox and dropped the magazine, quickly thumbing out all seven rounds onto the floorboard. He set the empty pistol on the seat poncho, then stepped out of the truck in his briefs, slipping a "Pelt and Herb" t-shirt over his head while Rat and his toadies rolled the rusty "new" wheels towards his old truck.

"Nice panties," Rat said. "Those standard issue for Coast Guard fags?" Then he hollered at the others: "C'mon boys, get them new tires on the man's truck before he calls his admiral on us."

"What do I owe you?" Tucker said, wincing at the sun, which finally decided to appear from behind the clouds.

Rat clicked his tongue. "Well, that's the thing, see. We can cut this two ways: one, you gimme two hundred for the tires—mounting 'em, coming out here twice, plus the installation and gas and all that," Rat said. And paused.

"Or?" Tucker said, warily.

"Or ... " Rat said, smiling like the entrepreneur-negotiator he apparently thought he was, "You can tell me where some of them 'seng patches is that your granddaddy used to go to and we can call it even." He crossed his arms.

All work stopped on the truck as the other two stared.

"You see," he said, "the price is up real good on root these days. More than what me and the boys can make changing tires for jack-wagons like you."

"I heard it's out of season," Tucker said, scratching his head.

"What! Who told you that?" Rat laughed. "Nothin's outta season in these mountains, cuz." The others grinned and went back to their lug wrenches.

Tucker sighed. "To tell you the truth, I don't even remember the last time I dug any. I planted some a long time ago—but you probably already know about that, too."

"Naw, man," Rat said, nodding to the hillside above them. "You talkin' about what used to be in those woods up there?"

Tucker cocked his head and looked hard at Rat. "What do you mean?"

Rat looked at his cohorts and smiled. "Well, that patch *used* to be nice. What there was of it. Reckon someone else thought so, too. Not that we seen it or nothin'."

"Guess I know what happened to it now, at least," Tucker said.

Rat glared at him. "Better watch where you point fingers, boy. I'd have told you to your face if *I'd* have gotten it. What were you thinkin', anyway? Plantin' *there*. That's easy pickin'. Close to the road. Ain't the best spot. Tsk, tsk, Tuckie. Your grandiddy would've slapped you silly."

Tucker pursed his lips and looked over to make sure the fellas were getting his wheels on. "I didn't know what I was doing. Pretty obvious. Thought I was planning for my future."

"Yeah, well, we know what *that's* like," Rat said. "None of us ain't got no future around here ... lest we find some *new* 'seng patches." Rat's eyes pressed hard into Tucker's: "Like your Paw Paw had. You don't think I remember seeing what he used to bring in? C'mon now, Tuck. You tryin' to say I'm stupid or something?" He glared. "Where'd he used to take you'uns?" Then he smiled. "You can trust me."

Tucker grimaced. "I really don't remember—"

"*BullSHIT!*" Rat shouted.

Rat's friends stood up at his change in tone, tense and ready to gang up for the easy beat-down if Tucker made a move.

Rat shot an evil look at Tucker: "Gun's still in the truck, right?"

Tucker glanced quickly at the other two, as one of them dropped his wrench, dove into the truck and grabbed the pistol. "I got it!"

Tucker shrugged and shook his head as the delinquent backed away from the truck, training the barrel of the pistol with a shaky hand at Tucker's chest. Tucker held a *do-I-look-scared?* gaze long enough to make the crank-head even more jittery. The man's eyes darted to Rat as if to say: *What do you want me to do?*

"Careful with that, dipshit. Don't want no one gittin' shot ... yet," Rat snickered. "I ain't in no mood to shovel out no grave this early in the day." Then his sallow eyes trained on Tucker's. "So. What's it gonna be, ole buddy?"

Tucker weighed out his options and chose truth with irony: "Man, I've been back, what? Less than a week, now? Got no money. House burned out. Living in that old truck—it being the only thing I got—and the hopes of getting it running again."

"Yeah, so?"

"So don't you think that if I had any idea where a big patch was, I'd have been in the woods by now and sold it?" Tucker let that notion sink in. Then he pointed to his truck. "You think I like sleeping in there? Not having a house or a family? You think I planned on coming home to this nothin'?" He spun around with his arms outstretched.

Rat considered that for a moment, but pressed: "Where's granddaddy's old book, huh? Bet you can't wait to get that truck running to those secret spots of his."

Tucker cocked his head.

Rat said: "Oh. You think I don't know about his little brown book? That old man kept directions to every damn patch in the county. I seen it. His own little treasure map. So ... you wanna show me where it is?"

"Be my guest." Tucker turned to the pile of burnt out rubble, inviting Rat to: "Dig in. If you find it, let me know and we'll *both* go diggin'."

Rat's gaze darted between Tucker and the ashy ruins of the home place. Tucker saw his wheels turning and added, "If you can find a spoon or a fork in there, let me know. Be nice to have something to eat with."

Rat grunted and stared for a beat more at the pile of charred beams before turning to his buddies: "Y'all done yet? Drop that jack and let's get outta here …" He turned to Tucker: "That'll be two-hundred."

Tucker's shoulder's sagged as he exhaled—glad to have avoided a fight in his underwear—and started for the truck.

Rat blocked him.

"Don't think I ain't got my eye on you," he warned. "You turn up with so much as a tiny ole two-prong, and I'm doggin' your ass. I'm a gonna get that 'seng out there." He waved in the direction of Paul's Peak while keeping his eyes glued on Tucker's. "Every bit of it. Don't even think about screwin' me over. I've done worse, too."

Rat continued to glare as Tucker reached into the truck and pulled out his wallet—counting out the cash and slapping it into Rat's hand.

"Pleasure doin' bidness," Rat said. "By the by, sorry to hear about your brother," he added with fake sincerity.

"Thanks," Tucker said flatly, ready for Rat to make good on his departure.

Rat turned to his buddies. "Ole Danny-Dan must have been jerkin' off so hard he couldn't let go long enough to grab the fire extinguisher."

The miscreants roared with laughter as Rat soaked up their adulation.

When he turned back to meet Tucker's eyes, he met a fist instead, which cracked across his chin, spinning him into the mud.

The one holding the gun took his eyes off Tucker to watch Rat flail on the ground. Tucker made a quick step and grabbed the barrel of the weapon— pulling it down and twisting the pistol out of the man's grasp with one hand, while impacting the side of his neck with a solid chop with the other. The big dumb kid hit the ground, face-first, next to Rat, catching the side of a cinder block with his open jaw. He howled, rolling side to side grabbing at his face.

Tucker then pointed the gun at Rat's other accomplice and cocked the hammer of the empty Colt for effect.

"It's cool, man!" The terrified punk raised his hands in surrender, wide-eyed and cowering as he backed away. "We're all good."

"Shut up!" Rat said, seething, as he rubbed his chin and pulled himself back to his feet while the other thug on the ground moaned: "I broke a tooth. He broke my damn tooth."

"You broke it yourself. Git up!" Rat said to his friend who spat blood as he wobbled to pull himself upright. Rat pointed a shaky finger at Tucker. "I won't be forgettin' this."

"Get the hell outta here, Harlan," Tucker said calmly but clearly.

Rat winced at his given name, but he and the boys regarded Tucker and the .45 pistol, then piled in the wrecker and roared away.

Business concluded.

Tucker walked to the mailbox to listen to the rattle of the tow truck's engine fade into the distance, making sure they were really gone and not coming back. After the adrenaline mellowed from his system, he walked back to the truck and shoved the pistol under the driver's seat—out of view this time. As he closed the door, he finally got a good look at his "new" tires—one still flat and none of them with any tread to speak of.

Tucker looked up at the road and sighed. "Should have just shot 'em while I had the chance."

Rat seethed as he kept the gas pedal on the tow truck pegged to the floor, rubbing his jaw in silence. Tucker had popped him a good one, he'd give him that. But Rat had been in fights—plenty. Growing up, he took more than a few beatdowns from his brother and most of his brother's friends, even some from friends of his own. Worse than just a lick, too. Before the law hauled Daddy away, he'd landed a few for his father to remember. The mean bastard even laughed about it, *respected* it almost. Rat gave as good as he got, but also knew when he was whooped, the feeling of which settled in him like a simmering coal in the bottom of a near-cold fire pit that never quite burned out, only needing the right conditions to reignite.

Rat would let this one stew, too. He knew how to get even. *Ain't that right, bro,* he thought as his eyes narrowed, picturing his brother's mangled face after their final run-in five years ago when Rat *took over* the auto shop, leaving his sibling mute and drooling in a care facility outside of Winston. The official report ruled it an accident. "Catastrophic mechanical failure" of the hydraulic jack. Sorry-assed Darron didn't even see it coming. If the chain hadn't broke, he'd of dropped it on him again, just for good measure.

Rat chuckled, hearing the muffled whimpers of his bastard brother from under the engine block as his blood mixed to black with the spilt oil on the cold concrete. Adequate payback in Rat's opinion for what Darron had doled out over the years. *Good ole Tucker Trivette ain't gonna be no problem,* he thought.

One of his buddies, preoccupied with the jagged nub of his lost incisor, spat into the floorboard from his busted lip while checking the damage in the side-view mirror.

The other sidekick stared at Rat, waiting for him to say something, anything. "You need some ice?" he said to break the silence. "Don't look swole too bad."

Rat just replied to the windshield. "Big help you'uns was. Chicken-shits."

"I didn't know he was gonna—"

"What? Kick your ass?" They both stared at the floor.

"I had that pistol," one of them finally said. "Shoulda—"

"Done what? Grow a pair? Shit, Army boy slapped you down while you were pissin' your pants. That's alright, though," Rat said calmly, mainly to himself.

Tucker had won this battle, but Rat felt confident he'd win the *war*. And it was a war as Harlan Ward saw it. Take a lick, get up, take it again if you have to, then wait. *Ain't gotta rush it.* Let that ache in the jaw settle in deep and hard—and hot. Wear that scar with pride just like the other ones, another notch in the belt or 'X' on the rifle butt that needed to be carved. The right time would come. Rat was sure about that. *No way that book burned up. That old man stashed it somewhere. Safe. Somewhere that wouldn't burn to the ground,* Rat thought to himself then laughed aloud.

"What?" his broken-toothed pal asked.

"Tucky Trivette might of put on some juice in the service, but he'll get what's coming to him ... Just like the rest of 'em."

"What you mean by that?"

"Shut the fuck up. Not even talking to you."

The dolts he ran with were too stupid to keep their mouths shut, anyway. So, there were some things he knew to keep quiet about. Rat's thoughts were his own. They had to be.

Didn't have to jimmy a lock or break a window, even. Back door was wide open. The drunk passed out on the couch hadn't even heard him come in. Didn't even wake up as he slapped Tucker's mama to the ground when she caught him rifling through the cabinets, her head cracking into the bedside table. He had panicked for a brief moment, seeing her head cranked at that angle as she bled into the floor. That just made the decision, the plan, easier, though. Open jar of shine on the floor, cans of spent cooking oil on the stove, piled up newspapers, a cigarette burning in the ashtray. Couldn't of fell into place any better. He continued checking every drawer, every closet, every corner of the house before the smoke got too thick to see. He slunk back into the woods as soon as the sirens got closer. Ducking under a laurel shrub, he sat hunched on an oak stump, watching it burn, even feeling the heat. Rat grinned again at the vision of that freak of a cripple running in to try and save the day—the look on his face. Poor bastard heaving his drunk daddy out the front door. Then the dumbass went back in. Too bad he didn't make it out. He'd a known where it was. I could have beat it out of him.

I need that book.

Buck Trivette's map ledger was something Zeb Greene told stories about back in the day. Back when Rat had followed him through the woods, poaching 'seng and hanging on Z's every word. The old man's journal was a local legend with the diggers. Z had even talked about stealing it at some point. *No telling how many honey holes are marked in those pages.*

Tucker knew where it was, no matter how much he lied about it. Had to. Rat figured his schoolmate would be in the woods soon enough. As broke as he was.

Rat nodded contentedly in the rearview mirror at the bright red welt still singing on his cheek then turned to his buddies. "Hand me the stuff."

One of the men opened the glove box and pulled out a sliver of aluminum stuffed inside an empty cigarette carton. Rat tapped out a short bump of sandy crystal onto his wrist and snorted it with flare.

"See," he said, wiping the residue on his knees. "Don't need no ice."

Twenty

The tire patch that Saul gave him to plug the flat made a rhythmic thumping on the pavement before eventually wearing down. Other than some squishiness in the brakes and a slight pull to the left, the old Dodge seemed to run like Tucker remembered. He made his way toward town and turned into the empty, hard-packed clay of the small brick ranch and parked next to the camper with the "For Sale" sign. From the outside, it looked to be in great condition. The lone scuff on its vinyl siding barely deserved notice.

Growing up, he had gawked at the convoys of similar RVs winding through town each summer and fall on the way to one of the many campsites off the Blue Ridge Parkway, leaf-lookers and vacation travelers—with plates as far away as Ontario. The idea of camping, though, had always been foreign to him. The great outdoors had been just a few steps off the porch his entire life. Why city folk traveled all that way just to park next to each other in cramped slots to "rough it" was beyond him.

The door on the small tow-behind opened easily. Tucker stepped in and walked through its narrow interior corridor, noting the stove and microwave looked almost new, his reflection warping on the shiny chrome of the sink faucet in the tight bathroom. The faint, musty whiff of humidity and plastic crinkled his nose as he opened the mini-fridge, but it looked clean as a whistle. A portable generator and a roll of yellow extension cord sat on the small dining table island, and the upholstery on the sofa had no signs of wear. There was even a small television mounted just under the pull-down loft. *This'll do just fine,* he thought— way more amenity than the bunk rooms he had shared with his shipmates.

As Tucker bounced on the couch, testing the cushions, a gentleman with scruffy gray stubble and unkempt hair stepped into the open doorway. "Sorry, sir," Tucker said and stood up. "Didn't look like anyone was home."

"Not a problem," the man said. "Wife's at Bible study. I was taking a nap. Heard someone pull up. What do you think? I know it ain't much."

"It's all I need for now," Tucker said, motioning to his truck. "Better than sleeping in that ole thing. Just got home from the service and need a dry roof."

"It's my brother-in-law's," the man said. "Bought it to take fishing, but he travels too much with his job. Barely used it. Wife told him we'd sell it for him."

"It's perfect," Tucker said. "But I don't know if I can give you what you're asking all at once. Can I put down two now and pay you the rest later? I'm looking for work. Hoping it won't be too long."

The man nodded. "You said the military?"

"Yessir. Navy."

"See much action?"

"No, sir. Just a lot of water."

The old man grunted with a hint of disappointment. "Well, me and the wife appreciate your service, whatever it was. Never know where they'll send you."

"No, you don't," Tucker agreed. "I got lucky."

The man nodded and stared off oddly over Tucker's head. "You got lucky today, too, son. How about we say two now ... and forget the rest."

"That's awful generous," Tucker said. "But I'd be able to pay you the rest. It's a fair price."

"Aw, this thing's just in the way. I'm sick of looking at it. You'd be doing me a favor. Something for your service. Keepin' us free and safe from them terrorists."

"That's a deal, then. Cash okay?"

"That'll be just fine. I'll try not to spend it before she gets home," the man said and winked.

Tucker pulled the cash from his wallet and handed it over.

"Door key should be there under the generator. Which probably needs some gas." The man shoved the bills in his back pocket and ambled back to the porch. "Good luck on finding work around here," he said and mumbled his doubts until he was fully inside.

Tucker backed the Dodge up to the trailer's coupler and cranked the wheel down to the ball hitch. Then he removed the wheel chocks and locked the hubs. While Paw Paw's old truck strained with the extra weight, Tucker pulled out of the driveway and shifted gears with zeal, hauling his new home behind him, anxious to set in place by nightfall.

Sure enough, by nine, Tucker washed off the last stubborn grease off his hands from the jack. Diffuse light through the window shades on each side of the trailer cast a halo around its immediate area. Beyond that, total darkness. The new moon all but invisible and intermittent streams of passing clouds blocking the stars. Katydids and peeper frogs chirped along the perimeter of the homestead, but the hum of the generator was the only sound Tucker could hear. He shivered as he splashed ice-cold water over his body, rinsing off the soap lather beside his new home. Luckily, the spring-fed spigot next to the house still functioned. Tucker had disconnected the hoses below the trailer sink, rigged a makeshift connection, and filled up for his bucket-bath. The aroma of beans and noodles wafted through the open door as his second helping simmered on the new stove.

Just beyond the Trivette mailbox, hidden in the darkness, a truck pulled slowly off the edge of the road, idling its engine, headlights off. The crickets and frogs ceased their chirpings temporarily as Tucker dumped the last bit of water over himself. He grabbed his waiting towel and scampered back up the short steps, closing the camper door behind his nakedness.

Soon after the evening wildlife renewed their trilling, the truck quietly turned around on the loose gravel, not switching on its beams again until reaching the main road.

Twenty-One

After a bath and full night's rest in a real bed—a dry one—Tucker popped awake in the compact sleeper space and took two quick steps into his "living room." He yawned as he pulled on a t-shirt and pants and heard a familiar clucking just outside. He peered through the tiny curtain covering the trailer door's window. The same lone chicken pecked through the scant crumbs rinsed from the cooking pan the night before.

"Not falling for that again," he said, shaking a finger at the bird. "Sneaky little bastard." He glanced at the pistol resting next to the microwave but reached for the box of Twinkies instead. Breakfast of champions. He unwrapped the brittle plastic tube and shoved its contents into his mouth as he began lacing up his boots. As the taste of rancid crème hit his palate, he gagged, spitting the rest onto the floor. "Godamighty!" he said, wiping the soured filling off his tongue with his sleeve. Tucker snatched the box off the table and found the expiration date, three years prior. "Didn't think these things went bad."

He scanned around the mostly-bare countertop looking for something else to eat. Beans and noodles again weren't gonna cut it. So, he quickly made a mental grocery list, shoved his wallet into his back pocket, and grabbed the keys to the Dodge.

As he pulled onto the main road, Tucker looked down at the gas gauge and frowned. Almost empty, again. He'd need to fill this tank before the one in his belly, which growled at the thought of biscuits and gravy. Sadie's wouldn't be open for another couple of hours, but maybe breakfast at the new shop in town was as good as Saul had said.

After savoring another slug from the oversized ceramic mug, Tucker decided that Saul was right. The coffee in the converted jailhouse was ten times better than the diesel fuel brewed in the carrier's mess hall. While he sagged when the waitress informed him that they didn't serve biscuits, Tucker smiled sweet as pie when he ordered his *second* ham and eggs-Benedict bagel. "To trying new things," he said, toasting her with his third cup of French press, and greedily shoving the last morsel into his mouth.

As Tucker wiped the yolk dripping from his chin, he gazed down the street through the rebar of the restaurant's jail window façade. The brick profile of the County Public Services building sat grim and plain against a steep mountain backdrop. "Why not," he mumbled to himself as he stood up to pay, leaving a healthy tip on the table. "What else do you have to do today."

Maybe Mr. Jim was right and the County Agent could explain where he had gone wrong with his *plantation* and give him some tips on how to salvage what was left. *If the geezer there even knows anything about ginseng.* Tucker envisioned a portly government employee with a short tie, twiddling his thumbs, wheezing between breaths, waiting for retirement. He could already hear the conversation: "*Well, no, Mr. Trivette. Can't say I know anything about that. I have some pamphlets on cabbage, though, if you're interested.*"

Tucker pushed through the double glass doors into the lobby. Racks full of crop brochures and gardening lined the walls, everything from beekeeping to yams—almost A to Z—including a flyer about "Pumpkin Field Day" and a sign-up sheet for farm insurance. There was nothing about ginseng. No surprise. He walked into the first office he saw, where a lone woman was just hanging up the phone, pretending not to be reading recipes in the *Southern Living* open on the table.

"Can I help you?" she said in a thick drawl as she slid the magazine under a bright yellow legal pad.

Tucker looked around furtively and spoke in a low voice: "Is there someone here I can talk to about ginseng."

The secretary grinned and pointed down a hallway, and mimicked his whispery tone: "Your secret's safe with me, hon." Then she said in a normal voice: "That way. First door on your right, sweetheart."

Tucker returned a wan grin then wandered down the corridor past colorful posters that decorated the hallway, one displaying wildflowers and their common names and another highlighting "Bird species of the Appalachians." The first plaque he came to read "Agriculture Agent." The door was open, so he knocked briefly on the jamb and stepped inside.

Allie spun around in a swivel chair. "Well, look what the cat dragged in."

"What are *you* doing here?" Tucker said.

"I work here."

"Oh!" he said. "*This* is the office you were talking about. Cool. Is your boss in?"

"My *boss?*" Allie said.

"Yeah," Tucker said. "The county agent or whoever it is who knows about ginseng."

Allie kicked back in her chair and propped her feet up on her desk. "Pray tell, why would you want to know about something as simple as that?"

"Uhh, I'd like to try growing some," Tucker said as he glanced around the office, still unsure he was in the right place.

"First time didn't work out so well, huh."

Tucker cringed. "I guess you *would* know about that."

"Yep," Allie said as she sat up. "I've got pictures of it in my desk, here. I use them as an example in my workshop presentations of what *not* to do." She reached into a drawer and held up a folder.

Tucker's brow furrowed deeper than a newly plowed field. "Presentations?" he said. "I mean, you're ... but ... where's the guy that—?"

"You're looking at her," Allie said, smiling at Tucker's confusion. "What's wrong with you, Tucker Trivette? No women in the Navy?"

"Sure, but ..." Tucker shook his head at his own stupidity. "You're him."

"Allie Gragg, your county agricultural extension agent. My *expertise* is the production of specialty crops—like ginseng," she said, standing and extending a hand for her sarcastic introduction: "So, how may I be of service to you, today, sir?" She raised her eyebrows and nodded semi-discreetly to the wall behind her desk.

Tucker squinted at the red and white embossed frame with two tassels and a photo of the bell tower above her diplomas—two degrees from North Carolina State University. One of them said "Master of Science".

"You did it," Tucker said, genuinely impressed.

"Yeah, but you better make it quick. This may be my last month. Come back and I'll be a memory here—unless I get this grant project approved," she said, pointing to her computer screen as she sat back down.

"Why? What happened?"

"Budget cuts. I'm newest. Last hired, first fired ... See ya." She threw a sarcastic wave then sat back behind her desk. Tucker took his cue and sat across from her as she said: "So, let's see if I can explain what you did wrong the first time. Okay to start there?"

Tucker nodded warily as she launched into her *professional* analysis.

"You probably didn't take soil samples, right?" Allie said.

Tucker shook his head.

"Soil's pretty acidic up there. Would've been a good idea to add some lime to bring the pH up a bit on that site, and some gypsum. Ginseng needs that, you know. It's a calciphile. *Loves* calcium. Without a soil sample, you'd never know," she sighed. "But that wasn't your biggest problem."

Tucker looked on, baffled. "It wasn't?"

"Nope," she said. "There's a lot of laurel up there, right?" She leaned forward, put on a serious face and said: "Let me ask you something. You and your granddaddy ever hunt ginseng in a rhododendron thicket?"

"No, I don't think so. He said there was no point in it," Tucker said.

Allie nodded. "And?"

Tucker said: "Well, there was a bunch in there, but I cleared it all out. I chopped and hauled brush for a whole damn week!"

"Doesn't matter," Allie said, sitting back. "Stands of rhodos reduce the mycorrhizal diversity in the soil *and* they're allelopathic, to boot."

Tucker crinkled his face. "They're *what?*"

"Sorry, Tucker. I should've known these big words would be too much for you. You being a seafaring type, and all."

She was having a tough time keeping a straight face—mainly because Tucker was turning a ripe shade of red. She was getting to him. Perfect!

He finally said: "Can you get off your high-horse long enough tell me how to grow the stuff?"

Allie shook her head. "Jesus, Tucker. Where were you when your granddaddy was teaching you and Danny all about ginseng. *He* learned. What happened to you? You must have been riding backwards on *your* high-horse back then."

Tucker looked at her, dumbfounded. "Why're you bringing Danny into this?"

"Remember at the hospital? I told you he used to come by. That's what we talked about: ginseng," she said. "Well, that and all kinds of things that grow in the woods. Native plants. Medicinal plants. Harvestable stuff."

"Wait. You helped Danny with this?"

"Hell, he knew more about it than I do. Should be him sitting here." Allie looked at the floor when she saw Tucker's expression change and turned off her sarcasm button. "I'm sorry, I shouldn't have even brought it up."

Deciding it was better to move on—but still jab back at her a bit—Tucker said: "So, what does all that mean, anyway? 'Allie-o-pathetic' or whatever you said. Plain English, please. That's something I *did* learn in the Navy."

Allie, sighed then continued. "It means that nothing grows under laurels. You would've done better planting your seed in that stand of poplars and maples on the other side of the mountain. Much better canopy—northeast facing—and the companion plants are right."

"And no laurels," he said.

"Right. Or rhododendrons. They're different species even though everyone calls every dark green bush a 'laurel' around here. They both suck for growing anything else around them."

"Okay, I get it. And?"

"Even then, you still would have needed to add some soil amendments if you were looking for any kind of return when you got back."

"Like fertilizer?"

"Yes. Depending on what the soil test said ... which you didn't take," she reminded. "Just phosphate or gypsum. To push them a little. Maybe some lime like I said. Just no nitrogen. Nitrogen makes the plant grow too quick. Makes the root slick-looking and you won't get a good price. Don't want to push them too fast. Planted ginseng needs some stress to make it grow like wild."

Tucker's mind was blown, and she could tell.

"And when you plant at any density, you can plan on dropping some serious money on fungicides to keep root rot and foliar disease from ripping through your patch. You following this?"

Tucker nodded slowly.

"A good seeding rate is around 10 pounds per acre. And you're talking a hundred bucks a pound for seed—good seed—not that crap they sell in the trapper catalogs. If your plants survive the first three years, then you need to think about repellants for the deer and voles. Turkeys—they'll eat your seed and the berry pods. And fences and security. That's your biggest 'pest' problem around here. People. Hell, you really need closed-circuit cameras. Signs won't keep the poachers out. Wouldn't have mattered out there where you planted, though."

"Tell me about it," Tucker said. "Someone robbed me blind. Took almost everything."

"What did you expect?" Allie said. "You were gone, what, seven years? You think *nobody* knew what you had going on out there? That patch was just a short walk through the woods. Harlan and his goons probably picked it clean two years ago before it was even close to mature."

"Harlan," Tucker shook his head.

"You got a gun?"

"Yeah. A pistol."

"That's a start," she said. "I'd recommend a shotgun or maybe an AR. Some of these pill-poppers are packing, and they're out digging as soon as the plants come up in Spring. They don't care a lick about the 'legal season,'" she motioned with her fingers. "You'd have to be in that patch every day once the plants got to any size. Main thing is the capital investment, though. You're looking at a few grand to get started. Are you pretty well set-up? Parents leave you a nice inheritance?"

The last bit of snark went over the line. Tucker's eyes narrowed. "Very nice. Thanks. No wonder you're still single." He stood up and went for the door so fast it caught her off guard.

"Wait! I'm sorry," Allie said to his back. But Tucker was gone. She heard the front door to the building shut, and her shoulders sank.

"Jeezus, Allie," she said aloud. "What are you thinking." Her cheeks went red and a hot tear escaped her eye. She picked up the folder and threw it against the wall. The "photos" that she had mentioned spilled out of it, but they weren't pictures—just copies of old soil reports.

Choking back raw emotions, Allie bent down to *deal with the mess she'd made* and thought back on the past several years, trying to make sense of it. Times had been tough for her as well. That Tucker had no idea wasn't his fault. She shouldn't have been so hard on him. *Shit.* But what did he expect? He had left home, too—and was gone longer. She had followed her own path and hadn't fathomed crossing his again.

Yet here he was. As headstrong as ever—but taller and more handsome, admittedly, than she would have expected. Tucker still had a way of pushing her buttons. After all these years. How could he get her riled like that?

Giving up on the scattered papers, Allie allowed herself a moment to recalibrate, sitting on the floor and leaning against the wall, not giving a damn if anyone walked in. Putting her life-thoughts in order was more important.

First, there had been college—no easy bargain. She hadn't known anyone; no one from her class went to State or anywhere that far off the mountain as far as she knew. She was the first in her family to even finish high school. And, though she felt up to the challenge, her first year was filled with self-doubt—fueled in part by the rude dorm mates who chided her "hillbilly" accent.

Something she lost by sophomore year through sheer willpower.

And the courses were tough, nothing easy about botany, biochem, calculus—all the requirements. She wasn't allowed an elective until her junior year, and by that point, she didn't even want one. She just wanted to finish. She settled on "urban landscape design" and got two unexpected results: one, she enjoyed the class immensely; but two, she knew she could never live in a big city. She would go back home, or to a similar small town, and thrive.

But school got easier—better, at least—and she started loving college. The harder the course, the more she liked it. By graduation, she knew that she had found her place in the world and chose to go on to the grad program in horticulture.

Then, her mom got sick.

It was fast and thorough, and left her father brokenhearted—literally. His first heart attack came just a week after the funeral. His second one came before her graduation, leaving him in the wheelchair.

Allie thought her life was over.

Mr. Hodges, the veteran county tobacco agent, up and quit, taking early retirement to move to Florida, leaving a position open at the Ag office. Allie applied and got it, to her great surprise. She could work and still be close to help her dad with the store. After trying to get him to sell, he confessed he wouldn't know what he'd do without that old store, and she knew what he meant. With her mom gone so recently, Allie knew she would not be able to handle his passing, too, so she ended up working two jobs.

Three really, she thought as she sat on the floor: the Ag office, the store, and caring for him. Though he refused most of her help, there were times when he had to face his limitations, and Allie was always there for him.

"If you only knew, Tucker Trivette," Allie said aloud. "If you only knew."

Done with that part of her recent history, Allie stood, gathered the rest of the papers, and moved to her desk, ready to shake it off. But when she looked in the still-open drawer, she stopped.

Tucker's letters.

She had kept them all—after reading them to Danny. "Aw, you keep 'em," he had said. Before the fire, he would bring them by, tucked under his short arm, and sit in her chair, spinning around and grinning, while she read Tucker's letters aloud. He probably had them committed to memory, but she guessed he just liked hearing a voice to his brother's words.

Allie was happy to oblige. The to-and-fro, their reading dance, and debates about how to farm in the forests, kept her grounded—helped her remember where she came from—*her* roots. Better times. Simpler times. Times gone forever, she figured.

Especially after the fire when Danny came with letters no more.

Twenty-Two

Tucker fumed as he slammed the Dodge into reverse and spun out of the parking lot. *What's her problem?* The back-and-forth repeated in his head like a broken, black-box recorder the entire drive back—without the useful data or answers. She *still* made him feel worse than a second-class citizen. His own RDCs, Navy drill instructors, had never even made him feel that low. Allie would have made a fine one, he thought. But he had to give it to her—she did know her stuff when it came to growing stuff.

He grudgingly acknowledged that she knew him, too. "What's *my* problem?" he asked himself aloud. "You screwed up. You're broke. And you need a job," he answered. Gas for the truck and the gourmet breakfast had drained his reserves even further.

As Tucker turned off the main road and passed Clint's house, he noticed a farm truck in his neighbor's driveway and saw figures moving through the Fraser firs on the nearest hill. Clint was back.

Tucker braked and reversed into the driveway. He stepped out of the truck and shaded his eyes from the sun as he gazed at the mountainside full of seven to ten-foot-tall Christmas trees. Flashbacks of sore forearms, bee stings, and sunburns made him shudder.

A group of four men in baggy, long-sleeved shirts and wide-brimmed hats made their way through the rows of trees, swinging shearing knives as they went. Tucker laughed aloud at the shiny metallic sign erected on the edge of the field closest to the house: "*Windburger's* Choose and Cut." A cartoonish caricature of Clint in a red suit and green hat shaped like a Christmas tree pointed up the hill.

Tucker nodded at the misspelled sign as Clint ambled down the hill to greet him.

They gripped hands firmly. "That supposed to be you, Santa?"

"They did a great job, eh? Didn't even have to pay for it since they messed up my name so bad."

"Catch any fish on your trip?"

"Didn't hook a one. But I caught a lot of zzz's. Good to see you, son."

Clint looked like he hadn't aged a day since Tucker left home. His steely eyes squinted under the brim of a faded Farm Bureau cap. Balls of muscle under the bushy, gray hair on his forearms proved that Clint could still keep pace with his hired help. "Been wonderin' when you were gonna pay me a visit."

"I had a few things to get straightened out first."

"Imagine so," Clint said, taking off his cap and wiping his forehead. "Real sorry about what happened over there. Know it wasn't what you were expecting to come home to."

"You could say that." Tucker said. "Bit of a shock to say the least. But it's good to be back. All things considered."

Clint patted him on the shoulder. "It's good to have a neighbor again."

"And this neighbor needs a job. Could you use some help?"

"You remember how I like 'em?"

"Tight, but no shoulders, leave the leader eight inches above good buds, cut out all the horns, and pull any cones, right?"

"I think that'll do just fine." Clint grinned as he pulled a set of pruning shears from his back pocket and handed them to his grown protégé. "I'm payin' these boys eight an hour and a steak dinner at Sadie's on Friday nights. Can't give you any more. Wouldn't be fair."

"Sounds good to me. I'm happy for the work."

Clint pointed up the hill to his lead man. "Carlos there will get you going. See if you can keep up. They're good men. Don't care what anyone 'round here says, these boys'll outwork anybody. Can't find nobody local that'll shear trees no more. Young'uns these days either leave the farm or get into trouble." He squeezed Tucker's shoulder. "It's good to have you home, son."

Tucker joined Clint's crew at the end of a row halfway up the hillside, and nodded an introduction. He guessed Carlos to be in his late twenties—thin and muscular with jet-black bangs camouflaging most of a jagged scar that looked like it began somewhere beneath his wicker sombrero. The other three younger men eyed Tucker, whispering in Spanish as they shared swigs of water from a sap-stained thermos and opened up foil-wrapped tortillas from paper sacks in the shady edge of the field—their shirts and fingers caked with polka dot splotches of rosin.

Carlos handed Tucker a spare knife and pointed to the first tree in the row. "So, amigo, show us what you got," Carlos said.

Tucker had sheared countless trees in his youth, but understood that wouldn't cut muster with these guys. He'd have to prove his salt.

Tucker gripped the handle of the shearing blade and methodically worked around the bushy tree counterclockwise, keeping his swing—and the blade's sharp edge—away from his kneecaps. He tipped off the ends of the eight-footer's branches and inspected its overall shape as he went. The other three men eyed him, still whispering, while Carlos chuckled and provided a play-by-play commentary in Spanish, studying Tucker's progress like a contest judge. Halfway around the tree, Tucker accidentally lopped one side of the tree too deep and scowled at his own handiwork.

The men snickered.

"Yeah, yeah, I'm a little rusty. Didn't say I'm a pro."

"That's good, *jefe*, because you're not. Your brother was much better." Carlos said, then winced. "Sorry. No disrespect." The other men lowered their heads.

"It's okay. You're right. He was," Tucker said with a sad smile, then shook off the flood of emotion the best he could. "I could use some practice."

"Here, let me show you, Trucker."

"It's *Tucker*. Only one 'r'," Tucker said.

Carlos looked at his other associates and muttered something in Spanish under his breath to lighten the mood. Tucker had picked up enough from his Latino shipmates to know what a *cabron* was.

"Hablo un poco de español, '*jefe*'," he replied with a passable accent. "And I'm not a dumbass. Just slow. Like I said, haven't done this in a while."

Carlos looked at Tucker and then back to his compañeros and smiled. "Okay, friend," he said, as he motioned for Tucker to pass him the machete. Tucker handed it to him. "Watch and learn. It's all in the wrist. You're single, right? You know the motion."

Tucker shook his head, nodding as the others laughed. Carlos tipped the entire circumference of the next tree in just a few deft strokes and tossed the knife, handle first, back to Tucker.

"Bienvenido, amigo! Welcome to our humble hillside," Carlos said as he threw his arms wide and gestured towards the thousands of trees remaining. "That's Benicio, Santos, and Francisco—my cousins and brother-in-law," he said, pointing to his field mates. They each nodded and grinned.

"So, what part of Mexico are y'all from?" Tucker said.

Carlos shook his head. "No part, ese. We're from Miami. Except Benicio. He's from Tegucigalpa. Don't even know any Mexicans."

"Whoops." Tucker grimaced.

Carlos chuckled, as he dug into his lunchbox. "Moved out here to get away from some things."

Tucker noticed half of a swastika peeking through the rolled-up sleeve on Carlos's left forearm and roman numerals on the tanned skin of his right wrist. He also saw another knife tucked into Carlos's pants—one not for shearing.

"Got a girl and a baby here, man. Don't need the trouble these bring no more," he said, looking at his ink and rolling his sleeves back down.

He pulled out a stuffed tortilla and handed it to Tucker.

"Wow," Tucker said. "This looks great. I could use some more breakfast."

"Breakfast? This is lunch, *cabron*," Carlos said. "We start earlier than some of you gringos go to bed!"

His pals laughed as Tucker took a bite of the homemade mass of cornmeal and beef and mumbled: "Mmm. Delicious. Gracias."

"De nada," Carlos said as he set down the thermos and began shearing the next fir in his row. "But you won't thank me by the end of the day, '*Tucker*.' Señor Clint wants the rest of these clipped today so we can start on the other field tomorrow." Then he turned back around and said, "Hey, wasn't there a guy named Tucker who made a cool car? Only like fifty of them? Saw a movie about that. Could make a nice ride out of one of those. The *chicas* love a weird car, yeah?"

Tucker laughed along with the rest of them even though he didn't get the joke. He figured he would soon enough.

The little radio in the travel trailer spewed classic, country tunes out of its three-inch speakers from an FM station out of Tennessee as Tucker took another hot swallow of bourbon from the nearly-empty bottle. A twenty-dollar bill, a few single fives and some change scattered on the table in front of him was all that remained of his bankroll. He rubbed his sore forearm and frowned.

While thankful for the work Clint had thrown his way and the amicability of his new-found amigos, setting up his new residence and transport had drained most of his final paycheck. A few hundred bucks a week working Clint's Christmas trees would pay the bills, but not much else. To come so far and wind up right back where he started with even less than he had to begin with just pissed him off.

Tucker poured another slug of whiskey down his throat and stared at his indignant reflection in the tiny trailer window, then at the bottle. He began swirling the clear brown liquid, creating a mini-whirlpool that crept up the sides of the glass and slowly began reaching into his head. He tilted the bottle around and around until his fingers shook with the introspection and cheap mash finally getting the better of him.

Flashing like quick edits of a b-reel, Tucker saw his father, blurred and grotesque, staggering across the invisible screen of his mind in a rerun. There were no words, just a rapid-fire recollection of sound and smell—anger and drink—mixing in a haze of cigarette smoke.

"What the hell are you doing!" he yelled at the ceiling and hurled the bottle against the thin wall, rattling the trailer, changing the radio station to static. The wash of distilled vapor emanated into the air sinking deep into his nose, the familiar burning stink causing a shudder as a dozen somber memories triggered in an instant.

A sinking self-loathing came over him as Tucker stared through the cabin window past his reflection into the jet black night. He rubbed the sweat beading his hairline with his open hand and opened the door to blink free of the past as the cool outside air wafted into his moist eyes. He took a long draw of it and exhaled with a heaving chest. Before dwelling too long, he began picking up the glass, but the faint tinkling of the fragments gathered in his palm nearly broke him again. How many mornings had he swept shards from the floor? How many more had he tweezered out of Danny's feet? *"What are you doing, Tucker?"* he thought.

After tossing the largest pieces in the trash, he guzzled some water, put on his shoes and got in the truck. As he weaved along the short drive to Clint's house, he saw that his neighbor's porch light was still on. He pulled off the road, parking crookedly in the driveway.

"That you, Tucker?" said a voice from the porch as Tucker stepped out of the truck.

"Don't shoot," Tucker said jokingly, closing the door and raising his hands. He heard Clint chuckle so he started for the rock steps. "I was hoping you were up."

"Ah," Clint said from his rocking chair, dog-earing a page of the book that he set in his lap. "Takes a while to get to sleep at my age. Just enjoying the evening."

Tucker tromped up the steps, holding onto the rails for balance.

"How you getting along out there," Clint said.

Tucker tried his best not to slur his words and belched quietly into his shirt. "Wonderful. Got everything a man could wish for. Except a phone. Was wondering if I could use yours?"

Clint stared at him with a curious look, then waved him toward the door. "In the hallway, son. Might have to jiggle the plunger on it. Sorta like the toilet. Sticks sometimes."

"Thanks, Clint."

Tucker wobbled into the cabin, bumping against the doorframe, and wiped more sweat from his forehead. It felt twenty degrees warmer inside the house. He fished a small folded piece of paper from his wallet and dialed the scribbled number.

He sighed thankfully as he heard his friend's voice on the other line.

"I need your help," Tucker said.

Twenty-Three

The bottom of Tucker's left foot throbbed from the shard of whiskey bottle removed earlier in the morning—one he missed before passing out. While the ache in his foot and hangover still lingered, being in the woods again would clear his head. He had shot out of bed, narrowly missing the roof of the trailer, remembering the route Paw Paw had driven them to harvest ramps early one Spring—pointing out a stand of young ginseng plants covering a slope. *Was I even old enough to drive, then?* he wondered.

Tucker's truck puttered along a higher-altitude stretch of the Blue Ridge Parkway, the narrow and well-groomed scenic road that meandered over four hundred miles through the mountain peaks of western North Carolina and Virginia. The crispness of the air at this elevation and the thought of digging a pile of root he could convert into some operating funds numbed most of the pain. The tourists took advantage of its many pull-offs to snap photos along the split-rail fences, cow pastures, and picturesque overlooks. The locals often used the Parkway to access some of the better trout fishing streams—or for short-cuts across the county when it wasn't clogged with rubbernecking dentists on their Harleys.

Traffic was sparse on this particular section—Tucker had only seen one other parked vehicle since he left the trailer—a brand new SUV with Georgia plates and a snorkel for serious off-roading craning from below the engine to above the windshield. He chuckled, guessing its four-wheel drive had never been used either. Probably one of the overly-serious fly-fishermen from Atlanta who'd drive hours just to park on the shoulder of the road, flicking their lines no more than twenty feet from their new truck. The catalog-bought fly rods and fancy tennis-racket-shaped nets dangling from name-brand tackle vests gave them away every time, as no self-respecting local would ever order tackle from a magazine. Tucker shook his head. He and Danny used to bring home stringers full of native brookies from tiny creeks emerging from beneath hidden springs with no more than a five-dollar Zebco and a can of yellow corn.

He strained the memories from his youth searching for the gravel pull-off he was looking for. Just before crossing the over the state line, he drove past the sign: "National Park: Collection of Plants, Animals, or other Materials Prohibited." State jurisdiction didn't matter here; this area was patrolled by Park Service cops—Feds. Not the run-of-the-mill deputy who might be in the woods on their day off for the same reason he was. At least one unlucky tourist each November got busted cutting their Christmas tree from the median, and more than a couple deer hunters had lost their rifle after dragging a carcass out of the woods along this same route. Park Service didn't care where you shot it; if it died on Federal land, there it was supposed to remain. Better to forfeit your meat than your Winchester.

Tucker wasn't worried about rangers, though. The ones who monitored the Parkway were too few and far between. Besides, he and Danny and Paw Paw had dug herbs in the deep woods of Forest Service property for years and never crossed paths with anyone, other than the occasional bear hunter looking for a lost dog.

"This looks like the spot," he said to himself as he parked just off the shady turnoff, glancing beyond the shoulder, which was empty of hurled appliances common off other slopes of other country byways. Federal taxes kept the Parkway clean enough to keep the tourists delighted to come back year after year.

Tucker gathered his gear and hopped a crisscrossed fence of stacked locust rails into the pristine wilderness. At least Parkway lands weren't being chopped up for vacation homes, he thought.

While it had been over a decade since he had been herb hunting in earnest, it all came back to him like he had never left. As soon as the light dimmed from the road's edge where the canopy began intercepting most of the light, Tucker's eyes tuned into the forest floor. He inhaled the terroir of mellowing loam and leaf as his vision narrowed to dissect and identify each snapshot of green through the lens of his memory, methodically scanning forty-foot lanes to his left and right. Grass and gravel fell away from the shoulder slope replaced by Virginia Creeper vine and locust at its edges, straining to hold on to the parsed beams of sun. As he made his way deeper into the shady expanse, fern and other wide-leafed plants spread across the earth to capture droplets of radiance trickling to the ground.

Fallen trees and dead, yet still sturdy, chestnut trunks were minor obstacles, giving him pause to check the footing of his deck loafers—he had forgotten his boots—but he moved through the brush with quiet efficiency as the mid-afternoon sun peaked and began sinking. The further he went, the righter the woods looked, the hip-high understory clearing out as tree trunks grew taller and wider. An hour into his hike, he found what he was looking for: three and four prongs of palmate leaves peeking above the other sun-hungry foliage that capped the cove's rich mulch.

He saw one, then another. Like deciphering a word-scramble, the more he concentrated, the more he saw—clusters of the precious plant. As he paused and scrutinized the verdant landscape, he noticed several more patches stretching up to the ridge well above where he stood.

Jackpot! How had this place not been discovered?

Throngs of ginseng plants grew interspersed discreetly between taller bunches of black and blue cohosh shrubs that lined the two-sided holler, halved by a clear stream bubbling across algae-covered stone. Though still early in the season, each plant had a healthy cluster of berry pods with fruits at the cusp of ripening. He remembered Paw-Paw munching them like pomegranate pulp as they used to hike the woods. "Keep you tickin' all day," he had said. Tucker pinched one off and popped it in his mouth. Its strong, bitter juice made him cringe with each crunch.

As Tucker pulled the screwdriver out of his back pocket, he hesitated before the steel tip of his improvised digging tool hit the soil, feeling a pang of guilt for the *sacrilege* he was about to commit—Paw Paw's lessons echoing in his memories. *"You only dig 'seng when the berries are ripe so you can put them seeds back in the ground. That way there'll always be more to come back to."* Plus, off-season harvest—on federal lands—was a felony.

There was that.

But Tucker brushed aside thoughts on the transgression, financial straits trumping ethics this time. No way he'd pass up this windfall. He went to work on the first plant on the edge of the patch closest to him and carefully exhumed each tentacle of it from the soil—taking care not to damage the neck or yank too hard, to ensure that even the hair roots made it out of the ground intact. That lesson he did follow. Once he had the entire plant in hand, Tucker gently shook off the loose dirt and placed the tuber into the plastic grocery bag he pulled from his pocket, nodding in self-approval.

It felt good—right—to be digging again.

As always, the tallest plants had the most striking roots—gnarled, hand-sized monsters with three-inch long necks or better—mother plants, some probably thirty years old, or more. The "old timers" surrounded by younger, smaller sprigs—the subsequent generations, germinated from seed fallen to the soil or carried and buried by chipmunks to take root—progeny propagating and spreading over decades throughout the rich cove.

Tucker moved from plant to plant in several plots and within a couple of hours, working quickly but carefully, he had filled his bag. *Not too shabby*, he thought as he wiped loose dirt on his pants leg, the dimming light signaling it was time to go.

"Eat your heart out, Harlan," he said aloud as he hefted the harvest. At least two pounds. If Z was buying root early like Jim Gragg had said, Tucker knew he'd be a couple Franklins richer. Plus, he had only dug a small portion of what was there. He smiled as he glanced around in the dusk at what still remained. *Barely got half of it*, he thought. He'd be back, and soon.

As he walked out the same direction he came, Tucker took note of the shape and species of the trees he passed, noting landmarks and breaking off green limbs of saplings every forty or fifty steps to trace his way back.

Just before emerging from the forest, he heard tires slinging gravel close to where he had parked as an engine roared away. Branches and shadows obscured his view, but it didn't sound like a Park Service cruiser. With the coast clear, Tucker bounded up the shoulder, jumped the fence, and hopped back into his truck to head back to avoid anyone being any the wiser.

Tucker decided to offload his product on a quiet weekend night, hoping Mr. Jim was right about Z's amenability to off-season transactions. While most ginseng dealers only bought root after September first's opening day, per the law, Z apparently made a good living for himself buying throughout the summer—early—from those who needed the money but couldn't afford to wait.

With a steady influx of trades from pawn junkies who never reclaimed their gold, he had plenty of cash to pay diggers, at a reduced price of course, and could afford to sit on the valuable root until the Asian buyers came knocking in the fall. Stiff fines and jail time were the penalty for buying out-of-season if undercover Fish & Wildlife agents happened to catch you, but Z was cautious—only dealing with those he knew.

Of course, he knew everybody.

The single incandescent bulb on the pole above the roof flickered, throwing quick shadows onto Zebulon's "Pawn and Gun." Tucker parked his truck next to the other one in the otherwise empty lot and saw light trickling through the front window from the recesses of the concrete hut. The crooked "Open" sign on the door never indicated if the shed-style shop really was or not. Z didn't keep regular hours and never touched the sign.

But Tucker heard low voices mumbling inside, so he knocked briefly, opened the door and stepped inside. The square interior was strewn with dusty guitars and mandolin parts, a few power tools, and rectangular glass cases containing an assortment of goods that Z had bartered for over the years.

Three other men at the end of the long counter turned quickly and ceased their muted conversation. The door rattling shut behind Tucker made the only sound as Z peered up at him from a loupe affixed to one eye. A handful of class rings and other jewelry littered the glass top in front of him.

"I been expecting you. What took so long?" he said.

Tucker looked confused. He wasn't expecting to be expected.

Z really wasn't expecting him either, but Tucker didn't know that. Z liked catching folks off guard—especially when they were coming in to trade.

And he knew what was in the bag in Tucker Trivette's hand the moment he saw it.

"You look like your gran'daddy," Z said, popping the lens out of his eye with a squint. "What can I do you for?"

Z's hair fell across one shoulder in a neatly braided ponytail that reached to middle of his torso. The sun wrinkles on his cheeks and the gray in his goatee added a mix of age and hard-earned wisdom to the ice-blue glint of his eyes. His clean khaki pants and collared shirt contrasted the impression Tucker remembered of him as a kid: Outlaw.

The other three men looked Tucker up and down as they stepped back to give him room to approach the counter. One of them spat brown juice into a plastic Mountain Dew bottle; another slid three gold links back into his pocket. The third squatted his oversize frame onto a tiny stool like a pumpkin swallowing a peanut. The motley trio didn't seem in any rush to conclude their business with Z, so Tucker casually passed his bag across the countertop.

"Hmm," Z mumbled as he began opening up the sack. "You find what you were lookin' for?"

"Uh, yeah," Tucker said. "Was a pretty nice patch. Didn't have time to get it all."

"No," Z said, looking up him. "I was referring to the world. You left for the service, didn't you?"

"Oh, that," Tucker said, nervously. "Yeah. I guess. Saw a lot. That's for sure."

"Hmm," Z said again as he poured the bag on the table and began inspecting each root.

"Someone said you were in the market," Tucker said as he looked back over his shoulder.

"Had someone call from California today, as a matter of fact," Z said.

Two of the men wandered to the opposite wall and leaned against its blocks with arms crossed—still staring at Tucker. The other one dismounted from his seat and sauntered towards the door, looking out the window.

"Where'd you get these?"

"Don't really feel like advertising," Tucker said, trying to play it cool.

"They look good," Z nodded. "I'm gonna have to zap 'em with the light, though. See if they're legit. Not from no Fed land."

"Yeah, I heard they paint 'em now," Tucker said and swallowed hard, biting his lip.

"It's the law," Z said, shrugging. "And Chinese won't buy no dyed root."

That was the main reason.

Tucker felt a dribble of sweat run from his armpit down his side. He never had a reason to be nervous when selling root with his grandfather. This felt different: out of season, with Zebulon Greene, a weekend night, in front of three brawlers who, for all he knew, were waiting to see him pocket some cash and follow him home.

Tucker watched Z reach back and grab a flashlight with a green lens from the shelf behind him—next to a revolver with a handle wrapped in tape.

Z glanced up at Tucker to make sure he was watching and turned the light on—passing the beam across the roots spread across the glass. Tucker did *not* see him wink to the other men or see his other hand reaching under the counter to flip a hidden switch.

A piercing WAH-WAH-WAH-WAH sound engulfed the small shop as the overhead fluorescents went off and blue strobes flashed from each corner of the shop. Tucker's eyes went wide and he froze trying to consider his options. He saw the front door blocked by the largest of the rogues, who looked like he was waiting to tackle the *criminal* on his way out.

The deafening sound of the alarm and the flashing lights disoriented Tucker to the point that he just turned in circles, then looked at Z.

"I didn't know. I didn't see the sign!" Tucker pleaded—yelling over the din of the sirens, certain that the law would rush in to arrest him at any minute.

Z flipped the toggle again, stopping the alarm as he and the other men broke into doubled-over, hee-hawing, full blown laughter. The chawer's spit bottle ejected half its contents when it hit floor.

Tucker was not amused. "What? Is that supposed to be some kind of damn joke?"

Z finally settled enough to say, "Just messin' with you, kid. I don't care where you got it. It's all good with me."

The men laughed more as Tucker hung his head, relieved and embarrassed, the butt of a joke he might have pulled, himself. He let go an appreciative chuckle and said, "Yeah, you got me. I think I peed myself just a little."

"That's a good'un, huh," Z said.

"Just give me my money," Tucker said, wiping the sweat off his hands.

Z reached into his pocket, eased a couple of hundreds out of a rubber-banded roll and slapped them into Tucker's hand. "That's pretty ginseng, boy," he said. "You come back with *that* anytime."

Tucker gripped Z's hand—and the bills—firmly before heading out of the shop. The screen door smacked back into place and Tucker heard the men continue their chortling—they'd be telling that story for a while.

Twenty-Four

Wei Ling returned empty-handed after yet another round of fruitless confrontations with the herb distributors she relied on to keep her father happy—and to maintain her elite lifestyle. Ginseng imports had secured Wei's family fortune for generations. Its discovery in the New World by a French Jesuit missionary over three hundred years ago had opened up the supply chain from the West that her family and other members of the ginseng cartel had capitalized on for the last two centuries.

Her father would expect their warehouse in San Francisco's Chinatown to be filled with exports from their Canadian and Wisconsin suppliers. Ginseng farmers there pushed the crop under shade cloth with tilled soil and fertilizers in as little as three years. This lower-grade root sold for low price per pound, but in bulk it commanded the lion's share of the market. Most of it entered Asia via Hong Kong to be ground into powders at local apothecaries or chopped and sliced for tea and other traditional recipes—consumed daily by over a billion customers in China and Korea. However, a drought in the upper Midwest had withered this year's harvest. A shortage would put a major kink in Wei's supply line, disrupt current orders, and throw the market into turmoil. Price fluctuations already were scaring off her go-to local brokers from committing to a firm sale—similar to rice, soy beans, or any other commodity.

The disruption in farmed root also affected the price of *wild* ginseng, causing it to spike. American ginseng, distinct from the Asian species, foraged out of the Appalachian forests, held a smaller percentage of their overall business but was the most lucrative as it took a lot longer to reach an acceptable harvest size—ten years minimum. Revered for its mythical *yin* energy properties, these scarcer roots, which complemented the *yang* of their Asian counterparts in traditional Chinese medicine, were carefully sorted and packaged to be relished by China's elite—sometimes for thousands of dollars per pound.

When market conditions for the prized root were tight and the Hong Kong supply depleted, the price shot up. Way up. Millennia of over-harvesting the native plants from northeastern China—ginseng's range on that continent—had pushed the wild root there to the brink of extinction, wild-harvesting forbidden in China for decades. In America though, there remained enough hidden under the canopy of deep forest to create fervor and demand from the street peddlers on Wing Lok Street to the high-end ginseng boutiques in Beijing and Shanghai.

Wei knew her consolidators were holding on to what little surplus they had from last year's harvest to see what might happen. The wild diggers and middle-men brokers along the east coast preferred to sit on their caches until inventories had sold off abroad, increasing their chances of cashing in big—just as Wei would do when she could finally secure the inventory. With her father and brother busy across the ocean for at least several more weeks, she could afford to wait.

The space her family rented at the edge of Nob Hill was convenient to Chinatown, but the three-block walk took a toll in high heels. Her self-admitted vice for the latest fashion and her need to make impressions in the district won out over comfort. Her father had even refused to fly her driver out with her to San Francisco. She never quit asking, though. Wei punched the key code into the panel on the door and quickly kicked off her Jimmy Choos.

As she crossed through the short foyer into her spacious office that adjoined their domestic warehouse, she gasped in surprise at the man sitting on her brand new Italian sofa. He rose slowly, with a discontented look, to straighten out his suit.

"*Bába*," she said, chiding: "What are you doing here? I hate it when you don't let me know you're coming. You said it would be another month."

Her father began to reply in Chinese but Wei interrupted him: "You're in America, Father. Please—speak English … It's good practice," she said to lighten the dark mood her father had carried across the Pacific.

Andy Ling glared around at the artwork and new couch in her over-decorated office space, and continued in English: "Yes. But it is obvious that you need no practice—spending money."

He walked to the window overlooking an expanse of gray concrete floor strewn with empty pallets. "Hmm," he mused. "What is that?"

"I don't know," Wei said, straining to see. "What are you looking at? There's no one out there."

"Exactly," he said, opening the warehouse door—his voice echoing angrily: "No one here. No product. No workers sorting it. No barrels ready for shipment. *Nothing*. Where is the product?"

Wei shrugged her shoulders and began to answer, but Andy interrupted: "I know you enjoy your ... independence. But that is something *earned*." Then he paused before telling her, "I believe the family interests would best be served with you home."

Wei shook her head in protest. "No. The *family* needs me here. I know the city. I know the market. I am working on it. It is just taking some time. It's the off-season, still. Product is difficult to find. And I can't control the *weather*."

"You cannot find when you do not look," Andy said, pointing at her face with two fingers. "You play here in America when you should work. So you are returning home to work. No more talk."

He turned around, stepping back into her office. Wei followed close behind and grabbed his shoulder. "What if I bring in a special shipment? More than I ever have, eh?" she said.

"No," he said flatly and turned back around.

"Please, Father. I will prove it to you. I promise," she pleaded.

Andy paused for a moment to hear her out.

"I will bring you *barrels* of wild root," she said. "The most valuable. As you know, I have secured a new supplier." This was a lie of course, as she hadn't even bothered trying to contact the young man from North Carolina. "And he has promised *plenty* of root. If I don't deliver, then I will come home. No discussion. Give me this chance," she said. "Please, *Bába*."

As his only daughter, while he would rather have her home, married and bearing grandsons, Andy did appreciate her interest in the United States and relied on her to secure the bulk of his American ginseng. While his son managed certain aspects of the business well, Wei certainly had a gift when it came to getting what she wanted.

He turned to leave again. "One chance. One month. Then home."

Andy shut the door to her office, leaving Wei alone in the empty warehouse.

Wei snapped her phone shut and quickly jotted a couple of notes in the eel-skin ledger on her desk and slammed her pen down. She sank in her chair, relieved. It had taken her the better part of the week to track down where exactly in North Carolina to find Tucker Trivette. A distant cousin had married a serviceman who had a friend of a friend at the San Diego base who knew someone in the personnel office who pulled his file. Contacts. She made a mental note to send them a gift basket for their help. While she could barely understand the gruff, southern accent from the rude woman at the post office who delivered Tucker's mail, Wei played the part of the naïve Fed-Ex clerk to a T. She would travel there to meet him in person to secure the shipment. *Personally.* There was even a direct flight to Charlotte. That would get her close enough.

Tucker's ginseng would make up for the lack of product coming in from her other sources. Since her father's ultimatum, she had beaten the bushes and threatened her local contacts for a solid week with animated diatribes and theatrical tantrums at their inability to fill the order she needed—berating their mothers, ripping up checks in their faces—earning her the nickname *Tiger Lily* by vendors in the district. As the representative of the highly esteemed guild, she felt free to accost them without the worry of losing face, cash being the currency of respect here. The distinctive clacking of her heels on the tile and concrete floors—a metronomic ticking, like a time bomb—sent the traders scurrying to the back corners of their shops and warehouses. She hunted them down and gave emphatic scoldings, but they all told her the same thing: no root was coming in to pass up the chain, simply an issue of supply and demand.

She understood. This was business. But it hadn't frustrated her any less. At least she knew how to find the young American. She would prove to her father that she could be a rain-maker on her own and earn enough favor to stay here, in the beauty of the San Francisco Bay and its mountains, which did remind her of Hong Kong—but with more freedom. While it lacked the frenetic, metropolitan bustle of her hometown, she felt at home in Nob Hill and commanded a greater presence in Chinatown. She was the big fish in the smaller pond, here—the only representative from her family—and liked being in control, absent her father and brother.

As she stood up to leave the office for her mid-day macchiato, Wei's confidence evaporated as her brother and two of his goons entered the room. Her brother grinned at her from behind a pair of gold-rimmed Bulgaris while his thicker and more muscular escorts stood in the doorway with emotionless stares. Their bulky suits contrasted her brother's tight jeans and silk crew-neck.

"Are you kidding me?" Wei barked. "Such an unnecessary trip for you and your *gorillas*. Father sent you to keep an eye on me, eh?" Despite the hubris in her voice, she immediately raised her guard.

While an equal in verbal ferocity face to face—in front of her father—her brother's temper could get out of hand. It always had, even more so with her father often away on business. Her mother and the well-paid nannies seemed too scared to do anything with Chin when he flew off the handle. Wei learned to bear the bruises in silence. Father would scold occasionally, but Chin, the golden son and heir apparent, rose beyond most reproach. Wei learned to challenge him in other ways, though. "Good to see you, too, Wei," he said sardonically in a choppy accent.

Before she could insult his *Ingrish,* Chin reached down and snatched the phone out of her hand.

Wei exploded with insults as she lunged to get it back.

Chin responded even more forcefully, pushing her back into the couch. She gasped in shock and launched at him again while he kept the phone out of reach with one hand and deflected her with the other. His two henchmen took a few measured steps into the room—out of curiosity as much as habit. Her brother shot her a look that said "better let it go," as she lashed out at him with more expletives.

"Enough!" Chin finally shouted in a voice angry enough to startle his sister into submission. He held a finger in her face, seething. Wei dropped back into the sofa and sulked, muttering obscenities under her breath, as Chin began scrolling through her calls. Then he opened her ledger and grinned.

Twenty-Five

Tucker and the tree crew knocked off early, having pruned an entire block of trees on a field Clint leased from another neighbor. Santos, the more allergy prone of the *Four Amigos*, as Tucker called them, had hacked his way through poison-ivy vines to get to the field the day before and spent the morning bathing in calamine lotion. Despite being a man down, the remaining team worked through their mid-morning lunch break and left the field just after noon—giving Tucker plenty of time to return to the woods by the Parkway to finish what he had started.

He parked in the same turn-off, but was prepared better this time with a large backpack slung over one shoulder—empty except for a bottle of water, a granola bar, and several plastic bags. Plenty of space to stuff his harvest. After strapping a folding shovel to the side of his pack—for more expeditious digging around the larger plants—he grabbed a smaller-bore digging stick he had whittled to better extract the finer roots from the soil without damaging them, laced up his boots, which he remembered to bring this time, mentally checked off his operational efficiency list, and set off.

Within minutes, he caught his old trail, quickly finding the broken saplings whose leaves had already begun to wilt. "Follow the bread crumbs, Tuck," he said to himself with an assured grin. *Two more small ridges, past the big chestnut stump, down the hill and I'm there*, he thought with confidence as he easily stepped over the same logs and rocks that he had stumbled through before in deck shoes.

As Tucker reached the *holler* he was looking for, he noticed marks on the ground he hadn't seen on his first trip. Leaves were stirred up in random strips scattered through the area. *Turkeys maybe?* Then he saw footprints in the soft loam of the cove—not his. At least two different sets.

He stepped more cautiously, analyzing the soil for clues.

Then he spotted the dig holes. "Dammit," he muttered. As far as he could see up both sides of the creek, widespread clusters of conspicuous craters dotted the ground like mini-grenade detonations. Tops of ginseng plants lay scattered about the entire forest floor as if they had been hit by a weed-whacker.

Tucker shook his head. He'd been had. Someone followed him. No way anyone had just accidentally stumbled onto the same place with the same intentions. As he remembered hearing someone scratch away in the gravel when he had returned to his truck, he groaned at the memory.

Then a twig snapped behind him.

"Keep your hands where I can see them and don't move," a gruff, female voice said.

Tucker's gut tightened as he turned to face a uniformed Park Service Ranger with her hand on a holstered Glock. Based on her athletic build and the focus in her eyes, Tucker could tell she wasn't afraid to use it. He also noticed her male partner approaching from his three-o-clock from behind a large poplar. They must have flanked him as soon as he stepped into the woods.

"Do what she says, boy," the male ranger said as he got closer to Tucker. "Let me see your hands."

Tucker quietly complied as Sgt. Brad Chatham, according to the name plate on his shirt, approached him like a linebacker stalking a quarterback. Tucker marveled at the ranger's size. The man stood at least six foot-six and his chest was thicker than the trunk of a hundred-year-old maple. Chatham turned Tucker's hands over and back and looked him up and down. Tucker thought the man better suited to a Steeler's uniform than the olive drab Park Service standard issue.

"You play ball?" Tucker asked with a smile, trying to earn some points.

Chatham ignored him and said to his partner: "Hands and pants are clean. Hasn't dug any. Yet."

He looked back at Tucker with no humor in his eyes.

"Maybe not today," she said. "He may be clean, but he's a digger. Isn't that right?"

Tucker stayed mum.

"You're the one who hit this patch yesterday too, aren't you," Chatham added.

"Patch of what?"

The female ranger rolled her eyes. "Do we look stupid?"

Her badge read "Lt. Deidre Drubbon." *Sounds about right*, Tucker thought. "I don't know what you're talking about," he said—not quite a lie. He hadn't been there *yesterday*. "I was just looking for some morels." A decent cover story on the fly, under pressure. He hadn't even rehearsed.

Ms. Drubbon paused and cocked her head at him in a way that said *"Really?"* Then she said: "You do know it's illegal to pick, harvest, collect, or remove *any* plant material from this area. You're on Parkway land. *Federal* land."

"You can't dig mushrooms?" Tucker asked, genuinely surprised.

"You didn't see the sign?"

"What sign?"

"The sign you drove right past before you parked down there," she said as she pointed in the direction of the road.

"Where are you from?" Chatham asked.

"Here," Tucker said.

"So you're local," Drubbon said.

"Born and raised. Base of Paul's Peak," Tucker said smiling coyly. "What about you?"

Her partner looked at Tucker like he had just insulted his mother.

"You dig a lot of morels," she said more matter-of-fact than a real question.

"Used to. Hunted 'em with my grand-dad," Tucker said.

Truth.

"So you know what they are and where they grow, right?" she continued.

"Yes, ma'am. Grew up in the woods." Tucker had no idea where the inquisition was leading, but he played along.

She put her hands on her hips and looked at him hard. "So you'd know better than to bother looking for 'em this time of year, right? Last ones faded out months ago. Season's long past."

Busted.

Tucker hoped she didn't see him gulp, but she just nodded to her partner. "Check his bag." Then she continued with sarcasm: "You must be lost, then, or something."

"Yeah, right," Chatham replied as he shook the water bottle, two bags, and screwdriver out of Tucker's pack.

"Mmm-hmm," Drubbon said as she grabbed the tool and held it up with two fingers in disgust, like a bag of dog turds. "Never seen anyone use one of these to get at morels, but sure is handy for digging 'seng, isn't it?"

"You on drugs?" Chatham said to Tucker.

"No way. I don't do that stuff."

Chatham and Drubbon looked at each other.

"Let's take a look in your truck, then," Chatham said as he motioned for Tucker to lead the way back out of the woods. "Never know what we might find."

"Last year we pulled up to a couple fixing a flat just down the road from where you parked," Drubbon said as they walked.

"Yep," added Chatham. "Seemed friendly. But didn't want us anywhere near their van."

Drubbon continued, "Turned out to be a mobile lab."

"Toddler was in the cab playing with needles," Chatham said, staring at Tucker.

Tucker shook his head and said, "That's awful."

If they thought he meant it, they didn't let on.

As they got back to the road, Tucker stood aside, showing the respect to officers he had learned in basic training, while Drubbon rummaged through the old Dodge.

"Nothing in the ash tray, dash, or under the seat," Drubbon said as she shut the passenger door.

"Told you," Tucker said.

"Except for this." The ranger held up an empty whiskey bottle.

Tucker shrugged.

"No lipstick on it though, so must not be his," Chatham said.

Tucker grunted a chuckle—*good one*—but the rangers didn't.

"Like he said: you got lucky this time," Drubbon said. "We find you out here again—"

"Or anywhere else," said Chatham.

"You'll be trying to sell that morel story to a Federal circuit judge who doesn't know and doesn't care how good they are sautéed with butter," Drubbon said with a quick grin then got serious again. "He'll take your truck *and* keep you in jail."

"I understand," Tucker said. "But I swear I didn't know it was illegal to hunt morels. When did that start?"

"Why don't you quit while you're ahead, son. You gonna pull the veteran card next?" Chatham said as he nodded at the "Go Navy" bumper sticker on the bumper of the truck.

"That was my grandpa," Tucker said. It seemed clear that his own *veteran card* wouldn't matter with these two, anyway, but the timing might. "I just got back last month from my own tour. Guess I need to get current on all that's changed while I was gone."

The two rangers seemed to hear what he was saying, and since he didn't appear to be a troublemaker, ambled back to their patrol vehicle, taking time to climb in, start up, and pull away with a last warning glare.

Tucker nodded goodbye and stood in silence by the side of the road until they were out of sight. While happy not to be cuffed and stuffed in the back of their SUV, he was still upset that somebody else—*several* somebodies—had beaten him back to that stash. Bastards. *Probably damned Harlan and his flunkies.*

When he could hear their green and white Ford Explorer no more, Tucker clambered into the cab of his old truck and took a steadying breath. As he cranked it up and shifted into first, he drew up a mental map of other areas he could try—if he could find them. The deep places where his grandfather used to take him, the ones in the journal.

While some of the old landmarks from his Paw Paw's scribblings might be reclaimed by the earth by now, the book would have at least given him some starting points. If the sites hadn't fallen victim to logging crews, or *other* poachers, he could salvage a living while he figured out what to do next.

Twenty-Six

Clint dropped the crew off for lunch on his way to the feed store the next county over to pick up his fertilizer order. While Tucker was grateful for the extra tamales that Benicio's wife, Isa, packed for him each day, Sadie's brisket sandwich was a welcome change. Santos and Benicio had inhaled their barbecue plates even before Sadie yelled to Tucker: "Order up!" Carlos and Francisco joked with each other in Spanish as Tucker joined them at the table.

They had begun the day just as the sun rose on one of Clint's first-rotation fields, shearing big trees—twelve- to fifteen-footers destined for shopping malls and the high-ceiling McMansions in the northern Atlanta suburbs. Pruning Fraser firs of that size required a step ladder to reach the highest branches and two-handed loppers to finish the top work. The leader had to be cut to the proper length and the trees' horn branches, competing leaders, removed to maintain an overall symmetrical pyramid shape to the ground. While balancing on the ladder, the crew pulled cones by hand. Depending on the weather the year before, some trees, or in this case the whole field, were overburdened with the upright, sap-drenched appendages. While many growers didn't bother fooling with them, these trees were already sold to Clint's most finicky customers who demanded perfection, which meant no cones. The time-consuming work in the full sun to pluck them certainly worked up an appetite.

"Best barbecue in the county, eh amigo?" Carlos said.

"The *only* barbecue in the county," Tucker joked weakly. While the *amigos* bantered jovially, seemingly unfazed by the manual labor, he was spent.

"You gonna make it, Tucker?" Carlos observed. "You look pretty tired, hombre. Where's your spirit of Christmas?"

They all grinned as Tucker held up his stained hands. Even after scrubbing with a kerosene-soaked rag, the remaining sap looked like a skin condition.

Tucker turned his head towards the window to the rumbling sound of a large engine, followed by the hiss of air-brakes. Through the window he saw the red Trailways bus parked just outside the post office. Tucker slid his chair back quickly and darted toward the door.

"I didn't mean to piss you off," Carlos said.

"I'll be right back," Tucker said as he left the diner.

He stopped in front of the blocky chrome front fender and tried gazing through the glare of the windshield. The side door creaked open, but nobody came out. Tucker sighed and turned back to the restaurant to finish his lunch.

"Wait a minute, wait a minute. Can't find my bag. Hold on," a familiar voice said from inside the bus.

Tucker turned back, grinning, as his friend made an ungainly waddle down the stairs hefting a bulky pack and hopped onto the dusty curbside, catching himself against the bus door.

"Easy there, big fella. I know you're half blind," Tucker said.

"I was asleep," Sam said as he grabbed his old buddy in a headlock.

"You can sleep in these things?" Tucker said of the bus.

"Like a baby," Sam said. "Told you I wasn't flying."

Sam's eyes crinkled and blinked behind the thick lenses as they adjusted to the light and he looked around, checking out his surroundings with a perplexed look.

"Where am I?" he said glancing up and around at the peaks that framed the town. "Looks like downtown Birmingham, circa 1850."

"It's home," Tucker said. "Got some big plans to line the pocketbook."

"I think I heard that one before," Sam said. "And how's that been working out?"

"That's why I called," Tucker sighed. "You hungry?"

"Now, what kind of question is that?"

Tucker picked up the bag—which felt loaded with whole hams—put his arm on Sam's shoulder, and guided him toward Sadie's as the bus pulled away.

Carlos and the others had finished their meals, chatting quietly at their corner table as a few more locals arrived for lunch, and everyone's eyes followed

Sam as he and Tucker approached the register. Other than the occasional tourist who wandered in by accident, the hole-in-the-wall rarely had outside customers.

"Barbecue plate *up*," bellowed Sadie. The wattle under her round chin quivered every time she spoke.

"You call that barbecue?" Sam said to Tucker after thoroughly inspecting the pile of hash.

Sadie glowered.

"Put it on Clint's bill," Tucker said.

She scoffed before turning back to the pit as Tucker led Sam to the table and Carlos stood to put plates in the trash, nodding greetings to Tucker's friend.

"Carlos, this is Blind Sam."

"Hola, amigo," Carlos said as he stared through Sam's lenses to see if he might indeed be blind. "Nice to meet you. You're going to be working with us in the field, eh?"

"Do what? What field?" Sam said cocking his head at Tucker.

Before Carlos could respond, a voice from near the door sneered: "What in *the* hell have we here? Looks like the Jew-Nited Nations."

Rat and his three-man cadre strolled over to the table. The Latinos tensed. "Hey, you know why Mexican and Black jokes all sound the same?" Rat said to his friends while staring at group around the table.

Sam squinted to see who he might have to lock horns with first. Tucker and the others returned blank looks.

"Once you've heard *Juan*, you've heard *Jamal*," Rat said.

His buddies cackled at that one, and a chortle or two came from other customers—before their wives kicked them under the table. But the silence that followed made everyone in the restaurant uncomfortable.

Then Sam started laughing. Really laughing. He horse-laughed so loud that even Francisco, the quietest of the work crew, began laughing, too. Sam then put on his best hick accent, while still grabbing his sides and said: "Daammnn, you're funny, boy. I ain't *never* heard that'un. I get it! Once you've heard *Juan*—that's y'all," he said, pointing at Carlos and his cousins, "You've heard *Jamal*—that's *me*." He pointed both thumbs at himself. "That's hilarious. HEE-HAWW."

Sam shook his head and pointed at Rat, cackled again, and slapped the table. Everyone in the restaurant, including Rat's goons, stared at Sam—wondering what might come next.

Sam then suddenly stopped laughing and stood straight up. His countenance went from hilarity to dead serious. "You were joking, right son?"

Rat's friends each took a step back.

"Who you callin' 'son,' *boy?*" Rat said.

"Ah, there's another good one I didn't see coming. Must be new material from the last Klan meeting. Card-carrying fools, here," Sam said, flatly, then sat down and took another bite from his plate while keeping his eyes glued on Rat, just in case.

Rat turned red before turning towards Carlos: "You think you can come in here and steal jobs from Americans?"

"I *am* American, *jefe*," Carlos said calmly as he stood up. "I was born in *Los An-heh-less.*" He emphasized each syllable with his accent. "That's a big city, eh? In *America*. Probably never seen one'a those."

"I know where it is, *heff-ay*. You just keep to yourselves. With your own kind," Rat said.

"I know, I know," Carlos taunted. "You're just upset that since us *güyes* moved up here, you mountain boys can't find no more five-hundred dollar cars or big easy country girls, anymore. Am I right?"

Tucker thought Rat's head was going to explode, but Carlos calmly continued: "What? You think I want to go to a Contra dance with one of *your* women? You don't even know what a *Contra* is. Francisco's wife is Nicaraguan. She can give you some thoughts on that."

Francisco's shoulders tightened up, his eyes burning into Rat's.

"I don't give a flyin' damn what *San Francisco* or any'you Messicans think about nothin'," Rat said and then looked at Sam. "You neither."

"Must be the barbecue," Sam said to Tucker as he took a bite from his fork and winced.

"He makin' fun of our barbecue now?" said one of Rat's cronies as he put his hand on a sheath at his side.

Tucker noticed Carlos slowly reaching into his belt and Santos eyeing the shearing knife leaning against his chair. To keep the situation from escalating, Tucker put a gentle hand on Carlos's shoulder, "No es nada, amigo. *Este puto tiene chilito*," Tucker said, holding out his thumb and forefinger an inch apart.

Carlos and gang erupted in laughter. Even Sam got the dick joke and smiled as he turned his attention to the French fries. "Hmm. Not bad. Must be the possum grease up in here."

"If you ain't gonna order nothing, the door's right there," Sadie chimed in at Rat's crew. Her nephew, Perry, stood beside her with his apron balled in his hand like wadded paper. Perry worked nights at a lumberyard across the border in Tennessee. He was even bigger than Sadie and had a square jaw that could take a lick from a tire iron. But that might just make him mad.

Rat and his buddies looked at each other. Outmatched, in numbers—and wit—Rat extended a middle finger as he and his gang left the restaurant. He spat on the floor on the way out and mumbled, "Just wait," under his breath.

Sadie shouted from the pit, "Hey, don't you be spittin' on my floors, now, Harlan Ward."

Rat turned his head to her with daggers in his eyes, but saw Perry take a step forward. He gritted his teeth and kept moving. Sadie and the rest of the customers gave a sigh of relief and Perry retied his apron.

"Feels like home already," Sam said as he belched into his sleeve, acting like nothing had happened. "So, what else am I helping y'all do?"

Which brought grins back to the tree crew.

Twenty-Seven

The experienced shearers traveled across each row in unison, taking just inches off multiple branches with every swing as they quickly circled the trees—singing *corridos* and country music as they went. Sam sweated through his first shirt in under an hour, stumbling along the steep terrain, butchering six-foot Frasers as he went. His crash course on tipping left a swath of destruction in his first row, which Tucker followed behind in an attempt to repair.

Sam stopped in the shade at the end of the field and stared at the acre of trees they had just finished. His eyes followed the rows up the field to the ridgeline, estimating how many they had left.

Thousands.

"You made me come all this way up here to Hillbilly Holler for this?" He looked at Tucker for an explanation. "Almost broke my leg twice in those giant squirrel holes."

"Whistle pigs," Tucker said.

"Do what?"

"Whistle pigs. Ground hogs. Those are ground hog burrows. You don't have them in 'Bama?"

"Yeah. We got 'em. Armadillos, too. Never heard one whistle, though."

"They do when you plug 'em with a .22."

"Ah, I see. And then Sadie serves them with coleslaw, right?"

Tucker laughed as Sam bent over to catch his breath, watching sweat drip from his nose.

Tucker passed him a jug of water and slapped him on the back. "What's wrong? You forgot what an honest day's work feels like."

"Don't know about honest, but yeah. It's work, alright."

"You'll get it sooner or later," Carlos said as he joined them, unfazed by the heat and the labor. "We're moving. *Vamos.*"

Tucker smiled weakly at Sam as they lifted up the barbed wire for each other and crossed the fence through a short patch of woods.

"So where did you two meet," Carlos said as they hopped over the trickling creek that separated the two fields.

"In the Navy," Tucker said. "Sam, here, taught me how to swim."

Carlos cocked his head at Sam in disbelief.

"Ain't afraid of snakes, neither," Sam winked.

"So what he teach *you?*" Carlos said to Sam.

"How to freestyle," Sam said. He began beat-boxing then stopped suddenly, looking at Tucker who was about to join in: "Don't even think about it."

"*Cabrones*," Carlos said, shaking his head and laughing.

Under the group's tutelage, Sam finally got the hang of the shearing knife and destroyed fewer trees as the day went on. A stream of curses periodically disrupted the rhythmic clinking of machetes on fir tips as Sam twisted his ankles on stumps and more groundhog burrows hidden under the thick orchard grass.

They finished up their work for the day as the sun set behind the farthest mountain on the horizon—all limbs intact. As Carlos and crew hopped out of the truck at Clint's barn and waved goodbye for the day, Sam squeezed a river of sweat from his shirt and scarfed down the cold, leftover tamales from the crew.

"Not bad, huh?" Tucker said.

"Better than that damn barbecue," Sam said, licking his fingers.

"See you boys tomorrow," Clint said.

"Say what?" Sam said.

"First thing," Clint said.

Tucker took a small step away from Sam just in case he still had the energy to swing at him.

"Dammit, I even got sunburnt," Sam complained as he cautiously pulled back the sleeves of his t-shirt. As Tucker rummaged through his backpack, Sam poured the last of his water bottle over his head as he leaned against the trunk of an ash tree whose limbs breached the canopy, opening to the sky far above them. While he welcomed the cooler transition of the shady, mature woods, the shearing work of the last few days and the up and down maneuvering through laurel thickets and creek-crossings throughout the morning had taken its toll on Sam's ankles, wrist, back … and morale.

Tucker had parked the Dodge on the edge of the dirt road where Saul's tract of uncut timber connected with Clint's property on the other end. Tucker figured it was as good a place as any to start. In his youth, he and Danny and Paw Paw had traipsed through this same area for ramps, mayapple, and bloodroot. Plus, he had no interest in a repeat encounter with the Park Service rangers anytime soon. So far, though, "Phase Two" of Sam's *training* had been fruitless. After the one day of shearing work had turned into the whole week, Tucker was running out of ways to convince Sam it would all be worth it.

Clouds obfuscated the exact location of the afternoon sun as it slipped just behind the undulating peaks as Tucker glanced down at the wobbling needle to get his north bearing. He gazed into the expanse of forest beyond. The conditions looked right, but after hours of hiking, he was starting to have doubts himself.

"You know, Tuck, I could've stayed home and parked cars all week for extra cash."

"This ain't work, Sam. Once we get into a patch, it'll get in your blood. You'll see," Tucker reassured. "It's like finding five dollar bills scattered in the woods."

"Feels more like losing twenty pounds," Sam said.

Tucker turned and looked at Sam's waistline. "You can afford it."

Sam scowled. "So explain to me again what the hell we're looking for?"

Tucker tilted his head to the sky.

Sam seemed confused. "Why're you looking up? Thought the stuff grows on the ground?"

"The trees tell you where to look. Poplars and maples, there. That's good. Cucumbertree, too. There's a tangle of grapevines up in that ash. That way," Tucker said, pointing ahead to a large swath of low-lying vegetation that sloped into the trickling draw of a spring-fed creek. "There. Green means go."

"What is it?"

"Money," Tucker said as he galloped to the edge of a patch of verdant growth and pointed at the ground. "See this? This is what we're after."

"Weeds," Sam muttered.

Tucker pinched off the stalk of the foot-high plant and twirled it in his fingers. "See how the stem comes up to a point and then branches off here," he pointed to each leaf that ended in a splay of five serrated leaflets. "This one's a three-prong. Some'll have four. And then there's the five-prongs or more. Those are like unicorns. I've only seen one."

"Weeds with leaves," Sam said, more unimpressed.

"You'll get the hang of it, once you train those bottle-rims on 'em."

Tucker grubbed around the base of the plant and carefully extracted the five-inch long mass of wrinkled root, holding it up for Sam to inspect.

"That's it?" Sam said. "And the Chinese pay good money for it, huh?"

"Good money," Tucker said. "This is a nice one. A few sacks full of these and we'll be sitting pretty. Z said prices were going up."

"Z?" Sam said, chuckling. "What kind of redneck, end-of-alphabet name is that?"

"The kind that pays cash."

"If you say so," Sam said, unconvinced. "What do they do with it? The Chinese?"

"Eat it. Drink it. Smoke it, maybe," Tucker joked. "Hell, I don't know. It's medicine. Paw Paw used to chew on a slice every day."

"Let me try it," Sam said.

Tucker snapped off a sliver from the end of the root, exposing its milky white interior, and passed it to Sam, grinning. "You ain't gonna like it."

"Hmm," Sam said as he nibbled a bite. "Tastes like a raw turnip ..." Sam said at first, then his face twisted as the full intensity of its flavor hit him, "... that came out my ass. Whew!" He spat the rest out in disgust and shivered. "Show me how to find another one."

"You try," Tucker said. "Look for the prongs."

Sam peered into the emerald mass below him and pointed. "There?"

"No, that's sarsaparilla."

"What's it worth?"

"Next to nothing these days. Folks here used to dig it to make skin salves," Tucker said. "A man can still make a living in the woods if he knows what he's looking for. My grandpa dug a bunch a different *weeds* his whole life. Kept him and us in cash when times were tough."

"Hmm," Sam said, looking around. "What about that one?"

"Buckeye. Seedling."

Not ready to concede defeat so soon, Sam took three steps forward and ran his fingers along the leaves of another plant on the ground: "This has to be it. Looks just like it."

"Poison-oak."

Sam withdrew his hand as if he had stuck it in boiling water.

"You allergic?" Tucker said as he walked over and plucked up the toxic plant by its stem.

"Isn't everyone?"

"Not really," Tucker said. "But I wouldn't recommend messing with it if you're not sure. Better clean your hands in case you need to take a leak. Definitely don't want a rash down there."

Tucker unscrewed the top to his water bottle, offering it to Sam.

"They say you got a few minutes to wash it off before it GETS YA!" Tucker said as he jabbed the plastic bottle at Sam, making him jump.

"Dammit, Tuck. This Mayberry crap's wearing thin."

"Here," Tucker said, pulling a hotel-sized soap bar out of his pack. "Use this."

Sam trotted over to the small branch that cut through the cove and washed his hands. After shaking them off, he sat down in the middle of a cluster of weeds just above the rocky bank of the creek.

"We ain't never gonna find enough of this *jin-sang* stuff to make a difference. I can't even tell what it looks like," he said, defeat creeping into his voice, now. "I don't think I'm cut out for this little enterprise you drug me up here for, Tuck. I'm a city boy."

Tucker topped off his bottle with the cold, spring water just upstream and nodded sympathetically. "I gotta agree. You ain't too good at this."

"At least you're encouraging," Sam said. "You really know how to build a man's confidence up, don't you?"

Tucker nodded, glancing where Sam was seated. "Careful, there."

"What?" Sam said.

"You're sittin' on a snake."

As Sam sprung up, Tucker laughed. "Bet you can't swim either."

"That ain't funny, Trivette," Sam said, holding his chest. "I think my heart just exploded."

Still chuckling—all the while scanning the forest floor—Tucker suddenly took a few steps to one side and lifted up the nearly flattened top of a large four-prong ginseng plant, displaying to Sam, who said: "You gotta be kidding me."

"Right under your fat ass the whole time. If it *were* a snake ..."

"Yeah, yeah, alright, give me that thing," Sam said as he snatched the plant out of Tucker's hands. "I ain't letting this go until I find some on my own."

"Where there's one, there's more," Tucker said. "And we're down low. Since the creek's right here, start looking uphill. I bet you'll find another one. Maybe the mother plant that this one came from."

Sam took a few steps, grunted, brought his index specimen up to his face, and looked at the ground again, comparing the leaves.

"Here," he said. "Got one. Now what do I do?"

"See! That wasn't hard was it? Use this, but don't shank it," Tucker pitched him a screwdriver. "Dig it out carefully. Dealers won't buy it if you slice it all to pieces."

"There's another one," Sam said with a hint of excitement in his voice.

"I hear you," Tucker replied. "I got three more right here. Finally, a *patch*."

From there, the two of them moved through the ground cover, squatting methodically as they spied more and more.

Tucker snickered at Sam's prostrate digging form, exhuming his finds more carefully than an archaeologist. Sam grunted at him: "You said be careful, right? I'm being careful!"

A snap of twigs in the distance caught Sam's attention. "You hear that?"

"Deer," Tucker said, unbothered, as he kept busy unearthing root from soil.

"You sure?" Sam said, cocking his head to hear better.

"Maybe a bear."

"For real?"

"Oh, yeah. They're up here. Black bear though—not grizzlies." He sensed Sam's apprehension. "They won't bother us."

"What do you do if you come across one?" Sam said.

"Make a bunch of noise. Yell like you're calling up hogs."

"And how, kind sir, does one call up a hog?"

"Like this: Soo-wee! Soo-wee! Go on, bear. Git!" Tucker hollered into the woods like he had seen Paw Paw do when he was a kid.

Sam burst into laughter. "I know how to call a pig, man. Just wanted to see you do it."

"Appreciate that," Tucker said. "I was county champion."

"For real?" Sam said again, but impressed.

"Champion liar," Tucker said, and together they laughed.

The pair searched the grove thoroughly. It wasn't El Dorado, but Tucker was pleased with the small bulge in their sack—enough to make the trip worthwhile. As he tightened the straps to his pack to move on, Sam staggered to the top of the next ridge and sat down.

"So what's the plan?" Sam said wearily as Tucker made his way up the hill. "You trying to prove something or we getting out of here soon. Feels like Miller time to me."

"We should be hitting a crossroad before too long. Maybe another three miles," Tucker joked.

"Three miles? Tucker, you better be ..." Sam trailed off, staring through the woods, trying to focus through his steamy lenses.

"What?"

"I may be half-blind, but is that what I think it is?" Sam hopped up and scampered off at a good clip.

"I thought you were tired," Tucker said as he scrambled up the slope trying to follow Sam, who bounded through the underbrush toward a clearing. "You saw 'seng from way over there? Not bad."

Sam shouted back: "Like you said, 'green means go'."

Tucker finally caught up to him at the edge of the gap. Sunlight poured into the space through an opening in the canopy no more than forty feet across at its widest. Sam stood on the edge of the crater of a tip-up mound from the large, fallen oak tree that had created the open corridor. They both stared into the discreet field of two-meter tall, lime green stalks.

"Screw those roots," Sam said. "We just hit the mother lode."

Finely serrated leaves spread from each shrub like miniature palm fronds, and beads of plump, rosin-heavy buds glistened like tiny jewels on the fifty or so plants neatly arranged, and obviously cared for, in the small field-nursery.

"Oh—" Tucker paused "—shit."

Twenty-Eight

"You talkin' about a cash crop, this is *it!*" Sam slapped Tucker in the chest.

Tucker ignored him as he scanned the ground for trip-wires and the surrounding tree trunks for trail cameras—or worse. While he didn't see any conspicuous booby traps, Tucker knew better than to stick around to admire little hidden gardens in the woods like this one.

"I don't think we wanna be here."

"Why not?" Sam grabbed the nearest stalk and tugged its shallow roots easily out of the ground. "See what I'm sayin'? Gotta be worth two, three, maybe ten grand, here. I bet that P? Or T? ..."

"Z," Tucker whispered, checking the ground for claymores or makeshift punji stakes of plywood embedded with nails.

"Yeah, him. He'd pay for this too, right? That's what I'm guessing." Sam saw Tucker cautiously peeking around trees. "Ain't nobody here, man. Relax."

Tucker said, "Shhh!" peering into the woods behind and around them. Sam went silent but continued running the dollar math in his head.

When nothing stirred, Tucker grinned: "Okay. Let's make it quick and git." He dropped his pack and snatched up the first plant he came to, handing it to Sam.

"That's what I'm talking about," Sam said as he crammed a gummy wad of foliage into Tucker's bag. "Smell that. I had *this*? I'd'a been a wealthy man never saw the inside of a damn ship."

As each of them tugged the roots of another cash-bush out of the soil, a familiar voice floated into the opening: "Well, well, well. Look at who we have in our honey patch."

Tucker and Sam spun to find Rat walking toward them with four other wiry men behind him. They both froze.

"Knew I wasn't hearing no deer," Sam said under his breath to Tucker.

"And I left the pistol under the damn seat." Tucker shook his head then said to Rat: "Sorry. Didn't know this was yours."

"Don't really matter, does it," Rat said as he stepped in closer to Tucker and glanced around. "I see you ain't got the Mexican mafia with you this time."

"You sure about that?" Tucker tried to sound convincing.

"I told you from the git-go, I'd be hound-doggin' your ass," Rat said. "We knows you ain't got back-up this time, Tuckerino."

His buddies laughed.

"This's gonna be ugly," Sam whispered to Tucker. Then he turned to Rat: "We can put 'em back in the ground. Roots look good still, don't you think, Tuck?"

Rat didn't smile. "You can't put paste back in the tube, boy. Them plants is dead. Need to be hung up to dry, now," he said glaring at their hands. Then he focused hard on Sam: "Like you."

Tucker and Sam looked quickly at each other, then threw the plants at Rat's face, coating him with sticky bud and dirt, and took off running into the middle of the field.

"Git those sons a' bitches," Rat yelled.

One of Rat's posse hurled himself into Sam, knocking him over while another jumped in, landing a couple of kicks to Sam's ribs. Tucker, seeing his partner hit the ground, squared off with one of his pursuers and landed a solid blow to the man's face—sending him reeling—but got blindsided by another from a fist to the side of his head. Rat flew into the melee catching Tucker with a knee to the gut, doubling him over. Punches and saliva flew while grunts and curses rippled through the woods. The hillbilly that Tucker connected with wiped blood from his nose and pulled a buck-knife from his belt. Then:

CHOOM!

The blast was close and took everyone's breath away—putting an immediate end to the brawl as they all ducked for cover.

Tucker grimaced, holding his side from the knee blow and propped himself up enough to see who was down—hoping one of the idiots had stepped on a mine—evening the odds to a fairer fight.

"Look there," Sam said, with a pained grin and a trickle of crimson leaking from his nose.

Everyone—Rat included—turned to see Clint standing at the other edge of the clearing with a halo of gun smoke hanging over his head as he pumped a new round into the sawed-off 12-gauge at his hip. "Drop that blade, boy," he said to the young man squared off with Tucker. "Or I'll drop you."

Tucker saw the shiv hit the dirt. That was *close*, he thought.

"What 'chu boys doin' in my field?" the old *tree farmer* said nonchalantly, but Tucker recognized the look in Clint's eye.

"This ain't your land!" Rat said defiantly, even while outgunned.

"Boy," Clint said, barely moving his lips: "You plant yours on your own land?"

"So you're *admittin'* this is yours." Rat just couldn't help himself.

Clint turned the barrel to Rat's face. "Why? You got something to say about it?"

Rat's dilated pupils fixed on Clint's. "Guess I don't."

"Good," Clint said. "Maybe you ain't as stupid as you look." He pulled out a roll of twine stuffed in his belt and pitched it to the ground in front of the bruised and dirty group.

"What're we supposed to do with that?" Rat said.

Clint grinned, "Pull 'em up, wrap 'em, and march 'em out. All of it. Early harvest, I reckon."

Tucker realized quickly that they were a lot closer to "civilization" than he had thought as he and Sam followed behind Rat's crew and Clint in single file down a meandering foot path along the edge of a narrow power-line cut adjacent to the woods. Clint kept the scattergun trained at their backs as he led them to a gravel road not a half-mile from his hidden stash. He jumped down into the lane and looked both ways before whistling for everyone else to do the same. Sweating profusely, they adjusted the bundles of twine-wrapped weed on their shoulders and slid down the dirt bank before hurrying across and dipping below the other side of the road back into the woods along a fence line that bordered a field of a neighbor's Christmas trees.

While Rat and the others focused on the trail ahead, grumbling about their predicament, Tucker noticed another, more discreet patch of greenery just downslope from the trail they followed. Pot wasn't the only cash crop that ole Clint had squirreled away in the woods. Several dozen four-prong ginseng tops peeked above the ground weeds uniformly interspersed within the otherwise sparse understory in at least a half-acre portion of the holler below them. Tucker shot a quick look at Clint who maintained his gaze—and his shotgun—straight ahead. Danny had been right all those years ago. Their neighbor had plenty of secrets.

After another five minutes of walking, they dipped under the two strings of rusty barbed wire and exited into one of Clint's fields of Frasers, which provided good cover from the road and any peering passersby—his old tobacco barn just ahead.

Clint hustled his pickup harvest crew across the gap between the trees and the outbuilding, and Tucker pulled the chain on the heavy double doors. Everyone filed in. Clint motioned toward an empty stall with his barrel and each of them dumped their bundles onto the aged, hemlock tongue-and-groove boards, kicking up a fine dust that settled onto the cob-webby tobacco stakes littering the floor.

Rat and his gang turned around sheep-faced. Clint gestured for Tucker and Sam to step aside and leveled the shotgun at the others.

"You ain't gonna shoot us in your barn," Rat said with a concern in his voice that replaced its usual temerity.

"Might," Clint said. He nodded at Tucker and Sam without breaking his gaze on Rat. "These two probably got enough left in 'em to dig holes for you pill-heads. Make good compost. Ain't nobody around here gonna miss you."

Rat snapped a look at Tucker who sniffed the real fear on Rat's face.

"How about we make a deal," Rat said in a softer tone.

"How about you shut your mouth," Clint said.

The rigid tone of Clint's voice made Tucker believe his neighbor's threat might not be empty—that and the grip he held on the Winchester.

"You each take you one of them plants. Right now," Clint ordered.

Rat and his clique looked at the bundles of weed—then at each other, then back at Clint, and then down at the plants, confused.

"Now. Move it!" Clint said, steel in his eyes.

Rat and each of his boys jumped at the command and grabbed up a stalk.

"That ought to be a few hundred worth. Not quite ripe, but good enough. Decent compensation considering you compromised my grow for the season. And that ain't even the interesting part," Clint said.

"You got more?" Rat said.

Clint shook his head. The tweaker had moxie—he would give him that.

"The hell's wrong with you?" Sam said, shaking his head at the whole group. "Your brain's been cooked, son."

Tucker snorted.

"Go on. Git," Clint waved them to the door.

"How're we supposed to get back to town with these?" one of Rat's friends said.

"*That's* the interesting part," Clint winked. Then he turned serious: "I ever see you near my property again, I ain't gonna be shooting leaves off trees."

Rat's gang shuffled out of the barn. Two of them giggled nervously at the fortune of their misfortune. The others, including Rat, still believed they were going to get a load of buckshot in the rear. Rat looked back at Tucker, defeated and defiant at the same time.

The bushy green tops bounced behind them with each step as Clint kept an eye from the barn, through the pasture, and on to the main road. It looked like the fools actually decided to walk the black top straight back into town.

Clint shook his head and laughed. Hard this time. Tucker and Sam joined in—relieved.

"You don't think they'll tell somebody?" Tucker said.

"Probably," Clint said. "So, let's get to it."

Twenty-Nine

The golden brown sap came off their hands with the orange pumice scrub Clint kept next to the well-house. After washing up, Tucker and Sam joined Clint on his wide porch to enjoy the final glow of the waning sunset.

Sam propped his legs up on the crooked, locust footstool and dabbed an ice cube on his upper lip from the empty mason jar beside him. "That's good tea, sir," he said. "Good as my mama's—and that's good."

Clint poured him a refill from the antique pitcher and topped off Tucker's glass. "Wife's recipe. She always was proud of her tea. Little things," he said. "Made a heckuva pound cake too. I gotta watch the sugar these days, though."

A steady hum in the distance caught their attention and they each turned towards the road, hearing the engine before they saw the vehicle. Soon after, Sheriff Hicks' patrol car pulled into the driveway.

"Mmm-hmm," Clint said. "Right on schedule." While Tucker and Sam shifted nervously in their rocking chairs, Clint stayed calm as a millpond. "Howdy, Marty," he said, as Hicks stepped out of his car, adjusted his belt, and walked up the stairs to the porch where Clint greeted him with a firm handshake and a smile.

"Clint," the sheriff said and nodded to Tucker. "Boys." His eyes rested on Sam.

"This here's Sam, Sheriff," Tucker said. "Buddy of mine from Alabama. Up here for a visit."

"Sam," Hicks tipped his hat and pointed at Tucker. "You keeping this one straight?"

"As an arrow, sir," Sam said.

Hicks looked them both over, their clothing still filthy from the afternoon's exploits. "Looks like y'all two run into some trouble."

"I ain't used to these mountains, sir," Sam stuttered. "Fell off a cliff—small one—and Tucker here had to drag me out."

"I fell off too," Tucker added, unconvincingly.

"Umm, hmm. Find any 'seng?" Hicks said, trying to contain a grin.

"I think it's out of season, sir," Tucker said, taking the high road. "Just giving my ole buddy here an introduction to mountain life." Tucker tapped Sam's boot with his, and Sam discreetly pushed the bag of root next to his foot behind the potted geranium between the rocking chairs.

"Well, Marty, what can we do for you this evening?" Clint said.

"We got a call." Hicks looked at each of them—implying but not accusing. "You mind if I take a look around?"

"Help yourself," Clint nodded towards his barn. He knew the caller had been very specific; and Hicks knew that Clint knew. The sheriff returned a thank-you tip of his Stetson and trotted down the steps, then moseyed through the field to the tobacco-house. Tucker and Sam shared a quiet look at Clint who remained impassive.

From the porch, they saw Hicks swing open the wide doors to the barn and peer in. Tucker and Sam had stowed all of the bud-heavy weed under the barn, concealing the seam of the trap door with hay. The scent of the fresh bales of fescue masked the sweet stench of the contraband squirreled away in the hidden subfloor. Hicks only lingered a moment, shut the doors to the barn, and returned to the porch.

"Well," he paused. "Pretty much what I suspected: false alarm."

Tucker and Sam stared straight ahead, afraid to say anything. A bead of sweat crept down Tucker's brow.

"Care for a quick taste, Marty?" Clint said.

"Don't mind if I do," the sheriff said as he took off his cap. Clint pulled up another chair.

"It's good tea. You'll like it," Sam nodded as he finished off another glass, his hands nervously rattling the ice in the jar.

Hicks nodded silently, staring at the distant peaks, as Clint returned from inside his cabin with a quart jar full of clear liquid and several small jelly jars that he passed to each of the men. He unscrewed the lid and poured everyone a taste.

Clint raised his glass. "To makin' a living."

"To makin' a living," Hicks repeated before tilting the glass to his lips.

Tucker and Sam clinked their small jars and shuddered as the corn liquor snaked its way down their throats, ending with a warm burn in the gut.

"Smooth, huh?" Clint said. He and the sheriff didn't even flinch.

"You tell that cousin of yours from Georgia, he sure knows how to drip," Hicks said.

"I'll do that," Clint winked. "One for the road?"

"No, thank you, I'm still on—aw, heck, why not."

Clint poured him another, and Marty pounded it back like the first.

"Sorry to bother you'uns," he said before standing up and adjusting his service belt. "Boys. Stay out of trouble."

"Yessir," Tucker and Sam replied at the same time.

"Let ole Clint here be your muse," Hicks chuckled as he walked to the car, slid in, and drove off.

Tucker turned to Clint. "I didn't know you had family in Georgia."

"I don't," Clint said, as he refilled their glasses.

Sam's additional bulk tested the occupancy limit of the travel trailer. He bumped into both walls while changing clothes, while Tucker bobbed to the Dixie Chicks spilling from the tinny radio speakers as he cooked dinner on the compact stovetop.

Sam looked into the pot and scowled. "What. Is. *That?*"

"Spam and macaroni," Tucker grinned. "Soul food."

"The hell it is," Sam said with disgust. "Looks worse than the chow at boot."

"I'm on a budget, remember."

"How far is it back to Sadie's. I'll buy. *And* fly." Sam rummaged in his bag for his wallet. "She do anything besides barbecue?"

"She's only open for lunch."

"Dang," Sam said. "McDonald's?"

"There's one the next town over," Tucker said as he burned his tongue on the pasta. "Ouch! About an hour's drive."

"Almost worth it," Sam said. "I do have a couple more of these." He pulled out a crinkled wad of aluminum foil and unwrapped a couple of biscuits. "Mama packed these for the road. Homemade. Maybe they're not too stale."

Tucker spooned out a portion of his concoction for each of them and propped himself up with a pillow on the bed. Sam squeezed himself into the couch and finished dinner in one bite and two slurps. "Well ... that was worse than it looked. But I guess it'll have to do." He nodded outside. "That hen put out any eggs?"

"Good luck," Tucker said. "I'm frying up that whole bird if I ever catch it."

Three quick knocks on the trailer door startled them. Tucker stepped to the window to see. "Who is it?"

"Got that map you asked about," a muffled voice replied.

"Ah! Come on in. Didn't hear you pull up." Tucker held the door for Saul as he stumbled in carrying two paper deli bags and a cardboard tube.

Saul glanced around the tiny trailer and nodded to the stove. "Well, it looks like you ate already, but my order from Katz's came in and thought I'd share—not the bagels, though. Not sharing *them*. Best in New York. Who knew they'd ship all the way out here. Guess I should have brought more. Didn't know you had company," Saul said as he acknowledged Sam.

"Saul, Sam. Sam, Saul," Tucker said. "Yankee prepper from Florida, meet Navy buddy from 'Bama."

"Pleased to meet you, Sam," Saul said. "Alabammy, eh? How do you like it here in the mountains?"

"I feel about as welcome as Ms. Parks did on that bus," Sam quipped.

"Hah! I like him already," Saul said to Tucker, then turned back to Sam: "The feeling is mutual. The locals love us 'Floridiots' here, too. You like pastrami and rye?"

"Sir, I'm so hungry I'd eat the sawdust ass from a hobby horse."

"Well, then, help yourself."

"Thanks for bringing the map," Tucker said.

"No problem. Hope you find what you're looking for. Gentlemen, you enjoy your evening. I'd stick around, but three's a crowd—especially in this soda can. Plus, I finally got an antenna up strong enough to grab a signal. Time to catch up on my *Baywatch* reruns."

"Thanks for the sandwiches," Sam mumbled through his full mouth.

While Sam picked through the crumbs in the bottoms of the bags, Tucker pored over the black and white copy of the aerial map spread across his mattress. He hoped it could point them to some better foraging grounds—and trigger clues from his memory on the hidden hollers he had visited with his grandfather years ago. Roads, farmhouses, logging trails—*anything*; if he and Sam could get to some of those spots, they might have a chance of striking green gold.

Tucker strained to remember any of the markers he'd recognize, but couldn't make heads or tails from the map. Then he noticed the hazy date etched in the corner of the plat—1964. "Good grief."

Sam wandered over from the couch, still licking his fingers as he peered over Tucker's shoulder. "What's the problem?"

"No wonder nothing looks right. This map is ancient," Tucker said as he rolled it back up to shove in the tube. "Worthless. I give up. And I gotta pee."

"World's your personal urinal," Sam said. "At least out here." As Tucker squeezed by him, Sam put his hand on his shoulder. "Man, we need to talk," he said.

"What's up?" Tucker said as he continued to the door.

"I'm gonna head home," Sam said.

"Wait, What? Really? Why?" Tucker said, genuinely surprised. "We're just getting started."

"This huntin' stuff in the woods ain't for me, man. Plus, there's the ticks and the poison-ivy." Sam shuddered, but remained sincere. "I'd love to help, but I got a job back home waiting for me. And my girlfriend ... my mama's cooking ... you know what I mean."

"Are you sure? I mean, you just got here," Tucker said, feeling a pang of regret for pushing his friend so hard so quickly.

"I'm sorry, man," Sam said and looked at the floor. "I hate to leave you in a tight." But it was obvious that he simply didn't believe Tucker's notion that hidden patches of plants could pull a man out of poverty. Then he looked back up at Tucker with a grin: "Don't get me wrong. I mean, it's not every day you can trim Christmas trees, find weed, throw down with hillbillies, and drink moonshine with the law, but I ain't cut out for this."

Tucker sagged. "I understand. It's not for you. But, hey. You came when I called. We tried." Tucker gave Sam a half-headlock-half hug, then slowly opened the door to the trailer to look up at the sky. There was no moon, and even with the light behind him, he could see the blanket of night illuminated with the stars.

"Hey, Sam," he said, as he took step, "I bet you don't get a view like this in Birming—"

Tucker twisted his ankle, stumbling to the ground before he finished his sentence, and landed on his side. "Oww! Dammit."

Tucker pulled himself up and grabbed up the bag on the step that caused his fall.

"What did I do this time?" Sam said from the doorway.

"I tripped on that bag of—," Tucker hefted the full sack in his hands, confused. It felt much heavier than it had before. "Damn, how much root did we *dig* today?"

"Hell, I don't know," Sam said. "I sort of forgot about it after getting punched in the face."

Tucker grunted and scooted around the side of the trailer to empty his bladder—sad that Sam was giving up, but happy that they had something to show for the circus that the day had turned out to be.

As Tucker began to close the trailer door, he heard the chicken clucking rapidly as it fled across the lawn through the shadows at the edge of the light. Something had spooked it. Tucker strained through the darkness to see what critter might be in pursuit, but whatever it was had slunk back into the obscurity of the evening.

"Probably a raccoon. Serves you right, devil-bird. Save me the pullet!" Tucker shouted into the black before zipping up to walk back inside.

Tucker lifted the sack again, staring at its contents through the bag from the overhead ceiling light. It looked and felt like more than twice as much as they had hauled from the woods. Maybe he was just tired, he thought, then smiled at the *currency*. "A shame you're leaving, Sam. You know, turns out you're pretty damn good at this."

"Nice try, but nope."

"Seriously. This is a nice haul. I didn't think we ended up with that much. Especially after tying up with those boys. Figured we'd have spilled half the bag."

Sam laughed. "I did get excited after seeing those *other* plants."

Tucker hoisted the ginseng into the refrigerator and sighed. "Don't worry. I'll mail you a check for your share of these."

"You keep it. You're the one with bills to catch up on."

Thirty

"Hmm," Z said after scrutinizing the roots. He looked up with suspicion at Tucker's smug grin. "These look real good. You and that black feller you was running with find all this?"

"He finally got the hang of it. Then he left. Wasn't his thing," Tucker said with regret in his voice.

Z grunted. "How does three-fifty sound?"

"Sounds like a good start."

Z tilted his head, taking Tucker's response for a cocky ploy for a higher price—which would have been a mistake. Z didn't negotiate when it came to ginseng. He kept close tabs on the going rate with other small-time dealers in the region to make sure he was in the ballpark, in or out of season. And he never came out on the short end—although the digger typically did.

After seeing the look in Z's eyes, Tucker said, "No, no, I mean, I'm gonna bring you more. A lot more."

Z nodded with a hard stare. "Good. I'm trying to fill an order. Buyer will like these. You get on some of your granddaddy's old patches?" he pried.

"Nah. I got a few of my own." Tucker said with mock confidence. "Paw Paw's spots gotta be picked clean by now. Would need a map to find them anyway."

Z tilted his gaze at him. "Hmm. Ain't a lot coming in this year. Gettin' harder to find and the law got their eye on the Parkway."

"Yeah. That's what I heard," Tucker said, looking away.

"Be in the woods myself if I was a younger man. Knees about give out. Can't get up and down the hollers like I used to," Z said, reaching for the wad of cash in his pocket.

"Jim Gragg told me you sell starter roots," Tucker said. "If a man wanted to grow his own."

Z nodded. "Smart. Where you gonna plant 'em?"

"I thought you just said I was smart?" Just like a secret fishing hole, he didn't share that kind of information, no matter how much he wanted to brag.

Z raised an eyebrow then counted out the payment, peeling off one of the fifties and shoving it back in his pocket. "That's for the rootlets. Come on around back. I got some to get you started. Just put 'em in a good spot this time. Not where any damn fool can find them."

Tucker shook his head. "Does anyone *not* know about that."

Z led him through the back of the store, past two cardboard containers of rifle barrels and a cracked, wooden ammunition crate that spilled brass and lead onto the poured cement floor. He opened the back screen and Tucker followed him past a pile of stuffed trash bags topped with ponds of rainwater writhing with mosquito larvae. A skinny, one-eyed mutt on a chain perked up and growled at Tucker as he sneaked past.

"That's Hoss. Don't mind him," Z said as he pulled a battered, plastic grocery sack from within a heap of fermenting garbage. "Wouldn't pet him, though. He don't even like me."

Just along the edge of the wood line that bordered the property of the s tore, Z turned up a small foot path which began a sharp ascent up the rugged slope. Within a few paces into the deeper shade, Tucker noticed a neat, square-shaped area carved out of the brush and brambles with small, green two-prong ginseng tops tightly arranged in distinct beds emerging from a staked mat of mulch and straw.

"Don't you tell nobody about this. I don't bring folks back here," Z cautioned, then pointed. "Most of these I started from seed, but them over there's from roots that come in to the shop that're too small for me to sell. I put them back in good dirt and they grow out nice. Here ... and other places."

Tucker heard the pride in his voice, and the plants did look healthy. Much better than the miserable few left in his own woods. "Do you fertilize them?" Tucker said.

"Heck no," Z said. "The harder they grow, the wilder they look. And the more they're worth. They need to suffer. Seng's like a man. Hard livin' builds character. Wisdom, even, if you make it that long. Takes time. You get old enough, you'll understand."

Tucker held on to the wistful look on Z's face a moment and considered the truth in his words—words from a man he had always viewed with contempt.

Z continued: "Those up in your woods, though, suffered a bit too much. Before they got took, anyway," he said with a grin. "If you move what's left into better dirt, they'll do just fine. Black dirt. Not that rocky, red shit."

Tucker nodded at the advice as Z gently cleared away the straw and mulch and popped out rootlets with his pocket knife, pinching off the small tops and dropping them into the plastic bag, counting as he went. Within a few minutes he handed Tucker the bag.

"Keep these in the fridge until you plant 'em. Don't wash the dirt off neither. They'll keep a good while like this," he said. "Waller you out a shallow trench and lay 'em in there and cover 'em back up. Should be growing your own seed in a year or two."

"Appreciate the advice," Tucker said, shaking the bag. "And these."

"I never did think much about plantin' 'seng when I was your age," Z said. "Was easy enough to find when I was comin' up. Mountains were full of it. A man used to could fill up bags of it. Never see another soul. Then folks started puttin' up signs and gates. Can't hunt it like you used to could." He spat on the ground.

"Your gran'daddy was one of the last purebred 'sengers around here. Good man. Knew his stuff. Didn't care for me much, though," Z said and hardened. "For good reason, I reckon."

Then he turned sanguine. "Things changed. Most of the diggers ain't got no respect anymore, these days." He pointed at the bag of tiny roots in Tucker's hand. "Nothing but thieves pulling up even that size trying to sell 'em for a quick buck. Folks don't start replanting it, it'll be gone. Your granddaddy knew this."

Z looked up at the mountains and then back at Tucker. "Course, you keep bringing it in, I'll keep buyin' it," he said. "Them Chinese is paying good money. They've done dug out all of theirs and they're offering top dollar for ours. Price is gonna hit a high this year. If a man could find himself a patch a 'seng—a big patch—where it ain't been dug out, this'd be the year to find it. I'd look a little harder if I was you."

Tucker nodded and thought to himself, *I know where one patch is.*

Tucker swirled what was left in the whiskey bottle and threw back another shot for luck—and for the liquid courage needed to do what he had contemplated since leaving Z's.

Tucker had seen plenty of big plants in Clint's woods on the march back to the barn with Rat's gang in tow. There had to be a few pounds of root in Clint's holler ripe for plucking. With the price of ginseng pushing upwards, as Z said, if Tucker could harvest enough and save enough, he'd put a down payment on a tractor and start farming himself—maybe plant some of his own Christmas trees. Why wouldn't he? He had the land and Clint seemed to be doing just fine at it.

It would be stealing, though. From his neighbor. Just as bad as Rat and his ilk. While the needle in Tucker's moral compass swung from one pole to the other, the heady buzz from the liquor numbed his misgivings. *I'll make it up to him*, he thought. After he got his own ginseng patch replanted—now that he knew how to do it right—he'd repay Clint. *Why should I even care, though? Clint grows dope. How is poaching 'seng any worse? He probably won't even miss it.*

Tucker snatched up his empty bag, flashlight, and a screwdriver and stumbled out of the trailer into the night. The new moon hid the shadows as he cut through the woods, under a fence and over two ridges. He paused when he saw the faint glow of light through a single window in Clint's cabin—then moved on.

Staying low, Tucker skittered along the dirt road that he had crossed a few days before. He shone the flashlight back and forth along the banks and finally noticed the skids of clay and footprints where he and Rat's gang half-slid down the loose bank before crossing the road.

The bouncing of the light coupled with the booze gave Tucker a giddy rush as he rustled and stomped through the underbrush and emerged onto the thin path through the forest, barely discernible in the dark. He shined the beam downslope and saw what he came for.

The patch of bright green tops glistened with a fine mist of dew, making them easy to pick out from the other low-lying herbs. Collectively, their expanse of four prongs of leaves looked like crowds of leafy umbrellas, drooping slightly, symmetrically extending from the stalks. Green cluster-balls of ripening berries rose above the center of each one.

Beautiful.

Tucker's excitement—and state of inebriation—sent him sprawling downslope after tripping over the large wad of a Christmas fern. He slowly stood up and retrieved the flashlight, which had slipped from his grasp and half-buried itself in leaves. Then he checked his back pocket to make sure he still had the screwdriver, which had jabbed him in the meat of his ass as he fell. After shaking off the dizziness from the tumble, he squatted by the first plant he came to and began digging, giggling as he worked.

He tottered from one plant to the next, jabbing the flathead into the soil at the base of each plant, prying the roots out as quickly as he could and tossing them into the bag. His haphazard stabbing and pulling damaged as many roots as he pulled out whole, but greed muddied any feelings of remorse as he hurried from one to the next.

After a frantic half hour, Tucker paused for a moment on his knees, breathless and queasy, and looked behind him. Even in the dim rays from his small light, it looked as if two bears had waged war in the holler. Broken and mangled ginseng tops littered the ground amidst rustled leaves, and his dig pits pocked the entire cove.

Tucker slowly stood up and wobbled over to each spot, kicking leaves to bury the severed stems in the mulch. Halfway through the sad attempt to cover his tracks, a wave of nausea sent him back to his knees. He retched twice before spewing a stream of bourbon-vomit into a stump hole, hunching on knee and elbow, waiting for his gut to relent.

As he stood back up and wiped his mouth with a sleeve, he heard a distinct, metallic clacking sound behind him. Then:

KABOOOM!

The simultaneous blinding flash lit up the cove as Tucker screamed and splayed himself flat to the ground. "Don't shoot! Don't shoot!" he squealed.

As the echo of the cannon-like blast subsided, Tucker shielded his eyes from another, more focused, light on his face.

"Tucker? What in God's good name are you doing down there?" Clint's voice came from behind the beam.

Tucker rolled over onto his stomach and threw up again. Then he stood up. "Just digging some 'seng."

"You call that diggin'?" Clint said in disgust as he passed his light around the area Tucker had destroyed, shaking his head. "Boy, your Paw Paw would'a tanned your hide treatin' them plants like that. Probably ruined every single one of them."

"I'm sorry, Clint," Tucker said with a hiccup. "I drank too much."

Clint lowered the flashlight. Tucker could tell he wasn't smiling.

"Yeah. I can see that."

Thirty-One

Hiking back to Clint's place, Tucker had to stop to puke twice more. His neighbor didn't look back until they were almost to the cabin. Tucker leaned over the railing of the porch and dry heaved several more times as Clint fetched him a quart jar full of icy well water. Tucker rinsed his mouth and spat over the deck, then chugged down half the jar while Clint stared at him with a mix of sympathy and disappointment.

"That's just gonna make it start all over again, ya know."

Tucker said, "I guess I'm gonna need it."

He couldn't bear to return a glance for too long, but Clint finally motioned for him to have a seat. Tucker sank into the rocking chair, shame reddening his cheeks, as Clint leaned the shotgun against the door jamb and stepped to the porch railing.

He crossed his arms and stared into the night. Tucker continued to sip water, hoping for the buzz to return, and fixed his gaze on the wood slats of the decking. His stomach calmed some, but his head ached with each blink of his eyes. His pride would be sore for longer.

It seemed like a solid hour to Tucker, but only a few minutes passed before Clint spoke up. "Figured it was you. Hoped it was you. Thought it might be those other boys for a minute. Be diggin' a hole if it was. I could see your light dancing in the woods a half mile away." He paused for a moment, then took a seat next to Tucker. "I caught your brother down there too, once."

"Really?"

"Right before the fire," Clint leaned back into the rocker and stared into space. "Saw his light, too, from the porch here, bouncing up the road for minute or so. But he was smart enough—sober, rather—to shut it off. He was settled in good just down the holler from where you were, bent over a plant, when I let loose with the Winchester. I bet he jumped five foot in the air before he tore out into the woods. That's when I saw it was Danny."

"So, he got away?"

Clint shook his head. "I'd already called the law. Couldn't take it back. Thought he was that Ward boy sneaking over trying to dig me out. Those boys had already hit another patch—'least I think it was them. One of the deputies come and picked your brother up on the road right close to the house. Didn't even have no root on him. Hauled him away in handcuffs. If I'da known it was Dan, I never would've called. I just knew he was gonna get a beatin' when he got back home ... So I went to the jail and bailed him out."

Tucker cast a slight grin.

"He was on a bunk in the cell by himself, all spread out, staring at the wall—'til he saw me. Looked like a puppy when you catch'em pissin' in the floor." Clint shifted in the rocker. "I felt bad for the boy and didn't understand. Danny knew as much about 'seng as your granddaddy did. Probably more."

"That's what Allie said, too."

"Heck yeah. Boy took to it like Mozart to music. Magic touch. Had him a nice little patch not too far from the one you got into. On my land!" Clint laughed. "More elsewhere, I'd reckon. Probably all stole now." Clint waved his arm.

Tucker considered the long hours Danny spent in the woods. He thought Danny was just dodging his chores and their parents. "Why do you think he did it?"

"I think those other boys put him up to it," Clint said.

"Who?"

"Those boys you and your buddy were fightin' with—Harlan and his bunch. Danny ran around with 'em for a while. They was dealin' with Zeb Greene."

"Z was dealing drugs?"

"No, no," Clint explained. "Them other boys was gettin' into that on their own. Don't think Danny ever messed with the stuff, but them others was running around diggin' 'seng for Z. Probably to pay for the drugs."

Tucker suddenly felt even worse. He imagined Danny hanging out with that crowd, no other friends, and no real family to speak of. Picked on and harassed, trying to fit in and impress that group of losers by leading them to patches they could bring in for cash. Rat and his gang would have been relentless and cruel.

"That's why Danny was in your patch? For them?"

"My guess." Clint shook his head. "Don't know why else. Why get into mine, though? 'Less he didn't want 'em knowing where his was. Hell, everyone knows about mine. That patch you was in been hit more times than I can count. Plants come back every year though. And I'll set a few back there from around the farm to keep them poachers lookin' there instead of poking around ... other places." Clint shot Tucker a wry look. "It's just a hobby for me. I just like looking at it. But for those boys, it's how they get by. Ain't got no real jobs or nothin'.

"Anyway, I had Danny here at the house after the deputy let him go. Called Hicks on vacation and he vouched for him. They didn't file no charges since I came and got him. Tried to keep him here for a while, in case your daddy was to go off. Didn't wanna take him back home."

Clint took a deep breath then continued in a somber tone. "We was sittin' right here when we saw the glow off in the distance. Didn't look right. When we realized what it was, Danny took off on foot while I called 911. Took three times before dispatch finally picked up, then my truck wouldn't start. Finally got it to turn over and I got there about the time the chief did. Your daddy was layin' on the porch, shirt burned off—spoutin' gobbledygook about Danny running in and startin' the fire, wanting something from your Paw Paw, and other nonsense. Feh." Clint waved his hand dismissively.

"Hicks told me that, too," Tucker said.

"Hell, that fire was blazing before he ran off to it. Me and the chief dragged your daddy off the porch about a minute before the roof came down. Nothing else we could do. Too hot."

"I had no idea," Tucker shuddered, imagining the scene.

"Should've told you before. But I don't like to talk about it. Can't forget that smell. Your daddy," Clint stood up shaking his head. "I wish I could've done more for him."

"Can't say I feel too bad." Tucker's lip quivered. "Daddy was no good. We both know it. But Danny ... "

"Danny gave his life trying to save your mama," Clint said. "God rest their souls."

"I should've been there for him." Tucker choked back tears.

"Son, you were doing what you had to do. Don't ever feel bad about that. Served your country proud. Came back a man." Clint slapped him on the back firmly and squeezed his shoulder. "Still a work in progress, though."

"Thanks, Clint," Tucker said. "I'm real sorry for getting in your 'seng. It won't happen again."

"I'm guessin' not," Clint said stone-faced.

"I hope you see it in you to let me keep my job with the trees," Tucker said with sincerity. "I need it."

"You getting any better at it?" Clint grinned faintly, lightening the mood.

Tucker grinned. "A little."

Clint stared up at the ceiling of the porch: "Like Conrad said: *It's only those who do nothing that make no mistakes, I suppose.*"

"That's not true," Tucker said. "Look at Rat."

"No," Clint said. "That's different. Mistakes are meant to be learnt from. Ever hit yourself with a shearing knife again?"

Tucker shook his head.

As he stood up from his chair, he looked directly at Tucker. "Didn't think so. But some folks never learn. Sweet cornbread and stupid are two things can't be fixed."

"Is that Mark Twain?" Tucker said.

"Nope—that's Clint," he said as he went back inside, and shut the door.

Thirty-Two

Tucker heard tires on the gravel near the mailbox and a few seconds later saw Allie pulling into the yard. His head still throbbed from the night before—and now *this*—*two* unexpected visitors in one day. What could Allie have to shred him about that she hadn't already?

But he put on a happy face—as happy as he had in him—and stood from the trailer steps where he'd been trying to clear his head, soaking up as much hangover-reducing sun as possible. Tucker started to meet her halfway as she shut down her Bronco and climbed out.

"Hey," she said. "How's going? What's up?"

"Oh, the usual," Tucker lied. "What are you doing here?"

"Well, it's nice to see you, too."

"Sorry," Tucker said. "Guess I meant to say: What brings you out this way?"

"Got company?" Allie said as she glanced at the rental company logo on the sedan parked next to his truck.

"Uh, yeah," Tucker replied as nonchalantly as he could. "Navy friend decided to swing by. Sort of a surprise visit. They're washing up."

"Oh," Allie said and started to turn. "Well, I can come back another time."

"No, please. Since you came all the way out here," Tucker said.

"I won't be but just a minute. Just felt like I needed to clear the air. About everything. I've been thinking."

"Yeah?"

Allie decided to cut to the chase. "Look, Tucker, we've been friends since grade school, right?"

"First grade."

"And that's a long time."

"It is."

"So we need to stop this."

Tucker wasn't following. "Stop what?"

"This thing—that's going on. Between us. It's just ... it's not cool. And it's not necessary."

"Okay," he said, trying to understand. It's probably the hangover, he was thinking—or other things on his mind, like his other visitor.

He glanced at the trailer while Allie was gathering her steam, then she said: "You've always been special to me ... Even though I might not have been the best at showing you that, and I think, I mean I think I've been, I don't know, kind of special to you, too."

Now, Tucker's head really pounded. "Allie, just say it. Whatever it is. Please."

"Okay," she said, steeled up—and went for it. "I think we need to bury this thing with us. I don't even understand how it got started or why it's been this weird for us for this long. But, I hate the way I've acted since you got back, and I want to apologize. I want the best for you, and I think I can be there if you ever need help. When Danny and I used to talk about ... stuff ..."

Allie's words slowed to a mumble as the trailer door quietly opened and out stepped Wei, a small towel wrapped around her petite frame as she dabbed her slick, black hair with another. "Oh, hello! You must be *Allie-son?*" she said as if she was meeting her best friend's fiancé for the first time.

"Oh, brother," Tucker said looking to the ground. "So, this is Wei. She's a friend of mine from Hong Kong."

"Navy friend, huh?" Allie flicked her eyes to Tucker, with venom.

"So nice to make your acquaintance!" Wei said. "Tucker told me *all* about you. You didn't tell me your girlfriend was so *pretty*. Is she joining us?" She turned and looked at Tucker. The ear to ear grin on her face, along with the skimpy towel, made Allie blush, or maybe angrier. Tucker couldn't tell, and, as usual with Allie, couldn't find the right words to explain what was actually going on, so he sat there with shoulders shrugged.

Allie shook her head imperceptibly at Tucker a moment with her mouth half open. Then she turned around, her expression morphing from astonishment to indignation. "No, sorry. Seems I'm interrupting," she said. Before Tucker could figure out what to say, she stormed back to her Bronco and hopped up into the driver's seat.

Tucker finally said, "Wait a minute. What about you and Danny? You didn't finish."

Allie extended her middle finger, cranked the engine, spun the tires, and sped off.

"I think she finished," Wei said, matter-of-factly.

Tucker watched until Allie's car was out of view then sighed. "So much for the olive branch," he said.

"So, she's *not* your girlfriend?" Wei said, innocently.

"Not that I know about," Tucker said. But Allie's reaction made him wonder: Was that jealousy? That would be something. Or had Danny and Allie been seeing each other? *Surely not,* he thought.

"Well, I'm sorry I scared her off," Wei said. "But. We have unfinished business. Let's talk ginseng. I'd like to see what you have."

Tucker stood for a moment thinking about everything Allie had said. But now he had bigger fish to fry. Wei had made the trip from California for one thing, and it wasn't for a romp in a travel-trailer. It almost made him laugh that Allie thought that, but he dreaded what he now had to confess to Wei. Her arrival had surprised him enough. Tucker had juggled greetings, small talk, a 'tour' of the travel trailer, the story of his house burning, his work in the Christmas trees—everything possible to avoid the truth. He had dodged that since the moment she stepped out of the rental car, as he tried to figure out how to spill the beans while she freshened up. But then Allie showed up, making his head spin even more. Tucker decided to come clean before things went any further.

"Listen," he began as Wei stepped back inside to dress. "I really appreciate you coming all the way out here, and I certainly made some big promises back in Hong Kong—"

"I know. That's why I'm here!" she said. "I worked hard to track you down."

Tucker could see her through the crack in the door pulling her arms through her shirt sleeves in one motion while reaching for her pants and immediately regretted what he was about to say: "Yeah, about that ..." He winced as he said: "I don't have any ginseng."

There was a terrifying pause, then Wei slung the door open, half-dressed and livid. "What do you mean?

"It's gone."

"You don't have it? You *lied* to me? I came here for *nothing*? You said—"

"Whoa, whoa, whoa. I didn't lie. I told you what I really thought I had ... *then*. I planted a ton of seed just up there." Tucker pointed to the hillside. "But when I got back, it was gone. Someone stole it. Even tried finding the old places I knew about and that didn't pan out either. I'm really sorry. I don't know what else to say. I had no idea you'd show up out of the blue."

His explanation did little to assuage Wei's anger and disappointment. "My father will be furious," Wei seethed. "*I* am furious! I cannot believe you *lied*." She zipped up her black leather skirt and paced in the narrow doorframe. "Father is unaccustomed to such disrespect. When you betray him, you betray *me*."

"I said I'm sorry." Tucker shook his head.

"Useless *gweilo!*" Wei slammed the door behind her.

After a moment, Tucker heard the muffled dinging of a cell phone followed by acrimonious chatter in Wei's native tongue. After what sounded like an expletive-laden "Goodbye!" the door swung open again. Wei was fully dressed and even more perturbed. "My *brother* followed me here. Father sent *him* to do *my* work. He too is *very* upset with you."

"I don't even know him!" Tucker said, his own anger growing.

"Well, he is here to collect on *your* promise."

"He's *here?*" Tucker said, the reality just hitting him. "Why is he here?"

"I told you!" Wei shouted. "To buy all of your ginseng!"

"I already told you, I don't have—," Tucker stopped suddenly and thought for a moment.

"What?" Wei said, impatient but hopeful.

"I know someone who does," Tucker said. "Where is your brother right now?"

"I don't know. Some place in town. Furs and herbs?"

Tucker sighed. "Okay, I know where he is. Just ... follow me."

As Tucker approached the Pelt and Herb, he saw Wei's brother Chin and two other stocky men leaning over the hood of a BMW looking over a map like lost tourists. Tucker whipped the truck alongside them followed by Wei, who lit into her brother as soon as she stepped out of her car.

He returned her Chinese excoriations at full volume.

The screen door flew open as Jim Gragg and Allie appeared.

"What the hell is going on, Tucker?" Allie said. Chin and Wei paused for a moment and looked at Allie. "Why don't you and your new girlfriend take your friends and your squabble somewhere else? Say … Hong Kong," she said.

"That's his girlfriend?" Mr. Jim said, eyebrows raised.

"What? No!" Tucker and Wei replied in unison.

"Didn't look that way back at your trailer," Allie said.

"She came to buy ginseng," Tucker said. "Her *and* her brother."

"Yes, ginseng," Chin said. "We buy Mr. Tucker's whole crop."

"See?" Tucker said.

Allie realized the mess Tucker was in—and laughed.

Tucker's head dropped to his chest, but Chin grew angry all over again. "Take me to ginseng farm, now."

"I-don't-have-a-farm," Tucker said, exaggerating to make sure Chin got the point.

Chin's thugs took a few steps closer and Allie said dryly, "I can vouch for that."

Her father added, "Everyone in the county can vouch for that."

"Thanks, guys," Tucker said, oozing sarcasm.

"What do you mean?" Chin said and looked at Wei. "What are they saying?"

And as if that wasn't enough, he repeated it in high-decibel Chinese.

"I'm taking you to someone who has some," Tucker said.

Mr. Jim thought that Tucker meant him and said: "I don't have any, son. Season ain't started, yet. You know that."

Tucker didn't know what to say—but Allie did. "Oh, wait. You're going to take them to *Z's*?" She shook her head. "Yeah, that's a great idea, Tucker. Z can sell them some elephant ivory and bear penis while he's at it. At least that's probably in season." She laughed openly, agitating Tucker and confusing her father even more.

"He's into that now? Good lord above," Jim said.

"No, Dad," she said. "Just … I got this. Go back inside, okay?"

"Okay," Jim shrugged and turned back into the store.

Chin said, "You have ivory too? Why did you not mention this before?"

"What?" Tucker said. "No ... just ... damn, Allie!"

Allie laughed again. Then she stopped and said: "You're out of your mind, you know. You want to go to jail for *them?*"

"I'm trying to save my ass, here, Allie," Tucker said.

"Good luck with that," she said and went back into the shop, making sure the screen door slammed.

Tucker sighed and turned to Chin. "Just—follow me," he said, gesturing for them to get back into their cars. "You need a ride?" he said to Wei.

"I will go with my brother." Without looking again at Tucker, she opened the passenger door to the BMW. Chin grinned victoriously at Tucker and got in to drive as the bodyguards slid into the back seat.

"You are out of your mind, Tucker Trivette," he said to himself as he hopped in the truck.

The sedan pulled in alongside Tucker in front of Z's "Pawn and Gun Shop" next to another beat-up truck parked by the front door. Tucker recognized it and groaned. "What's he doing here?" he mumbled and shut down the Dodge.

Tucker strode into the shop leading the group of Asians. "You ever work?" he said to Rat.

"No more than you," Rat said as his buddies chuckled.

Rat and two of his crew hovered over large brown grocery sacks on the back table. Tucker figured they were full of plucked buds from the plants Clint had *gifted* them. Maybe Z traded that, too. At least Rat's gang would be more mellow on the weed than they were on crystal.

Rat eyed Chin and his retinue with cautious contempt as they walked into the dimly lit shop. Chin casually looked into the cases of curios as they approached while his handlers gawked at the rack of semi-auto rifles adorning the side wall. They paid no mind to Rat's group other than the one with the buck knife on his belt—they would take him out first if it came to that.

"My, my, *my*," Rat said, ogling Wei. "Gotta say, Tuck, this 'uns a lot better looking than your four-eyed darkie buddy. What does she want? I might just have it."

Wei ignored him completely, while Tucker let go a sigh of disbelief and said, "Where's Z?" with as little emotion as he had in him.

"Right here," Z said as he came through a back entrance and shut the door behind him. "I've been expecting you'uns. What took you so long?"

Wei and Chin gave Tucker a vexed look. They had no idea who the man was.

"My family is very much interested in—" Wei began.

"We are here," Chin interrupted, pushing Wei aside, "To buy ginseng, yes? You have product?" Chin nodded to the bags.

"That's good timin'. Hell yeah, I do," Rat said confidently. Then he looked over at Z. "If it's alright with you."

Z casually shrugged and nodded, letting Rat have his moment in the sun.

Rat grabbed one of the paper bags from his fellow diggers and proudly opened it.

Chin lowered the sunglasses onto the tip of his nose and squinted closer to see. His eyes went wide at the twisted mass of creamy brown and yellow rhizomes.

Tucker shook his head at Rat. "You son of a bitch. Wonder where you got that?"

"Oooh. It was a nice patch," Rat sneered. "Just off the Parkway, past the state line."

The hairs stood up on Tucker's neck and he felt his face get hot.

"Funny thing," Rat continued. "Looked like some jackass had dug some already, but he left way more than he took. Guess he didn't make it back in time. His loss—our gain."

Tucker fumed.

"You have more?" Chin piped up.

"Greedy little chink, ain't ya?" Rat said.

"Shut up, Harlan," Z said.

Rat bit his lip as Chin sorted through the bags while Z retreated into the recess of his shop and pulled off a burlap sack covering a cardboard barrel. He rolled it forward towards the group.

"It's still early," he said. "But there's this, too."

The earthy scent of the pure, terroir of soil and root wafted into the shop from the nearly full container as he pried off the top.

Chin and Wei looked into the barrel and then at each other. Chin's face lit up. "We will buy all of this and any more that you procure. But you sell only to us."

Zebulon raised a brow: "I'm amenable to that. Long as the price is right."

"That's right," Rat chimed in. "Money talks and bullshit walks. Right, Z?"

"Shut up, Harlan," Z said.

Rat and his peers looked away.

"We pay top price," Chin said and then shook his head. "Therefore, we do not negotiate."

"As long as the price is the one I give to you, then we won't have no problems," Z said. "Should be some zeros behind the number, too. You know as well as I do what it's worth this year."

Chin bowed up at the *insult*, but Wei touched his arm and said, "We respect your offer and will accept your price, here in *America*." The last part was for her brother. She continued looking at him as she said to Z, "I'm sure you will be fair."

Chin said something to her under his breath, but Wei simply nodded and smiled at Z, who returned the gesture.

"Yes, I'm sure I will," Z replied. Then he turned to Tucker. "You can go now."

Tucker's looked at Z. "What?"

"That's right," Rat said. "Let the big boys do bid'ness."

"Shut up, Harlan," Z said even more firmly, without looking at him. "Ain't gonna say it again." Rat lowered his head knowing Z's next rebuke might come with a fist, or worse.

"Now, wait a minute," Tucker said. "I brought 'em to you." He looked at Z then Wei, hoping she'd say something. "I should get a commission or something, right?"

Wei looked back at him, unmoved. She had what she and her brother had come for—less than she had hoped, but it was impressive nonetheless.

"I think you find a big patch, bring me some of what you did before, and we'll talk. In the meantime ..." Z reached under the counter and pulled out a small, stained cloth bag and shoved it across the counter. " You left this here."

Tucker looked down at the small sack—a digger's bag—and then back up at Z.

"What's this?" Tucker said as he picked up the musty clutch and began to open it. "I don't think I—"

Z reached over and clasped his hand around Tucker's knuckles, and pushed the pouch solidly into Tucker's chest, staring into his eyes. "I said, here's your damn poke. Don't leave your shit here no more."

Tucker gripped the bag and held Z's insistent gaze for a moment, then slowly backed away as Z relinquished his hold with: "Now, get outta here."

"Yeah, sure, sorry about that," Tucker conceded quietly, still baffled but not stupid. "Must have forgot it last time," he added for effect.

Rat said, "Dumbass," and his gang smirked.

Tucker glared at him, then turned to Wei, and with a curt and sarcastic bow, said "You're welcome," before walking away, kicking the door open on his way out.

At his truck, Tucker tossed the bag through the open window onto the seat, hopped in, cranked it up, jammed it into reverse, and tore out of Z's parking lot. Not only had the ungrateful lot treated him like a chump, but Rat and his gloaters had robbed him of a solid stash of root and were being paid a premium for it. Everyone scored from the deal except him. "What the hell?!" he yelled.

Tucker began driving a beeline towards the liquor store. He gripped the plastic ridges in the steering wheel until his knuckles whitened. "Gonna tie a good one on, tonight, boys! I deserve it!" he yelled through the open window. As soon as the words escaped his lips, he slammed on the brakes, weaving to the edge of the road, and came to a jarring stop. Other than the creaking pops of the engine at having accelerated then slowed so suddenly, the only sound he heard was his own breath. His chest heaved in anger as he looked at himself in the rearview. "That's exactly what Dad woulda done," he said to himself, nodding his head. Tucker released his grip on the wheel and stared at his shaking hands, then back to the mirror as he calmed. "You ain't giving up *that* damn easy." And it would have been that damn easy, he thought.

Tucker rubbed both eyes with his damp hands, put the truck into drive again, and looked back before reentering the lane. As he made the U-turn towards Paul's Peak, he picked up the small tote in his free hand, shaking out its contents as he picked up speed. The corners of the square object grabbed the sides of the sack, but finally slid out into the floorboard. He glanced down, went off the road again, then swerved back onto the blacktop when he realized what it was:

His grandfather's journal.

Tucker slammed the brakes, slid two wheels off the shoulder, and shut off the truck. He reached down and picked up the worn maroon and brown book and held it in his lap—low, so no one could see. It still bore a peppery scent from the fire, the char on a portion of the front leather jacket smudged black onto Tucker's fingers. The rest of it seemed intact, as tough as the man who once carried it.

Tucker looked back at the direction of Z's. "Where the *hell* did you get this?" he said aloud as he riffled through the pages, then stopped and opened the cover again—turning the first few pieces of worn paper, seeing his grandfather's scrawled cursive.

He looked once more through the rearview then drove directly home.

Time just stands still when you're huntin' ginseng. If I get lost in the woods, I don't care.

Travis Cornett
Boone NC

Part III

Thirty-Three

Hunched over the small table in the trailer, Tucker opened the scuffed leather binding under the dim light of a propane lantern. The generator had run out of fuel, but Tucker was too eager to delve into his only remaining family heirloom to waste another trip into town.

The logbook had been gifted to his grandfather by "Pa Paul," Tucker's great, great grandfather, in 1930 per the faded calligraphy of the inscription. Paw Paw couldn't have been more than six or seven years old. He smiled at the crude charcoal-pencil portrait of the old cabin, before the porch addition, and lollipop-shaped trees adjacent to it—the orchard that Tucker had heard about as a kid. Paw Paw occasionally spoke of the freak ice storm that brought down every apple tree around the house long before Tucker was born. *"Pa made sider,"* the only written entry, in a child-like scrawl, below the outline of a cartoonish apple.

The next pages were dated at the top of each weathered margin, but there were gaps of several years—missing layers of time, when Paw Paw perhaps shelved the book for one reason or another, Tucker supposed. Each page read like redacted chapters of a history book. His grandfather's early years, absent any nostalgia. Life back then was work without much respite, as reflected in the meager prose.

Further in the chronicle, prosaic notes about life on the farm transitioned to more detailed musings. Time taken in the sketch work as his grandfather became more serious about his craft, more intent on proper documentation. Descriptions of the woods where he foraged appeared more colorful and precise along with his renderings of bark, leaf, and root—from days before fences, pavement, and progress chopped up the uninterrupted landscape.

The progression of entries went from being organized by date to the names of locales never designated on any formal map—just folkloric places that only natives like him would recall. Tucker remembered a few. He had been to places like Four-Top and the grassy bald on top of Skinner's Knob. Tucker even remembered catching trout from Bearberry Creek as a boy. Several sites were close by, an easy walk. But, there were many others, farther away, that Tucker couldn't place—ephemeral creeks with names he didn't recollect, alongside sketches of old chimneys and other structures reclaimed by the forest; moonshine stills, sugar-tapping shacks, and smokehouses, long-since disappeared, that his grandfather sheltered under during multi-day sojourns.

A few headings were adorned with the renderings of forest herbs, which forced Tucker into paying closer attention. Impressed by his Paw Paw's artistry, Tucker could easily make out the orbed leaves of galax, the mace-like flower heads of sarsaparilla and spikenard, and the pithed bark of fire cherry. His grandfather's smeared pencil-illustrations of ginseng highlighted the shape and venation of the plant's leaflets, the dimple of wrinkles within its stress rings, and fine hair roots, which framed the edges of several pages.

Then it got interesting.

Scribbled numbers appeared beside the later entries. Pages in the second half of the book consisted of columns of numbers accompanied with notes squeezed into every possible corner and margin. Coded memos accompanied each description and sketch. The strings of numerals made little sense at first. But after several minutes poring over their potential hidden meaning, a light bulb went on in Tucker's head just as the glow from the delicate ash of the lantern's mantle began to fade. The arcane numbers jumped out at him with complete clarity—*those are lat and long coordinates.* Finally, a language Tucker could understand. "You're an idiot, Tucker," he said out loud. Paw Paw had been a Navy man, too.

Tucker smiled as he saw other complementary descriptions he had hoped to find—less cryptic terms and abbreviations like "*lbs*" and "*ozs*," and "*big patch!*" with a double underline.

As he ran his finger down the page, he felt texture, too—subtle indentations in the paper—made by a pocketknife, toothpick, or twig. Scratching softly with his pencil, Tucker discovered the faint but decipherable checkmarks next to some and "Xs" next to others.

"Hmm," he said, smiling at Paw Paw's cleverness. As he reached the end of the journal, the last entry stretched across the entirety of the final two pages. A map.

The unsophisticated graphic plainly depicted Paul's Peak, in miniature—the wilderness and contours of the ridgelines that continued beyond it—with small Xs and checkmarks at various locations. The last thing that caught Tucker's attention before the last bit of propane light sputtered out of the lantern was a dark blob of scribbled ink in one corner of the diagram with the words 'laurels and pines' written below it.

In someone else's handwriting.

Thirty-Four

Tucker packed his bag of provisions carefully, stuffing enough canned beef stew, jerky, and trail mix to last three days. His canteen could be refilled from the clear water that bubbled from springs and seeps running through most hollers. The tarpaulin stuffed in the bottom of his pack could serve as a tent, or just a ground cloth if the weather cooperated. It had taken more than half a day to sort through the pile of poster tubes in the archives room at the county tax office to find the most recent topographical maps of the area. He even found the updated map of Saul's place. A compass dangled from the Paracord wrapped around his hand, and the Xeroxed map copy jutted from his back pocket.

Tucker cross-checked the latitude and longitude lines with Paw Paw's journal three times before finally matching up two quadrants adjacent to the Trivette and Winebarger properties and the one Saul now occupied beyond the back side of Paul's Peak. The large swath of land fell within the national forest boundary and would take at least a day to hump into, maybe more to hike back out, if he got lucky. Tucker had wandered this far into the bush in his youth, but never alone—Paw Paw had always led the way into the deeper ranges of the forest.

His boots left prints in the dew-flecked Timothy grass, as he set off uphill through the field to the first sagging fence at the wood line. The water bottle in his pack sloshed with each step as he climbed past the first ridge and upwards to the peak. Weeks without regular PT drills had taken its toll; the steady incline of his march with a full backpack burned his calves and brought on a heavy sweat, even in the cool humidity of the early morning.

But excitement fueled his ascent, with hope replacing doubt each time he opened his grandfather's journal. If one of Paw Paw's "big patches" of 'seng remained untouched, hidden in one of the many deep hollers, his financial worries would at the very least be put on hold for a while. So, Tucker was determined to keep looking until he hit pay dirt.

Upon reaching the peak, he stopped to catch his breath and pulled out the topo map. After checking it against his compass and the notes in the journal, he sipped from his thermos and began working his way back down the north slope of the mountain—turning west at two large, forked oaks with three brittle strands of barbed wire embedded deep within the heartwood.

According to Paw Paw's notes, there should have been three trees—a corner boundary of the original property line. But one had fallen. Lightning strike. Its shattered trunk lay rotting beyond what remained of the fence wires disappearing under it into the forest floor. Tucker wondered how many more benchmarks had vanished altogether over time. The farther he went, the more he relied on the precision of his navigation skills—and luck.

From the boundary corner, Tucker turned north again, counting paces and looking for the ruins of a low rock wall—remnants of a homestead older than history that the forest had reclaimed even before Paw Paw began chronicling his travels. Within a few hundred steps he found it—the hard way—by twisting his ankle in the loose pile of stone and landing hard on one knee to keep from falling on his head.

"Dammit." Tucker cringed as he steadied himself enough to roll up his pants to check the damage. While only a trickle of blood oozed from the scrape against the rock, a golf ball was already rising, signaling a coming bruise that would ache even more in the morning. He splashed enough water on his knee from his bottle to rinse the abrasion, then limped to a larger rock to remove his pack.

Following the rock wall to its end at the base of the mountain, Tucker found a wallowed-out spring head that surely had once supplied water for the family of settlers who had lined it with flat rocks. He gingerly pulled off his boot and sock and soaked his ankle in the pool until the cold water brought numbing relief.

Twenty minutes later, after tightly retying his boot, Tucker hoisted the backpack straps over his arms to tackle the next leg of his quest—straight up the south face of the next mountain. Judging by how tightly the contour lines stacked against each other on the plat, the steep terrain would show little mercy on his tender ankle. But he didn't need the map to tell him that. When he looked up at the summit, the back of his head bumped the top of his pack. *Too bad I don't have any rappelling gear,* he thought.

Tucker began snaking his way slowly along the profile of the slope—following a deer trail that meandered like a switchback up the near-vertical face. His sore ankle and the effort needed to haul himself up the grade forced him to take small breaks at each bend before forging up the next incline.

Thin, crumbly topsoil offered little support, with the hillside too steep for sitting. Gravity his main foe, the scree rocks he tried to use for balance spat out from under his boots, whirling downslope, their knocks echoing as they impacted other stone below.

Halfway up the slope, pulling himself along one step at a time using the thin trunks of saplings, Tucker came suddenly upon an outcropping of granite concealed by a patch of laurel shrubs. He immediately tensed, scanning the ledge for the first, most obvious risk: snakes—timber rattlers, specifically. Despite the superstitions, they didn't always shake their tails in warning, and a bite would ruin his week—at best. Luckily, nothing scaly lounged on the ledge.

Next, Tucker took stock of the concave opening sheltered by a thin shelf that widened into a burrow deep enough that he couldn't see where it ended. Then, he noticed the scat—and froze again. Large, black seed-laden droppings littered the mouth of the lair. A bear's diet of dewberries—recently expelled. This had to be its home cave, its territory.

Apart from the thumping of his own heartbeat in his temples, Tucker heard nothing more. Pausing a moment to settle his nerves, he shifted his pack and resumed the climb. The jolt of adrenaline boosted his energy and awareness, but he knew it would be short lived; he still had a long way to go—straight up.

Tucker belly-crawled to maintain his grip on the unforgiving debris, maneuvering under laurels that were formed into a green battlement like a snake-fence. After scurrying over the top lip of the wall, he collapsed in a pile of perspiration and profanity, ankle throbbing and legs burning with the effort of the last hour's climb.

After several minutes, he stood up, weak-kneed, dusting himself off and uncapping his jug, pouring water into his mouth and over his head. While not very flat or insulated from any weather that might spawn on the horizon, this spot was as good a place as any to spend the night. He was too tired to look for a better site, anyway.

The small fire built to heat his canned meal spiraled wisps of smoke upwards into the night. Fortunately, the wind was calm, and no mosquitos pestered him at this altitude. He wolfed down his dinner, balled up a t-shirt for a pillow, and propped his ankle onto the pack by his feet, which dulled the twinge. Before long, his eyelids grew heavy.

No sooner than he started to doze off, a faint rustling below his makeshift campsite shook him out of repose. His ears piqued as he grabbed a flashlight and peered over the edge of the ridge.

The sound ceased.

To be on the safe side, Tucker hurled the empty stew can into the void—to see if anything stirred, as well as to curtail the chance of a nosy bear visiting in the middle of the night to rummage the empties for leftovers. He heard the tin container bounce a good distance, then he listened closely again.

Nothing.

Confident he could rest undisturbed, between weariness and the gentle popping of the embers, Tucker leaned back, falling asleep before he knew it.

Tucker broke camp before dawn. The clear sky full of stars made him yearn for the sextant, although its bulk and lack of uninterrupted views made it impractical for the mountain's rolling profiles. The compass from his pack would suffice. There was Orion, perched as a canon in its low angle on the horizon, beginning its creeping parade to the west, soon to disappear with the sun. He ran an imaginary line from its belt until it intersected Aldebaran, Taurus's ruddy star. Going the other way, he noted Sirius. The flashbacks to the lectures in A-school brought a tired smile to his face.

He took a pair of readings and jotted notes into the book, then closed it. But before stuffing his bedroll back into the pack, he opened the journal again, some hint of imagery jostling his memory. Flipping to the last entry, he nodded from the pages to the sky. Faint dots smattered into the paper, pencil-smudges at first glance, mirrored the image in the eastern heavens. Within the crotch of the cover crease, three *stains* in an angled line, Orion's Belt. To the left, Betelgeuse, or "Yettel-geeze" as his navigation instructor had pronounced it in its proper Arabic, and Rigel, on the right—smack dab in the middle of the 'X' of his destination.

Before heading in the direction dictated by the constellation and mimicked in his grandfather's notes, he unzipped to pee into the residue of his fire—no need to waste his drinking water—and kicked dirt over the hissing coals. According to his calculations from the crude schematic, he figured to be just a couple ridges shy of his goal: the stand of *laurels and pines*.

Even though most old-timers believed that ginseng didn't grow in pine stands, Tucker knew better. Paw Paw had hunted 'seng with success in many old conifer groves, and Tucker now believed his grandfather was leading him to a spot that punched yet another hole in that theory.

Men and nature had shaped this landscape over the centuries. Much of the forested vastness of Appalachia had fallen under the axes of Tucker's ancestors, followed by fires that ravaged the slash residue on clear-cut hillsides. As the decades passed, progeny from root, acorn, and seed reestablished the bare ground. The few remaining "virgin" forests endured only due to the inaccessibility of steep slopes that kept even the bravest of axe-men at bay.

When the last giant chestnut trees, which had once dominated the prehistoric canopy, disappeared from blight in the early 1900s, scattered stands of lofty pines freed, from the chestnuts' domination in the overstory, took their place—untouched anomalies of nature trying to restore some sense of order and balance to the mayhem that man had wreaked.

White pine had long been valued for its strong, light wood since before the Revolution. Prized by shipbuilders, masts constructed from its tall, self-pruning boles adorned most vessels of the New World. Clint had explained all this to Tucker. In colonial days, the British marked the best trees with hatchet-slashes in the shape of an arrow, reserving the mightiest of the mast-pines for the crown and its Royal Navy—causing much consternation amongst the colonists who logged them in earnest to build the nation. Clint had a framed replica over his mantle of a folded flag from the Pine Tree Riots of the late 1700s. The Brit's "Broad Arrow" policy led to the War of Independence as much as the tea tariffs did in Boston. "That ain't in most history books," Clint had shared.

As he moved more briskly along towards the final waypoint, the tops of evergreens came into view, with a thin band of laurels stretching across the ridge in their foreground. Tucker's pulse quickened as he scaled up the swag and reached the thin seam of rhododendron hedge that opened up into a narrow vale of large conifers. This had to be it.

Branches snapped behind him.

Tucker spun around, dreading the thought of being followed yet again. Craning his neck as the pops and snaps of twigs persisted in the brambles, Tucker readied himself for a fight, or flight, even though he didn't look forward to, or have much energy for, either option. His ankle still panged with every hard step.

After a moment, he glimpsed a tan figure shuffling towards him between a witch-hazel bush and a blind of maple saplings. He unsnapped the leather sheath of his axe and waited.

A muffled snort echoed in the forest and Tucker breathed a sigh of relief.

He grunted back at the buck that finally emerged from the thicket—a big one. Its antler's eight spiked tines hung on vines like a hay fork as it shook its head—as much at Tucker as to free its head from the brush. The deer watched Tucker's every move as it sized him up. Tucker stamped and bellowed again—wishing he had a rifle. A stag that size would fill a freezer for half the winter and make a nice trophy for the wall, too.

"Today's your lucky day, big fella. Move along. I don't have an issue with you and I don't feel like running."

The massive animal stared at him a moment longer, then a squirrel on a nearby tree chimed in, chittering to protest the buck's, and Tucker's, presence. The deer flicked its ears as it turned to the squirrel, then back to Tucker, before it shook its neck again and bounded away, exposing the white flash of its tail as it hurtled without effort over the laurels in its path.

Tucker glanced around the holler to make sure he was the only large mammal left in the immediate area. The coast looked clear, but the squirrel kept up its racket.

"What?!" Tucker leered at the noisy critter before sliding down the smooth slope to the base of the holler and entering the stand below.

The texture of the forest floor transitioned from crunchy hardwood leaves to beds of thick, evergreen needle-mulch. Throughout the understory, he also noticed the tell-tale companion plants his grandfather trained him to look for: wispy, white fronds of black cohosh flowers waved in the light breeze, and lush Christmas ferns speckled the ground.

Then, he saw the ginseng. Plenty of it.

Tucker smiled at the swatch of large three and four prong plants spreading in natural symmetry throughout the narrow vale—far more plentiful than his Parkway find—replete in mother-plants and progeny, the product of generations of successful seed dispersal.

The journey of a single seed was tough. His grandfather had likened it to sea turtles hatching on a beach and making their run to the sea. Not many made it. It was no small feat for a plant to survive and grow to maturity—much less hundreds of them in a single location. From the time berries ripened and fell in early autumn, the seed had to make it to the soil without drying out on an oak leaf or being eaten by a rodent intent on building its winter stores. Then it needed two cold winters for the embryo within to mature and germinate, and its tiny stem had to push through the leaf litter and competition from other herbs to grab splashes of sunlight—which came at a premium below the canopy of mature woods. This was a healthy stand with ideal growing conditions.

Not enough to retire on, but it was a dang good start. He unclipped the rucksack from his waist, set it beside the nearest white pine, and began digging in earnest. The deep loam, formed by more than a century of needle-shed compost, was a pleasure to work in. After effortlessly probing around the first few roots with his screwdriver, Tucker abandoned the tool—opting to go bare-handed. Even the hair-roots could be lifted from the light, fluffy topsoil of rotted needles with minimal tugging.

In less than two hours, Tucker dragged his root-laden tarp to the other edge of the woodlot, gawking at the still-plentiful supply of smaller plants he'd left for future harvest. He pulled out Paw Paw's book and made his own notes as he sipped the last drops of water from his bottle, grinning wide at his good fortune.

Tucker stood up to stretch his back, dust off his knees, and to begin looking for a stream to refill his canteen. Moss-covered rocks below him hinted at a hidden spring.

He paused in the dense silence of the deep forest to admire his handiwork spread out on the tarp—a respectable haul that, even dry, would yield a good five pounds or more. *"Not bad for a single trek,"* he thought. The sense of accomplishment that swept over him felt good.

Then a voice above him shattered that contentment.

Thirty-Five

"Damn, boys. Lookie what I found!"

Tucker sagged. He didn't want to look, but slowly turned to face Rat and five of his buddies lining the top of the hill—reinforcements. Based on their filthy clothes, they had struggled up the same steep slopes, probably tracking him not long after he left the trailer. One cradled a carbine in his arms, some version of a ranch rifle with a bench-vise saw job on the barrel to make it even lighter; another had a cheap revolver stuffed in his belt.

Tucker considered making a lunge for his pack and the pistol inside; but they'd surely plug him before he could get a round off. He eyed the hatchet on the ground next him, but the old "knife to a gun fight" trope came to mind, so Tucker resigned himself to defeat, again.

"If it ain't my ole buddy, Tucker," Rat said, sauntering down to him. "Where's your four-eyed nee-gro pal?" Two of Harlan's grubby *pals* scanned the woods like they expected Sam to appear any minute.

"He'll be along with—"

"Don't give me that shit, dawg," Rat interrupted. "That boy tucked tail back home the other day. Watched him get on the bus. Whattaya think, I'm stupid? I know ever-thing goes on. Like when our *friend* takes to the woods to get in our 'seng."

"This ain't yours, Harlan," Tucker said through gritted teeth.

"It is now," Rat said, looking down at the tarp, all but licking his lips, pupils wide from what he snorted—the only way they could have kept up, Tucker thought to himself. *And me with a bum ankle.* Cold comfort, but something.

Tucker gave in to anger and reared back to take Rat's head off before two simultaneous shots echoed, with rounds hitting the mulch, spraying him and Rat with clods of dirt. Tucker, shielded his head, while Rat ducked, more annoyed than scared. "The fuck, Randy!"

The two with the guns looked at each other, each surprised that the other fired. The one holding the rifle clicked on the safety with wide eyes and a shaky finger.

"Cut that shit out," Rat said and turned to Tucker, nodding down at the tarp. "We'll be takin' that. And we appreciate all your hard work. I just want you to know that from the bottom of my cold, dead heart." Without taking his eyes of Tucker's, he then gave a one-word command: "Boys."

Two of Rat's posse immediately scooted down the embankment and gathered up the corners of the tarp. "Gotta say, me and the boys enjoyed our little hunting expedition. You were 'bout as hard to track as a gut shot deer. Left more crumbs than Goldilocks." Rat chuckled and tossed the empty can of stew at Tucker's feet. "About hit me in the damn head with that."

"Sorry I missed."

"Was a nice buck there, too," Rat said. "Jumped at you, huh. Jester would've shot it, but that would've given up our 'tactical advantage,' right? Ain't that the military term?"

Tucker glared as Rat gave orders. "Tie him to that tree." Rat nodded to a large, smooth-barked beech on the slope—above the pines and facing downhill. "He gives you any trouble, shoot him."

Tucker offered token resistance as four of the thugs wrestled him up the hill and rammed his head into the tree, opening a gash on Tucker's scalp. As blood flowed across the bridge of his nose and dripped onto his boots, they secured him firmly, facing the deep holler below. Then, they stretched his arms behind the tall beech, wrapping his wrists and body with duct tape and rope—encircling the trunk at least four times. The one cradling the carbine maintained a sinister grin on his face, flicking the safety on and off again for effect.

"These is real nice," Rat said as he inspected the roots, dropping them into a canvas sack he had brought for the occasion. "Ought to bring a nice dollar. Thank you, Tuckie. Candy from a baby."

Tucker watched in a daze as the motley bandits turned up the tarp and poured the rest of the booty into the bag. Rat then casually picked up Tucker's pack and dumped out its contents. The pistol fell out first. Rat shook his head at Tucker. "Tsk-tsk," he said. "Someone might get hurt with this." Rat grinned and stuffed it in the back of his pants.

Then his eyes widened as Paw Paw's journal fell to the ground. He picked it up triumphantly and shook it in Tucker's face. "Umm-hmm," he crowed. "Been lookin' for this. Had a feelin' it didn't get burnt up."

"Rot in hell," Tucker said and spat.

"Will do. And I'll see you there—later," Rat said with a laugh as he thumbed through the old pages. "Yeah, boy. Maps and everything. Just like I thought. I'd say we're about set." He stuffed the small book into his pants and said, "Let's go, boys. It's a long haul back." His buddies all laughed with him and started back over the hill.

Tucker glared. "You can't leave me tied up like this, Harlan. I could die out here," He wiggled in his bonds to make his point.

"Yeah, I imagine so. Heard coyotes last night while we was humped up at the bottom of the mountain. Gotta say, that 'un was a bitch to get up. I commend your persistence." He stared at Tucker with intense and icy eyes, his remorseless conclusion reached without much hesitation, and Tucker knew he was serious this time. Rat pulled Paw Paw's pistol out of his pants, cocked it with his thumb and held it within a few inches of Tucker's face.

Tucker winced, thinking a bullet was coming, wondering if he'd even hear the shot.

"Hmmph," Rat grunted. "I thought you might mess yourself. Guess you do still have some balls." He looked around at the isolated spot, then at his posse before backhanding Tucker in the groin with the butt of the pistol.

The air in Tucker's lungs released in a gasp as bile rose to his throat and his chest heaved within the wrapped tape as he struggled to regain a breath.

Rat let the hammer down on the pistol, grunted again, and started up the hill after the others. Without looking back, he said over his shoulder, "You stay put now, Tuckie. We'll see you on the *other* side." Another laugh, and he was over the top.

The moment they were out all of sight, Tucker wrestled furiously with the tape on his wrists and arms to no avail; it felt like they used an entire roll.

The way they had tied him up, his feet almost dangled, and he couldn't get any leverage. "Dammit, Harlan! Come back here and cut me loose!"

No reply.

"Harlan! I know you can hear me." Nothing. "HARLAN!"

A single shot rang out in the distance—Harlan's answer. Or maybe they dropped that buck.

Tucker closed his eyes, as much to calm himself as to pray, then strained to hear footsteps, snapping branches, or any other sound, hoping someone in the 'hunting party' might have had second thoughts. He heard nothing. No one was coming back. And no one else knew he was here. *I didn't tell anyone where I was going,* he thought. Saul or Clint might be inclined to pay a visit to the trailer, wondering where he was, but that might be days. The rising panic in his gut and the hard knock to his head and balls churned Tucker's stomach and sent white streaks across his field of vision. He dry-heaved twice and passed out.

Tucker came to with his head throbbing and throat burning with thirst. Based on the falling shadows and dim angles of the blurred sunlight, evening was coming quick. One of his eyes had almost crusted over with dried blood that had seeped down his face from the gash on his forehead. He could just make out his backpack and its contents littering the slope below him—including his hatchet—the only instrument he possibly could use to cut his binds. Out of reach.

While he hadn't given up completely, his morale was sinking into a morass of resignation. His arms, pinned from his shoulders, had gone all but numb, and his toes tingled with a sensation like there were holes in his socks. He cursed his predicament and thrashed against his bonds one last time, then he was done— his energy sapped from the long hike, the hours spent digging, and the struggle with his captors. They had tracked him. Just like the bucks they'd poach out of the deep forest to later parade through town on the hood of their muddy 4x4s. There would be no such fanfare for him.

This far into the woods, no one would hear him even if he could muster enough voice for a scream. Maybe if he was lucky, some bear hunter would come across his remains one day, still clinging to the trunk of the smooth beech trunk on which he expired. Desiccated leather on bone.

For the last few moments of the fading afternoon light, Tucker stared down into the holler, then up at the high canopy. This really was a beautiful spot to die. The old growth poplars formed a cathedral around the cove. And there was the heart-shaped burl on the gigantic oak he could just see on the other ridge. Tucker grinned at the irony. It hadn't changed from over a dozen years ago when his Paw Paw led him and Danny here the first time to dig a pile of ginseng root. He had been just a kid but remembered with crystal clarity the looming hulk of the sow bear and the guttural sounds she made approaching the tree where Danny shook branches at her cub. Paw Paw had been so calm.

As he slipped in and out of consciousness, his thoughts drifted to his grandfather—a true mountain man who had taught Tucker everything he knew about the woods, who inspired him to leave these mountain hollers and see the world, challenging him to use the stars to guide his way home. Paw Paw, whose worn journal pages had led him here to stake a claim for his future.

All of it for naught. They had taken everything. A legacy lost.

Tucker mumbled a brief, raspy prayer and accepted his fate as he heard coyotes begin howling just over the next ridge, excited by the blood scent of wounded prey in the air.

Maybe it would be quick, he thought as he passed out.

Tucker came to again in the predawn murk with a steady scratching sound from behind—the sound of someone, or some thing, sawing at the manacles embedded into his wrists.

"Harlan? That you? Thank God," Tucker said, hoarsely.

No one replied.

"I need some water. I knew you couldn't just—." As the cut bindings gave way to his weight, Tucker lurched forward, rolling to a stop at the base of the next tree on the steep slope. He looked up at the silhouette of a slim, quiet figure above him.

It wasn't Rat—he wouldn't have kept his mouth shut this long. Tucker raised his tingling arms and wiped away matted blood from his eyelashes, straining to see beyond the twinkling flashes in his line of sight. He could just make out the blade of a knife extending from one arm, and an empty sleeve dangling from the other.

"Danny?" Tucker whimpered, thinking he was lost in a dream state—or dead. He shook his head and a spasm of pain ripped down his shoulders. He hurt too much to be dead.

"You okay, Tuck?" Danny said in his same soft drawl.

"Is that really you?" Tucker said, struggling to right himself on numb, weak ankles.

"I reckon so," Danny said as he shimmied down the slope and caught Tucker with his one arm just as Tucker's legs crumpled. His fingers wrapped around Tucker's forearm like a vise.

"I thought you were dead," Tucker sobbed, embracing his brother with the little strength he had. "What are you doing here? How'd you find me?"

"Watched you digging for a while from up on that ridge. Then I left. Got hungry."

"Can't believe you're here," Tucker said weakly. "I'd a died on that damn tree."

"You was fine at the time," Danny said. "Figured you'd be in there a while. Then I heard a shot. Didn't seem right. Thought I'd better check it out," Danny said as he hoisted Tucker back up the slope. "Didn't know Rat and them boys was on you. I came up from the other side. Had to wait 'til they was all the way gone. Them boys done you wrong. I thought you was dead. Thought they'd shot you for sure."

Tucker shook his head, "Would've been if you hadn't a come ... Dead I mean ... Wait, come back from where? Where've you been?" Even in the faint light, Tucker could see rippled scars across his brother's face. "That from the fire?"

Danny grunted, supporting Tucker's weight like it was nothing. "Can you walk?"

"I think so," Tucker said. "Might need a hand, though."

"Well, good ... I got one."

Tucker thought he saw a smile as he painfully chuckled and limped after his brother to the crest of the ridge.

Danny guided him for what seemed like an hour across the rugged slope. Tucker had so many questions but could barely keep his eyes focused on each step. They finally reached a spot where the shadows retreated from large rocks jutting from the ground. At the craggy base of a huge boulder, Danny paused to pull away a tree top that covered the entry-way into what seemed like a solid stone face. He motioned Tucker through the narrow opening, following the slightest sliver of dawn entering the chamber. Danny sat Tucker down on something soft and, as Tucker's eyes adjusted to the light, he saw Danny draw water from a dented tin pail next to a smoldering fire pit.

"Here. Drink this," Danny said, holding a cup to Tucker's lips.

Tucker grimaced at the bitter fluid at first—then drained the rest of it and held up the cup for some more. "What is this place? This is where you've been all this time?" Tucker groaned.

"You rest, now," Danny said, and walked out of the cave, re-sealing the door opening with the hemlock bow. "We'll talk later," he said from outside.

Tucker reclined on the makeshift mattress. As his eyelids sagged, he thought about the unlikely series of events over the past ten hours, and before he knew it, fell fast asleep.

Thirty-Six

Tucker awoke staring at a rock ceiling stained amber by the thin haze of wood smoke hanging in the air. He sat up uncomfortably on the narrow canvas cot. Danny stoked the small fire within its cobblestone hearth while he puffed on a corn cob pipe. Tucker could see more clearly how the scars on his brother's face disfigured most of one cheek and wrapped around the hairline of his forehead to above his ear, where Danny's scruff of jet-black hair draped over the bare spots.

"You smoke now?"

"Just to pass the time," Danny said as he raked orange coals beneath a bubbling coffee kettle.

Tucker reached up to touch the tender knot on his head and grimaced.

Danny said, "Didn't think you were ever coming home."

"Sometimes, I didn't either," Tucker said—the two of them conversing as if no time had passed at all. "But I'm back."

"I know. I saw you was back at the home place," Danny said.

"You saw me? There?"

Danny nodded

Tucker looked at the ceiling again. "Well, damn, Danny ... why didn't you come out and at least let me know you were alive?"

"I's here in the woods," Danny said, as innocently as ever.

Tucker couldn't help but chuckle. "Come on. Well, why didn't you let me know about the fire? Mom and Dad?"

"You found out, didn't you?" Danny shrugged, unaffected. "Didn't know where you were. Hadn't heard from you in a while."

"I wrote letters. But you never wrote back," Tucker said.

"Yeah. Guess not," Danny said. "Ain't much of a writer."

Tucker glanced around the cave where Danny had been living—for a while, it appeared. A small gas-cylinder lantern hung over a neat pile of river rocks. Two crates supported a mold-stained sheet of discarded plywood creating a table, and a large, blocky stone draped with deer hides made a stool.

The cot Tucker rested on had been pieced together with poplar saplings interlaced with strips of bark and encased with burlap. A lever action rifle leaned against one side of the entryway.

Tucker said, "That's Paw Paw's old varmint gun."

"Reckon it is," Danny said as he dipped a cotton rag into the kettle, then grabbed handfuls of leaves from two different glass jars and stuffed them into the cloth. Twisting the poultice on each end, he pressed it against Tucker's head. "Hold this here a bit."

"What is it?" Tucker asked.

"Horse chestnut, dandelion root, witch-hazel," Danny said. "Good for a whump to the noggin."

Tucker must have missed that lesson from Paw Paw, but the hot compress took the ache away almost immediately. He pointed at the side of Danny's face. "You really did get burnt pretty bad. You use this stuff for that, too?"

"Cinders got me on the way out of the house." Danny rubbed his fingers across his face. "Oak bark and elm. Witch-hazel. Plantain. Took a long time. Healed up alright, but I don't look purty no more."

"Aw. Just gives you more *character*," Tucker said, downplaying the disfigurement.

"Hmph. You say so. Reflection ain't hard to take in the creek. A mirror might scare me though," Danny seemed to say to himself.

Tucker changed the subject. "So, you been living here ever since, huh?"

Danny said, "Going on close to year now, I think."

"Really?"

"Ain't so bad. Well, winter weren't much fun. About froze to death. Kept a fire goin' in here the whole time and still got cold. Had plenty of wood, but I could've used an extra blanket." Danny grinned wide. Then I got a couple deer." He nodded at the furry hides folded neatly in the corner. "They'll keep you toasty."

"What about this other stuff?" Tucker said, nodding to a shelf with canned goods and cloth sacks.

"Folks sell me stuff from time to time ... well, Zeb Greene, mostly—only, I reckon."

Tucker shook his head in disbelief. Z sure knew how to keep a secret. But Tucker saw it now—Z protecting his own. Danny, an outcast just like him. *Hell, me too,* he thought. Some secrets weren't always selfish, just part of the unspoken code among brethren, trumping law and logic. Tucker had been gone long enough not to see it—here. But it's just like the Navy, Tucker thought. You watch out for your own. To hell with the rules. Those were the written law. Theirs was a code that carried more weight than scripture. Z's law, *their* law, his and Danny's. They had to be followed, no matter the penalty man might impose.

"So, you trade him 'seng?"

"Not just 'seng. I bring in morels, branch lettuce, ramps—and purslane for them Mexican fellas—they cook it like collards. Not bad with a slab of fatback, neither. Z trades it all. A man can make a good lick if he knows where to look. Some days I make a hundred dollars or more."

"In a day?" Tucker said, amazed. He could barely claim that much to his name. "What do you spend it on?" he asked, glancing around the cave.

"I don't, much. Bullets. Beans. Rest is under the mattress, like Paw Paw did."

"Better than the bank," Tucker mumbled. "But ... why? I mean, why all the way out here? Alone like this?"

"Heard they was saying I started that fire. Figured I'd lay low. I been coming up here since before you left. Since I was a young 'un, I guess. Nothing else I could do. I just had been in jail."

"Yeah, I heard."

"Wasn't gonna go back," Danny said as he looked at the ceiling. "It gets lonely sometimes. But I'm used to it. Don't have much need for people. Not with everyone gone and you off in the Navy and all."

Tucker hung his head. "I'm sorry. It was just something I had to do. Pa was so drunk and crazy and—"

"I understand. You ain't gotta apologize for nothing. Life gives us what it gives us."

Tucker almost couldn't believe what he was hearing from his little brother—the one who had lived in the woods for a year.

"I didn't set that fire, Tucker. I drug him outta the house. I tried to get Mama out, too … but she was already …" Danny hesitated. "I just stayed here. It's pretty nice once you get used to it. Peaceful and all."

"No one to bother you here, for sure," Tucker said and Danny nodded.

After a moment to weigh his own emotions, Tucker said, "I don't think anyone blames you for the fire. Everyone thinks you're dead. Clint told me what happened that night. Said he caught you digging in his ginseng and then—"

Danny's hackles flew up. "Shoot, I wasn't digging his 'seng! I was pickin' his berries. Old man Clint just lets 'em fall off to the ground. Them's pretty plants, what's left of 'em. Old plants. No need for that seed to go to waste like that. I make sure they *all* come up."

Danny huffed, then continued. "But Deputy just had got me locked up, then Clint bailed me out. Then we saw the fire. I didn't know what to do. That's why I run off."

Tucker nodded like he understood. "I'm just glad you're here. When we get back, we'll get that fire thing sorted out."

Danny shot Tucker a worried look. "I ain't leaving here, Tuck. I ain't spending no more time in no jail. Not for no fire I didn't start."

"You won't go to jail. Hicks even told me it was an accident. You know as good as me that Mom always smoked in bed. But hell, jail can't be worse than living in a damn cave. It's *like* a jail in here." Tucker looked around at the rock walls surrounding them.

"Heck, no. This is paradise, here. It's home." Danny grinned. "Better than your place. I seen that little trailer."

"So, you were spying on me."

"Just making sure you's okay, is all," Danny said and grinned. "Even left you and your big black friend a present one night."

"I knew it!" Tucker cackled. "Me and Sam couldn't have dug that much."

"You tripped right on it," Danny snickered. "Fell on your face like an ole drunk."

"You got me good on that one," Tucker laughed along with his brother. "In a way, that's what got me fired up to come looking for more."

"And you made your way up here," Danny said. "Guess you figured out Paw Paw's scribbling. Some'a mine too, maybe."

It took a moment for Tucker to catch on: "*You* gave the journal to Z."

Danny nodded and went back to the kettle to pour a hot cup of water. "Wanted you to find what you were looking for—maybe find me."

Tucker shuddered with a wave of emotion. "I'm glad you did. Real glad."

Danny grinned and said: "I got something else to show you, too. You got someplace you gotta be or anyone to get back to? Some girl, maybe?" he teased. "Allie's sweet on you, still, you know."

Tucker bristled. "Hah! If she was, I think that ship sailed. But sounds like you two got along good, though. She said y'all talked a lot."

"Yeah. About the woods," Danny said. "She knows her stuff."

"That's what she said about you."

"Shoot, Tucker. She's your girl. Always has been."

Tucker thought about that a long minute. His brother was right even if Tucker didn't want to admit it. When he finally looked up, Danny said, "I wasn't the only one keepin' an eye on you."

"Who, Allie?" Tucker said as Danny grinned again.

"Oh, she's been watchin' you like a catbird does razzberries." Danny finally burst into full-fledged laughter, causing his older brother to blush.

"When did you learn to dream up lies like that?" Tucker said.

Danny's laughter stopped abruptly. "I don't never lie, Tucker. Paw Paw taught us better'n that." Then he nodded at Tucker's shoulder. "Taught you enough to get that right, I guess."

Tucker rolled up his sleeve and glanced at his tattoo. "Yeah, the guy did a pretty good job, don't you think? I sketched out like I remembered. 'Course, it's everywhere over there. It'd blow your mind how much 'seng there is."

Danny smiled. "I reckon so."

Then Tucker suddenly remembered: "Damn! I gotta get back to town before Harlan sells those roots. Bastard stole the whole haul. If you hadn't come along, I'd be broke *and* dead."

"I know," Danny said. "He's a bad feller, Harlan. Ain't gonna come to no good end. You don't have to worry about that, though. It's long gone." Danny's face appeared stiff from the scar tissue, which made his features hard to read.

"I need that money, Danny," Tucker said. "Mom and Dad took everything I had. Everything the Navy gave me. I gotta start over. I wanna try growing it for real. Get a proper patch. Farm trees, too. Work Clint's while I get started. You can help me! Hell, you worked trees better as a kid than I do now."

"You weren't no good at the trees, that's for dang sure." Danny chuckled, then settled again. "You got the book with you? Paw Paw's book?"

"No, dammit," Tucker shook his head. "Rat took it, too."

"Aw," Danny said. "He won't get far with it."

"I did."

"Yeah, but all they did was follow you," Danny said. "They can't figure them symbols out like you did. You had to know Paw Paw to know how to do that." He stood. "Let's take a walk. Got something to show you. Get that ankle fixed up proper, too."

"I really gotta get back and stop Rat—"

"No," Danny said, looking sternly at Tucker. "I got something to show you. Now, come on."

Flustered with his little brother's impatience, Tucker said, "My ankle's fine. Just needs a little rest."

But Danny was already outside.

Tucker peeled the cloth from his forehead, throwing the compress aside, and limped after his brother.

Danny gingerly wrapped the strips of cotton rag that had once been a t-shirt around Tucker's ankle after squatting at various stops in the forest, collecting material to stuff inside the homemade bandage. The dressing made walking cumbersome at first, but the combination of the folk remedies pressed against the joint provided enough relief for Tucker to keep up, as he followed Danny to whatever he was so intent on showing him.

Danny moved through the woods quietly and with purpose. Strong. Transformed since Tucker had last seen him from a rambunctious country kid to a seasoned and studied veteran of the hills—a mountain man, like their grandfather. Tucker watched Danny analyze the details of every nook and cranny in the landscape. His boots barely made a sound as he shinnied up each ridge, waiting for Tucker to catch up.

After a half hour of trekking, they arrived at a promontory. Danny waited patiently for Tucker to catch up, resting on a hornbeam whose rippled trunk matched the sinews and musculature of Danny's forearm, both ironwood. A high wall of impenetrable rhododendron stretched in each direction, and as deep inward, as far as Tucker could see—a laurel hell—impassable except for fools or outlaws.

"Where do we go now?" Tucker said, catching his breath.

Danny gave Tucker a quick nod and plunged under the first branch straight into the thicket. Tucker took the first steps cautiously, but as he entered the shady depths of the tangled weave of stems, the shrubbery opened like an arbor trellis.

Tucker noticed cut stumps purposefully cleared, creating a byway through the labyrinth. At a slight stoop, he maneuvered through it easily to keep pace with Danny's long strides.

Within a few minutes, they reached the end of the coppiced tunnel where it opened into a spacious gorge of massive, mature poplars and maples bordered by the expanse of laurels on all sides. Tucker was first awed by the beauty and size of the trees—a rare sweep of gorgeous timber left untouched by saws, a true virgin stand.

Then the deep green of the understory caught his eye. Rows upon rows of mature ginseng plants stretched as far as Tucker could see, with glistening, red berry pods—the size of golf balls—suspended just above them.

"Been plantin' them seeds since we were little," Danny said.

Tucker's mouth opened wide, but no words came to him.

"My secret little stash," Danny beamed.

Tucker stared in awe at the uncountable thousands of parasols in miniature, blanketing the valley as they nodded in the faint breeze.

"How did you—" Tucker shook his head in amazement, "—do all this?"

"One a Paw Paw's old spots," Danny said. "I just planted more. This's the one I drawed out in the back of his book. You was in the small one. I've been tendin' to this one since before he passed. Adding to it. Plantin' every year. Except that time you took them seeds from under the porch." Danny smiled at Tucker. "Watched you kill yourself trying to get'em in the ground. That was funny. Remember it like yesterday. Moved most of 'em in here after you left for the Navy."

Tucker looked up at Danny and shook his head. "I knew there should have been more in that patch. Allie said I messed up. Told everyone about it, too, I guess."

"Well," Danny said, "This here's better dirt. Safer spot, too. Rat and them boys'll crawl all over any woods as long as it's close to a road. I was the one told 'em about your patch. Even showed 'em once. Showed Allie, too. To keep 'em all off my trail. Sorry." He winked.

Tucker nodded, then laughed. It all made sense now. "How'd you keep it alive?" he said, stunned at the sheer quantity. Ginseng never grew like this in a natural stand.

"Learnt lots of tricks—the hard way. Voles will get in 'em bad some years. So will deer. They'll eat your tops, but don't bother the root too bad. Turkey'll rob your seed after plantin' if you let 'em. Made my own traps and spray to keep the critters out. Shot a bunch, too. Gotta keep watch. Root-rot and leaf blight will get 'em if it rains too much. Allie helped me with that. Gave me some ideas. I like her. She's smart. Hauled a sprayer up here. Gets a good breeze through here even after a rain. Keeps the blight out."

Tucker shook his head as Danny rattled on about his favorite subject.

"We ain't even that far from the house. You just took the long way," he laughed. "Them laurels hide it nice. That'll keep Rat and them other boys out of it. They ain't gonna find it 'cause they're too dang lazy."

Danny laughed at their indolence then said: "Take what you need, Tuck. If you want it."

"No way, Danny. You did all this," Tucker said, feeling tears rise. "This patch is worth a fortune." Then he had another thought. "But this ain't our land. How would we even get it out without the law taking notice?"

"Hell, they never come up here."

"Park Service's is on to me already, so they might."

Danny gave Tucker a quiet look. "You didn't know, did you?"

"Know what?" Tucker said.

"All this is ours," Danny said. "This land. From here to the house. Paw Paw never told you that story?"

"What story? What do you mean?"

"Paw Paw's daddy kept it when the government took the rest for the national forest. Inholding they call it. It's on the Forest Service maps. Don't even show up on the county ones. Was a handshake agreement, Paw Paw said, but the iron markers is still in the ground. I found all but one. Six hundred acres or more. He never told mom and dad. Afraid they'd wanna log it. Sell it. This is ours, Tuck. Every bit of it."

Tucker's mouth dropped open again as he considered the value in just the timber alone. Paw Paw and his secrets.

"I ain't got no use for all this," Danny said, nodding to the ginseng. "Got all I need. I just like growin' it. Like he did. Plenty to share. Lot of them plants is from your patch, anyway."

Tucker tried to grasp what his brother was offering. "If you're really willing to share it with me, I know someone who'd be real interested in buying it."

"It's a lot," Danny beamed. "Probably gonna need some help."

"Let me worry about that."

Thirty-Seven

Z gave Rat and his boys a frosty look as they stepped in front of Z's other *customers*—his regular trio. An assortment of antique revolvers spread across the glass countertops. Rat and one of his lanky cronies pushed the pistols aside as they proudly hoisted the full sack of their haul onto the table.

The gun traders' looks went from threatening glares to wide-eyed surprise when they saw the impressive snarl of roots bulging out of the top of the bag. They glanced at each other, then stared again at the crusty group and its hotshot leader, keeping their gaze fixed on Rat.

"You best watch who yer givin' that Devil-Eye to," Rat told them.

One of the men chuckled as he spurted brown into his bottle and turned to Z with a cynical look that said: *"Who does this kid think he's talkin' to?"* Z exhaled slowly and nodded to the older men who stepped aside to let Rat approach.

"Might need the big scale this time, Z," Rat smirked.

Z stared a blank moment, then retreated to the back of the store, returning with a heavy, spring balance that he placed on the counter. Furrowing his brow, he began loading into the scale tray. He had a good idea where, or at least from whom, they had *acquired* it.

"So? How much you owe me?" Rat said, his tongue swishing back and forth between the corners of his mouth.

Z regarded him coolly, then looked at the scale after mounding on the last handful. "Looks like about sixty-two hundred worth—give or take."

"I'll take!" Rat said and faced his partners. "Yeah boy, now that's a good day's work, ain't it?" The other fools grinned like school-kids. "You got enough in your wallet for that?"

Z pulled a thick wad from his back pocket and slid the whole roll across to him. "That's five. Come back tomorrow and you can get the rest."

Rat sneered as he snapped off the rubber band and began peeling off bills.

As Rat riffled quickly through the cash, Z warned: "Man can get a bad rep in these mountains, he ain't careful. Another man might not wanna trade with him he hears the wrong story. Bad for business."

"Preach to someone who cares, Z," Rat replied. "Now, I'm gonna hold you to what you still owe. Come tomorrow, if you ain't got it—"

"You'll do *what?*" Z said slowly with a look that burned a threat of death into Rat's beady eyes. Z pinched off turds bigger than this punk, and his patience had worn thin.

Rat twitched, but kept up the act to maintain his cool in front of the lackeys. "Come on now, old buddy, you know the game. You want more good root like that, you gotta pay up. Otherwise, I'll have to find my own Chinaman. Would hate to cut you out of a share of high quality product like this."

Z dismissed the comment with a wave, motioning to the cash that Rat still thumbed between his filthy fingers. "What are you gonna do with all that?"

"That's my bid'ness."

"It'll all be up your nose in a week," Z said.

Rat glowered but wiped his nostrils in case it was obvious.

"Another thing," Z said, looking at him directly to make sure Harlan caught his drift, "Certain folks don't show up, Sheriff's gonna be askin' around."

"Let 'em ask. I ain't know nothin' about nobody." Rat played it calmer than he even thought he could, caught up in delusions of grandeur; but most of his gang stared at the floor. "Come on, boys. We got a party to tend to."

Z shared a stoic look with his fellow pistol-peddlers as Rat and company left the shop, waiting a moment to make sure they were gone before picking up the phone.

Thirty-Eight

The Sheriff's patrol car pulled down the drive onto the Trivette property and came to a stop next to Tucker's truck. Hicks shut off the engine, stepped out of his vehicle, and approached the trailer. Nothing stirred inside after a few knocks on the vinyl door. He put his hands up to the small window to hide the glare as he peered inside.

"Tucker Trivette, you in there?" he said and knocked again—still nothing. A faint voice piqued his attention. Hicks looked first toward the road, but then circled to the back of Tucker's trailer to follow the sound and stared up the slope.

"Sheriff! Hold up!" came a distant voice from the wood line.

"That you, Tucker?" Hicks shouted.

"It's me. I'm coming." Tucker shouted as he emerged from the trees and tramped down the grassy slope, favoring his ankle with his backpack slung over one shoulder.

He reached the driveway out of breath. Only then did Hicks see the gash on Tucker's head. The wound had clotted but still oozed and probably needed a few stitches. The bloodstains streaking Tucker's shirt and the caked dirt on his pants legs painted him like an earthquake survivor.

"God almighty, son. What happened to you? Fall off another cliff?" Hicks asked facetiously, but still concerned. "You alright?"

"It's a long story, sir, but you need to arrest Harlan Ward. Tied me to a tree out there and left me to die."

"Hang, on. What are you talking about? That where you been? In the woods? We got an anonymous call this morning to do a welfare check. Said there might be trouble."

Tucker cocked his head. "Well, there's more to it than that. But first, I wanna press charges against Rat and his boys, now. They came at me with guns, stole my ginseng, and would've killed me. Took my pistol, too. You need to arrest him. All of 'em. Conspiracy, theft, whatever. Attempted murder!"

"Now just hold on a minute, son. How long you been out there?" Hicks said.

"Couple days. I was—"

A female voice interrupted Tucker mid-sentence at full volume from the cruiser's CB receiver: "*All units, be advised we have multiple 10-89s at Sixth and Cherry.*"

"Ah, hell. Now what?" Hicks cued the receiver on his chest: "Roll medics. I'm in route. Tell Lucas at the coroner's to meet me out there and hold any other traffic on this until next-of-kin are notified."

"What's that all about?"

"Hop in. Might concern you, too."

Reds and blues flashed like synchronized disco lights against the siding of each doublewide as patrol cars and EMT wagons flanked the scene at haphazard angles. Tucker stepped out and leaned casually against the cruiser. As Hicks entered the chaos behind a medic wheeling in a stretcher, the wind kicked up. A distant reverberation of thunder began low and distant, gaining volume as it spread from its origin. Tucker looked towards the graying sky as his nose picked up the intimation of moisture forming in the air. A storm was coming.

As a deputy finished tying off the crime tape to the row of mailboxes, stretching it across the entire loose gravel parking area, Tucker saw Hicks emerge from the trailer, ducking under the ribbon.

"What a mess," he said.

"What happened?"

"One dead, two more heading to ICU."

"Do what?"

"Overdose, looks like. That group that Harlan runs with. Just got done interviewing the other two that could still speak. Sounds like they took what they stole from you and cashed in one helluva party. Enough spilled on the table in there to kill every one of 'em twice. See it all the time these days."

"And Rat?" Tucker said.

Hicks shook his head. "Not here. His buddies say he took off earlier in the afternoon. Solo." Hick's could see the anger boil in Tucker's face. As the deputies exited the trailer escorting one of Rat's shirtless accomplices in cuffs, Hicks nodded and said: "Don't worry. We'll find him soon enough. Told that one he'd be up on at attempted murder. He sang pretty quick. Corroborated your story."

Hicks exhaled. "Always another one to take his place, though. Way things are around here. Economy and all. Speaking a which—what are *you* doin' for work?"

"I've got some plans."

The sheriff raised his eyebrows and pointed at Tucker's head, but left it with his usual: "Well, stay out of trouble. And get that seen about. Derek, here, will give you a ride."

"Where we going?" Deputy Derek said as he tossed the yellow tape roll into his car.

"Can you take me to the Ag Center?"

Rat's heartbeat thumped beneath the thin skin of his greasy temples as he hunched over the creek on all fours, slurping from the rocky pool to douse the desert of his throat. Handfuls of the stream water cascaded from his stringy hair, cooling his cheeks, but not his eyes, which glowed with fierce intent from within the dusky circles ringing their sockets.

It was so much easier going it alone than babysitting his posse of tagalongs and listening to their idiotic banter. He had set off on his own after Randy went limp in the bean bag and the others became incoherent. Lightweights. He had warned them about mixing their candy. They didn't listen. No matter. Whatever he found this time would be his, alone.

He had returned to the same trail, traversing most of distance in less than half the time it had taken with his gang of bumbling morons in tow, the chemistry in his system fueling the gaunt muscles in his legs up and over the mountainsides like a bobcat.

As he reached the peak of the next ridge, he pulled Buck Trivette's journal from the small of his back and opened it up to the last page, mumbling to himself: "See, that's a different spot. Weren't no big laurels where we found you, was there, Tucker?" His eyes darted furiously from one feature to the next on the page. "This one here's different. Bigger." He slapped the book shut and scrambled up the next mountain, stopping along the way to gas up with another quick snort from the half-crumpled Marlboro box in his shirt pocket that was slowly disintegrating from sweat.

He could barely contain his excitement as he shimmied up the final escarpment, facing a wall of rhododendron that stretched forever, it seemed. At its edge, he leaned against a thick poplar and cracked the book open again, tracing the drawing with a discolored fingernail. A creeping smile stretched across his face from thin lips. Adjusting his belt to secure the journal on one hip and the stolen pistol on the other, Rat dove into the confines of the thicket.

He spent the next hour on his belly, crawling and cursing under the latticework of branches, their brittle stems doing their best to thwart any forward momentum. He paused hearing a rumble of thunder and the intermittent slap of heavy drops tapping their warning beats above him. While the twisted trunks entwined him in their clutches, flexing and releasing as the growing wind bent their tops, he couldn't feel the breeze, yet. Each inch he gained, it seemed like the dense laurels closed their grip tighter, choking the air beneath. With his elbows poking through their brittle leaf-shed, sleeves and knees bleeding through torn jeans, his pulse quickened as a sheet of lightning flashed through, showing the gap to the other side. He scrambled the last few yards to exit the expanse, the claustrophobic shrubs seemingly happy to eject him.

From the prone position, he could see it.

"Eureka, bitch," he said as he stood. Even through the driving downpour, he could see the tops of the ginseng plants dancing from the cascade of raindrops falling on each frond through the canopy above. Rat turned his head to survey the expanse of loot as far as he could see; the end of the cove now obscured by the rain. "Oh, my. These been taken care of!" he said, licking the rain and greed from his lips.

"Yes, they have," said the figure stepping into his field of vision.

"Damn! Where'd you come from!" Rat said as his shoulders jumped on anchored legs.

"Why'd you come here?" Danny said with an eerie calm. Rat recognized the voice, but had to squint through the deluge to see for sure.

As lightning flashed above them, Rat saw the scars rippled across Danny's face. The empty sleeve.

"Holy hell, if it ain't Danny-boy Trivette!"

"Yep."

"Could've sworn you were burnt up."

"Nope. Got out."

"Got-damn, son. It don't look like it," Rat's body shook as he slapped his knees, laughing. "I just gotta say it: You look like Freddy fuckin' Kruger!"

Danny said nothing.

"That fire was hot. I made sure of it. Thought I saw you burn," Rat said with a wicked sneer.

Danny's head cocked to one side. "You were there." It wasn't a question.

Rat thought he saw confusion for a moment, but it was hard to read Danny's taut expression through the rain.

Thunder echoed across the entire mountainside and Danny moved forward, quickly.

Then Rat saw into Danny's eyes.

It wasn't confusion.

"Hey now, you need to back off," Rat warned as Danny reached him.

Rat's footing slipped in the growing mire of the hillside as he turned his head to reach for the pistol in his belt.

Before he could touch the handle of the Colt, Danny lunged in front of and around him, with the long arc of his arm returning to his side as he passed. The knife was so sharp, Rat didn't even notice at first.

"What did you do?" The words formed in Rat's mouth as he tried to speak, but nothing came out other than a gurgle. He looked down at the crimson heat spreading from his collar to his navel. Finally realizing what happened, he grasped at his throat trying to cover it, his overworked heart gushing the life from his body in short arcs like an uncapped oil drain as his arms and legs grew cold. He sank to his knees as his pulsing stream mixed with the runoff flowing downslope.

Danny faced him, waiting for the look of terror and vengeance to dissipate from Rat's eyes as he finally slumped over. Danny stood over him a minute longer, then yanked the book and pistol free from Rat's belt before turning slowly away to fetch the shovel.

Thirty-Nine

Tucker waved to the deputy as he pulled out of the county parking lot. "This should be interesting," Tucker mumbled as he opened the double doors to the building and met Allie in the lobby.

At first, Allie's eyes narrowed, but before an angry frown could fully form, Tucker's bruises and filth replaced it with concern. She nearly dropped the stack of brochures when she saw the damage up close.

"Oh, my god. What happened?" Allie asked as she delicately reached for the goose egg on Tucker's forehead. She pulled her hand away as he cringed.

"It's a long story."

"Have anything to do with all the sirens?"

"Not directly," Tucker said, indirectly.

"Where have you been? You look like *shit* ... and smell like it, too."

"I got something to show you," Tucker said. "It's important."

"What is it?"

"Can't explain. You just gotta see it. Trust me," Tucker said.

"Uh, okay," Allie said, still wrinkling her face at the shape he was in. "Where're we going?"

"Can you drive?"

Tucker helped Allie pull off her backpack and set it atop the hollow stump beside him to keep it from wicking moisture from the damp ground. The storm had been quick and fierce, disjointed, barely raining a drop in town, but soaking every inch of land behind Paul's Peak.

They stopped briefly to rest and sucked down water from their canteens.

"How much farther?" Allie said flatly.

"Almost there."

"You said that two hours ago."

"You sound like a kid," Tucker giggled.

"Not funny anymore. Not that it ever was."

"I promise it'll be worth it. Trust me."

"You keep saying that, and I don't." Allie pointed at his face. "And you look like an ogre with that thing."

Tucker touched the angry contusion on his forehead and clenched his teeth. "Don't have a BC powder on you by any chance?"

Allie huffed and rubbed her calves. "If I did, I'd have already taken them."

After berating Tucker the first three hours of the trip and almost turning back twice, Allie finally gave up on getting the big secret out of him. Tucker wanted to spill the beans, but he and Danny had agreed to wait and let her see for herself. She wouldn't have believed them anyway.

Tucker saw into her exasperation. "You gonna be okay? Seriously?"

Allie groaned, physically exhausted from the hike and mentally exhausted from the emotional roller coaster of the last few days. She gave Tucker a smug look. "Are we almost there, *seriously?*"

"We're close," Tucker said as he leaned against a mossy boulder, careful not to slip. He looked blankly into the distance for a minute before saying, "Woods are nice out here, aren't they ... Quiet."

Allie snorted. "You're unbelievable, Tucker Trivette. Bringing me this far into the woods to give me a line. And a bad one at that," She took another long draw from her water bottle while he stared at her. "What? Why are looking at me like—"

"Would you be quiet just for once so I can do this?"

"Do what?" she said.

Tucker turned to her and slowly pulled the plastic thermos from Allie's lips while staring into her eyes. Her face went from annoyance, to confusion, to a look of longing that she hoped he returned.

Then he stabbed her cheek with his index finger.

"Ow!" Allie said, rubbing her face. "What was that for?"

"Got her," Tucker said, scraping the mosquito from his thumb.

Then he leaned over her and smiled widely, brushed the hair back over her ears, and gave her a soft, sweaty kiss between her eyebrows. Allie gazed up at him without saying a word, but her face got hotter than it already was.

"Best I can do," Tucker chuckled, then got serious again. "I'm really glad you're here, Allie. What can I say? I need you."

Allie blushed and tried to regain her composure.

"Have for a long time," Tucker said as he picked up her pack and held the straps open for her to slide her arms through. "I'm just an idiot sometimes. Thick as spring fog."

"You waiting for me to disagree with you?" she said, but with kindness and hope underneath.

"Shut up," Tucker said, smiling, and touched her lips. "Let's not ruin this, huh?"

He let the moment lie, then took her hand and gently pulled her up. She let him—and smiled back.

They made the final climb together with Tucker pushing Allie's rear to propel her up the steep slope. As they came across the top of the ridge, there sat Danny, leaned against a red oak, legs crossed, whittling the end of a twig. Waiting for them.

"Hey, Allie," he said in an understated tone as he stood up.

It took less than a millisecond for the shock to sink in as her mouth gaped open in a silent scream.

"What's the matter?" Tucker snickered. "You look like you just saw a ghost."

A squeal finally escaped her, and Allie threw her arms around Danny, sobbing, and clinging to him, swinging from side to side.

"Hey, Allie," Danny repeated, patting her shoulder awkwardly—not accustomed to the attention.

"Oh my god! Is that really you?" she wailed then immediately turned to Tucker and punched him fully in the shoulder. "And you're an asshole! Why didn't you tell me?"

"Easy," Tucker said, rubbing his arm. "I just found out, too. Right, brother?"

Danny grinned. "We got something to show you."

Allie fanned her eyes, firing off questions faster than Tucker or Danny could even answer.

"Just hang on a minute," Tucker said. "There's something else. You gotta follow us."

"More hiking? You have to be kidding me."

As the trio broke through the gap in the maze of hedges and the cove's hidden bounty came into view, Allie stood silent with her mouth agape, shaking her head for what seemed a full minute.

"So what do you think?" Tucker said, suppressing a grin.

"I've never seen ... anything like ..." she began. "How did you—?"

"I didn't," Tucker said. "He did."

Danny nodded without a sound, kicking the leaves by his feet.

"There's so *many*. It's *beautiful*," she said.

"I think she's impressed," Tucker said to his little brother.

"You never told me you were growing it like *this!*" Allie said. Then she punched Danny hard in the chest.

"You never asked," Danny grunted as he slumped over catching his breath.

"What do we do now?" she said.

"I don't know," Tucker said. "You're the expert. You tell me."

Allie grinned wide. "Got a screwdriver on you?"

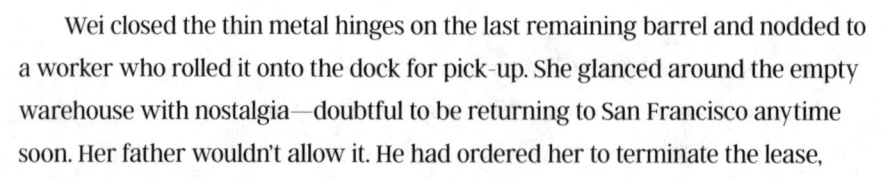

Wei closed the thin metal hinges on the last remaining barrel and nodded to a worker who rolled it onto the dock for pick-up. She glanced around the empty warehouse with nostalgia—doubtful to be returning to San Francisco anytime soon. Her father wouldn't allow it. He had ordered her to terminate the lease, finalize the last invoices, and return home to Hong Kong.

For good.

She had managed to scrounge a scant amount of product from the resident root-hawkers in Chinatown. But her brother had done even worse. Chin spent the last uneventful week failing to secure even half of the expected volume. Their competition—another member of the *guild*—had been one step ahead of him, scooping up the best of the drought-decimated Wisconsin crop, leaving her family far behind the curve this buying season.

Bàba was not happy.

Wei sighed as she reached for the toggle on the master switch for the overhead fluorescents of the warehouse.

"Miss me, yet?" a familiar voice echoed in the cavernous expanse. She turned to find a backlit figure standing next to the exit door of the depository.

"Tucker?" Wei said as she squinted. "What are you doing here?"

"Took a while to figure out which one of these was yours," Tucker said glancing around the vacant space.

"Seriously!" Wei exclaimed. "*What* are you doing here?"

"I heard you were in the market for some ginseng or something."

"I was," Wei said, crossing her arms. "Someone lied to me, though. Stood me up. Said they had a farm full of it and didn't. I have to go home now. Leaving tomorrow, back to Hong Kong." Her tone was unapologetically nasty.

"That's a shame," Tucker said with a smirk. "I hope it's a refundable ticket."

"What do you mean?" Wei cocked her head, deeply suspicious.

The garage door at the end of the warehouse suddenly rattled open and a windowless cargo van pulled into the empty area. Wei's last remaining worker shrugged his shoulders as the van pulled in, coming to a stop in front of her. A large black man with thick glasses grinned widely and waved from behind the wheel.

"Who is that?" Wei said.

"One of my *associates*," Tucker said as the passenger door opened and Allie slid out.

Wei stiffened and shot a glare at Tucker.

"I believe you already met the other one."

Allie strode over and shoved a manila folder into Wei's arms. "I think this is all you'll need. Certification documents for the whole load. Legal this time, too." She waited for Wei to respond; when she didn't, Allie said: "Inspector signed off on them in North Carolina last week. I assume you have the export permit from Fish and Wildlife?"

Wei nodded, inspecting each sheet of the dossier as Sam got out of the van and opened up the back door. He rolled out several barrels from the cargo hold and popped their tops so Wei could see into each cardboard cylinder packed to the rim.

Wei carefully lifted a small handful from each barrel—her eyes darting between the ginseng and Tucker.

"This is—" Wei stumbled with her English. "*Incredible.*"

"Told you she'd be impressed," Tucker said to Allie who rolled her eyes.

Sam continued shuttling the load from the van down the ramp and motioned to Tucker: "You gonna help or what?"

"Sorry," Tucker said, enjoying the moment. He saw Allie getting jealous all over again. "How many you got left?" Tucker knew exactly how many there were, but relished the look on Wei's face.

"Nine," Sam said bluntly. "Come on, man. You made me count 'em a half dozen times before we left."

"Oh yeah, I forgot," Tucker said. He turned to Wei as he stepped into the van to reel off another container: "I hope you're still in the market. We drove an awful long way."

"Hungry too," Sam chimed in. "Got any recommendations? Drove right through Chinatown. Smells real good down there. Almost missed the turn trying to read the menus. They were in Chinese, but the pictures looked damn good. Got a hankerin' for some of that General Tso's chicken."

"Who is he?" Wei said again.

"Blind Sam. Well, he's not really blind. But he *is* always hungry. And we call her 'The Boss'." He nodded Allie's way.

Allie rolled her eyes again.

Wei shook herself out of disbelief and tried to regain composure.

"Got a scale around here somewhere?" Tucker asked but didn't wait for a response: "Not that you need one. Each empty barrel tares out at four point one pounds, and there should be around thirty-two point eight pounds of product per barrel ... on average. Just guessing."

Wei gave up on her attempt to not appear impressed. She approached Tucker, stoically at first, then leaned up and threw her arms around his neck—and squealed. She then stepped back and straightened out her business suit, as Allie looked on, a bit incredulous.

"Sorry," Wei said to Allie. "That was just business. Let me get your payment. Boss Lady." She walked back towards her office.

"Will this take long?" Allie called out. "Tucker and I have *business* to get back to at home." Tucker blushed and Allie punched him hard in the chest.

Wei stopped long enough to turn with a wide smile at both of them before entering her office, returning quickly with a three-ring-binder. She folded a perforated sheet in the ledger book, ripped out the pay stub, and handed it to Tucker.

It was all he could do not to look at it. "I know it's a little late in the season, but it took longer to get here than we thought. Lot of work to get it out of the ground and dried properly. And Sam really wanted to see the Grand Canyon. Might have some more in a couple of months. You know, if you're still interested," Tucker said playfully.

"As I said before, we pay top price and are happy to purchase all that you can procure," Wei said in her best business voice.

Tucker leaned over and gave Allie a solid kiss on the forehead as he handed her the check. She glanced at it, grabbed his hand and squeezed the blood out of his fingers.

"Y'all need a room?" Sam said, shaking his head.

Allie handed Sam the check. "Maybe."

Sam's took off his glasses to read the number that overflowed from the small white square on the check. Tucker saw him grab his chest.

"Told you," Tucker winked then said to Wei: "Let me know when you wanna come out for the next load. You got my number."

Allie said, "You've got *my* number. It's in the folder."

Sam stared at the check again as he got in to drive and said, "Sam's House of Brisket: So good, you'll go blind. Whattaya think?"

"I think I'd eat there every day," Allie said.

"You can cater the wedding," Tucker said and winked.

Allie punched him again.

Forty

Tucker casually strolled into the bank and approached the counter. While Gloria chatted with a customer outside through the teller intercom, he could see the manager with another client through his open office door. Tucker flashed a wide smile that caught Gloria by surprise when she turned around from the window.

"Good morning, Gloria. I certainly hope you're doing well," Tucker said with a tone that shocked her more than seeing him in the bank again.

She shifted uncomfortably in her stool at the sincerity. "Well ... Thank you," she said more like a question. Then she asked, "Is there something I can help you with?"

"Just need to cash this," Tucker said, as he slid the folded bank draft to her. He turned his attention to a stack of deposit slips, and shuffled them on the counter, awaiting her reaction.

Gloria unfolded the check and began to write out a receipt when she took a closer look at the amount. She stopped suddenly in disbelief. "Is this some sort of a *joke?*"

"I'll take it in large bills, please."

Gloria looked back down at the check and then back to him, not knowing how to react. "I'm gonna have to talk to the bank manager."

"You do that."

Gloria rammed the stool back behind the counter and hurriedly entered the manager's office, interrupting his meeting, as Tucker watched with a glee he could barely contain.

After a moment, they both joined Tucker at the counter. While Gloria pouted as she looked on, the manager graciously said: "Mr. Trivette, unfortunately we don't keep much cash here at this branch for withdrawal. Certainly *that* much cash. However, I'd be happy to help you open up an account and get this deposited for you. I assume you are certain that this comes from a reputable source?"

"Why don't you call and check? I won't be offended. I completely understand the protocol. Phone number's right there," Tucker said and pointed to the top corner of the slip. "I don't have anywhere else to be."

The banker apologized to his other client and picked up the phone. Within less than a minute, Tucker heard "Okay. Thank you," as the banker hung up and walked back out of his office with a wide, polite smile. "Well, as you said, this note is legal *and* tender. How about we get that account paperwork going for you, hmm? Gloria can help you get started and I'll join you after I finish up with this customer. Won't take a minute."

"Well," Tucker said and paused for effect: "On second thought, I'll probably just take a drive down to Charlotte. I think it's obvious that I'm going to need a bigger institution—one that's equipped to handle my level of banking needs. Not so sure I want to do business here after all. You understand, right, Gloria?"

Tucker gently took the check from the banker's fingers leaving him speechless. But the look on Gloria's face was even better.

Tucker turned to leave and waved without looking back.

The remaining tops in the secluded grove had yellowed and wilted, the first cold snaps of fall leaving a scant few with balls of red berries contrasting the flaxen consistency of the withering foliage. Despite what had been harvested, plenty of roots still laid buried throughout the grove.

Tucker and Allie moved quietly through the woods together, stopping to dig any plants whose tops still touched—thinning out the stand, making room for the others to flourish. They also collected rootlets growing beneath the mature plants—second, third, and fourth generations from seed fallen to the ground before Danny could claim them. Tucker had carefully chosen and prepared another planting site—in a secure location, far away from the main roads, and in black soil. He was doing it right this time.

With winter coming, Tucker decided to wait until spring to start construction on the new home place—a traditional two-story farmhouse with a wrap-around porch. Tucker would ask Danny at that point to move back, into the new digs, but not before. He knew he'd just get a no. Saul had already bulldozed the site, hauling away the rubble from the homestead—erasing old memories to be replaced with new ones.

A cool wind drifted into the alcove from the north, chilling the air.

"A fire would be real nice," Allie said to Tucker, squeezing his arm.

Tucker dropped a few rootlets into his poke and stood up. "I'll get one going."

He kissed her gently on the top of the head and grasped her hand, leading her to the sheltered tent site just within the bordering laurel thicket.

Danny watched the two of them leave the holler from the other side of the stand and smiled. It was good to have Tucker back. And good that he and Allie had finally come together—good the way everything had turned out. The way it was supposed to.

As he walked the full perimeter of the hidden cove, admiring the remaining crop and enjoying the peace of the evening, Danny stared for a moment at the small pile of flat stone stacked in the far corner of the plot. The bloodroot he had planted around it would look real pretty come springtime. Just a mound of rocks removed from the ginseng beds that would hardly draw any attention.

Tucker didn't know. He didn't need to. No one did. The evil beneath was buried deep. Less it spread. Just like Paw Paw would've done.

Danny leaned down to pluck off the last cluster of burgundy berries from a nearby plant. He poked small holes in a semi-circle in the ground with his index finger and dropped a seed in each hole, covering them with leaves—then stuffed the rest in his pocket and grinned.

Wait until they see the other patch.

The End

Afterword

American ginseng *(Panax quinquefolius)* remains the most sought after forest medicinal plant in North America and is an integral part of the history and culture of Appalachia. Ginseng is listed on the Convention on International Trade of Endangered Species (CITES) of Wild Flora and Fauna and faces continued pressure due to overharvesting in the wild for its export to Asia, where it is valued for traditional, wide-ranging medicinal applications.

If you happen to own a nice open patch of older-growth hardwood forest in the foothills or the mountains, I encourage you to plant some seed to keep this special plant and its traditions going forward. The best technical resource I can recommend for the cultivation of ginseng is by Dr. Jeanine Davis and Scott Persons: *Growing and Marketing Ginseng, Goldenseal, and other Forest Medicinals*. For more information on the history and tradition of this special plant, I highly recommend *Ginseng, The Divine Root*, by David Taylor. If you consider donations to worthy conservation causes, please give to United Plant Savers. They're working their butts off to conserve ginseng and other rare medicinal plant species that are slowly (some quickly) disappearing.

Acknowledgments

Serendipity, friendships & acquaintances ... and bourbon. I wonder how many cool things get created from that recipe. Every good story has an even better back-story.

I have had the pleasure of working over the years with many landowners, diggers, growers, and scientists who are working to preserve ginseng—for conservation and for profit. I'm from a little town in east central Alabama, so I didn't grow up in Appalachia, where folks still hunt herbs to make ends meet or to carry on family traditions. However, the 'sengers here in western North Carolina, where I've called home now for close to 20 years, graciously let me into their world, and their stories helped weave this one. Thank you. Especially to Travis—my ginseng mentor.

As an Extension agent in a small mountain county, I get to visit and meet a lot of really interesting folks. A few years ago, I took a call from a homeowner with some property who had questions about setting out some ginseng on his land. Those are my favorite kinds of calls. This particular landowner happened to be Glenn A. Bruce, one of several talented writers & artists who have made the North Carolina mountains their home. Treat yourself and order a copy of *The Maples*. Glenn weaves a good yarn. Along with his many novels and short stories, he also writes screenplays. He wrote the movie, *Kickboxer*, which I watched no less than a dozen times with my buddy Richard Turner in our formative years as teenage martial-arts-flicks-aficionados. So, that was cool. I mentioned to Glenn that there had never been a movie made (that I knew of) that had incorporated ginseng in any meaningful way—which is sort of surprising, considering the history, economy, and culture of this truly mythical plant. I remember him saying: "Well, if you come up with a story, let me know."

    I jotted the bare bones of the storyline that night in the margins of Town of Boone Tree Board minutes from April 2015 after two bourbons and a soak in the hot tub. My wife, Silvi, thought it was pretty good. Later that week, I typed it all out and gave it to Glenn. To my welcome surprise, he was intrigued, and after a couple months of conversations and idea swapping on additional characters and plot lines, he had cranked out a screenplay. In my enthusiasm and complete naivety as to 'how the industry works,' I emailed it to Anson Mount (the star of AMCs *Hell on Wheels*), who I had met as an undergrad at Sewanee. You know, because Hollywood movie-stars that you knew back in college are chomping at the bit to jump on randomly emailed screenplays. Anson replied back: "Do a novel first and see if it gets legs." So, I asked Glenn if he'd help me with it and he did.

    A year after typing "The End" the first of many times, I met Shari Smith of Working Title Farm. Glenn had mentioned that she had just published Radney Foster's first book, a collection of short stories, and was hosting a reading & book signing here in Boone. She happens to live here, too. That was convenient. Of course, I went. As an AM DJ back in high school at WACD in Alexander City, Alabama, Radney Foster was the first country artist whose music really migrated me to the genre—before then, I was a Prince and U2 and Guns N Roses teenager. So, I got to hear Radney play acoustic versions of a few of my favorites and pitched the novel to Shari. She was interested, and there you have it. Serendipity, friendships, and bourbon.

    I would like to express my sincere gratitude to Glenn A. Bruce, who expressed enough interest in the original idea & storyline to create the screenplay, '*Sang*, which served as the road map for this novel. Appreciate you taking the time to teach me the tricks of the trade, and the non-tricks (there's nothing tricky about writing and editing. It's work. Most of it. The rest of it was a lot of fun ... and more work); for your extensive mentoring, editing, and story building, expertise on crafting dialogue, and for the conversations in the old farmhouse on Schull's Mill. Would still love to see this make it to the big screen, someday.

Appreciation to Mike Jasper, Bettie Bond, Ross Young, Max Hagaman, and Sandy Lebowitz who read early versions of the novel and provided excellent critique.

To Mom and Dad, thank you for always supporting where I've wanted to go ... even when you weren't so keen on the idea. It all worked out.

Thanks to Shari Smith, publisher and friend, who believed in the story. I'm so very proud to be a Working Title Farmer.

And to Silvi, Cristian, and Lucas for putting up with this little project. Y'all are the best things in the world.

Big love.

~ Jim Hamilton

Based on the screenplay, 'Sang, by Glenn A. Bruce
Story by Jim Hamilton and Glenn Bruce
©2019